Michelle Reid grew up on the southern edges of Manchester, the youngest in a family of five lively children. But now she lives in the beautiful county of Cheshire, with her busy executive husband and two grown-up daughters. She loves reading, the ballet, and playing tennis when she gets the chance. She hates cooking, cleaning, and despises ironing! Sleep she can do without, and produces some of her best written work during the early hours of the morning.

Trish Morey is an Australian who's also spent time living and working in New Zealand and England. Now she's settled with her husband and four young daughters in a special part of South Australia, surrounded by orchards and bushland, and visited by the occasional koala and kangaroo. With a life-long love of reading, she penned her first book at age eleven, after which life, career and a growing family kept her busy until once again she could indulge her desire to create characters and stories, this time in romance. Having her work published is a dream come true. Visit Trish at her website at www.trishmorey.com.

Jane Porter grew up on a diet of Mills and Boon romances, reading late at night under the covers so her mother wouldn't see! She wrote her first book at age eight, and spent many of her high school and college years living abroad, immersing herself in other cultures and continuing to read voraciously. Now Jane has settled down in rugged Seattle, Washington, with her gorgeous two sons. Jane loves to hear from her readers. You can write to her at PO Box 524, Bellevue, WA 98009, USA. Or visit her website at www.janeporter.com.

D1342252

30128 80356 599 6

Mediterranean Mavericks

MICHELLE REID

TRISH MOREY

JANE PORTER

MILLS & BOON

All rights reserved including the right of reproduction in whole or in part in any form. This edition is published by arrangement with Harlequin Books S.A.

This is a work of fiction. Names, characters, places, locations and incidents are purely fictional and bear no relationship to any real life individuals, living or dead, or to any actual places, business establishments, locations, events or incidents. Any resemblance is entirely coincidental.

This book is sold subject to the condition that it shall not, by way of trade or otherwise, be lent, resold, hired out or otherwise circulated without the prior consent of the publisher in any form of binding or cover other than that in which it is published and without a similar condition including this condition being imposed on the subsequent purchaser.

® and ™ are trademarks owned and used by the trademark owner and/or its licensee. Trademarks marked with ® are registered with the United Kingdom Patent Office and/or the Office for Harmonisation in the Internal Market and in other countries.

First Published in Great Britain 2018
by Mills & Boon, an imprint of HarperCollins*Publishers*
1 London Bridge Street, London, SE1 9GF

MEDITERRANEAN MAVERICKS © 2018 Harlequin Books S. A.

The Italian's Future Bride © 2006 Michelle Reid
The Greek's Virgin © 2006 Trish Morey
At the Greek Boss's Bidding © 2007 Jane Porter

ISBN: 978-0-263-26877-5

0818

MIX
Paper from
responsible sources
FSC™ C007454

This book is produced from independently certified FSC™ paper to ensure responsible forest management.

For more information visit: www.harpercollins.co.uk/green

Printed and bound in Spain
by CPI, Barcelona

THE ITALIAN'S
FUTURE BRIDE

MICHELLE REID

CHAPTER ONE

IT WAS like playing Russian roulette with your sex life: place a loaded invitation in the barrel, then shoot and see if you scored a hit.

Everyone was doing it, Raffaelle Villani observed cynically—the young and nubile, complete with breast implants and carefully straightened and dyed blonde hair. They circled the room eyeing up likely victims, picked the richest man they could find, then primed him and fired their lucky shot.

Or unlucky, depending from which side of the fence you viewed it.

Some you win, some you lose, he mused as one eager player tried the deal on him only to be rewarded with the sight of his back.

Contempt twisting his lean golden features, he beat a retreat to the furthest corner of the room where the bar was situated. Discarding his untouched glass of champagne, he ordered a glass of full-blooded red wine to take its place.

Functions like this were the pits and he would not have come but for his stepsister twisting his arm. He owed Daniella a favour for pulling him out of a tricky situation recently with a woman who had been about to become his latest lover—until Daniella had whispered in his ear that the woman was married with a small son.

It turned out that she had even lied to him about her name. Discovering that she was actually the ex-catwalk model Elise Castle, now married to the heavyweight Greek Leo Savakis, had not made Raffaelle feel good about himself.

Married women were not his bag. Married women with small children were an even bigger turn-off. As were neat little liars who pretended to be someone they were not. Elise Castle ticked the boxes in all three categories and the hardest part of it all had been accepting how thoroughly he had been duped by a pair of innocent blue eyes and a set of good breasts that had been her own.

Or maybe not, Raffaelle then contended. Perhaps the breasts and the blue eyes had been just more lies the beautiful Elise had fed to him. Fortunately he had not managed to get close enough to find out.

But he still owed it to Daniella that he'd managed to get out of a potentially scandal-spinning tangle before it had exploded in his face.

He was into gun metaphors, he noticed. What a great way to spend a Saturday night.

Where was Daniella—?

Straightening his six-foot-four-inch frame up from its bored languid slouch against the bar, Raffaelle began scanning the sea of bodies milling about in front of him for a glimpse of the sylphlike figure belonging to his beautiful stepsister.

He found her almost instantly. Her glossy mane of black hair and the red dress she was wearing made her virtually impossible to miss. She was standing with some smooth-looking guy over by a wall on the other side of the room, and it came as a shock to Raffaelle to see that she was playing the game like all the rest!

She was pouting, her pose distinctly saucy, her breasts pushed up almost against the guy's chest while he looked down at her with one of those lazy I'm-interested-smiles on his handsome face.

Were Daniella's breasts her own—?

The question hit Raffaelle's brain and made him curse softly because he didn't care what Daniella's breasts were made of. She was not and never had been his type. And anyway, as his stepsister, she was and always had been off limits.

She was also getting married in two months, to one of his closest friends. But there she stood, coming on to another man!

Annoyance launched him away from the bar with the grim intention of going over there and hauling her away before one of the other kind of circling vultures here—the press—noticed her and ruined the foolish creature's life.

'Mr Villani?' a husky female voice spoke to him. 'I'm really sorry to bother you but…'

Raffaelle spun on his heel to find himself staring down at yet another nubile young thing with the requisite blonde hair and good breasts. His expression turned to ice as he looked down at her, though the way she was looking up at him through tense, apprehensive, big blue eyes almost made him think twice about turning his back.

More so when the pink tip of her tongue arrived to nervously calm the little tremor he could see happening with her lips.

Nice lips, he noticed. Full, very pink, very lush lips.

'Do you think I could h-have a word with you?' she requested nervously. 'It's really important,' she added quickly. 'I need to ask you a big favour…'

A favour? Well, that was a novel approach. Raffaelle felt the corner of his mouth give a twitch—and thereby did the worst thing he could have done, by allowing a chink of interest to stop him from walking away.

Her silky hair hung dead straight to her slender shoulders and she possessed the most amazing pearly-white skin. He sent his eyes skimming down her front to her cleavage where two firm, plump very white breasts balanced precariously inside the tiny bodice of the short and skimpy pale turquoise silk thing he supposed he should call a dress. She wasn't tall by his standards, but she had a pair of legs on her that did not need the four inch heels she was wearing to extend their fabulous length.

Cosmetically enhanced or not, this one was probably the most appealing package in the room tonight, he accepted as he lifted his eyes back to the pair of pink lips to watch them tremble some more as she waited for his response.

When he still did not give one, she took a step closer, her too-blue eyes lighting up with appeal. 'You see I have this—problem…'

She was going to touch him. His stupid hesitation had given her encouragement to believe that he was interested.

Raffaelle stiffened, each well toned muscle in his long lean framework abruptly tightening up.

'No,' he iced out.

Then turned on his heel and strode off.

Cold, rude, arrogant swine, Rachel mentally tossed after him in stinging frustration. Did the too-tall, dark and disgustingly handsome devil think he was so special that he didn't need to be polite to a woman?

Well, you're not my type, Mr Villani, she told the long length of his retreating figure. Especially if *his* type was the kind of women doing the rounds here tonight.

Rachel's blue eyes turned bitter as she flicked them round the gathered assembly of the famously rich and beautiful—in that order, money being the biggest attraction here tonight. It was a trade fair for the beautiful people to ply their wares in front of London's wealthiest, though it hid under the more respectable title of a Charity Fundraising Event.

She should not have come here. If Elise hadn't convinced

her it was the only way to get close to a man like Raffaelle Villani, she would not have been seen dead at a do like this.

'He likes them blonde and slinky,' Elise had said. 'Notoriously can't keep his hands off. You only have to read down the list of his last fifteen girlfriends to know the man has no control when he's faced with blonde hair and a great pair of legs.'

Well, not in my case, Rachel thought heavily as she gave a grim tug at the hem of the dress Elise had made her wear. 'You have to look the part,' her half-sister had insisted. 'When you pay the extortionate price for tickets like these it means you have to look as if you can afford to throw good money away.'

The silly price of the tickets was one thing, but a five figure sum dress only earned its price tag if it looked good on the wearer.

Rachel felt as if she looked like a very cheap tart.

'Hello, beautiful…' The unremarkable hit line arrived as a hand squeezed around her waist at the same time and a pair of lips arrived at one of the straps which held up the dress. 'Having trouble with the dress? Can I help?'

His teeth nipped at the shoulder strap. Rachel heaved in a thick breath of disgust. 'Take your hands and your teeth off me,' she iced out, then broke free and walked off without giving the guy a single glance.

She'd taken about five steps before she realised she'd inadvertently walked in the same direction as Raffaelle Villani.

And there he was.

She stopped dead.

He was in the process of disentangling a lovely young thing wearing red from the possessive clutches of another man. The vision in red turned to pout a protest at him, then flung her arms around his neck and kissed him full on the mouth.

So much for him preferring them blonde, Rachel thought cynically. The creature he'd just claimed and was now kissing was hot-lipped, glossy and black-haired.

Oh, God, she thought helplessly, what was she going to do if she did not manage to pull this off?

'You're drunk,' Raffaelle informed Daniella.

'Tiddly,' his half-English stepsister insisted with a smile gauged to melt his irritation away.

It did not succeed. 'Admit to being drunk, *cara*,' he advised as he grabbed both of her hands and dragged them down from around his neck. 'It is the only excuse Gino will accept for what you have just been doing.'

'I haven't been doing anything—!' Eyes the colour of warm dark chocolate opened wide and tried their best to look innocent.

'You were hitting on that guy,' Raffaelle accused her.

'We were flirting, that's all! And what do you think you're doing, Raffaelle?' she protested when he took hold of her hand and turned towards the exit.

'Taking you home,' he clipped out. 'I don't know why I let you talk me into bringing you here in the first place.'

'For some fun?' Daniella offered up.

'I don't do this kind of fun.'

'That's your big problem, Raffaelle,' she informed him as he trailed her behind him. 'You don't *do* anything these days other than work yourself into the ground.'

'My choice.'

'To be a grouch.'

A nerve ticked at the corner of his mouth because she was right: he was becoming grouch—a bitter and cynical grouch.

'All because one woman managed to con you into believing she was pure sweetness and light…'

'As you try to do, you mean?'

'I *am* all sweetness and light!' Daniella insisted. 'And that wasn't very nice,' she complained. 'Nor do I lie or cheat.'

'Tell that to Gino not to me,' Raffaelle countered. 'If he had seen the way you were preparing to wrap yourself around that guy, he would call the wedding off.'

'But Gino isn't here because he prefers to be halfway across the world playing the hot shot tycoon.'

'However, the press *is* here—'

Raffaelle stopped walking as a sudden thought hit him. He swung round to pierce her with a hard stare.

'Is that what this is about?' he demanded. 'Did you drag me out to this thing—which is nothing more than an overpriced knocking shop,' he said with contempt, 'so that you would be caught on camera playing the vamp with some other guy just to punish Gino, knowing that *I* would be on hand to haul you out of trouble before you got yourself in too deep?'

'I hate him,' Daniella announced. 'I might even decide not to marry him. I'm supposed to be the love of his life yet I haven't set eyes on him in two wh-whole weeks!'

The small break in her voice did it. Raffaelle heard the fight with tears and released a sigh. 'Come here, you idiot.' He pulled her into his arms. 'You know Gino worships the ground you walk upon but he is busy trying to free himself up for that long glorious honeymoon he has planned for you both.'

'He even sounds like he would rather be doing something else when he rings me,' she sniffed into his shirt front. 'I'm not a doormat. I refuse to let him wipe his feet on me!'

Raffaelle shifted his stance.

'You're laughing at me!' Daniella choked out.

'No, I am not.'

What he was actually doing was staring over Daniella's glossy dark head into the cynical blue eyes of the blonde who had approached him a few minutes ago. She was now standing about ten feet away being buffeted by the milling crowd but not noticing because she was too busy looking at him as if he was a snake.

A sting injected itself down the front of his body. The confusing signals she was giving off dressed—or *un*dressed—like she was, while glaring at him like that, were setting his senses on edge.

Who the hell was she, anyway? Why had he not hung around long enough to find out?

Did he want to know?

His eyes cooled and hardened. No, he didn't, he answered his own question. Expensive tarts in expensive dresses were ten-a-Euro to buy in this room. He did not need to buy his women. And this one was more the type for the guy who was approaching her from behind right now and eyeing her up and down as if she was his next tasty snack.

And tasty said it, he found himself reluctantly admitting as he ran a glance down her front until he reached the place where those two fabulous legs came together.

Was the hair at her crotch the same pale gold colour as the hair on her head?

He shifted again, was vaguely aware of Daniella talking into his shirt but didn't hear what she said. That damn inconvenient thing called sexual curiosity was trying to take him over, heating him up like a pot coming to the boil.

The blonde stiffened, tugging his gaze back to her face to clash with the shocked look in her eyes. He realised then that she knew what he had been thinking, her pearly-white skin suffused with heat.

Feeling the spark too, *cara*? his glinting eyes mocked her. Well hard damn luck because I am not buying.

The approaching man had reached her—a tall fair haired good-looking guy who stepped right in behind her and ran his fingers up her bare arms to her shoulders, then bent to murmur something in her ear.

She quivered—Raffaelle saw it happen. As she slowly blinked her eyes and turned her head sideways so she was no longer looking at him, he watched her sumptuous pink mouth tilt into a smile.

She turns on for any man, he observed grimly.

'Hi,' Rachel said, still stinging at the way Raffaelle Villani had just looked at her as if she was a sex object put on show to be bought.

'Hi to you too,' Mark returned. 'No luck with the appeal approach?'

'Look at him,' she sighed, glancing back at Mr Villani who was now in the process of curving the clinging dark-haired woman beneath the crook of his arm.

What was he, six-three—six four? Rachel found herself giving him a thorough once-over. He had a great pair of shoulders inside the black dinner suit he was wearing, and a mean pair of long powerful legs. His bright white dress shirt gave the honey-gold tones of his skin at his throat a warm, tight, healthy glow that annoyingly made the tip of her tongue grow moist.

He was supposed to be a fantastic athlete, so Elise had said. Watching him as he began guiding the dark-haired woman through the doors which led to the hotel foyer, Rachel could see why. He moved with loose-limbed grace, languid and supple but firm. If you stripped him down to a pair of running shorts she would be prepared to bet you wouldn't see a single ripple of unwanted flesh.

Marital status: single. Age: thirty three. Loves snow-skiing and water-skiing. Owns his own sexy powerboat which he races at the weekend when he has the time. Owns homes in London, Paris, Monaco and, of course, his native Milan. Plus a huge private skiing lodge inside the very prestigious Gigante Park, where he likes to his spend part of his winters refining his no doubt amazing skills on the ski slopes. Inherited his wealth from his heavyweight banking family, then went on to triple that fortune with shrewd investments which pushed him and the Villani name right to the top of the rich list.

He was, in other words, a tall, dark, very good looking, very *rich* Italian male with a sinful amount of sex appeal and all the conceit and arrogance that came with such an impressive pedigree.

It was no wonder he'd cut her out without giving her a chance to explain herself. A man like him was just too darn precious about his own status as the most eligible catch on the block to think of questioning if a woman might want to approach him for any reason other than to latch on to his great body and his lovely money.

Well, Mr Villani, Rachel told his elegant back. Self-obsessed millionaires are ten-a-penny these days. You only have to look around this room to see that.

But men of honour were a very rare breed indeed.

'I thought Elise said he was only into blondes,' she said to Mark. 'But you can't put a hair between him and that black-haired female, so what chance did I have of getting in there?'

'You idiot,' Mark said. 'Don't you know who the brunette is? That's his flighty stepsister, Daniella Leeson of Leeson Hotels fame. She's about to marry his best friend and that other hotel heavy, Gino Rossi—Don't you ever read any of the stuff I print?'

Rachel gave a slow shake of her head, still watching Raffaelle Villani as he paused in the foyer, framed like a masterpiece between the two open doors. He was helping his stepsister on with her coat now—all care and attention.

Gorgeous face in profile, honesty forced her to admit. With fantastic high cheekbones and black eyelashes so luxurious she could see even from this far away, how they hovered like sexy dark shadows just above those golden cheeks.

When he'd done with the coat he turned his stepsister round

and lifted her chin with a gentle finger, then smiled as he murmured something to make her smile back at him.

So he possessed killer charm too, when he wanted to unleash it, Rachel saw, and did not like the stinging flutter she felt suddenly attack the lining of her lower stomach.

Was this the side of him he'd used on Elise to make the silly fool risk her marriage for him? The way Elise told it, he had done all the chasing while she'd tried to keep him at arm's length.

No chance, Rachel denounced. There was no way any woman could hold this man at arm's length if he did not want to be held there. It was no wonder that poor Elise had dropped like a shot duck into his hands.

'I've ruined everything,' she murmured dully. 'Look, they're leaving.'

'The hell you have,' Mark said brusquely. 'We can't let Elise down after all of this planning. I can still rescue this.'

Grabbing one of her hands, he began pulling her towards the foyer.

'The trouble with you, Rachel, is you insisted on trying the wrong tack on him then blew it. This time you do it the way we planned it, okay? So listen,' instructed the man who got his highs hunting down and catching the rich and famous at their worst. 'I'm going to grab the lovely Daniella's attention. All you have to do is to move in on him the moment I move in on her. I can give you ten seconds at most, so don't hang around and, for God's sake, don't let yourself think! This will be our last chance.'

Their last chance…

They'd reached the foyer by now and Mark's instructions were playing across her tense chest muscles like sharp hammering throbs. Raffaelle Villani and his stepsister were already turning towards the main exit doors.

'Hey—Miss Leeson!' Mark called out. 'Where's your future husband tonight?'

Daniella Leeson paused, then turned on the delicate heels of her shoes, saw Mark with a camera already up at his face and switched on a false smile.

'He's…'

'Get going,' Mark muttered sideways at Rachel.

As if in a dream Rachel let Mark's urgency take her over. Her legs felt like jelly as she moved in. Raffaelle Villani was only just turning to watch his stepsister pose for the hated paparazzi so he didn't see Rachel coming at him from one side. Stepping right in front of him and without daring to think, she threw her arms up and clasped his face between her fingers, then stretched up on tiptoe and crushed her mouth against his.

She didn't know which of them was the more shocked as heat hit her body like mega-watt high voltage. His grunt of surprise vibrated against her lips. Lights flashed, her skin burned, her fingertips tingled where they pressed against his warm satin tight skin.

Seconds. It took too many seconds for his brain to relay to Raffaelle what was happening and by then her mouth was fusing hot against his. His hands leapt up—it was automatic to close them around a small waist with the intention of pushing her away.

A camera flashed.

He pulled his mouth free, found himself staring down at the same blonde who'd approached earlier. '*Madre de Dio*. What do you think you are doing?' he raked out.

The flash hit him again. She was staring up at him, all big blue apologetic eyes and smudged pink lipstick and her fingers had shifted from his face to the back of his neck.

'Sorry,' she whispered breathlessly. 'But you left me with no other choice.'

She began to pull away. The camera was still flashing. Instead of aiding her withdrawal, Raffaelle tightened his grip on her waist and made her stay exactly where she was.

He was blindingly, blisteringly furious. 'No choice about what?' he bit down at her.

She wriggled against him in an effort to free herself. What happened next made her breath catch and he knew why it did. She was plastered against him like a second layer of skin and the extra physical pressure had brought their lower bodies into contact.

'*Dio*,' he cursed again.

'Oh, God,' Rachel echoed. 'Y-you—you're…'

'I don't need you to tell me what I already know!' he raked out. 'I just need an explanation as to what the hell you think you are trying to pull off with this!'

'I…'

'Okay kiddo, let's go.'

Let's go…Raffaelle lifted his eyes to the photographer, wondered why he hadn't noticed the camera dangling round his neck before. Then answered his own question with a twist of his mouth. He had been too busy looking at her to notice him in any detail.

'Some set-up,' he gritted.

'Please let me go now.' She tugged at his iron grip on her waist.

'Not even if you decide to faint,' he incised, sparks flying from his eyes as he watched Daniella turn towards them and her eyes give a startled blink.

Indeed, he agreed with her surprised expression. The photographer was already shooting out of the door.

'You,' he raked at his attacker, 'are coming with me to explain yourself.'

Without giving her a chance to protest, he reached up to yank her claws out of his neck, then let go of one hand and used the other to begin hauling her towards the exit.

'Raffaelle—!' A bewildered Daniella called his name as she hurried after them.

Outside a cool breeze hit his angry face.

Just angry—? He was bloody blindingly livid. His instincts must be dulling for him to get caught out like this.

'Please…' the blonde pleaded.

'Be silent,' he snapped out and his hand tightened its grip on her wrist. He felt her wince; he didn't care. Dino, his chauffeur, drew his limo up at the kerb and climbed out of the car.

Raffaelle strode towards it with his captive almost tripping up behind him on her flimsy sparkling spindle-heeled shoes. 'Grab a cab and take Miss Leeson home,' he instructed his driver.

'But—Raffaelle—?' his stepsister wailed in protest.

He ignored her. He ignored everyone, including the blonde who was still desperately trying to get free. Opening the front passenger door to the limo, he tried to propel her inside.

She dug her heels in. 'I'm not—'

He picked her up and bodily put her into the car. When she tried to get out again, her mouth opening wide with the intention of screaming for help, he bent swiftly and smothered the sound with his mouth.

He didn't take pleasure from hard angry kisses, he told himself, particularly when he'd just been hit on by a woman who deserved a slap not a kiss. However the kiss gave him a hell of a lot more satisfaction, especially when her muffled scream rolled around his mouth and sent his tongue chasing it.

She quivered. She tasted of champagne and pink lipstick.

By the time he yanked his mouth away again she'd sunk into trembling shock.

'Now, listen to me,' he incised as he locked the seat belt around her. 'I don't know how much your partner in crime was paying you to pull off that stunt, but in case you did not notice, he was not the only sleaze-gathering scum working the room back there. The pack has scented a story and is about to descend on us.'

On that hard warning he straightened, slammed the car door shut, then strode round to the other side while Rachel twisted her head to stare dazedly at the press pack gathering at the main hotel doors. By the time she'd absorbed all of that, Raffaelle Villani had folded himself into the driver's seat next to her—a lean, dark, hard-muscled male with aggression bouncing off him.

His chauffeur had left the engine running. He snaked out a hand and threw the car into drive. They took off with a jerk just as the press pack tumbled over each other with their cameras flashing. Rachel watched as the whole debacle played out like a comic strip. Even his stepsister had her part to play. She was standing by the kerb staring after them while the chauffeur was politely trying to urge her into the back of a black cab.

Mark was nowhere.

Thanks, Mark, Rachel thought helplessly, visualising her darling half-brother rushing off to file his scoop without giving a second thought to what he had left her to face!

Rachel flicked a scared glance at the man sitting beside her, then shivered. If murder had a look to it then he was wearing it.

'Please stop the car so I can get out,' she begged and didn't even care that she was begging.

He didn't answer. Lips clamped together, he sent the car shooting out into the main stream of traffic. Several car horns blared in protest at his pushy arrogance. He ignored those too.

'Look, I know you're angry,' she allowed shakily. 'And I know that you have every right to be, but—'

'*Grazie*.'

'This is kidnap!'

'So sue me,' he gritted. 'That could be fun.'

Fun—? Rachel trembled and shivered as she sat tensely beside him. None of this had been *fun* from the moment she'd allowed Elise and Mark to talk her into it. One minute she'd been perfectly content, hiding away in Devon nursing her broken heart, the next minute she'd found herself staying up here in London with her half-sister and being embroiled in her complicated love-life!

'It w-wasn't what you think—'

'You don't know what I'm thinking.'

'I am *not* being paid to—'

'Hit on me?' he offered when those very same words dried in her throat. 'It is a relief to know I still have some natural pulling power then.'

He had loads of natural pulling power. That was his problem.

'Are you always this obnoxious when you've been caught off your guard?' she flared up on the back of pure agitation. 'So I hit on you—what's new there to a man like you? From what I hear, half the women in Europe have done it at some point in your blessed life—and not all of them because of your sex appeal!'

He sent her a glinting look. 'Did I hear a hint of scorn in your tone then?'

'Yes!' she flicked out. 'Men like you stroll through life as if you own it. You do what you want when you want to do it. You pick your women on looks alone and don't give a care whether they have feelings you could actually wound!'

Something sharp hit his voice. 'I wounded—you?'

'You mean you don't know?' The sarcasm was out before she could stop it.

They'd stopped at a set of traffic lights and he turned in his seat. Instantly the sheer size and power of the man flooded over Rachel like a simmering hot shower. She could feel his eyes skimming her face and her body as he checked her out while flipping through his huge data bank of women, trying to pinpoint who she was. Any second now and he was going to make a connection he could have made hours ago if he'd been more observant.

Rachel felt the stinging temptation to lie, if only to really confuse him, but— 'No,' she said finally.

Someone just like you did that to me, she added inside her head. Then she flicked him a hard resentful glance, heaved in a breath and saved him the bother of further taxing his no doubt phenomenal brain power.

'Elise Castle,' she breathed out.

CHAPTER TWO

THE name had its desired effect, Rachel noticed bitterly, as a long thick silence stretched between them and he didn't say or do a single thing.

She held her breath again while she waited for him to recover and begin spitting out a barrage of angry questions—but still nothing came.

In the end she took the initiative and broke the silence. 'The name means nothing to you?' she gibed.

Other vehicle headlights swished past the car windows, lighting their faces momentarily. Illuminated, she saw only the cold steel of his eyes as they fixed hers like lashing daggers and he kept his silence. In the darkness her gaze dropped for some reason to the single line straightness of his mouth.

A mouth that already felt disconcertingly familiar. She could still taste it. Her tongue even made a passing swipe at her lips in response to the thought.

Headlights lit up the car's interior again, dragging her attention back to his eyes. They'd narrowed and were watching her like a hawk waiting to pin its next victim. Rachel's breathing fell into small jerky fits. Her heart was pounding. He was frighteningly exciting to look at, all well cared for male with just the right balance between sensational good looks and raw masculinity.

Her mouth had to part to aid her quick breathing. He dropped his gaze and the result was a tingling quiver across her lips that sent the tip of her tongue nervously chasing it. Sexual awareness was suddenly alive and cluttering the atmosphere. Rachel felt her breasts grow heavy, their tips pushing out with a terrible knowing sting. He flicked those eyes back to hers again and he knew—he *knew*!

Then the traffic lights decided to change, demanding that he set them moving. She watched as if mesmerised as his dark head shifted back into profile, watched his long-fingered hands as he flipped the car into a slick right turn. More seconds ticked by and her chest felt as if it was burning beneath the pressure she was placing on it by barely breathing at all now.

'The name means plenty to me,' he finally answered. 'And you are not Elise.'

No, Rachel knew she wasn't Elise. She was her younger, less pretty, more sensible half-sister.

More sensible—when? She then scoffed at that. Sensible women did not get themselves into situations like this. Sensible women steered clear of the complicated love lives of others—and especially of frighteningly sexy men like him!

Sensible women did not fall in love with handsome Italians with a rich repertoire of words of love and a killer seduction technique—yet she had done it.

She had to close her eyes as an image of Alonso suddenly appeared in front of her. Tall, dark, beautiful Alonso, who had been so warm and attentive and flatteringly possessive when they had been out together, and so excitingly intense and passionate when naked with her in bed. They'd spent six glorious weeks living together in his apartment overlooking Naples. He'd vowed he loved her. 'I love you—*ti'amo mia bella cara*…' he'd murmured to her in his rich, dark, accented voice and she'd known without a doubt that she loved him.

Rachel shivered.

It was only when the time had come for her to return to England and he'd said, 'We had a wonderful time, hmm, *amore*? It is a shame it now has to end,' that she'd understood what a stupid, gullible, naïve fool she had been.

'I said you are not Elise,' this other Italian with the rich, dark accent prompted.

Rachel opened her eyes and let the real world back in. 'No,' she agreed. 'But very few people will be able to tell that from behind…'

A bell of understanding suddenly clanged loud in Raffaelle's head. Next to come was an action replay of the way this woman had thrown herself on him, followed by several camera flashes. Like a wild beast sniffing danger in the atmosphere, he picked up the scent of a deliberately constructed scandal involving him and the very married Elise.

But it was a scandal he believed he had already diverted. As far as he was aware, the lovely Elise had seen the error of her ways after his last spiked conversation with her on the telephone before he'd broken all contact with her and made his quick exit from London back to Milan. The grapevine, via Daniella, said she had not been seen on the social circuit since.

So what was *this* devious creature up to? Why had she gone to so much trouble to make out for the camera that she was Elise?

'Explain,' he commanded.

Not this side of midnight, Rachel thought tensely and clamped her lips together. Having come this far, she was not about to scupper everything by getting Mark's story pulled before going to print.

She'd already revealed more than she should have done.

'Look…' she heaved out instead. 'You're not an idiot, Mr Villani. You must know you're asking for trouble taking me against my will like this—so just stop the car and let me out now.'

'Not a chance in hell,' he refused.

And the way he turned his head to slide his eyes up her legs had Rachel tugging jerkily at the short skirt of her dress. She knew that look. It was as old as the human race. She'd let him see her attraction to him; now he was looking over the goods on offer.

'If you honestly think—!'

'Changing your mind about the hit, *cara*?' he taunted. 'Wondering if you might have bitten off more than you can chew with me? Well, let me confirm that you have done.' His voice hardened. 'You made the hit. I bought it. Now you are going to play it my way.'

'You're crazy,' she whispered.

Maybe he was, Raffaelle conceded. But no woman—*no woman*—played games with him and got away with it!

'I'm getting out of this car—' Rachel reached for the door handle. The automatic lock gave a clunk as it fell into place at the same time that he increased their speed.

True—true unfettered fear began to scream in her head as it finally began to sink in what a stupid, crazy, dangerous situation she had managed to get herself into here. What did she know about Raffaelle Villani, other than the details fed to her by Mark and Elise? How did she know he wasn't some kind of mega-rich sex maniac prowling Europe unhindered because his money could buy his victims' silence.

Just as he said, he had bought her…

Her skin began to creep, her fingers closing tightly around her small clutch bag so they felt the reassurance of her cellphone.

How much time did she need to call the police before he reacted?

She dared a quick glance at him, heart hammering, fingers tensely toying with the clasp on her bag. He didn't look like a lunatic, just a very angry man—which he had every right to be, she was forced to admit.

'Your partner in crime did not hang around to protect you,' he taunted grimly next.

He had to mean Mark. 'You don't—'

'Unless he is in one of the cars following behind us, that is…'

Cars—? Rachel twisted around to peer through the rear window.

'There are three back there I can pick out as belonging to the paparazzi,' she was told. 'And there are most likely more of them following not far behind them.'

Twisting forward again, she stared at him. 'But why should they want to follow us?'

'You are not that naïve,' he derided the question, flicking his eyes from the rear-view mirror and back to the road ahead. 'Or you would not have chosen Raffaelle Villani to pull your life-wrecking stunt.'

Life wrecking—? 'N-no.' Rachel gave an urgent shake of her head. 'You don't understand. This was not—'

'Not that it matters,' he interrupted. 'We are here now.'

As in *where*—? Even as Rachel thought the question, one of those shiny new apartment blocks that flanked the river loomed up close. With a spin of the wheel he sent the car sweeping on to its forecourt. He stopped it hard on its brakes and was already out of the car and striding around it to open her door.

Rachel didn't move. She was trembling like mad and her heart was thundering. She didn't look at him either, but just stared starkly ahead.

'Do you get out yourself or do I have to lift you?' he demanded.

Since she'd already learnt the hard way that he was perfectly willing to do the latter, swallowing tensely, Rachel took the more dignified choice, unfastened her seat belt and slid out of the car.

It was an odd sensation to find herself standing close to him. Nor did that sensation make any sense because she'd stood this close once already tonight and thrown herself right against him a second time, yet he hadn't felt this tall or as powerfully built or as dangerous as he did right now.

She shivered, panicked and was about to make a run for it when car doors started slamming. The paparazzi had arrived right behind them and were already piling out of their cars.

Raffaelle bit out a curse, then he was wrapping her beneath the hook of a powerful arm.

Cameras flashed. 'Look this way, Elise—!' one of them called out to her.

But she was already being ushered through a pair of doors. 'Keep them out,' Raffaelle instructed the security man manning the foyer.

Before Rachel knew what was happening, he'd marched her into a lift and the doors were closing the two of them inside.

It had happened so fast—all of it—everything! And she'd never felt so afraid in her entire life. Her head was whirling and her legs had gone hollow. The panic had not subsided and it sent the heels of her shoes screeching shrilly beneath her as she spun round, then she lifted an arm and hit out at him with her bag.

He fielded the blow like a man swatting a fly away. 'Calm down,' he gritted.

But Rachel didn't want to calm down. Hair flying about her slender neck as she struggled with him, 'Let me go—let me go!' she choked out.

Then she threw back her head and opened her mouth to scream.

Only it didn't arrive. Nothing happened. The scream remained just a thick lump pulsing in the base of her throat. And he didn't attempt to smother it like he had done outside the hotel but just stood there looking down at her while she stared up at him.

It was crazy—the whole evening had been crazy, but this

was *the* craziest part because it felt as if they'd both suddenly been frozen in time.

The panic receded. She forgot to breathe. As far as she could tell, he wasn't breathing either and he was frowning as if he too couldn't understand what was going on.

Gorgeous frown, she found herself thinking. Gorgeous black silk-hooded eyes. In fact he was, she saw as if for the first time, altogether totally breathtaking to look at. His facial bone structure was striking—the high forehead and good cheekbones, the long narrow nose and perfectly symmetrical chin.

And his eyes weren't really grey, but an unusual mixture of green flecked with silver. His skin was amazing, a tightly wrapped casing of honey-gold her fingers remembered with a tense little twitch. The satin-black eyebrows, those luxuriously long eyelashes that were hovering just above the cheekbones, and the mouth…

Don't look at his mouth, she told herself tautly, but she didn't just look, she stared at it. Slender, smooth, slightly parted. The tip of her tongue snaked out to wipe away the now familiar tingle she felt take over her own lips.

He breathed. The warmth of his breath brushed her face, scented with the heady fruits of a rich dark wine. She tried a tense swallow, looked back into his eyes and saw what was coming. He was going to kiss her. Not to stop her screaming or even in anger, but because—

Oh, God, she wanted him to!

He muttered something in Italian. She released the strangest-sounding groan. In the next second he'd captured her mouth and they were kissing—really kissing. Not stolen, fought-for, punishing or smothering kisses, but like two greedy, hungry lovers with a swift, hot, urgent necessity.

Their tongues flickered and slid in a wild, erotic dance of hungry heat. Without caring she was doing it, Rachel lifted her arms up over Raffaelle's shoulders and arched closer until she could feel every inch of him pressing against her, from his hard-packed chest to powerful thighs.

He was so pumped up and solid, his hands moving on a restless journey over the silk dress covering her slender body to the bare flesh of her shoulders, then back down to her small waist again. She became aware that she was purring like a well stroked kitten. He breathed something harsh, then picked her up with his hands and started walking without breaking the kiss.

Her hands were in his hair now, raking his scalp and scrunching its smooth style, the swollen globes of her breasts nudging at him high on his chest.

This should not be happening. This *should not be happening!* a shrill voice screamed inside her head.

The panic returned; Rachel yanked her head back at the same moment that he did the same thing.

Like two people who did not know what the hell was happening to them, they stared at each other again, her eyes wide dark pools of shocked horror and confusion, his blackened by stunned disbelief. Her mouth was burning, her lips still parted and pulsing and swollen as she panted for breath.

He put her down so abruptly she almost toppled off the thin heels of her shoes, her fingers trailing around his shirt collar then down the front of his jacket where they clung, because they had to, to his black satin lapels.

Anger burned now. A thick, dark, intense anger that pulsed from every hard inch of him as he used a key to open a door. Rachel had not noticed that they'd left the lift, never mind crossed another foyer to reach the door!

Manoeuvring them both inside, he kicked the door shut with a foot before peeling her off his front. She staggered dizzily. He walked away down a spacious hallway, then disappeared through another door.

She wanted to faint. She wished she *could* faint. She wished the floor would open up and swallow her whole. Every inch of her body was still alive and buzzing with excitement and a shrill ringing was filling her head.

The ringing stopped abruptly and she blinked. Then she heard his voice ripping out words in sharp Italian and realised the sound had been coming from a phone. She caught Elise's name and reality came tumbling over her like a giant snowball, dousing every bit of heat.

It took real willpower to make her trembling legs walk her down that hallway. But she needed to know what he was saying and to whom he was saying it.

The door was flung wide open on its hinges and she stilled in the opening, staring starkly across a spacious living room with wall-to-wall glass on one side and an expanse of warm wood covering the floor softened by a big creamy-coloured rug. Everything in here was clean-lined and modern. He was standing beside one of several black leather sofas that were carefully placed about the room.

His back was to her. He had a land line telephone clamped to his ear and his hair was still mussed. Her fingers tingled to remind her who had done the mussing. As she continued to stand there, he lifted up a set of long fingers and mussed it up some more.

'Daniella—' he snapped out, then stopped and sighed.

Whatever his stepsister said to him then made his voice alter, the snap going out of it and low, dark, soothing Italian arriving in its place, aimed to apologise and reassure.

Me too, please, Rachel wanted to beg. Reassure me too that this is all just a big nightmare.

But it wasn't and her heart was still beating too fast. The low dark flow of his voice seemed to resonate directly from deep inside his chest before reaching the rolling caress of his tongue.

Oh, God. She put a set of trembling fingers up to cover her

eyes. Did all Italian men have deep, sexy voices, or was it just that she had been unlucky enough to meet the only two that could do this to her?

Then an impatient 'Daniella,' arrived again. 'Take my advice and call Gino. Take your bad temper out on him, for I am in no mood to hear this.'

He had switched to English. Rachel dropped her hand in time to watch his shoulders give a tight shrug.

'If *Elise* upstaged you then count your blessings that she was more interesting to the cameras than you and your behaviour were five minutes before!'

Elise…Rachel tensed as a sudden thought hit her. If Raffaelle's stepsister had been fooled tonight into believing she was Elise, then maybe, between them, she and Mark had managed to pull this off!

Rafaelle's voice returned to smooth Italian. Rachel listened intently for the sound of Elise's name being spoken again but it did not happen. A few seconds later he was finishing the call.

Raffaelle put the phone down, then flexed his wide shoulders. He could feel her standing somewhere behind him but he did not want to turn around and find out where.

He did not want to look at her.

He did not know what the hell she was doing to him!

With an impatient yank he undid his bow tie, shifted his stance to angle his body towards the drinks cabinet, then plucked with hard fingers at the top button of his dress shirt as he strode across the room. His jacket came next. He lost it to the back of a sofa. The silence screamed across the gap separating them as he flipped open the cabinet doors and reached for the brandy bottle.

'Drink—?' he offered.

'No thank you,' she huskily declined.

Husky did it. He felt that low sensual voice reach right down inside him and give a hard tug on his loins.

'Keeping a clear head?' he mocked tightly.

'Yes,' she breathed.

Pouring a brandy for himself, he turned with the glass in his hand. She was standing in the doorway in her turquoise dress, with her arms held tensely to her sides. Her hands were gripping the black beaded bag she had tried to hit him with in the lift and her blue eyes were telling him that she was scared.

Some might say that she had asked for everything that was happening to her but Raffaelle was reluctantly prepared to admit that he had been behaving little better than a thug.

He took a sip of his drink, grimly aware that what had broken free in the lift was still busy inside him. He wanted her. He did not know why he wanted her. He'd been tempted by sirens far more adept at their craft than she was without feeling the slightest inclination to give in.

Yet he did—want to give in. In fact the want was now a low-down burning ache in his gut.

She wasn't even what he would call beautiful. Not in the classic Elise-sleek-catwalk-fashion-sense, that was. There again, neither had Elise been catwalk-sleek by the time he'd met her. And this woman's face did not possess the same striking bone structure that Elise had been endowed with. The eyes were the same blue but the nose was different—and the mouth.

The mouth…

Lifting the glass to his lips, Raffaelle half hid his eyes as he studied the mouth, wiped clear of pink lipstick now and still softly swollen from their kiss in the lift. Elise's mouth was a wide classic bow shape whereas this mouth was shaped more evocatively like a heart and was frankly lush. And Elise was taller, though he would hazard a guess the lost inches would not show on a photograph as this one had stretched up and plastered herself against his front.

The dress was expensive—you didn't live most of your life

around fashion conscious females without being able to pick out haute couture when you saw it. But it did not fit her. It was too tight in places, like across those two white breasts that were in danger of falling out of it, and it hugged the rounded shape of her slender hips like a second skin.

'Turn round,' he instructed.

She tensed in objection.

'I am looking for your likeness to Elise,' he informed her levelly. 'So humour me and turn around…'

She did. Raffaelle grimaced because he would have been prepared to swear that right now she would rather spit in his face than comply with anything he wanted her to do. The passionate kiss in the lift coming hard on the back of the way she'd looked at him in the car had made her so uptight and defensive he could almost taste her hostility towards him even as she stood there with her back to him.

And that was just another thing about her. Elise might have been a damn good liar but she had not possessed a single spark of passion or spirit. She'd been quiet and surprisingly shy for someone who had earned her living sashaying along catwalks and posing for glossy magazines.

But that was thinking with hindsight, because he had not known who Elise really was at the time. And he was looking in the wrong place if he expected to find the very married ex-model's nature in a woman who was definitely not her.

The back view did it, though. The back view with the straight hair and the narrow shoulders and tight backside told him exactly why this woman believed she could get away with pretending to be Elise from that angle.

'Had enough?' She spun back to face him so she could fix him with an icy stare.

It made him want to grimace, because if she was allowing herself to believe that such an expression was going to hold him back she was sadly mistaken. Despite the frost, she'd switched him on and now, he discovered, he was not feeling inclined to switch himself off again.

In fact he was beginning to enjoy the sexual sting that was passing between them.

The way he was standing there with his glass in his hand and his eyes half hidden, he reminded Rachel of a long, lean jungle cat lazily planning the moment when it would pounce.

Still dangerous, in other words.

The loss of his jacket wasn't helping. The bright white of his shirt only made his shoulders look wider and his torso longer and tougher, and the way his loosened bow tie lay in two strips of black either side of his open shirt collar kept on drawing her eyes to the triangle of golden skin at his throat.

Rachel's throat went dry. Oh, please, she begged, will someone get me out of here—?

Because looking at him was recharging the sexual buzz. She could feel it moving through her blood in a slow and sluggishly threatening burn, scary yet exciting—like a war she was having to fight on two fronts.

'Don't you think it is time that you told me your name?'

Rachel tensed, her eyes flicking into focus on his face. Then a strained little laugh broke in her throat because it hadn't occurred to her that he didn't know who she was.

'Rachel,' she pushed out. 'Rachel Carmichael.'

Something about him suddenly altered. For some unknown reason she felt as if the air circulating around him had gone as tense as a cracked whip. And the eyes—the eyes were not merely hooded now, they'd narrowed into sharp eyelash-framed slits.

'Well, hello, Rachel Carmichael,' he drawled in a very slow, lazy tone that made the hairs on the back of her neck stand on end. 'Now this has just become very interesting...'

'Why has it?' she asked warily.

'Why don't you come and sit down so we can talk about it?'

She had the impression that the jungle cat in him had just sharpened its teeth. Taut as a bow string and balanced right on the balls of her feet now, Rachel wondered if this would be a good time to try to make a run for it.

But the idea lasted for only a moment. He had not brought her up here to his apartment to let her get away before she had given him an explanation as to why she'd set him up tonight.

Making herself walk across the room took courage, especially when he watched her all the way as if she was performing some special provocative act designed purposely to keep his attention engaged.

Oh, God, did he have to look so sleekly at ease and so gorgeously interested?

Beginning to feel disturbingly hollow from the neck down, if she did not count the sparking sting making itself felt, Rachel picked one of the black sofas at random and sat down right on its edge.

The skirt to her dress immediately rode upwards to reveal more slender thigh than was decent with a peek of her stocking lace tops. Unclipping her fingers from the death grip they had on her bag she gave a tug at the dress's hem, only to notice to her horror that its bodice wasn't doing much to keep her modesty covered, either.

And still he stood there watching her every single move, deliberately, she suspected, building on the sexual tension that was fizzing in the air. Her heart was pounding. She refused to look up. She wanted to swallow but would not allow herself the luxury of trying to shift the anxious lump lodged in her throat.

Then he moved and she jerked up her head, unable to stop the wary response, only to feel almost dizzy with embarrassment when she saw how he was looking at her.

'I will have that drink now,' she burst out, desperate for him to turn away so she could pull up the bodice of her dress without him watching.

One of those sleek black eyebrows arched in quizzing mockery at her abrupt change of mind about the drink. He knew what she was trying to do. It was scored into his eyes and his body language.

'What would you like?' he asked politely.

'I don't know—anything,' she shook out.

He turned his back. Rachel feathered out a tense breath and hurriedly rearranged herself. In all her life she had never felt so out of sorts and out of place as she was feeling right now, sitting on this sofa, wearing this dress, with that man standing only a few feet away.

She was nobody's luxury appendage—never had been. She'd always left that kind of thing to the more beautiful and capable Elise. Playing the role given to her tonight had been tough on her pride, from the moment she'd donned the whole image. And the only man she'd ever thrown herself at in her whole life before tonight had been Alonso, and, she recalled with a grimace, he'd been more or less crawling all over her by then anyway.

And Alonso hadn't been rich. He'd just been a very junior car salesman with good lines in smart suits and a tiny apartment. He drove flashy cars but he didn't own them, and he'd earned less money than she had earned picking fruit on a farm just outside Naples.

A glass appeared in front of her. Glancing up, she unclipped one of her hands from her bag and took it with a mumbled, 'Thanks,' then sat staring at it wondering what the heck was in it?

'Splash of vodka topped up with tonic,' he provided the answer. 'And it is not spiked with something lethal, if that is what the frown is about.'

'I wasn't—'

'Then you should,' he intruded curtly. 'You don't know me, Rachel Carmichael. I might go in for drug-enhanced love-ins. How old are you, by the way?'

Rachel blinked. 'Twenty-three. Why, what has my age got to do with anything?'

'Just curious.' He sat down right next to her sending her spine arching into a defensive stretch.

Raffaelle saw it happen and smiled. The air circulating around them was alive with an ever increasing sting of awareness. He could feel it. He knew that she could feel it. What he could not figure out was *why* it was there and what he was going to do about it.

Liar, the dry part of his brain fed back.

'Okay…' Relaxing into the sofa, he stretched out his long legs. 'Now, start talking.'

Talking… Sending her tongue round her dry lips, Rachel looked down at the bag she was still clutching in one hand and made a small shift of her wrist so she could see the time on her watch.

It was just coming up to midnight. How long did Mark need to do his thing with his digital camera, write his accompanying piece, then file it with the newspaper via the Internet?

She looked at her bag with the comforting feel of her cellphone inside it, and wondered if she dared take it out and ring him to check?

Great idea, she then thought heavily. As if Raffaelle Villani was going to let her contact anyone until he had his explanation.

'Sit back and relax,' he invited.

What she did was stiffen up all the more. 'I'm perfectly relaxed as I am, thank you.'

'No, you are not. There is tension—here…' A finger arrived in the naked taut hollow between her shoulders, sending her spine into another muscle splitting arch as if she'd been stung by an electric shock.

The sensation flung her, gasping to her feet. 'That wasn't—necessary,' she protested.

'You think not?'

'No.' Taking a few shaky steps away from him, she put the glass to her mouth and sipped while he watched her through half hidden eyes and a knowing smile on his lips.

'We share chemistry, *cara.*'

Rachel laughed thickly. 'That of kidnapper and victim.'

'And who do you believe is the victim here—?'

Just like that, with one smooth question, he brought the whole madness which had made up this evening tumbling down to where it really belonged.

For which of them was the real victim? Certainly not her, she had to admit. He had every right to be angry. She had no right to be anything at all.

On the short sigh that quivered as it left her, Rachel finally took responsibility for her own misdemeanours. It was no use trying to pretend she was innocent when she wasn't. Or to wish Raffaelle Villani a million miles away because he'd ruined all their plans when he had stopped her from getting away back there at the hotel.

He was right about the chemistry too. Just turning to look at his long, lean, relaxed sprawl, giving off all kinds of innate sexual messages, sent her insides into an instant tight spiral spin.

Then—okay, she told herself grimly, let's keep this strictly to business, then maybe the—other—stuff will die a natural death.

On that stern piece of good common sense, she lifted her chin, pushed her eyes upwards to fix them on his face, then she steadied her breathing and plunged right in.

'As I just told you, my name is Rachel Carmichael,' she reminded him. 'Elise is my half-sister. W-we had different fathers, hence the different surnames…'

CHAPTER THREE

HE DID not move. He remained relaxed. His eyes told her absolutely nothing and his mouth held on to its smooth flat line.

So why did Rachel get the unnerving impression that he had already worked most of that out?

'Elise has been out of the modelling scene for over five years now since—since she married Leo Savakis—'

'And gave him a son.'

Rachel could only nod, pressing her lips together as she did so, because she knew without him adding that dry comment, how badly all of this reflected on Elise.

'Leo is an…awesome guy,' she continued. 'He is the very hands-on head of the Savakis shipping empire as well as being a respected international lawyer, expert in British, Greek and American corporate law—'

'Skip the CV. I know about Leo Savakis,' he coolly cut in.

Of course he would know about Leo. Most people who moved in high business circles would have heard about her brother-in-law's remarkable career.

'He's a very busy man.'

'Aren't we all?' drawled this high mover—in the business world at least.

'S-sometimes Elise feels—neglected.'

'Ah,' he sighed. 'So I am to get the sob story before you lurch into the ugly part.'

'Don't mock what you have never suffered, Mr Villani!' Rachel flared up in her sister's defence. 'When you've gone from being the face on every glossy magazine to a stay-at-home wife and mother with no identity to call your own, then you might begin to understand!'

He didn't even bother to respond to that heated outburst. 'So she feels—neglected…' he prompted instead.

'And lonely.' Once again Rachel steadied her breathing. 'When Leo works abroad he prefers Elise to stay put in London or on his island in Greece. He says it's all to do with security,' she explained. 'He's made enemies in his line of work and…'

'Naturally feels the need to protect his wife and his son.'

'Wouldn't you?' Rachel flashed.

He raised a black satin eyebrow. 'Are you working in defence of Mr Savakis here or his poor neglected wife?'

'Both,' Rachel declared loyally. 'I *like* Leo…'

But she wouldn't want him as a husband, she added silently. He was too overwhelmingly unreadable and dauntingly self-controlled. He adored Elise though, she was certain of it. It was just that…

'He's been virtually living in Chicago for the last twelve months, working on a high-profile case that only allows him back home for the occasional flying visit.'

'Hence poor Elise feeling lonely and neglected—'

'If you don't stop being nasty about her, I'm going to leave!'

He shifted his shoulders against the black leather, then moved his legs, bending them out of their lazy sprawl so he could rest one ankle on the other knee. Rachel's eyes were drawn to the lean bowl between his hipbones where the expensive black fabric of his trousers sat easily against—

Oh, please, someone help me! she thought despairingly and wanted to run away again.

He moved a hand next, lifting it up so he could stroke a long finger across the flat line of his lips. Above the stroking finger, his grey-green eyes feathered a ponderous look over her in a way that further fanned the sexual charge.

Did all Italian men have an ability to seduce just by using body language, or was it just her misfortune that they affected *her* like this?

Disturbed by the whole hectic physical war going on here, Rachel put some distance between them by walking across the room to stand staring out of one of the huge plate glass windows. London—the River Thames, Westminster and Tower Bridge—lay spanned out before her in a familiar night scene.

Behind her his silent study pin-pricked her spine.

He had not even bothered to challenge her threat to leave. It was as if he knew she was becoming more and more trapped here by the sexual pull and he was enjoying feeding it.

One of the friends she'd made during her stay in Naples had once claimed that Italian men could seduce you and make you feel wonderful about falling in love with them without so much as considering falling in love themselves. It was the Italian way. Apparently you were supposed to feel blessed that they'd bothered to notice you at all.

Because they were conceited and arrogant by nature, so confident in their prowess as mighty lovers, that the suggestion that they might not assuage your every sexual fantasy never entered their minds or their beds. Such an uncrushable self-belief was seductive in itself. Rachel had fallen for it with Alonso. Now here she was, feeling the pull again and with a much more dangerous beast than Alonso ever had been.

It was time to put it to death, she told herself.

Turning from the window, she looked back at him. 'Leo knows about your affair with Elise,' she announced.

And saw death happen to sexual promise as he flicked those eyes into sharp focus on her face.

'He was sent photographs of the two of you together in a restaurant here in London, then later being very intimate on a dance floor,' she pushed on.

His tight curse brought him to his feet.

'Elise got upset—'

'Naturally,' he gritted.

Rachel bit down hard on her lower lip. 'She denied everything, which was a bit stupid when Leo was standing there with the photographic evidence,' she allowed. 'F-fortunately the photos were dark and very grainy and she insisted that the blonde in them could be anyone.'

'She lied, in other words.'

'Wouldn't you have done in her place?'

His dark head went back. 'If I was so miserable in my marriage that I needed to look elsewhere for—company, I would be man enough to say so *before* the event!'

'Well, good for you, Mr Villani,' Rachel commended. 'It must be really great to be so sure of yourself that you *know* what you would do in any given situation! Well, Elise *lied*,' she stressed. 'And, right off the top of her head, she suggested that the woman in the photos could even be me. Leo wasn't impressed—I don't normally look or dress like this, you see—'

He flicked her a cynical look. 'Another liar in the family, then.'

'Yes,' Rachel sighed, seeing no use in denying it. 'I had been staying with Elise in London for a while to—to keep her company while Leo was away. She was so low and depressed I encouraged her to go out with an old f-friend from her modelling days and—and enjoy life a bit instead of moping around the house waiting for…' She stopped, shutting the rest of that away where it belonged.

By his expression she knew he knew what she meant.

'Anyway,' she went on after a moment. 'She took me up on the offer and really started to cheer up and be her old self! But I had no idea she was out there enjoying herself with another man…'

'Oh, call it as it is, *cara*, we had the hots for each other.'

'You don't need to be so crude about it!' she said heatedly.

'What happened next?' He was striding across the room towards the brandy bottle to replenish his empty glass and there was nothing languid in his movements now.

'Elise told Leo that *I* had been seeing someone while I was staying with her…'

'A someone who just happened to be me—?' Brandy splashed into the glass.

Rachel watched it and mentally crossed her fingers and hoped he had the steady head for it. 'She was fighting for her marriage.'

He swallowed the drink. 'So did Savakis call you up to demand confirmation and you lied to him for your sister's sake?'

'Leo didn't do anything.' Ignoring his sarcasm, she kept strictly to the point. 'Instead he chose to let the subject drop.'

'Generous man,' he drawled. 'Or a sadly besotted one.'

The idea of Leo being either generous or besotted was so alien to Rachel that she had to stop and think about it and still couldn't get either scenario to fit the Leo she knew.

'Things have been—strained between the two of them ever since, and now…' Rachel gathered herself in before she revealed the next bit. 'Elise has just found out that she's pregnant.'

Raffaelle responded to this with an abrupt stiffening of his long body. The glass clenched between his fingers, he turned a narrowed look on her face.

'Do go on,' he invited softly.

Rachel wished she didn't have to go on but she knew that she did. 'W-with the timing and—everything, there's a big chance that Leo might not believe the baby is his.'

'You mean he does not know about it yet?'

'Not yet,' Rachel murmured.

'And is it his baby?'

'Yes!' she cried out. 'Unless you are wondering if it might be your baby?' she then could not resist hitting back.

'I know it isn't.' His mouth was as hard now as his eyes were like ice.

Rachel shivered. 'It's Leo's baby,' she repeated firmly. 'Conceived during one of his flying visits home. He'd only been there one night when he was telling Elise over the break-fast table that he was flying back to Chicago the next day. S-so she rebelled at his arrogant assumption that he could just fly in and—' The rest was cut off and smothered. But once again she knew that he knew what she was getting at. 'So Elise decided to punish him by telling him she had started her period and so was off limits…'

Because, as Elise had said, if Leo thought he could fly in just to ease his libido, then he could go back to Chicago and to libido hell!

'*Dio*,' Raffaelle muttered. 'The sly machinations of a selfish woman never cease to impress me.'

'Nor am I impressed by the casual attitude of a man on the hunt for sex!'

'Was that remark aimed at me?' he demanded.

'Does it fit?' Rachel lanced back. 'Did you or did you not hit on my sister because you fancied your chances in her bed?'

Guilty as charged. His teeth came together. 'I did not know that she was married,' he declared stiffly.

'And that's your excuse?' Rachel denounced. 'Why didn't you know she was married?' she demanded. 'She was a famous ex-model, for goodness' sake! Her face used to be seen everywhere. Her marriage made the front pages of every glossy there is!'

'Does she look like the famous model any more?' he hit back. 'You know she does not! She carries more weight now and her face has altered. And she did not exactly go out of her way to tell me who she was!'

'What did she do then—pretend to be Catwoman, complete with rubber mask?'

Rachel saw him make a grab at his temper. 'She used a different name,' he said.

A different name—? That was one small detail Elise had left out of her account of her reckless rebellion against Leo.

'What name—?' She frowned at him.

He looked at her, then dared to laugh, though it wasn't a very pleasant-sounding laugh. 'Does—*Rachel Carmichael* mean much to you?'

Rachel suddenly needed to sit down again. Walking on trembling legs to the nearest sofa, she sank into its soft black leather and put the glass to her equally trembling mouth.

'I see you recognise the name,' he drawled hatefully.

'Shut up!' she whipped back; she was trying to think.

The devious witch, the calculating madam! She'd gone out there on the town stuffed full of rebellion, using *her* name as a cover-up, while insisting that Leo's precious security guards remained at the house to guard her son!

'No wonder Mark dragged me back here,' she mumbled.

'Who the hell is Mark?' Raffaelle Villani rapped out.

'My half-brother—the one with the camera,' she enlightened.

'You mean you are related to one of the paparazzi?'

Rachel shifted uncomfortably. 'Mark and Elise are twins.'

He didn't bother to say anything to that, but just stood there glaring into space. The atmosphere was pretty much too thick to breathe now and Rachel was wishing she was wearing armour plating because she had a horrible feeling she was going to need it soon.

'From where?' he demanded suddenly.

Looking up at him, she just blinked.

'You said that your brother dragged you back,' he enlightened her. 'From where—?'

'Oh—Devon,' Rachel responded. 'I work there on the family farm—organic,' she added for no reason she could think of.

His raking scan of her was downright incredulous. 'You…are a *farmer*?'

Her chin shot up. 'What's the matter with that, Mr Villani?' she challenged. 'Does it bruise your precious ego to know you're about to be intimately linked to a poor farming girl instead of some rich chick with a three-hundred-year-old pedigree—?'

Silence clattered—no, it thundered down as both of them realised at the same time what it was she had just said.

'"Intimately linked—?"' he fed into that rumbling thunder.

Rachel bit down hard on her bottom lip to stop it from quivering. The thickened air in the room began to curdle—or was it the vodka she wasn't used to drinking that was beginning to make her feel slightly sick?

'Explain that,' he raked out.

'I w-will in a minute,' she whispered. 'I just need to—get my head together to…' say what still had not been said.

Abandoning what was left of the glass of vodka and her bag to the floor at her feet, she made herself stand up again, preferring to meet what was about to come back at her from an upright position with her hands free rather than have him loom over her like a threatening thunderclap.

Why did he have to be so intimidatingly tall and big?

She found herself sending him a plea for understanding with her eyes as she lurched back into speech. 'Elise provided this d-dress and the invitation to the charity thing tonight,' she explained. 'Then she was packed off to Chicago with her son this afternoon f-for a surprise visit to Leo, while Mark and I…'

'Set up the sting on me?'

Pressing her lips together, she nodded, deciding not to object to the latest label he'd hung on them because it was the truth, and there was still more to come.

'Tomorrow morning you and I will appear together in a Sunday tabloid—'

'Saying what—?' he bit out.

Oh, God, she groaned silently. 'S-something like— Raffaelle Villani goes public with his latest w-woman…'

Having to really bite down hard on her bottom lip now, Rachel searched the hard angles of his face for a small sign that he wasn't into murder—but she didn't see it.

'It was important to convince Leo that the woman in the photographs he has in his possession and the one who will appear in tomorrow's paper are the same person and *cannot* be Elise if she is in Chicago with him!'

And that was the bottom line.

Suddenly he was a tall dark stranger standing there. A man so cold and so very still it was as if he had pulled on the same awesome cloak of implacability that Leo always wore.

The silence gnawed. So did the heightened tension which began sapping the defences that had kept Rachel going through all of this.

'It should have ended there,' she pushed into the taut atmosphere. 'If you had behaved as predicted and let me get away from you, I would have disappeared back to Devon and tomorrow's tabloid spread would have become Monday's bin liner—over and forgotten about—and my sister's marriage would have been safe!'

It was the way it worked, Mark had said. Raffaelle Villani

would have no case to deny. He might bluster and demand a retraction from the paper but that would be all he could do. Elise's name would not be mentioned by Mark and other than Leo receiving hard evidence that his wife was not the woman in the grainy photographs with Raffaelle Villani, everything else would just—go away.

But this man had not reacted as predicted. He'd grabbed and held on to her. And the pap-pack had caught their scent. Now she was stuck here in his apartment with the pack no doubt waiting outside ready to pounce on her the moment that she tried to leave.

And where was her darling quick thinking half-brother? Putting his twin's needs first, as he always did.

Now Rachel hadn't a clue as to where it was all going to go from here except—

It was time to beg, she recognised starkly. Time to appeal to one very cold and angry Raffaelle Villani for his under-standing and co-operation, when deep down she knew they deserved neither.

She moved towards him. 'Mr Villani,' she murmured huskily, 'please, just think about it. I was actually doing you a favour too tonight because if Leo—'

'What the hell is—*this*?'

Rachel hadn't realised she'd lifted a hand out towards him in appeal until his long fingers were suddenly clamped around her wrist.

'W-what—?' she said jerkily.

Grim mouth flattening, he lifted up her hand until her fingers dangled in front of her confused face. She had to blink twice to focus on the diamond-encrusted sapphire ring twinkling back at her.

'Oh,' she said and swallowed. She'd forgotten all about the ring.

'You are betrothed—?' he enquired with blistering thinness.

'N-no.' Rachel shook her head. 'It—it's nothing; the ring is a f-fake, just w-window-dressing.'

'Window-dressing,' he repeated.

'Part of the look…' She was beginning to squirm inside again. 'Leo needed to see it if he was going to…'

'Believe you were not his wife?'

She nodded, then swallowed again. 'Elise's engagement ring is a big single yellow diamond. Th-this one is so glaringly different that it…'

Her voice trailed away, the hiss of his breath making it do so because she knew he had caught on.

'So, let me see if I have this clear,' he said grimly. 'You dressed yourself up to look like your half-sister—from behind, then you threw yourself at my neck, kissing me as if I am your…?'

He wanted her to say it. Her heart began thumping. He was going to make her confess the final full duplicity.

'L-lover,' she breathed.

'*Betrothed* lover?' His voice was getting softer by the second. Rachel licked her lips and nodded.

'And I was not supposed to issue an instant denial about this?'

'Th-there's a letter going to be h-hand-delivered here to you tomorrow along with the relevant newspaper,' she told him shakily. 'The letter will explain everything we have talked about and point out to you that to expose the photograph as a lie will leave you open to questions about wh-whose baby it is Elise is carrying.'

'*Madre de Dio*,' he breathed. 'You are truly devious.'

He was right and she was, but— 'This is serious, Mr Villani!' she cried out. 'You don't know Leo! He's one hell of a strict Greek! He's also an absolute killer expert on law! If he decides that his wife has been cheating on him with you and could be having *your* baby…for all your wealth and power, he will drag you to the courtroom and through the gutters along with Elise!'

He threw her hand away. 'I never touched her—!' he bit out angrily.

'Even this very trusting sister can't believe that!'

Her denunciation bounced off the walls and the sheets of plate glass while the air sizzled with his undiluted rage.

'One kiss, Mr Villani,' Rachel stressed urgently. 'One small kiss stolen from the wife of Leo Savakis and he will never forgive her, and you will find yourself stuck with the worst kind of enemy there is!'

He just turned and walked off, striding across the expanse of wood flooring and out through the door.

Rachel followed, quivering, shaken to the roots because it was only now, when faced with what this all meant to *him*, that she was beginning to realise how none of them had given much thought to how unfairly they were treating him in all of this.

She hurried after him. 'I'm so sorry…'

The husky quaver of her apology fell on stony ground. It had been such a useless thing to say anyway, so she didn't blame him for the filthy comment he threw back at her, as one of his arms flew out with an angry hand attached to it, which hit open another door to allow him to keep walking without altering his angry stride.

Rachel found herself coming to a trembling halt in yet another doorway. This one opened on to a shiny black and white kitchen and he was standing by a huge black mirror fronted fridge. One of the doors was swinging open, but by the way he was just staring Rachel received the pained impression that he didn't know what it was he was staring into.

'Please believe me when I say I did *try* to explain it all to you earlier—at the charity thing!' she tried again—frantically. 'I *insisted* to Mark that we should at least attempt to get your understanding and cooperation but…' she sucked in a breath

'…you wouldn't give me the chance to speak and then the whole thing j-just ran out of control!'

He slammed the fridge door shut and turned to face her. If her trembling legs would have let her, Rachel knew she would be running by now.

But—look at him, she told herself helplessly as he began striding towards her. He was so gloriously magnificent in his anger, his face muscles stretched tight across his amazing bone structure and his torso pumped up like a warrior about to begin a slaying-fest.

He reached for her.

She quivered. 'Y-you—'

He shut her up with his hard hot mouth to mouth that totally blacked out her brain. When he let her up for air again she was dizzy and disorientated, in no fit state to find herself being dragged by the hand down the hallway then out of the door to the lift.

His free hand stabbed the call button. Bright balls of panic spun in her head. He was going to throw her out. He was going to hand her to the wolves out there and—

'Please don't do this,' she begged him on the very—very edge of tears now.

He pulled her into the lift. They rode down with him standing there in front of her, with her wrist still his prisoner and the rest of her pinned against the lift wall by the steely glitter in his eyes.

'Think about it,' she begged unsteadily. 'You don't want to—'

He swooped and cut the words off the ruthless way, with another open mouthed onslaught that lost her the will to even stand.

But she had to stand. She had to follow where he pulled as they left the lift and crossed the foyer with a curious security guard looking on. Then a hard hand pushed open the main doors and Rachel lost the next few seconds beneath the glare of flashing flickering lights and the pandemonium of questions that burst out.

His arm was around her shoulders now, hugging her to him and keeping her upright.

'Smile,' he hissed and she smiled like an alien.

Then the words came, those low, smooth accented tones dryly confirming that no, as they could see, she was not Elise. She was in fact Elise's beautiful half-sister, Rachel Carmichael.

Then he let drop the big one, by calmly inviting their congratulations because they had just become engaged to be married.

The fake ring was displayed on her finger for the pack to snap to their greedy hearts' content.

How long had they known each other? Where had they met?

He answered all the questions with the relaxed humour of one who had all the answers, since he was merely duplicating facts from his short affair with Elise.

Breathing took on a shallow necessity aimed to maintain the fragile beat of her heart. The rest was a haze, a fog of nothing in which she must have performed well because no one suggested she was about to pass out or, worse, that she looked more like a horrified prisoner being hauled to the gallows than a happily betrothed future bride.

'Now you have what you came for would it be possible that you can do us a favour and leave us in peace?'

So lightly requested, so full of lazy charm. The pack laughed. He turned her within the iron grip of his arm. Silence hit with a deafening force as the doors closed with them back inside.

'Congratulations, Mr Villani, Miss Carmichael,' the eavesdropping security guard said with a grin.

If the man holding her clamped to his side said anything in

response then Rachel didn't hear it. She was too busy trying to decide if she was dizzy with relief because he hadn't thrown her out there to face the paparazzi alone, or if she was dizzy with fear over what was still to come.

They travelled back up in the lift. She was in shock. She had been totally incapacitated by a man locked into his own agenda. An agenda that involved him seizing control of a situation they—*she* had taken away from him.

His apartment door closed behind them. Rachel shivered. And still the ordeal did not end there. The arm propelled her down the hall and in through another door. *It* closed with a quiet deathly click and only then did she manage to find the strength to break free.

She had moved three shaky steps before it hit her that this was a bedroom. A very male bedroom with very masculine items scattered around it and a very large bed standing out like a threat, with its very dark plum-coloured linen upon which it was too easy to imprint the solid frame of a dark-haired honey-skinned man.

She turned. He was still by the door and watching her. Not one small gram of anger had softened from his face. Her skin gave a fizz of alarm-cum-excitement because, even in anger, the way he was looking at her was stripping her bare to her quivering skin.

'Why—?' she breathed.

'You wanted my co-operation and you have had it,' he answered. 'Now I want what I want, and you, Miss Carmichael, are about to pay your dues.'

He started closing the gap between them.

'No.' Rachel shook her head and began backing away. 'I won't let you do this.'

'Oh come on, *mi amore*,' he taunted coldly. 'We are betrothed to be married. You wear my ring on your finger and my impeccably mannered family is going to try not to be shocked that my bride is wearing farmers' boots to her wedding and straw to decorate her hair.'

'Very funny,' she muttered, looking about her for an escape.

'They will tread daintily between organic lettuce and—'

'Will you just stop this!' His words might taunt but the rest was now getting scary. 'Look,' she said quickly. 'I know you are angry—and I know that you have every right to be.'

'*Grazie.*'

'Oh, God,' she choked as his hands closed around her waist and the shock of feeling them there again lit up her skin. 'I'm *sorry* about *everything*, okay?'

His dark head began to lower. Rachel tried to arch away.

'Your heart is racing.'

'Because you're *frightening* me!'

'Or exciting you.'

No, frightening—*frightening me!* Rachel repeated—though only inside her head where a strange tumbling darkness was gathering, closing around her like a cold mist that began to take her legs from beneath her and brought forth a string of soft tight curses as she began to go limp.

CHAPTER FOUR

SHE came around to find she was lying on the bed and her head was pounding. Someone moved close by and she flicked open her eyes as Raffaelle Villani came to lean over her.

With a startled jerk she tried to get up but he pushed her back down again.

'Be calm,' he said grimly. 'I do not ravish helpless females.'

Well, forgive me for not believing you, she wanted to say but, 'W-what happened to me?' she whispered instead.

'You—fainted.' His mouth tightened as he said that and his eyes were hooded; in fact his whole face was hidden behind a tightly controlled mask that did not make Rachel feel any safer. 'You are also very cold.'

It was only as a soft cashmere throw landed across her that she realised she was shivering.

'I should not have taken you outside to meet the press wearing only that dress.'

The press. It all came flooding back like a recurring nightmare and she closed her eyes again. 'I can't believe you actually did that,' she whispered unsteadily.

Straightening up, *'Mi dispiace,'* he offered stiffly. 'I have no excuse for frightening you as badly as I did.'

'I wasn't talking about you playing the sex maniac!' She

sat up and this time he did not stop her. 'I meant what you just did down there in front of all those reporters.' She grabbed her dizzy forehead and stared up at him. 'Have you *no* idea what it is you've done?'

'I did what I had to do,' he stated coldly.

'Great,' she choked. 'You did what you had to do and managed to escalate this whole thing right out of control!'

'It was out of control long before I became involved. You said as much yourself.'

So she had. 'Well, we are now stuck with a fake betrothal, complete with a fake ring and all the other fake stuff that is going to come with it.'

'But your sister's marriage will be safe, which, of course, makes the subterfuge, sacrifice and lies worth it?'

The sarcasm was still alive if the frightening anger had lessened, Rachel heard, and went to get up.

'Stay there,' he commanded, turning to stride towards the door. 'Give yourself chance to—warm up a little and—recover.'

Recover for what? Rachel wondered half hysterically. She was never going to recover from this awful night for as long as she lived!

Ignoring his command, she moved to sit on the edge of the bed, then sat trying to calm the sickly swimming sensation still taking place in her head.

'I have to find a way to get out of here undetected so I can go home,' she mumbled, more to herself than to him.

Still, he heard it and paused at the door. 'Where is home when you are in London?'

Usually with Elise but, 'With Mark, right now,' she replied, then squinted a look at her watch. 'He will be worrying where I am.'

'Not so I noticed, *cara*,' he drawled cynically. 'Not that it matters,' he then dismissed, 'because from now on you will be living right here with me.'

'I will not!' she gasped out.

He had the door open now. 'If my freedom to choose what I do with my life has been curtailed, then so has yours,' he declared. 'So, until we find a way out of this situation which does not involve *my* loss of face, you and I, Miss Carmichael, will in effect be stuck to each other with glue. So lie down again and get used to it.'

With that he walked out, leaving Rachel gaping at the empty space he'd last filled with his cold anger, which was just as bad as the hot anger from before!

'But that's just stupid—!' she fired after him. 'Betrothed people don't have to live together!'

If he heard her he did not come back to argue and, after a second, Rachel slumped her shoulders where she sat, wondering dully if he didn't have a point. Now the press wagon was rolling, nothing was going to stop it in the near future without someone—or all of them—losing face.

She closed her eyes, wishing her head would just stop spinning now so she could think.

She needed to ring Mark. The whole story had gone bottom upwards and she needed to warn him then get his take on what she should do next.

Ignoring the swimming room, she got up then just stood looking down at her feet. Her shoes had disappeared. Tugging the throw around her chilled shoulders, she began searching for them but they weren't anywhere to be found.

He must have taken them with him. To stop her from making a bid for freedom? He had to be crazy if he thought her mad enough to run out there where the paparazzi waited—with or without her shoes!

She did find a bathroom, though, which she was sincerely

glad about, since she had not been near one for hours and hours. It smelled of Raffaelle Villani: clean and tangy, with a hint of spice.

Nice, she thought as she washed her hands in the basin. The kind of expensive scents you expected to surround a super-elite male. Then she supposed she must also smell super-elite right now, bearing in mind that her body had been pampered by a whole range of expensive products Elise had provided along with the expensive hairstyle and dress.

She caught sight of herself in the bathroom mirror then and was actually taken aback because she hardly recognised herself—that sleek blonde thing with dead straight hair and heavy make-up.

Well, she thought grimly as she viewed the thick licks of mascara that lengthened her eyelashes and made her eyes look bluer than they really were, everyone just loved to tell her that she had the potential to look almost as good as Elise if she'd only take time with her appearance. Now it seemed they'd achieved their dearest wish, only—

She was not and had never wanted to be Elise, had she? And that person she could see in the mirror was just someone pretending to be something she was not.

The fraud, in other words—the fake.

The pink lipstick had all gone by now, she saw, but her lips still looked fuller than she was used to seeing them. Fuller and sexier because of too many hot kisses shared with a complete stranger.

A stranger who was in for a big shock when he eventually got to meet the real Rachel Carmichael.

Releasing a sigh, she turned away from the mirror and went back into the bedroom to search for that other item that had gone missing—her bag with her cellphone inside it.

It wasn't in the bedroom so she let herself into the

hallway, then walked down it and into the living room. The dress did not feel so indecently short now that her ankles were no longer elevated by four-inch heels, she noticed as she walked.

She heard the bag before she found it because her phone was already ringing. It had to be Mark—who else? she mocked grimly as she followed the sound and found the bag lying on the floor by the sofa she'd last sat down upon.

Her half-finished glass of vodka stood alongside it. As she bent to get her bag there was a moment when she considered picking up the glass first and downing what was left in true Dutch courage style before she told Mark what had happened.

In the end she didn't need to tell him. Pushing her hair behind her ear, she put the phone to it.

'Rachel, what the hell are you doing in Raffaelle Villani's apartment?' Mark's voice all but pounced.

'How did you find out where I am—?' she asked.

'Because it's all over the bloody Internet!'

A sound from behind her made her turn to find Raffaelle Villani propping up the living room doorway. His shirt sleeves were rolled up now, revealing tanned muscular forearms sprinkled with just enough dark hair to make her wonder where else on his body it might be.

Her stomach muscles quivered. Her mouth went dry. Fluttering down her eyelashes, 'It's nothing for you to panic about,' she said huskily into the phone. 'I—I've been explaining the—situation to R-Raffaelle.' The name fell uneasily from her lips and she caught the way one of his eyebrows arched in mocking note of that. 'He—he's being very understanding about it as—as I told you and Elise he would be once he'd heard all the facts.'

There was a short silence. 'I'm coming to get you.'

'No—!' Rachel pushed out. 'It—it's better that you stay away from here.'

'Because I'm the press? Because between the two of you— you've come up with this crazy engagement announcement that is flying round Europe as we speak?'

That far, that quickly—? Rachel swallowed.

'I'm your brother first, Rachel,' Mark was saying angrily. 'And if that bastard is—'

'Well, it's just a bit too late to remember that, Mark!' she cut in. 'After the way you left me standing tonight, I wish I didn't have a brother!'

'I thought you were right behind me until I reached my car.' He had the grace to sound uncomfortable. 'When I did think to look back, the rest of my cronies were piling out of the hotel and I couldn't see you anywhere, so I assumed you'd disappeared in the other direction.'

'And, happy with that very stupid idea, you just went home without me to post your scoop.' Wasn't that just typically Mark?

'I had a deadline,' he grunted.

I had a *life*, Rachel thought angrily. 'Well, it's too late to come at me with the brotherly concern now.'

'Yeah, you're right.' He sighed. 'Sorry, Rachel. So he's okay with all of this, then?'

Straight from apology back to business, Rachel noticed. 'Yes,' she said.

He sucked in a breath. 'So when are you coming back here?'

'Coming back?' She looked at Raffaelle Villani. He was standing there, waiting to hear her answer as much as Mark was.

And she knew suddenly that she was going nowhere. She owed it to this man to play the game the way he had decided it would be played.

'I'm not coming back,' she said to Mark, but it was this other man's wry tilt of his dark head that held her attention.

'We—we're still talking through our options,' she added. 'So I'm staying here f-for now.'

'Just talking?' Mark asked silkily.

She couldn't answer, not straight away anyway, because there was something about the way Raffaelle was looking at her now that—

'Yes,' she said.

But the gap had been too long for her streetwise, cynical half-brother. She heard him let out a long breath of air. 'I hope you know what you're doing,' he said grimly. 'He isn't the kind of man you want to become mixed up with.'

Great advice, she thought, after the event. 'I'll call you—tomorrow,' was all she said.

'I had better go and ring Elise to tell her she can stop worrying.'

And that was Mark, Rachel noted bleakly, back to prioritizing in his usual way—his twin always being a bigger priority for him than she ever could be.

'Okay,' she murmured. 'Tell her I—'

'Great,' he cut in. 'Got to go now, Rachel. I need to change my copy before it goes to print. Do you have any idea how much you've messed me about by making that announcement tonight?'

The phone went dead. Rachel stared at it. And, for the first time since this whole wretched evening began, she felt the thick push of weak tears hit her eyes and her throat.

Raffaelle watched as she continued to stand there with the cellphone in her hand. She'd gone pale again and if her body language was speaking to him then it was telling him that she had just been tossed aside like a used bloody pawn.

Anger pumped at his chest. He wanted to kick something—her twin siblings, for instance.

'What did you expect?' he demanded brusquely. 'A full rescue, complete with armour and swords? You are not the main player on this chessboard, *cara*—Elise is.'

'I know that,' she whispered and sank down on to the sofa.

He breathed out a sigh. 'At least her unborn child will get to know its rightful father.'

He'd meant that to sound comforting but it had come out sounding harsh. She winced, pressing her lips together and dipping her head. Her hair slid forward, revealing the vulnerable curve of her slender white nape.

Raffaelle brought his teeth together, his tongue sitting behind them and tingling with a mixed-up desire to taste what he could see and the knowledge that it was at real risk of being bitten off if he did not take more care about what he said.

With a reluctance to let his mood soften, he pushed himself away from the door and walked towards her. She heard him coming and stiffened her spine. When he leant down with the intention of picking up her glass to offer it to her, she actually shuddered.

'Please don't start dragging me around again,' she choked out.

Was that what he had been doing—?

Yes, that was what he had been doing, Raffaelle realised, and straightened up with a jerk. 'I'm—sorry,' he said.

'Everyone is sorry.' She laughed tensely. 'Doesn't help much though, does it?'

He couldn't argue with that so he threw himself down on the sofa beside her and released another sigh. 'Beginning to feel more like the real victim now, *cara*?' He could not seem to stop the taunts from coming. 'It is a strange feeling, don't you think—being kind of frustratingly helpless? If we then start to wonder how our present lovers are going to feel when the news hits the stands, the sense of frustration really begins to bite.'

'You have a lover?' Her chin shot up, her slender neck twisting to show him blue eyes stark with horror and the glittering evidence of held-in tears. His inner senses shifted, stirring awake from what had only been a very light slumber anyway.

'Do you?' he fed back.

'Of course not!' she snapped. 'Do you really think I would have got involved in any of this if I had a lover who could be embarrassed by it?'

'Whereas I was not allowed to make that choice,' he pointed out. 'So stop feeling sorry for yourself,' he finished coolly. 'You are still less the victim here than I am, so—'

'And you are just *so* loving being able to keep saying that to me!' Rachel got to her feet, restless, tense without knowing why.

Then she did know and she turned on him. 'So who is she—?' she speared at him as if she had the right to ask such a question.

Which she didn't, as the mocking glint in his eyes told her.

But it did not stop her stupid brain from conjuring up some other leggy blonde creature with a very expensive pedigree draping herself over him while he lounged in much the same way he was now—all long limbs and tight muscles and rampant sex appeal waiting to be adored because it was his due.

She took in a short breath, despising the heat of jealousy she could feel burning in her chest, as if a few angry kisses and a sham announcement had given her exclusive rights of possession over him!

It did not, but nor did it stop her crazy imagination from imprinting her own image of him. Her heart began pounding out a suffocating rhythm. This time she couldn't even look away! And to make it so much worse, having been crushed against him more times than was decent, she could even smell his sexy scent in her nostrils, feel the warmth of his mouth and the possessive touch of his hands on her—

'There is no one—fortunately…'

His deep voice slunk into her brain but she had to blink to make herself hear the words he'd spoken—then blink again to make herself understand what they meant.

He meant that there was no other lover in his life right now. Her mouth fell dry and her legs went hollow.

'I was just curious as to whether you had a man hanging about in the wings of this charade, ready to jump out and cause me more trouble.'

'Well, there isn't,' she confirmed and spun away, hating to hear him make that sardonic denunciation of her character because she knew he had every right to suspect her of every underhand trick there was going.

'Good,' he said. 'So I can sit here and enjoy looking at my newly betrothed's fabulous legs without worrying if I am encroaching on someone else's territory.'

The aforementioned legs tingled. She moved tensely. 'We are not betrothed—'

'And the way the neat shape of her *derrière* is teasing me as it moves inside that tight little dress...'

Rachel swung round. 'Is this your idea of having fun, just to get your own back on me?'

'With compliments?' he quizzed innocently.

'Those are not compliments!'

'You don't like me to tell you that I like what I see—?'

'No—!' she lashed out.

'But it's okay for you to look me over as if you cannot believe your good fortune, is it?'

Rachel froze as a guilty blush ran right up her body and into her face. 'I w-was not—'

'Are your breasts your own?' he cut in on her insolently.

Her mouth dropped open in complete disbelief that he had actually voiced that question. 'How dare you ask me that?' she seethed.

'Easily,' he replied cynically. 'They look real, but who can tell by just looking these days—'

'They are real!' she choked out. 'And I've had enough of this—'

'No, you haven't.'

With only that small hint that something was coming, he sat forward and snaked an arm around her waist, then tumbled her down on to his lap.

Her cry of alarm doubled as a shimmering gasp when she found herself contained inside all of that long-limbed, hard-muscled strength.

'W-what do you think you're doing?' Her clenched fists pushed at his shoulders.

The gleam in his eyes mocked her. 'The way you keep looking at me, count yourself lucky that I lasted as long as I did.'

Oh, God, she'd been that obvious? 'You said y-you wouldn't do this—!'

'You are no longer helpless.'

He caught hold of her chin and pushed it upwards, his eyes hiding beneath half-lowered eyelashes as he waited for her lips to part with her next cry of protest—then he pounced, dipping his dark head to match the full pink quivering shape of her mouth with his.

So they'd kissed in anger. They'd kissed in a terrifying state of untrammelled lust. They'd kissed to shock and to subdue. But this—this was different. This contained so much hungry, frustrated, heated desire that it stirred her up more turbulently than any kiss she'd experienced in her entire life.

He explored her mouth so deeply that the feeling of being taken over completely drained her of the will to fight. Her clenched fists stopped pushing and opened to begin stroking in tight, tense, restless movements that only stopped when she found the warmly scented skin at his nape.

One of his arms held her clamped against him, the other stroked the length of her silk-covered thigh. Her dress had rucked up and the higher his hand glided the more she had to brace her inner thighs to try to contain what was happening there. And her breasts were tight, the nipples two stinging pinpricks pressing against the solid wall of his chest through his shirt.

Her fingers became restless again, one set moving to his satin cheekbone, then down in a delicate tremor to the corners of their straining mouths. He muttered something as he caught hold of her fingers and fed them down between them, until she was covering the hard ridge of aroused flesh pushing at his trousers. Frenzy arrived, a hot feverish frenzy of mutual desire that had been bubbling beneath the surface ever since their first kiss. Now it quickly spiralled out of control.

He caught hold of her hair and pulled her head back, his mouth deserting hers to wreak a trail of hot kisses down the arching stretch of her throat.

She was writhing with excitement, her skin alive to every brush of his lips and flickering lick of his tongue. A simple tug and the strap holding up her dress slipped off her shoulder. As clear air hit the thrust of her breast his mouth was continuing its delicious torment across its swollen quivering slope until he claimed the nipple with a luxurious suck.

An explosion of pleasure swept down from her nipple to low in her body, making her shudder, making her scythe out hot breaths as she clung to him.

Then his mouth came back to hers again and his tongue stung deep. Her deserted nipple was pulsating in protest at the loss of his exquisite suckling. She groaned into his mouth. He responded by lifting her up and bringing her back down strad-dling him without breaking the deep hot-mouthed kiss. She felt the thickness of his erection and couldn't stop herself from pressing into it. He encouraged her by clasping the tight mounds of her behind, now fully exposed because her dress was bunched to her waist. Flaming heat ignited between her thighs and she rocked her lower body, her fingers clutching at his silk-black hair.

When he stood up with her she didn't bother to protest. She knew what he was doing and where he was taking her. How he made it there without staggering she didn't know because his breathing was shot and his mouth had still not given up possession of hers.

The bed felt soft beneath her as he laid her down on it and she clung to his neck in case he decided to straighten and leave her, but he did no such thing.

Her dress was shimmied down her body. He stripped it from her legs with the deftness of a man who knew the easiest way to undress a woman without interrupting what was already happening with their mouths. There was no bra to remove— this dress was not the kind that permitted the wearing of one— and her stockings held themselves up, which left only her panties as a flimsy barrier to her complete nudity, but they stayed in place because he was now busy with his shirt.

She wanted to help; it was a feverish need that sent her fingers frantic as they tugged at shirt buttons, while his slipped lower to deal with his trouser-clasp and zip…

An impatient rustle of clothing, the fevered hiss of their breath, the heated scents from their bodies and the urgent touch of their fingers on newly exposed eager flesh…

And that deep drugging kiss just did not stop throughout all of it, not as she explored his muscle-packed contours or throughout each quivering gasp she made of pleasure when he explored her softer rounded flesh.

The impatient tug he gave at his shoes to remove them coincided with the reckless way that she dragged off his shirt.

Hot, taut satin skin adorned her hungry fingers once again, coated with a layer of male body hair. She scraped through it with her fingernails and felt him shudder with pleasure, her skin livening with excitement when she finally felt the full power of his naked length come to settle alongside her own. He was big and hot and amazingly, beautifully, magnificently built. Greedy for more, she rolled tight in against him and he accommodated her with a shift of his body that brought her into full contact with every part of his front.

The pouting buds of her breasts rubbed against the rough hair on his chest and she couldn't breathe for the tingling, stinging pleasure of it, yet she was panting, could barely cope with the thrills of excitement that went racing through her as he ran his hands down her spine and over her bottom and thighs to locate her stocking tops. He sent them sliding away with no effort at all. Her toes curled as the silk finally left them and he closed his fingers over her foot and used it to bend her leg over his hips.

Shock stung her into a quivering mass of pleasure when he captured one of her hands and fed it down to the velvet-smooth thickness of his penis, then urged her to stroke it between her legs.

He was big, a beautiful long-limbed muscular male with proportional length to his sex. She still had on her panties but she did not want them on; she wanted to feel him stroking like this against her with no barrier to dull the sensual ache.

Maybe he read her mind because he rolled on to his back, taking her with him, so she lay over him. Then he lifted her up and pushed her thighs together and ran his fingers into the scrappy fabric of her panties to stroke it away from the firm shape of her behind.

'Your skin is like silk,' he breathed against her urgent mouth.

When she caught the words with the flickering tip of her tongue he ran a forefinger into the tightly clenched crevice he'd uncovered and followed it all the way to the hot welcoming wetness between her legs.

He knew exactly what he was doing. Rachel just went wild as the dizzying tumult of thick, warm stimulation coiled around her senses. She moved with him in natural enticement and on a lusty growl he toppled her on to her back, then came to lie across her, their kiss completely broken for the first time.

His eyes were two intense black diamond orbs that he took from the burning desire suffusing her face to look down where his fingers now moved on her, following the path of pale dusky curls into soft female folds between her pearly-white thighs. The damp tip of his tongue appeared between his teeth as his dark head followed. For the next few minutes Rachel existed purely in the drugging eddy of his touch.

She was exquisite. The most receptive woman he had ever experienced. There was a brief moment when he let himself wonder what man had taught her to respond like this. Then, as something too close to jealousy ripped at him, he thrust the question away. His fingers made a slow sensual journey to search out her pleasure spots, allowing his thumb to replace his tongue in rolling possession of her taut little nub. He looked back at her face and watched her sink deeper into helpless response, urged on by his burning need to drive her out of her mind.

Her pale hair lay spread out across his pillow, her parted mouth warm and full and softly gasping, her lips dewy-red against the whiteness of her wonderful skin. Her eyes were closed, her slender arms thrown above her head in complete abandon and the two peaks of her breasts swayed and quivered as she moved her body in a natural sensual rhythm with his caress.

And his heart was thundering against his ribcage, the ache of his own steadily growing need pulsing its demand along his fully aroused length. She wanted to come. He could feel the anxious ripple of her inner muscles bringing her swiftly towards her peak. But thinking about another man making her feel this good made him determined to heighten her pleasure some more.

So he ruthlessly withdrew and, as she whimpered out a protest, he stripped her panties fully away. Without pausing, he then began a long slow, tormenting assault with his hands and his lips and his tongue over every inch of her smooth pale flesh. Dipping his fingers yet again into her hot sweet centre, he closed his mouth round one of her breasts. They were so perfect, two plump pearly-white mounds of womanly softness, with pink super-sensitive tips protruding from their rose-circled peaks. His fingers toyed with one while his tongue toyed with the other. She groaned and arched and gasped and quivered and tried to pay him back with the hungry nip of her teeth. Her hands were everywhere on him now, exploring and stroking, sometimes sending him into paroxysms of shudders when she decided to score her nails into his flesh.

By the time he covered her, she was nothing more than a shimmer of sensation and he took her face between his fingers, then urged, 'Look at me,' in a dark husky voice that made her tremble as she lifted her heavy eyelids and showed him dark blue passion-drugged eyes.

He was so very beautiful, she thought hazily. A dark passionate lover with the face of a fallen angel. Rachel held his gaze as he eased himself between her slender thighs and made that first slow silken thrust inside, surprise widening her eyes as she felt his girth and length. She was no virgin, but he was big so maybe experience had taught him caution with a new lover because she could see his fight not to give her all of him gripping the perfect mould of his face.

'Okay?' he asked huskily.

She nodded, her tongue making a circle of her lips as she willed her inner muscles to relax. With an erotic slowness that fanned the flames flickering between them, he followed her circling tongue with his own. Her fingers were clutching at the bunched muscles in his shoulders, her breathing reduced to short gasps of air as he pushed deeper still. She could feel the roughness of his thighs pressing along the length of her silkier thighs and the way his lean buttocks clenched as the first sense-shattering ripple of her muscles played along his length.

It was a slow, slow merging like she'd never experienced— a careful all-consuming invasion that sent her mind spinning off somewhere and her senses taking on a singing bright will of their own. She moved restlessly beneath him, wanting all of him—needing all of him—but where her hands clutched his shoulders she could feel their bulging taut muscles were trembling with stress as he held himself back. Impatiently she lifted her hips, closed her eyes, then let her muscles draw him in deep.

Nothing had ever felt like this, Raffaelle thought on a lusty groan as the full pressure of his hips sent her thighs spreading wider apart and she took him into that hot tight tunnel with a gripping greed which sent shots of sensation rippling down his full length.

He claimed her mouth with a devouring kiss and she kissed him back so desperately that he flung caution aside and allowed the powerful flow to take him over. Half expecting protest, he received eager encouragement instead as the tactile muscle play of her pleasure surrounded him in moist muscle-livened heat.

She was amazing, a pearly-white sylph with the moves of a siren. Her arms were wrapped around his shoulders, her fingernails scoring deep into his flesh. He moved with increasingly harder strokes and she moved with him, taking each driving plunge from his flanks with an exquisite contraction which rewarded each exquisite thrust.

Energizing heat poured into both of them, driving the whole thing right out there into a different world. The real excess began to build like an electrifying life-force that fine-tuned itself between agony and ecstasy, liquidising the senses and shutting down the brain. The white heat of her orgasm took her over, lifting her whole body from the bed in a quivering arch and holding it there while he thrust and shuddered and ground out hoarse words as she pulsed all around him and brought him to a shattering climax that carried them on and on.

CHAPTER FIVE

AFTERWARDS they lay in a tangle of slack limbs, racing hearts and heated flesh. His face was pressed into the pillow next to her head as he fought for breath and Rachel lay pale as death with her eyes closed, trying desperately to block out the wildly wanton way she had just behaved.

Hot sex with a stranger. Her insides turned over.

She had never done anything like this before in her life.

Which did not make her feel any better about any of it.

Nothing, she suspected, was ever going to make her feel good about it. This was Raffaelle Villani spread heavy on top of her. The man with a notorious reputation for getting off with long-legged blondes.

Now she knew what it felt like to be just one of a large crowd. Self-contempt engulfed her, followed quickly by hot suffocating shame.

Maybe she moved or maybe she even groaned. She didn't think she'd done anything but he suddenly shifted, levering up his torso so he could withdraw that all-powerful proof of his prowess from inside her, and the worst shame of all came when she was unable to still her damning quivering response.

At least the way he shuddered told her that he was experiencing the same thing.

Pushing up on to his forearms, he lifted his dark head off the pillow and looked at her. One of those thick silences seized the next few seconds while Rachel tried hard not to burst into tears. Her heart was still pounding, the desire to duck and hide away almost impossible to fight. It didn't help that his expression was so sensuously slumberous, like a man who was feeling very—very satisfied.

'I…'

It was the only word Rachel managed to drag free from the tension in her throat.

'You—what?' he prompted huskily, reaching up with a long, warm, gentle finger to run it along the trembling fullness of her pulsing lower lip.

'I th-think we got carried away…' She breathed the words out over his finger because he had not lifted it out of the way.

'Well, you carried me away,' he said with an odd half smile that did not seem to know whether to be cynical or just rueful about the whole thing. 'You were—special.'

'Th-thank you,' she mumbled unhappily.

'Quite an unexpected…gift to come out of this mess tonight, which makes me so glad I did not turn away from it when I had the chance…'

A gift—he saw her as a *gift*?

Cynical, Rachel named his half smile, and tensed as the warmth still sandwiched between their two bodies began to chill.

'Well, turn away now, Mr Villani,' she responded frozenly. 'Because it's the last *gift* you are going to get from me!'

She gave a push at his wide shoulders and obligingly he rolled away to lie on his side, watching as she scrambled off the bed, then began hunting the littered floor for something to wear to cover up her nakedness. Catching sight of her dress lying there on the floor in a brazen swirl, she shuddered, hating the sight of it, and made a wild grab for his shirt instead.

'You sound very certain about that.'

'I am.' Rachel had to fight with the shirt sleeves, which had become tangled inside out.

'We were really great together…'

'Well, you're such a great lover,' she flicked back. 'Better than most, if that gives your ego a boost.'

'*Grazie.*'

Get lost! she wanted to scream at him. A gift—a *gift*!

The shirt slithered over her now shivering body and she dragged the two sides together with fingers clutching at the fine cloth like tense claws.

Flushed, angry, and aware that any second now she was going to explode on a flood of wild, uncontrollable I-*hate*-myself! tears, 'Is there another bedroom I can use?' she asked, chin up, blue eyes refusing to do anything other than look directly at his smooth, sardonic, lazily curious face because she was determined to get away with at least some small part of pride intact.

'You don't need one. This bed is easily big enough for the two of us.' He was supremely content in his languid pose.

Refusing to get into an argument with him, Rachel turned to walk towards the bedroom door.

'I don't do one-night stands,' he fed gently after her.

She stopped, narrow shoulders tautening inside his oversized shirt. 'Neither do I…' she felt constrained to reply.

'Good. So we understand each other.'

'No.' Rachel swung round. '*I* don't understand!'

He was already off the bed and reaching for his trousers, so casual about his nakedness that she had to fight not to blush. He was incredible to look at: all golden and glossed by hard muscle tone, made all the more blatantly masculine by the triangle of black curls that swirled between his burgeoning pectorals and then drew a line down his torso to the other thick cluster curling around the potent force of his sex.

The stupid blush broke free when she recalled what that part of him had felt like erect and inside her. She tried to damp it all back down again but it was already too late because, as he was about to thrust a shockingly muscled brown leg into his trousers, he glanced at her and went as still as the dead.

Her breathing went haywire, her old friend panic rising up from places she did not know it could rise up from—her tender breasts, her taut nipples stinging against the cloth of his shirt and that terrible hot spot still pulsing between her legs, which made her draw in her muscles in an effort to switch it off.

He dropped the trousers. And she knew why he had. Seeing the way she was looking at him had turned him on like the floodgates opening on a mighty dam. What she'd thought potent before was suddenly downright unbelievable. He started walking towards her and she actually whimpered as she put out a trembling hand in the useless hope of holding him back, while her other hand maintained a death grip on the shirt to keep it shut across her front.

'No, please don't.' Her little plea came out all husky. Already her legs were threatening to collapse. 'We-we've made this situation messy enough as it is without adding intimacy to it—*please*!' she cried out when he just did not stop.

'I have just come inside you with the most amazing pleasure I have ever experienced,' his dark voice rasped over her. '*Intimacy* is here, *mia bella*. It is too late to switch it off.'

But it wasn't—*it wasn't*! 'I don't want—'

'Oh, you want,' he refuted. 'It has been vibrating out of you from the first moment we met. And I would be a liar if I did not admit to feeling the same way about you—so quit the denial.'

'Sex for the hell of it?' Rachel sliced back wildly.

'Why not?' Capturing her warding hand, he used it to draw her in close. 'We are stuck with each other for the next few months while this thing plays itself out, so why not enjoy what we do have going here which is not part of the lie?'

'If I walk out of here dressed like this and tell anyone waiting out there that I changed my mind because you just were not good enough—that should finish it,' she suggested wildly.

'Are you telling me that my finesse is in need of practice?' He threw back his head and laughed. 'Since we both know that you seem to be pretty much a natural sensualist, Miss Carmichael, I give you leave to teach me all you know.'

'What is that supposed to imply?' Rachel stared up at him.

He grimaced and she didn't like the cynical gleam that arrived back on his face. 'Either someone taught you how to give a man unbelievable pleasure or it just comes naturally to you,' he enlightened. 'I was attempting to give you the more honourable benefit of the doubt.'

He was daring to suggest that she'd been trained like a con-cubine to pleasure men—?

First a gift, now a trained whore. Rachel stiffened like a board. 'How dare you?' she breathed furiously.

'Very indignant,' he commended. 'But I have just had the life essence squeezed out of me by the kind of muscles I did not know a woman could possess and you kiss like a delight-ful, greedy, well-seasoned Circe, *amore*—dangerous, but I'm hooked.'

'I think this has gone far enough.' She went to twist away from him.

He spun her back, broke her grip on the shirt front and ran his two hands inside it in a sensual act of possession that claimed her slender waist. Two long thumbs stroked the flatness of her lower stomach and her flesh turned into a simmering sensory mass. When she released an agonised breath he watched the way her pale hips swayed towards him as if they could not stop from hunting out closer contact with the burgeoning jut of his sex.

'Look at you,' he murmured. 'You cannot help yourself. That deliciously damp cluster of curls I can see crowning your thighs is crying out to feel me there again.'

'No,' she denied, knowing it was horribly, shamefully true.

'If I do this…' he eased her in closer and gently speared a path between her thighs '…your slender thighs cling to me as if your life depends upon it…'

And she was clinging. Weak and helpless. He rocked his hips and her arms just lifted, then fell heavily around his neck as she gave herself up to the pure pleasure of it. Her head tilted back, her blue eyes dark and her soft mouth parting and begging for his kiss.

He did not hold it back. He ravished her mouth while other parts of him ravished the soft folds of warm damp flesh between her legs. It did not occur to her that he was as much a slave to what they were generating between them. To Rachel he was just displaying his contempt for her. Toying with her because the humiliation of being made such an easy victim of her half-sister's messy marriage still stung his ego and he wanted her to pay for making him feel like that.

This was payback—sexual payback. And he meant to make her keep on paying for as long as this thing took to pan out.

She was picked up and tumbled back on to the duvet. He came to lean over her, blocking out the light like a domineering shadow, everything about him so physically superior, strong, mesmerising—overwhelming yet so potently exciting at the same time.

His eyes glinted down at her, his face a map of hard angles built on arrogant sexual claim. She was about to be ravished a second time and the horror of it was that she knew she was not going to say no.

A telephone started ringing with the shrillness of a klaxon. Staring up into his face, tense and not breathing, Rachel thought for several seconds that he was going to ignore the call and continue with what he had started here.

Then his face altered, shutting down desire with the single blink of those long eyelashes, and he took hold of his shirt and grimly closed it across her breasts.

With that he levered himself off the bed, leaving Rachel to sit up and huddle inside the shirt while he went to recover his trousers and this time pulled them on.

He glanced back at her, nothing lover-like about him anywhere now. 'Get in the bed. Go to sleep,' he instructed.

Then he strode out of the bedroom, closing the door behind him, leaving Rachel coldly aware that she had just been put in her place.

As the *gift* in his bed, to use if or when he so desired it.

The telephone went silent. Unable to stop herself, Rachel got up and went to open the door as quietly as she could, meaning to creep down the hall and listen in on the conversation—just in case it had something to do with them.

She did not need to take another step from where she was. The door on the opposite side of the hall was open. He was standing in front of a desk with his back towards her and his trousers resting low on his hips.

'You think that ringing me at two in the morning will please me, Daniella—?' His tone did not sound pleased at all.

Rachel continued to hover, watching as his naked shoulders racked up tighter the more that his stepsister said.

'Daniella…' he sighed out eventually. 'Will you give me the opportunity to speak? I am sorry you have been hit by so many telephone calls,' he said wearily. 'No, the lady in question is not Elise,' he denied. 'She is who she has always been. It is everyone else who made the mistake. '

A lie. Another lie. Rachel felt the weight of every single one of them land upon her shoulders.

Raffaelle turned sharply, as if he could sense her standing here. She watched his eyes move in a possessive flow from her face to his shirt, then down her legs. The intimacy in the look conflicted with the coldness now in charge of his features. And she knew that not only had he brought himself under control, but she was now looking at the man she'd first met, undeniably attractive but cynical and hard.

On a wavering grimace Rachel dropped her eyes from him and stepped back into the bedroom. When Elise had picked him to have her rebellious affair with, she had chosen the wrong man, she thought heavily as she closed the door.

Pushing his free hand into his trouser pocket, Raffaelle suppressed the desire to either curse or sigh as he leant his lean hips against the edge of the desk while Daniella continued to yell in his ear.

He was angry with the interfering press, who were taking it in turns to call up Daniella in their quest for more information. He was also fed up because the whole thing was now driving itself like a train with no damn brakes.

And he was achingly bloody aroused and despising himself for feeling like that. Where did he get off, jumping all over a woman—a *stranger*—like some randy, feckless, uncontrolled youth—?

No wonder she'd looked at him just now as if he had crawled out from beneath a stone. No wonder she had gone back in the bedroom and shut herself away. She knew she was trapped; *he* knew he was trapped!

'No, Daniella,' he grimly cut in to her half-hysterical ranting. 'It is *you* who made the mistake two months ago. She was *never* Elise—have you got that?'

His cold tone alone had the desired effect.

'You mean you want me to *say* that I was mistaken?'

'No. I am telling you that you *are* mistaken.'

'So you *have* just got engaged to marry this Rachel Carmichael—the same woman who threw herself at you tonight?'

'*Si*,' he confirmed.

'Just like that—?' She was almost choking on her disbelief.

'No, not just like that,' he sighed out. 'I have been—courting Rachel over the last few months.'

'*Courting* her—?'

Bad choice of word. '*Seducing* her, then.'

Her struck silence made him grimace and he couldn't make up his mind if she was beginning to swallow the lies or simply being sensible for once and taking on board the grim warning in his voice.

'Is she pregnant—?'

'No!' he bit out, jerking upright from the desk and swinging round as a sting of stark alarm shot down his back.

Dio, he'd used nothing to stop it from happening, and he had not thought to ask her if she was protected!

What kind of crass bloody oversexed fool did that make him? Or her for not thinking about it—?

'And, since my personal life is no one's business but my own, *cara*, can I suggest a simple *no comment* from you would make me happy? Or, better still, Daniella—take the telephone off the hook!'

He cut the connection and tossed the handset back on its rest, then just stood there, not knowing what to do next.

Sex without protection with a woman he barely knew. Flexing muscles rippled all over him as he took on board the consequences which could result from such a stupidly irresponsible act.

With his luck tonight, she could already be in the process of conceiving his baby. Add all the other risks which came along with unprotected sex and he suddenly felt like a time bomb set to go off!

A growl left his throat as he turned back to the bedroom. Chin set like a vice, he pushed open the door. The room was in darkness. He switched on the overhead light and went to stand at the bottom of the bed.

She was nothing but a curled up mound beneath the duvet. 'I did not use protection,' he clipped out.

The mound jerked, then went still for a gut-clenching second. Then it moved again and she emerged, sliding up against the pillows, flush-cheeked—wary, defensive—sensationally delectable.

Dio, he thought.

'Say that again,' she shook out.

'I did not use protection,' he repeated tautly. 'I am not promiscuous and I have never taken such risks before in my life,' he added stiffly. 'I like to think that I can respect my…partner's history in the same way that she can respect mine.'

Rachel looked at the way he was standing there like some arrogant autocrat caught with his pants down by his bitch of a wife. Only his pants were up; it was his shirt that was missing and the bitch of a wife in this case was the *gift* he'd been handed and enjoyed thoroughly—before he'd thought to wonder where she had been before she'd landed in his bed!

As if it wasn't bad enough that she was sitting in the bed belonging to a man she had only met for the first time tonight, wearing his shirt and his scents and his touch on her skin—she now had to endure the kind of conversation that belonged in a brothel!

Next he would be asking how much he owed her for her services. Give him half a chance and she knew he would love to denounce her out loud as a whore.

Well, what did that make him? Rachel wanted to know.

'I am a clean-living, careful, healthy person,' she snapped out indignantly.

'I am relieved to hear it.'

He didn't look it. 'I don't sleep around! And if you hit me with one more rotten insult, Mr Villani,' she warned furiously. 'I think I am going to physically attack you!'

'My apologies if it sounded as if I was trying to insult you—'

'You did insult me.' She went to slide back down the bed.

'But we don't know each other.'

'You can say that again,' Rachel muttered.

'And it is an issue we need to address.'

'Well, you addressed it very eloquently,' she told him and tugged up the duvet with a *now go away* kind of shrug.

If he read it he ignored it. 'We have not finished with this.'

'Yes, we have.'

'No, Rachel, we have not…'

It was the alteration in his voice from stiff to weary that forced her to take notice. 'We still have the issue of another kind of protection to discuss.'

Another kind… Rachel froze for a second, then slid back up the pillows again, only this time more slowly as she finally began to catch on.

He put it in simple words for her. 'I did not protect us against—conception. I need to know if you did.'

It was like being hit with one hard knock too many; she felt all the colour drain from her face. 'I don't believe this is happening to me,' she whispered.

Taut muscles stretched as he pulled himself in like a man trying to field his own hard knock. 'I presume from your response that it is a problem.'

'I've told you once—I don't sleep around!' she cried out.

A nerve flicked at the corner of his hard mouth. 'You don't need to sleep around to take oral contraception.'

'Well, thank you for that reassuring piece of information,'

she said hotly. 'But, in my case, and because *I don't sleep around*, I—don't take oral contraception either…' The heat in her voice trailed into a stifled choke.

He cursed.

Rachel covered her face with her hands.

She had just indulged in uninhibited sex with a stranger without any protection; now his millions of sperm were chasing through her body in a race towards their ultimate goal!

Fertilisation. A baby—dear God…

Suddenly she was diving out of the bed and heading at a run for the bathroom. She thought she was going to be sick but then found that she couldn't. She wanted to wash herself clean inside and out!

Instead she just stood there with her arms wrapped around her middle and shook.

She heard him arrive in the door opening. 'I h-hate you,' she whispered. 'I wish I'd never heard your stupid name.'

Raffaelle shifted his tense stance, relaxing it wearily so he was leaning against the doorframe. He wanted to echo her sentiments but he did not think she was up to hearing him say it while she stood there resembling a skittish pale ghost.

'It happened, *cara*. Too late now to trade insults,' he murmured flatly instead.

She swung round to stare at him, blue eyes bright with anger and the close threat of tears. 'You think that kind of remark helps the situation?'

Pushing his hands into his trouser pockets, Raffaelle raised a black silk eyebrow. 'You think that your previous remark helped it?'

No, she supposed that it didn't.

Losing the will to stand upright any longer she sank down on to the closed toilet seat. 'I'm so horrified by what we've done.'

'I can see that.'

'I don't w-want a baby,' she whispered starkly.

'Any man's or just mine?'

Rachel looked at the way he was standing there in the doorway—*lounging* there half-undressed. A tall, lean, tightly muscled *supremo*, the image of everything you would want to grab from the human male gene pool.

Feeling something disturbingly elemental shift in her womb, she went on the attack. 'Being flippant about it doesn't help.'

'Neither does flaying yourself.'

She stared at him. 'Where the heck are you actually coming from?' she gasped out. 'You don't know me, yet you stand there looking as if you couldn't care less about what we've done!'

'I am a fatalist.'

'Lucky you,' Rachael muttered, pushing her hair back from her brow. 'Whereas I am wishing that yesterday never began.'

'Too late to wish on rainbows, *cara*.'

'Now you are just annoying.'

'I apologise,' he drawled. 'However, since we could well be in this for the long haul, I suggest you get used to my— annoying ways.'

'Long haul—?' Her chin shot up. What was he talking about now?

'Marriage comes before babies in my family,' he enlightened.

Marriage—? 'Oh, for goodness' sake.' It made her feel sick to her stomach to say it, but— 'I'll take one of those m- morning after pills that—'

'No, you will not,' he cut in.

She stood up. 'That is not your decision.'

His silver eyes speared her. 'So you are happy to see off a fragile life before it has been given the chance to exist?'

'God, no.' She even shuddered. 'But I think it would be—'

'Well, don't think,' he said coldly. 'We will not add to our sins if you please. This is our fault not the fault, of the innocent child which may result. Therefore we will deal with it the honourable way—if or when it comes to it.'

'With marriage,' she mocked.

'You must know I am considered to be quite a good catch, *cara*.'

Softly said, smooth as silk. A sharp silence followed while Rachel took on board what he was actually implying. Then she heaved in a taut breath. 'I suppose I should have expected that one,' she said as she breathed out again.

'I don't follow.' He frowned.

'The—you set me up for this accusation.' She spelled it out for him. 'The—you got me into bed deliberately so you could position yourself as the great millionaire catch!'

'I did not say that.' He sighed impatiently.

Oh, yes, he damn did! Inside she was quivering. Inside she was feeling as if she'd stepped into an ice cold alien place.

'I'll take the other option,' she retaliated and went to push past him. The hand snaking out of his pocket grabbed her by the arm as the other hand arrived, holding a mobile telephone.

'Let go of me.'

He ignored her and there was nothing relaxed about him now, Rachel saw as he hit quick-dial, then put the phone to his ear.

'Are we still under siege from the press?' he demanded.

He had to be talking to the security man in the foyer, Rachel realised. A new kind of tension sizzled all around them while he listened to the answer and she waited to find out where he was going with this.

The hard line of his mouth gave a twist as he cut the connection. Sliding the phone back into his pocket, he speared her with a hard look.

'The paparazzi is still out there,' he stated grimly. 'I do not expect them to leave us alone any time in the near future—understand?'

Rachel just stared at him, all eyes and weighty heart and pummelled feelings.

'Wherever you or I go from now on, I can almost guarantee that they mean to follow.' He made his point brutally clear. 'So think about it, *cara*,' he urged grimly. 'Do you want to take a walk out to the local all-night pharmacy and turn this thing into a tabloid sensation as the pack follow to witness you purchasing your morning-after medication—?'

Ice froze the silence between them as diamond eyes locked challengingly with frosted blue. Rachel thought about screaming. She felt like screaming! He really, truly and honestly believed that she was ruthless enough to calmly take something to rectify the wrong they had done, his wonderful *fatalist* attitude giving him the right to believe that his morals were superior to her own.

And why not? she asked herself starkly. What did he really know about her as a living, breathing person? Hadn't she flipped out the clever counter attack to his marriage deal? Wasn't she the cool liar and cheat around here, who could hit on a man and let him take her to his bed for no other reason than she'd fancied him?

Why not tag her as a woman who was also capable of seeing off a baby before she was even sure that there was one?

Hurt trammelled through her body, though, melting the ice and turning it into tears because she could not deny him the right to see her as a cold, ruthless schemer—she'd painted her own portrait for him to look at, after all.

He saw the tears and frowned. 'Rachel—' he murmured huskily.

She pushed his hand off her arm and walked away, only to pull to a hovering halt in the middle of the bedroom.

Nowhere to run. Nowhere to hide, she realised as her tears grew and grew. In the end she did the only thing she could see open to her right now and climbed back into the bed and disappeared beneath the duvet again.

Heart thumping, eyes burning, she pressed a clenched fist against her mouth to stop the choking sobs she could feel working their way up from her throat.

She heard him move. The lights went off. A door closed quietly. He had the grace to leave her alone with her misery and at last she let the first sob escape—only to jerk and twist her head on the pillow just in time to see him lift up the duvet and the warm dark shape of his now fully naked body slide into the bed.

Her quivering gasp was lost in the arm he used to draw her against him. Eyes like diamonds wrapped in rich black velvet searched her face, then a grimace touched his mouth.

'You're crying,' he said huskily.

'No, I'm not.' Squeezing a hand up between them, she went to brush a stray tear from the corner of her eye.

Or she would have done if one of his fingers had not got there before hers took the tear away; she could not hold back another small sniff.

'I would not have done it,' she mumbled.

'*Si*, I know that.' He sighed. 'We were fighting. You used your weapon well. I retaliated by cutting you to pieces. I apologise for doing it.'

'You're so ruthless it's scary.'

'*Si*.' On another sigh he sent one of his legs looping over her legs to draw her in a bit closer to him, then he caught her hand and pressed it to his chest.

She felt his warmth and his muscled firmness and the prickle of hair against her palm. It was all very intimate and very dangerous—especially so when she didn't try to pull away. The shirt formed a sort of barrier to stop the more frightening skin to skin contact, but—

She eased out a sigh of her own and tried to ignore what

was happening to her. 'I'm really sorry I got us both embroiled in this mess,' she whispered in genuine regret.

'But you did do it,' he pointed out with devastating simplicity. 'Now we have to deal with what we have.' He came to lean over her, suddenly deadly serious. 'And what we have is one story, one betrothal, one bed,' he listed. 'You will not, during the time we are together, give cause for anyone to question our honesty.'

'Our lies, you mean.'

He shook his dark head. 'Start believing in this, *cara*,' he advised. 'The fate of your sister's marriage rests on your ability to live, breathe and *sleep* the role you have chosen to play in my life.'

His life. Those two words said it all to Rachel. This was *his* life he was protecting. His reputation. His pride.

And why not—? she thought painfully. Her mouth quivered. The tip of his tongue arrived to taste her soft upper lip.

Rachel saw that grimness had been replaced with slumberous desire and knew what was going to happen next.

'No,' she jerked out.

But his tongue dipped deeper. 'Yes,' he contradicted in soft silken English.

'But I don't—'

'You do, *cara*,' and he showed her how much she did by trailing his fingers inside the shirt.

Her breast received his touch with livewire tingles. Don't respond! she told herself, but she did. Her mouth opened wider to turn the gentle contact into a proper kiss and the globe of her breast peaked pleasurably against his palm. It was terrible; she could not seem to control herself.

On a husky murmur he took the kiss back from her and from there it all began to build again.

It should have been a huge let-down after what they'd just

been fighting about—but it wasn't. What it was, was a slow, slow attack on every sensual front he could discover by using his lips and his tongue and the light-light tantalising brush of fingers. There was not a single millimetre of her flesh that was not gently coaxed into yielding its secrets—its every weakness exposed and explored until she felt like a slave to her own sensuality and an even bigger slave to his.

By the time he prepared to come into her, she was so lost in a hazy world made up entirely of him that she just lay there, watching while he produced the protection they'd both forgotten about the last time and expertly rolled it down his powerful length.

His eyes burned hers as he came over her. When he pushed inside, her groan brought his lips down to capture the sound. They moved together in a slow, deep, serious, dark journey, which left both of them totally wiped out by its end.

And, as sleep finally swept her into boneless oblivion, Rachel knew she had been totally taken over, ravished, possessed.

I wish, was the last conscious thought she remembered having and fell asleep wondering what it was she had been about to wish for.

She awoke cocooned in a nest of warm duvet and to the sound of a telephone ringing again. Only it did not sound loud, as if it was being muffled by the thickness of walls and doors. But the persistent sound pierced through her sleep like a sluggish pulse taking place inside her head.

She didn't open her eyes—didn't want to. Too many bad memories were already rushing back, the worst of them being the knowledge that she'd fallen into bed with a man she'd only met the night before, had hot, unprotected sex with him and now his physical imprint was so deeply stamped on her that she could still see him, hear him, feel him and smell him with every sensory cell she had.

The ringing stopped. Rachel let her eyes open. Daylight was shrouded by the drawn curtains but she could see just enough to know that the place beside her in the bed was empty and she breathed a sigh of relief.

At least she would have some time to get herself back together before she had to face him again.

Easing out of the bed, she rose to stand up with just about every muscle feeling the extra stretch as she looked around her for something to put on.

Her clothes had gone. So had the shirt she had been coveting last night like a last line of defence. What now? she asked herself. Were her missing clothes supposed to be sending her a message about where she fitted into his life?

Suddenly spying the cashmere throw he had used to cover her with the night before draped over a chair, she leapt on it and wrapped herself in it. The throw covered her from throat to ankle but she still felt like the wretched man's concubine, imprisoned for his exclusive use.

And he knew how to use her, she was forced to admit when her senses gave a tight little flutter in response to the thought.

Someone knocked on the door. She almost tripped over as she spun round to stare at it.

'Y-Yes?' she called out, puzzled as to why the heck he was bothering to knock when privacy had been something he had taken no heed of last night.

'Your things have arrived, Miss Carmichael,' a totally strange female voice announced. 'Shall I leave the suitcase here outside the door?'

'Oh—y-yes—thank you,' she answered, frowning because she didn't know what the woman was talking about.

She waited a few seconds before going to pull the door open a small crack to make sure the woman had gone before she looked down to discover the suitcase she'd hastily packed before leaving Devon was now standing on the floor. Clinging to the black throw with one hand and still frowning, she used her other hand to lift the case inside the bedroom and shut the door again.

Last time she'd seen this, it had been lying open and spilling its contents on to the spare bed in Mark's flat. So how had it ended up here instead?

Had Mark delivered it? Had he come here, then left again without bothering to see or speak to her to find out if she was okay?

Hurt thickened her throat as she heaved the case on to the rumpled bed and unzipped it. Inside it was everything she had brought up to London with her, plus all the extras that Elise had provided to help turn her into her look-alike.

There was also a piece of paper lying on the top of everything. Picking it up, she unfolded it to find it was a hastily scribbled note from Mark.

Did you have to send the chauffeur round to knock me up for your stuff at 6 o'clock in the morning? I'd only just crawled into bed!

Elise called you last night after I told her the good news, but your phone was dead. She and Leo wanted to congratulate you on your coming nuptials, if you get my drift. Call her later today so she can play the ecstatic sister for Leo's benefit.

I'm off to LA this afternoon for a few weeks. See you when I get back. Love M.

Mission accomplished, in other words, so it was back to normal life—for Mark anyway. No words of concern for how she was feeling. No sign of a rescue plan for her any time soon.

Rachel stared out at nothing for a moment or two. Then, as

a rueful grimace played its rather wobbly way across her mouth, she let the note fall on to the bed and turned her attention to selecting fresh clothes from the suitcase. At least she was now overloaded with expensive hair products and cosmetics, she consoled herself.

Dressed in a short bathrobe and fresh from his shower in one of the guest rooms, Raffaelle opened the bedroom door as the bathroom door shut with a quiet click.

He stood for a moment, viewing the evidence of her occupation, then walked over to the bed and picked up the note. His expression hardened as he read it. His eyes then drifted to the open suitcase, where it looked as if everything had been dumped in there at haste.

Did she feel deserted? She had to feel deserted because it was exactly what had happened to her.

Replacing the note where he'd found it, he turned then and strode across the bedroom to open the door which led into his dressing room. Ten minutes later he was dressed and letting himself out of the bedroom as quietly as he had come in while the running shower still sounded from the other side of the closed bathroom door.

CHAPTER SIX

IT TOOK nerve for Rachel to open the bedroom door and step into the hallway. She would rather be doing anything than facing Raffaelle Villani in the cold, harsh light of day.

Rubbing her hands up and down her arms in a nervous gesture as she walked, at least she looked more like herself, she tried to console herself. With Elise's image stripped away and her hair shampooed and quickly blow-dried, she'd seen the real Rachel staring back at her from the mirror—the one who wore jeans and a long-sleeved black knit top. Her make-up was minimal and her hair had reverted to its natural style.

All she needed to do now was to convince herself that she was the real Rachel, because she certainly did not feel like her inside.

She intended to go and hunt down her bag and her cellphone before she did anything else, but she never got that far. The door next to the kitchen stood open and, having glanced through it, she then pulled to a heart-sinking halt.

Raffaelle was there, standing by a long dining table. He was wearing a soft loose-fitting smoked-grey T-shirt and a pair of charcoal trousers that hung easily around his hips. And, if she had ever wanted to know the difference between expensive man dressed in a formal dinner suit and expensive man dressed casually, then she was looking at him.

The aroma of fresh coffee would have sailed right by her if he had not used that moment to lift a cup to his mouth. She was held transfixed by his height again, by his sensual dark good looks, by his mouth sipping coffee and his long golden fingers holding the cup.

Sensation quivered right down her front as each and every sense unfurled and responded to the sight of those hands, that mouth, the long legs and wide shoulders—to her exciting new lover. Her breasts grew tight and tender in her bra cups, her tongue grew moist in her mouth, her breathing stopped completely as a tight tingling erupted low down. It was like falling into a deep, dark pit of forbidden pleasures. She didn't want to feel like this but she could not break free from it.

Then he glanced up and caught her standing there staring at him. It was like being pinned to a wall by her guilty thoughts. Heat rushed up from her toes and through her body until it suffused her face to her hair roots while he just stood there with his cup suspended just below his sensual mouth.

The agony of mutual intimacy was nothing short of torture as she watched his eyes drop to the pair of simple flat black shoes adorning her feet, then begin a slow journey upwards, along well-faded denim that clung to her legs and her hips and the flatness of her stomach like a second skin.

His scrutiny paused right there and suddenly something else was adding to the turbulent mix. Rachel knew what he was thinking. She felt the muscles around her womb clench tightly as if it was acknowledging that it already belonged to him.

Maybe he saw the tightening because his eyes darkened. When he lifted them to clash with her eyes, the sheer power of what was passing between them put her into a prickling hot sweat.

He broke eye contact and she could feel her heart drumming against her ribs as he dropped his attention to her mouth, slightly parted and trembling, with its light coating of pink lipstick, then back to her eyes, looking out at him from a fixed hectic blue stare between quick flicks of mascara. Finally he let his eyes drift over her hair, where long and sleek straight had been replaced by a mop of silky loose curls that framed her still blushing face.

'Where did the curls come from?' he asked softly.

Forced into speech, Rachel had to moisten the inner surface of her lips. 'They were always there, just hiding,' she answered, lifting a self-conscious hand up to push the curls from her brow.

He continued to stare as the curls bounced back into place again. Shoulder-length straight now finished in a sexy blonde bubbly riot almost level with her pointed chin.

'They suit you,' he murmured.

'No, they don't,' she denied. 'But I was born with them, so…' She added a shrug, then stuck her hands into her jeans pockets and finally managed to drag her eyes away from him.

Raffaelle frowned as he watched the defensive body language.

'Is there any of that coffee going spare?' she asked.

'Sure,' he answered. 'In the kitchen. I will go and get it—'

'No.' She jerked into movement. 'Let me.'

She'd disappeared before he could stop her, fleeing like a scared fluffy blonde rabbit. It made him grimace—a lot of things made him grimace, like the tension she'd taken with her—the knowledge of what they'd done the night before. And the lack of awareness in her own natural beauty, for which he placed the blame firmly at her glamorous half-sister's feet.

Draining his coffee cup, he made the decision to follow her. Now the morning ice was almost broken he had no intention of letting it freeze over again.

She was standing by the coffee machine, watching it fill a cup.

'Here,' he said, striding over to offer his empty cup. 'I like it black.' He moved away from her before she had a chance to react to him. 'What do you like for breakfast—a fresh croissant? Cereal? Toast?' he listed lightly. 'There is some fresh orange juice in the fridge if you—'

'I don't want anything,' she cut in. 'Th-thank you,' she added. 'Just a caffeine shot then I will have to be going...'

'Going...' He turned slowly to look at her.

'Yes,' She was clearly refusing to look at him, staring down at her watch instead. 'I have a train to catch back to Devon and half the morning has gone already.'

'We've been over this,' Raffaelle reminded her. 'You are staying right here with me.'

'Yes, I know that.' She nodded, setting the blonde curls bouncing as she concentrated on the job of swapping her filled cup for his empty one beneath the stream of coffee from the machine. 'But I need to get some clothes if...'

'I will buy you any clothes you will need.'

Rachel stiffened. 'No, you will not! I have clothes back in Devon—and don't you *dare* make such a derisory offer like that again!'

'It was not derisory,' he denied. 'I was being practical.'

'Well, I'm trying to be practical too, and I can't just drop everything as if I don't have another life. I need a couple of days to—organise things with the farm.'

'You mean you actually run the farm yourself?'

More derision? Rachel stared at him but only saw honest disbelief in his face. 'Efficiently,' she stated coolly.

'So who is looking after it while you are here?'

'A—neighbour.' She frowned as she said that, wondering why she had put her relationship with Jack in such odd terms. 'But he has his own place to run, so I...'

Something altered in his demeanour, though Rachel wasn't sure exactly what it was.

'Use your phone to make your arrangements, as I have had to do,' he said coolly.

'God, you're so insufferable,' she gasped. 'It's all right for you. You're Mr High-flyer. You can order people about by phone, but I can't.'

Ignoring the high-flyer quip, Raffaelle walked towards her. 'You think?'

'I know.' Rachel nodded backing into the corner of the kitchen units as he approached, then feeling well and truly trapped by the time he towered over her. 'I've seen the way it works with Leo. W-when he needs something done he just throws his weight around by telephone.'

'But you need to be hands-on to water your organic lettuce,' he mocked.

'You don't need to be so derisive about it!' she flashed in her own defence. 'When this is all over with, Mr Villani, you might be unfortunate enough to have lost a deal or two because you weren't paying proper attention, but I risk losing my whole livelihood!'

'If you are carrying my child then this will never be over.'

Placed coolly into the argument, Rachel swallowed thickly. 'Don't start hitting me with the worst thing that could happen again,' she shook out huskily.

He went to say something, then sighed and changed his mind. Tension stung—antagonism that wasn't all to do with what they were arguing about.

'You said it was family-run thing,' he then prompted.

'It is,' she confirmed. Then she took a breath and altered that answer to, 'It *was* a family run thing until my parents were killed five years ago in—in a road accident. Now the farm is split three ways between me, Mark and Elise.'

'Which means that you do the work and they do nothing?'

'I like the work, they don't.'

'Loyal little thing, aren't you?' he mocked her. 'Has it not occurred to you yet that they are not very loyal to you—?'

Raffaelle wished the words back as soon as he'd said them. But it was too late. She'd already gone pale and she lost her cup so she could make a defensive fold of her arms across her front.

'My family loyalty is none of your business,' she muttered.

'You think—?' Anger with himself made his voice sound harsh. But since the anger was there now, he took a grip on her clenched left hand and prised it upwards. 'This ring on your finger demands that I should have your complete loyalty now.'

'It's fake.' She grabbed the hand back and thrust it beneath her arm again.

Things were starting to happen. Fights with women usually did end up as sexual battles and Raffaelle was beginning to feel the sexual pull. He reacted to it by snaking his hands around her slender nape and tilting her head back so he could claim her mouth.

She tasted of mint toothpaste and pink lipstick. He found he liked the combination. And she didn't try to fight him, which he liked even more. By the time he raised his head again, her arms were no longer defensively crossed but clinging to his shirt.

'This isn't fake,' he rumbled out deeply, still toying with the corner of her mouth. 'So let's forget about Devon and go back to bed. I don't know why we got out of it in the first place.'

'No.' She gave a push at him and when he released her she scuttled sideways. 'I've got things to do.'

'You mean you're running scared all of a sudden.' He grabbed her hand to pull her out of the kitchen and back into the dining room. 'If you are hoping to escape to a pharmacy in Devon,' he said brusquely, 'then first you should take a look at these…'

He brought her to a stop beside the dining table where a selection of the Sunday tabloids lay spread out.

Rachel froze, wondering how she had missed seeing them before. But she knew why she'd missed them; she'd been too busy drinking him in to notice anything else in the room.

In every photograph but one, she and he were standing outside the apartment block displaying the ring and looking convincingly loverlike and besotted. The only photograph that was different was in Mark's paper, which bore the clever caption, *'First public kiss for newly engaged lovers.'*

'My fifteen minutes of fame,' she jibed tensely, looking at the sleek stranger in the photographs, who happened to be her. Raffaelle looked no different than his tall, dark, handsome self and how he'd managed to pull off that smile without making it look cynical was worthy of a headline all by itself.

'This is set to last a lot longer than fifteen minutes, *cara*,' he responded dryly.

'Because you're newsworthy.'

'Which is the only reason why you hit on me in the first place,' he pointed out. 'This is what you wanted.' He waved a long finger at the photograph her half-brother had taken. 'I must admit you look very like your sister in that.'

The picture showed a clinch which looked like they'd been lovers for ever. That wave of tingling intimacy shot down Rachel's front again and she quickly shifted her eyes to the other more carefully staged photographs, all of which were accompanied by catchy tag lines aimed to turn them into tacky celebrity fodder.

'I did not want all the rest of this, though. That was your fault.'

'You cannot be so blind.'

It was the way he said it that made Rachel look sharply at him. It had been hard and sardonic—tones that repeated themselves in the expression on his face.

'Explain that,' she demanded.

'I meant nothing.' He went to turn away.

'Yes, you did!' She caught hold of his arm. 'And I want to know what you meant!'

He swung back to her, face hard, eyes angry. 'Did you never

think to question if your brother's cronies would know who his twin is? Of course they knew—' he answered his own question '—which is why they came after us and called out Elise's name. They saw you looking like her and him making his quick escape, then they saw a very contrived yet really juicy scandal brewing involving Elise, Leo Savakis and Raffaelle Villani in a gripping sex triangle. I can forgive you your naïvety, *cara*, if you are as shocked as you appear to be, but I will not forgive your stupid brother for not thinking this thing through and foreseeing the obvious outcome if I had not intervened!'

Rachel pulled out a chair and sat down on it. He was oh-so-sickeningly right. And the worst of it was that he seemed to have worked all of it out within seconds of her explaining it all last night.

'Now ask yourself how long you think it will take the press to sleuth out exactly who you are,' he persisted. 'And your fifteen minutes of fame becomes a roller coaster ride to hell and back while they dig into your past, with Leo Savakis waiting in the wings for you to fall off the rails and accidentally reveal it is all just a big ugly cover-up for his wife's transgressions.'

'You don't have to say any more,' Rachel whispered. 'I get the full picture.'

'Do you?' he rasped. 'Well, add this into the mix. Start running scared now and I will blow the whole lie sky high and damn your sister's marriage. I can take the heat of the repercussions if she cannot!'

He walked out of the room, leaving Rachel alone to stew on what he'd said. It didn't take long. He was right and she had been running scared when she'd made that bid to leave here and go back to Devon. But that had nothing to do with the lies, though they were bad enough. Her reasons did not even have anything to do with their stupid delving into unprotected sex!

It was to do with him and what he did to her. What he made

her feel. If he could affect her this badly in only one night, then she was going to be an emotional wreck by the time it came to the end.

If it came to an end, she then amended, recalling that marriage warning he'd made.

Raffaelle was pacing his study wondering what was the matter with him. Why had he bitten her head off like that?

Because she wanted to go home to collect some clothes and organise her life, or because she still persisted in defending her selfish family?

Or was it because she'd mentioned a man down there in Devon? A *neighbour* she had not bothered to mention before…?

He did not know. He did not think he *wanted* to know. Something was happening here that scared him witless each time he came close to looking at it.

He heard her moving about then and went to see what she was doing now. He found her in the living room with her bag in her hand.

'I—can't find my phone,' she said and she looked pale and defensive again.

'The battery was flat. I put it on the charger in my study. I'll go and get it…' Then he paused. 'Who do you want to call?'

Irritation ripped down his backbone because he knew it was none of his business who she wanted to call. By the expression on her face, she thought the same thing.

Still, she answered him. 'I will have to ring round a few people if I am not allowed to leave here—'

'No.' Raffaelle shook his head. 'We will do it your way, only we both go and we will use my car instead of the train.'

'But—'

'Ten minutes,' he said gruffly, turning away again. 'And don't keep me waiting. The sooner we leave, the sooner we can get back.'

He drove them in a silver Ferrari with the same reckless efficiency he'd driven the night before. But then, his driving had had to be nifty when they'd met with the paparazzi waiting outside for them to leave. They'd picked the car up from the basement car park but the moment they'd emerged on to the street they'd been spotted and all hell had broken loose as camera-toting reporters fell over themselves to get into their cars and give chase.

'I don't understand why they're still hanging around,' Rachel said after they'd lost their pursuers in a sequence of dizzying turns down narrow back streets. She hadn't dared speak before then in case she broke his concentration and they ended up hitting a wall. 'What do they think we are going to do? Get married on the apartment steps or something?'

'They don't know enough about you.' He sounded so grim that Rachel felt a cold little shiver chase down her spine.

'I hate this,' she whispered. 'I hated it when I used to get caught up in it with Elise. I don't know how you people live your lives like this.'

'We live in a celebrity-driven world,' he answered levelly. 'The masses are greedy for the intimate details of the rich and famous—or, for that matter, anyone who lives a high profile life. You have now joined the celebrity ranks, so get used to it, because this is only the beginning of it.'

The beginning of it…

After that Rachel did not speak another word. They reached the motorway and suddenly the powerful car came into its own, eating up the miles with the luxurious smoothness that promised to cut the journey time by half.

He stopped once at a motorway service station, led her into the café and bought sandwiches and coffee.

'Eat,' he instructed, when she stared at the unappetizing-looking sandwich he'd placed in front of her. 'You look like death and you have eaten nothing since you threw yourself at me last night.'

And I look like death because I hardly had any sleep last night, she threw back at him without saying the words out loud. Because out loud meant opening a Pandora's box full of what they'd been doing instead of sleeping.

The indifferent-tasting sandwich was washed down by in-different-tasting coffee. Rachel was surprised he ate his sandwich or drank the coffee. They just didn't look like the kind of food this man would usually put anywhere near his mouth.

When they hit the road again he wanted to talk. 'Tell me how your family works,' he invited.

So she explained how her mother had lost her husband to a long-term illness while the twins had still been very young. 'A few years later she married my father and then had me.'

'So what is the age difference between you and the twins?'

'Six years,' she replied.

'And who did the farm originally belong to?'

'My father. But he—*we*—never differentiated between Mark and Elise and myself. And it isn't really a farm,' she then added because she thought she better had do before they arrived there and he saw it. 'It's what we call a smallholding, with three acres of land, a house, a couple of greenhouses and a couple of barns.'

'Another lie, *cara*?'

Rachel shrugged. 'It's run like a farm.'

'And the…neighbour that helps you out when you need it—what does he do?'

'Jack owns the land adjoining our land—and his *is* a farm,' she stressed. 'He's been good to us since our parents died.'

'Call it as it is,' Raffaelle said. 'He has been good to *you*.'

Rachel turned to look at him. 'Why that tone?' she demanded.

His grimace stopped her from becoming hooked on watching his face. 'I don't think I want to elaborate,' he confessed.

'Suits me,' she said and, turning the collar up on her coat, she leant further into the seat and closed her eyes.

His low laugh played along her nerve endings. 'You are prickly, Miss Carmichael.'

'And you are loathsome, *Signor*.'

'Because I don't mind saying that I dislike the way your siblings use you?'

'No. You are loathsome simply because you are.'

'In bed?'

Rachel didn't answer.

'You prefer, perhaps, this Jack in bed as your lover because he is so *good* to you.'

He was fishing. Rachel decided to let him. 'Maybe.' She smiled.

'But can he make you fall apart with pleasure there as I can, or does he bring the smell of farmer to your bed, which you must overcome before he can overcome you?'

'As I said. You're loathsome.'

'*Si*,' he agreed. 'However, when I said that I don't sleep around I meant it, whereas you seemingly did not.'

Rachel turned her head and flicked her eyes open to look at him. Once a liar always a liar, she thought heavily when she saw the grimness lashed to his lean profile.

And a tease could only be a tease when the recipient knew he was being teased. Sitting further up the seat with a sigh, she pushed a hand through her curls and opened her mouth to tell him exactly who and what Jack was—when her attention was caught by a giant blue motorway sign.

'Oh, heck,' she gasped. 'We need to take this next turn-off!'

With a startled flash of his eyes and a few muttered curses, he flipped the car across several motorway lanes with one eye on the rear-view mirror judging the pace of the traffic behind them and the other eye judging the spare stretch road in front of them. By the time they sailed safely down the slip road Jack's name had been washed right out of Rachel's head by an intoxicating mix of nerve-fraying terror for her life and the exhilarating thrill of the whole smooth, slick power-driven manoeuvre.

'Which way?' he demanded.

Rachel blinked and told him in a tense breath-stifled voice while her senses fizzed and popped in places they shouldn't. What was it about men and danger that struck directly at the female sexual psyche?

He glanced at her and saw her expression and sent her a wide slashing masculine grin that lit her up inside like a flaming torch.

'Scared, *cara*?' he quizzed.

'You—you—'

'Had it all under control,' he smoothly provided. 'Which, in Italian terms, makes the difference between a mere good lover and a fabulous lover.'

Rachel knew exactly what he meant, which was the hardest thing to take. If he stopped the car now she would be crawling all over him in a hot and seething sexually needy flood.

It was everything—the powerful car and the reckless man and the adrenalin rush still singing through her blood. She tried to breathe slowly and lost it completely when he reached across to her and gently stroked her cheek. Static fire whipped across her skin cells, she whispered something and turned her head. Their eyes clashed. For a short, short split second in time it was like falling into a vat of writhing, hissing, snapping snakes.

He looked away. The smile had gone but the atmosphere inside the car had heightened beyond anything real. Rachel sat on her hands to stop them reaching for him and tried to pretend it wasn't happening while he drove on with a sudden grim concentration that only made everything worse.

She gave directions in short, sharp, breathless little bursts of speech that only helped to increase the tension. He said nothing but just reacted with slick control of the car. They were both sitting forward in their seats. They were both staring fixedly directly ahead. She knew where this was going to end up just as he knew it. And the agony of knowing was as tough as the agony of having to sit here and wait.

At last—finally they turned into the private lane which led to the farm. Winter fields barely waking up to early spring spread out on either side of them, neatly ploughed and ready to sow. The old farmhouse stood in front of them, its rustic brick walls warmed by a weak sun. Flanking either side of it stood the adjoining barns and behind the house they could just see the greenhouse's glass glinting in the weak sunlight.

In front was the cobbled yard where Rachel's muddy old Jeep stood tucked in against a barn wall. On the other side stood another car, a Range Rover, making Rachel's heart sink, though whether that was due to disappointment, because she knew what was buzzing between the two of them was about to be indefinitely postponed, or relief for the same reason, she refused to examine.

Raffaelle brought the car to a stop in the dead centre of the courtyard, killed the engine, then climbed out without uttering a word. Rachel was slower in moving, unsure if her stinging legs would hold her up if she tried to stand on them.

He couldn't know what was coming and she didn't know how to tell him. One glance at his face across the top of the car and she was almost bowled over by the strict control he was holding over himself.

His eyes were not under control, though. They looked back at her with a possessive glitter that showered her with sexual promise.

She parted her paper-dry lips. 'Raffaelle—' she began anxiously.

'Let's go inside and find a bed,' he said huskily.

She quivered and swallowed, then heaved in a tense breath in preparation to speak again. The front door to the house suddenly swung inwards, snatching her attention away from him.

He looked where she was looking, shoes scraping on worn cobbles as he turned then went perfectly still.

A man stood in the open doorway—a tall, well-built, swarthy-looking man wearing brown cords and a fleece coat. He was also a man easily in his fifth decade, with eyes like ice that he pinned on Raffaelle.

'Jack,' Rachel murmured, feeling trouble brewing even before she saw Raffaelle tense up when she said Jack's name.

Damn, why hadn't she thought about this before she'd teased Raffaelle about her relationship to Jack?

And, oh dear, but Jack did not look pleased at all.

She hurried forward. Raffaelle stood frozen as he watched her walk straight into the other man's arms. He was trying to decide whether to go over there and punch the bastard for taking advantage of a vulnerable young woman left alone here to cope on her own. Or to reclaim what now belonged to him, then tell him to get the hell out.

In the end it was the other man who took the initiative.

'Jack…' Rachel burst into nervous speech as she reached him. 'This is…'

'I read the paper this morning, Rachel,' he cut in, looking across the cobbles with a set of grey eyes that were as cold as Raffaelle's own eyes.

He put her to one side so he could walk forwards. Rachel could feel the suspicion coming off him in waves. Jack knew her better than most people, so if anyone was going to smell a rat about her surprise engagement then it would be him.

'I n-need to explain.' She dashed after him.

'Mr Villani,' Jack greeted coolly.

Nerves jumping all over her now, Rachel rushed into speech yet again. 'Raffaelle, this is Jack Fellows.' Her anxious blue eyes pleaded with him to understand. 'He's my—'

'Guardian,' Jack himself put in. 'Until she is twenty-five, that is.'

'Well, that is a new name for it,' Raffaelle drawled.

'Jack is also my uncle,' she said heavily. 'M-my mother's brother…'

'And the one who looks out for her interests,' Jack coldly put in. 'So, if you are the same Italian who broke Rachel's heart last year, then you had better come up with a good reason for doing it or Rachel will not receive my blessing for this engagement.'

Oh, dear God. Rachel wished the ground would open up and swallow her. It just had not occurred to her that Jack would make such a mistake!

Now Raffaelle was looking at her as if she was one of the devil's children and she couldn't blame him. It had to feel as if each time he turned around he was being forced to answer new charges that someone in her family planted at his feet!

'Raffaelle is not Alonso,' she muttered to Jack in a driven undertone.

'Was that his name?' Her uncle looked at her in surprise. 'I don't recall you actually ever mentioning it.'

That was because she hadn't. She'd just come back here from her trip to Italy looking and behaving like a woman with a broken heart.

Her uncle turned back to Raffaelle. 'My sincere apologies for the mistake, Mr Villani,' he said and offered him his hand.

But it was too late for Rachel as far as Raffaelle was concerned. She sensed his anger hiding beneath the surface of his smile as he took Jack's proffered hand.

Then he switched the charm on. By the time he had finished explaining who he was and what he was, and trawled out the same story about how and where he'd met Rachel, he had her uncle eating out of his hand. It was like watching an action reply of the way he had handled the press the night before. And all Rachel could do was smile benignly once more and be impressed by his performance, while knowing retribution was close at hand.

He coolly assured Jack that he was no fortune hunter out to marry his niece for her share in the family pile. He assured him dryly that no, not all Italian men were so cavalier with the vulnerable female heart.

And of course he was madly in love with Rachel—what man would not be? His arm snaked out to hook her around her shoulders so he could draw her in close to his side.

I'm going to kill you the minute I get you alone, that heavy arm promised. And Rachel believed it—totally.

Then he apologised to Jack that the news of their betrothal had broken in the papers before he'd had a chance to come here and officially request Jack's blessing.

It was his finest moment, Rachel acknowledged from her subservient place at his side. Jack was old-fashioned, with traditional values. She could see from her uncle's expression that in Raffaelle he thought he was meeting a man after his own heart.

Jack had to rush off then but he offered them dinner to celebrate.

Smooth as silk, Raffaelle thanked him but regrettably had to decline. Apparently he had to be back in London this evening—to attend an irritating business dinner.

Whether there was a business dinner, Rachel did not know. But, of course, her uncle understood. Busy men and all that.

And Raffaelle's ultimate coup was to gain Jack's instant agreement that everything here would be taken care of while Rachel was away, because of course Raffaelle wanted her with him.

'Just be happy, darling,' Jack said to her, then he kissed her cheek, shook Raffaelle by the hand and left them, driving away while they stood and watched him—with Raffaelle's arm still exhibiting its possession across her shoulders in a grip like a vice.

Happy was the last thing she was feeling by the time her uncle's car disappeared out of sight. The moment he turned them to face the house Rachel tried to break free from him but his grip only tightened as he walked them across the cobbles.

The front door opened directly into the farmhouse-style kitchen, heated by the old Aga against the wall. Coming in here should have felt comfortingly familiar to Rachel but it didn't. The door closed. The arm dropped from her shoulders. Moving like a skittish kitten, she took a few steps away from him then spun around.

'I…'

'If you are about to utter yet another lie to me—' he cut right across her '—then let me advise you to keep silent!'

CHAPTER SEVEN

HER heart gave a thick little thump against her ribcage. It was like looking at a complete stranger again—a tall, dark, coldly angry stranger.

'I was actually about to apologise for the…misunderstanding with Jack out there.'

'You set me up.'

'It w-wasn't like that,' she denied. 'Y-you were fishing for information and I stupidly decided to tease you about my relationship with Jack.'

'I am not referring to your desire to pull my strings by intimating there was another man in your life,' he said. 'Though using your uncle like that is unforgivable enough.'

'Then what—?' she demanded.

'Alonso,' he supplied. 'The Italian heartbreaker I have been set up to play substitute for in your desire for payback!'

'That's not true!' Rachel protested.

His angry eyes crashed into her like a pair of ice picks. 'Not only is it true but you are the most devious witch it has ever been my misfortune to come into contact with!' he incised. 'This was never just about saving your half-sister's marriage! You always had this hidden agenda in which I paid for the sins you believe your other Italian lover committed!'

'No!' she cried. 'I'm *not* that petty! Elise's problems are serious enough without you adding such a crazy accusation into the mix! And anyway,' she said stiffly, 'you are nothing like Alonso. In fact I couldn't compare the two of you in any way if I tried!'

'In bed, perhaps?' he grimly suggested. 'Did you close your eyes and imagine it was him you were driving out of his head with your thrust-and-grind gyrations and those exquisite little muscle contractions?'

'No!' she said hotly. 'How dare you? That is such a rotten thing to say!'

'Then who did teach you to make love like that?' He took a step towards her. 'How many men, *amore,* does it take to produce such a well-practised sensualist?'

Blushing hotly, she cried, 'I'm not listening to this—'

She turned towards the door that led through to the rest of the house. The way he moved so fast to slam a hand against the door to keep it shut had her shivering out a shocked gasp.

'Answer the question.' He loomed over her.

Rachel folded her arms. 'You so love to throw your weight around, don't you?'

'Just answer.'

Anger flicked her eyes up to meet his. 'Why don't you tell me first—how many women have slipped in and out of your bed to make you such a *fabulous* lover?' she hit back. 'What was that,' she mocked when he clenched his expression. 'Do you want to tell me it's none of my business?'

'I am thirty-three years old, you are twenty-three.'

'Meaning the ten year difference justifies the numbers you clearly don't want to give?'

His shoulders shifted. 'I do not break hearts.'

Rachel released a thick laugh. 'You wouldn't know if you broke hearts! Men like you don't go into sexual relationships with the care of tender hearts in mind, *Signor*. They go into them for the sex!'

'In your experience.'

She tried to push past him, but the muscles in his arm bunched to form an iron bar she could not pass. 'Yes,' she hissed out.

'Gained mostly from this Alonso guy who took only what he wanted from you and trampled on the rest?'

'Yes!' she said again. 'Happy now?' she demanded. 'Have you got the required information nicely fixed in your head? I've had *two* lovers. Both Italian. *Both* with their brains lodged in their pants!'

For some reason she hit out at him, though she didn't understand why she had. The feeble blow barely glanced off his rock-solid bicep. And she was beginning to tremble now and didn't like it—beginning to bubble and fizz with anger and resentment and the most horrible feeling of all—humiliation at the way Alonso had treated her!

So maybe Raffaelle was right: when she'd agreed to hit on him to save Elise's marriage some subconscious part of her had wanted to pay back Alonso.

'So I am playing the fall guy.'

He was reading her thoughts. She swallowed tensely.

He turned to push his shoulders and head back against the door. '*Dio*, I cannot believe I fell into this trap.'

Rachel struggled to believe that she had fallen into it all too. 'I vowed I would never go near another Italian.'

'*Grazie*,' he clipped. 'I wish you had kept to your vow.'

Rachel turned away and walked over to the Aga and put the kettle on to boil. Why she did it she hadn't a single clue because she knew she could not swallow even a sip of anything right now.

But at least the move put distance between them. Silence

hummed behind her while she removed her coat and laid it over the back of a kitchen chair. Outside a weak sun was trying its best to filter into the room through the window on to scrubbed pine surfaces that had been here for as long as she could remember, yet she still felt as if she were standing in an alien place.

'Where did you meet him?'

The brusque question startled her into glancing at him. 'Who—?' she bit out.

His shoulders almost filled the doorway, his dark head almost level with the top of the frame. His face was still angry, the clenched jawline, the flat mouth, the glinting hard eyes, yet its harsher beauty still riveted her to the spot and claimed her breath and sent the hot stings of attraction streaking through her veins.

'My heartbreaking rival,' he provided and moved at last, shifting away from the door to pull out a chair at the table and sit down.

'In Italy.' Rachel moved to the sink and began toying with the mugs left there to drain. 'I was working on a farm just outside Naples—w-work experience,' she explained. 'He lived there. We met. Within a week I was moving into his apartment…' Wildly besotted with him and madly in love. 'He told me he loved me and, like a fool, I believed him. When it came time for me to come back to England, he said thanks for the great time and that was it.' She picked out two mugs at random. 'Do you want tea or coffee?'

'Coffee—when was this?'

'Last summer.' Shifting back to the Aga, she put the mugs down and picked up the coffee jar, then suddenly put it down again.

It had been only last summer when Alonso had taught her a lesson about Italian men she'd vowed never to forget. Yet here she was, involved with another and threatening to make the same mistakes all over again.

'I need to—do a few things before I can leave here. Can you make your own coffee—?'

She had disappeared through a door before Raffaelle could say anything—running scared again, he recognised as he sat there listening to her footsteps running up a set of stairs.

Then, on an angry growl, he got up and went to stand by the window. One part of him was telling him to go after her and insist she finish telling him the whole miserable story about her Italian lover—her *other* Italian lover, he grimly amended. Another part of him was wondering why he was not just climbing into his car, which he could see standing outside on the cobbles, and driving away from this…fiasco before the whole thing leapt up again and bit him even harder!

Because it *had* bitten him already, a voice in his head told him. She could already be carrying his child.

'*Dio*,' he breathed. He could not remember another time in his life when he had been so thoroughly stung by a woman.

And he did not need all of this hassle. He had many much more important things he could be doing with his time than standing here wondering what she was doing upstairs where he could hear her moving about just above his head.

Leo Savakis was not really his problem—none of this was his damn problem—except for the as-yet-unconfirmed child. He did not need to hang around until they discovered the result of their mindless love-in. A telephone call in a month would make more sense than hanging around her like this.

Yet some deep inner core at work inside him was stopping him from getting the hell out of here.

Lust, he wanted to call it. A hot sexual attraction for a devious female with cute curly blonde hair and the heart-shaped face of an innocent but who made love like the most seasoned siren alive.

He had taught her how to be that person—that other Italian lover had tutored her on how to give the best of pleasures to a man, had then dumped her as if that was all she had been good for—a student of his sexual expertise and a boost for his ego.

And then there was that thing with *real* teeth which was biting at him. He was used to being desired for himself. He was used to being the favoured one women revolved around, waiting with bated breath to find out which one of them he would choose.

Arrogant thinking? Conceited of him to know that he only had to crook a finger to have them crawling with gratitude around his shoes?

Yes. He freely admitted it. His clenched chin went up.

With Rachel Carmichael he was learning very quickly what it felt like to come in as second best in the heart and mind of a woman.

He did not like it. It gnawed at his pride and his sexual ego. And if he needed to find an excuse for why he was still standing here instead of driving away, then there it was.

There was no way that he was going to accept second best to any other man. By the time this thing between them was over, his Italian rival was destined to be nothing but a vague shadow in her distant memory.

She'd gone quiet.

Raffaelle looked up at the ceiling. What was she doing up there—lying on her bed pining for the heartbreaker?

Rachel was sitting on her bed with her cellphone lying in her palm displaying a text message from Elise.

Thank you for doing this for me. I will love you always. Leo is over the moon about the baby. He's taking us to Florida on a long overdue holiday. I could not be happier. He sends you his congratulations! Tell R thanks for his understanding. Have a great time playing the rich man's future bride!

What a wonderful game, Rachel thought bitterly. What a great way to waste several weeks of her life.

If she still had a rich future husband to play the game with, that was. He could have come to his senses and made his escape while she was up here moping—driven away in a cloud of dust and offended pride!

Getting up, she walked over to the window that overlooked the courtyard. The silver Ferrari still sat there glinting in the shallow sunlight. Relief was the first emotion she experienced—for Elise's sake, not her own, she quickly told herself.

Then the bedroom door suddenly opened and she turned to see him standing there, filling the gap like he had filled the other door downstairs and her senses responded, reaching down like taunting fingers to touch all too excitable pleasure points and she knew she was relieved he was still here for no one else's sake but her own.

'*Ciao*,' he murmured huskily.

'*Ciao*,' she responded warily, searching his face for a sign that another battle was about to begin and feeling the taunting brush of those fingers again when she saw that anger had been replaced by lazy sensual warmth.

'Need any help?' he asked lightly.

'Doing what?' Rachel frowned.

'Packing.' Walking forward, his gaze flicked curiously around a room made up of countrified furniture complete with chintzy soft furnishings. 'I see no sign of it happening yet,' he observed. 'But then—' his eyes came back to hers '—maybe you have other ideas for how we can spend the rest of the afternoon—?'

It was like being tossed back into the pit of writhing snakes again.

Switch off the anger and let desire rush back in, she reasoned. 'I d-don't think—'

'Good idea—let's both not think.' He moved in closer. 'That

small flowery bed looks the perfect place to spend a few hours thinking of nothing at all but this…'

But this—but this… His arms came around her and his mouth took over hers. No one needed to think about doing this, although—

'Why?' she whispered. 'Y-you should…'

'Be turned off you because you keep showing me different faces?'

His fingertips combed through the curls on her head as if to remind her of one of those changes she had made once already today and—damn her, but Rachel felt herself almost purring into his touch like a cat stroked by its beloved master.

He saw it and, on a soft laugh, caught her full, softly rounded, inviting mouth. It was one of those bewitching, tasty, compulsive kisses that clung, tongue tip to tongue tip. She swayed closer and his hands caught her waist to feel the slender arching of her spine for a few seconds before he gently but firmly drew her back.

'You get to me, Rachel, you really get to me. Though God knows why you do, because I certainly don't.'

'Not your usual type?' She could not resist the dig because while he frowned at her she was tingling in places that should not do that—the nerve-endings along the length of her inner thighs and between her legs.

He shook his head. 'Not my usual anything,' he muttered. 'You answer back, you disrespect, you lie and you cheat without batting an eye.'

'I don't cheat—!' she protested.

'Then what do you call the woman I first met last night with the long straight hair and the couture dress?'

A cheat. He was right.

'Well, this is the real me,' she said as she took a step back from him. 'The one with curls and jeans and—if you give me the chance—the one constantly fighting with dirt beneath her chipped fingernails…' She looked down at her nails, frowning now because they looked so different from what she was used to seeing: clean, well manicured and—pink. 'I am not made to be a *femme fatale*, Raffaelle. I wasn't even that good at it last night, only you didn't notice it because you were seeing what you'd been conditioned to expect to see at a function like that.'

'You were damn good at what came afterwards,' he said brusquely. 'I'll take a rain-check on the *femme fatale* bit if I can have more of that.'

Her chin went up, blue eyes coolly challenging. 'And the cheating face I'm supposed to show to the real world? Does it pop on and off according to what you require from me?'

To her surprise he let loose one of those lazy sexy smiles that melted the hardness out of his face. 'I think I like the idea of that. I will keep the sensual curly-haired Circe all to myself while the rest of the world gets the *femme fatale*.'

'Complete with fake ring to go with the fake relationship.' Rachel heaved out a sigh. 'We shouldn't be doing this at all.'

'Too late for regrets, *cara*. We have been over this already. We are both into this up to our necks.'

'Not the sex part.'

'Yes, the sex part!' he contended. 'It is here. We have it. And since it is the area where you really do get to me, we keep it.'

'If I say no?'

His laugh was derisive. 'You would have to want to say no and you don't.' He lowered his head to toy with her lips again. Electrifying, seducing. 'Do you—?' he challenged her for an honest answer.

Since her lips were clinging and her hands had already found their way beneath his T-shirt to the satin tight warmth of his skin she could not very well give any other answer than a weak shake of her head.

'Then say it so I can hear it.'

'I want you,' she whispered, swaying closer to him again, wanting, *needing*, body contact.

His hands on her waist held her back. 'Say my name,' he insisted.

Say his name... Alonso was suddenly looming up between them again. She tugged in a tense breath.

'I did not think of any other man but you last night, Raffaelle.' She felt she owed it to him to tell him that.

His murmur of satisfaction brought his mouth back to hers again with a full-on hot, deep, sensual attack. At last he was letting her have what she craved the most—skin-to-skin contact with him. Her fingernails curled into satin-tight flesh, then followed the muscular line of his ribcage across his chest, then around to his back so she could punish him at the same time as she arched even closer.

He shuddered, deserting her mouth. 'You ruthless witch,' he muttered as he took a moment to grip the edge of his T-shirt and rake it right off. Hers followed suit before he would allow her any more of his mouth.

Like that they strained against each other, exploring with their hands, tongues and lips. He was perfect. No man should possess a body like his. Rachel tasted his skin, her hands moving possessively over his hair roughened contours while he stood there and let her enjoy him, encouraging her with kisses and slow strokes of his hands.

Neither of them noticed that they were still standing in front of the window. Rachel with her back to it, Raffaelle with the sheen of the sinking sun painting his skin rich gold with a hot coral glow. He buried his fingers in her hair and pulled her head back to receive the full onslaught of his kiss.

Lights flashed, explosions took place. In the dizzying urgency of two lovers who needed to move this thing on to its next passionate stage, they missed that those explosive flashes came from outside the window.

The camera-toting paparazzo, who'd picked up their trail where others hadn't, slunk off down the driveway back to his car parked in the lane. He was smiling, pleased with himself, while the two captured lovers continued what they were doing, Rachel reaching up her arms to wind them round Raffaelle's neck as he lifted her up so her legs could cling to his hips. The bed was two steps away and he toppled her on to it, then bent to rid of her tight-fitting jeans.

He stood back. 'Tell me what you want,' he demanded as he began to strip.

'You,' she whispered.

'And who am I?'

'Raffaelle,' she sighed out—then sighed again as the full burgeoning thrust of him was arrogantly displayed.

He made her repeat his name throughout the long hours that followed. By the time they drove away from her home the intimacy between them had evolved into something beyond sex.

They arrived back at his apartment mid-evening. Raffaelle cooked them a meal while Rachel unpacked her clothes, grimacing at the array of sleek designer hand-me-downs Elise was forever giving to her, which most women would kill to own, but which she had rarely ever had an occasion to wear. Now they took up all of her hanging space in Raffaelle's dressing room as if they reflected the person she was now.

But she wasn't, was she?

They ate in the living room, lounging on a rug with their backs resting against one of the sofas and the television switched on. Rachel ate while she tried to concentrate on what was happening on the TV screen when really she was already hyped up about what was to follow.

Crazy, she told herself. You know none of this is real. You must be mad to let him get to you this badly.

Then he reached out to pick up her wineglass from the low table in front of them and handed it to her and their eyes clashed. What was good or bad for her became lost in what happened next. He moved in to kiss her; she fell into the kiss. The glass went back to the table and they made love on the rug between bowls of half-eaten pasta with the television talking away to a lost audience. Afterwards he carried her, satiated and too weak to argue, to bed.

'The pots and things...' she mumbled sleepily.

'Shh,' he said. 'I will see to them,' and he left her there.

By the time Raffaelle came back into the bedroom she was asleep. When he slipped beneath the duvet he did not disturb her—he did not think he had the energy to cope with what was bound to ensue if he did.

He closed his eyes, wanting sleep to shut out the next few hours before he had to make any decisions about how they were going to tackle the rest of this. The great sex was one thing, but the realities of life still waited out there for him to deal with.

Lies built on more lies. Smothering the urge to sigh, he shifted his shoulders against the pillows. She moved beside him, turning in her sleep to curl in close to him, her soft breath warm on his neck and a cool hand settling lightly on his chest.

He looked down at it resting there, with its pale slender fingers and pearly-pink varnished nails, and his skin burned in response to what he knew it could make him feel.

Lies or not, she was in his blood now. A fantasy siren most men would kill to possess. He closed his eyes again and tried to hunt down that illusive thing called sleep. His last conscious thought was the grimly satisfying knowledge that she was almost worth the temporary loss of his freedom and the trail of subterfuge he was about to embark upon.

Unless Mother Nature decided to get in on the act.

He fell asleep on that thought.

The next day brought fresh problems to deal with. He had been drinking coffee in the kitchen and trying to put his head in order while Rachel still lay lost in sleep in his bed, when his housekeeper arrived and laid a tabloid down in front of him.

'I thought you might want to see this,' she murmured embarrassedly.

But one glance at the photograph was enough to send him into the bedroom. 'Rachel, wake up.'

He shook her gently, then watched as she did her trick of emerging from the duvet in that way which grabbed at his senses.

'We need to talk,' he said grimly, then dropped the paper on to her lap.

Silence hung for the next thirty seconds while he stood there waiting and she looked down at the newspaper. There was something disturbingly erotic about the way the photograph had caught them and he knew by the way she suddenly dropped her face into her hands that this was one intrusion too far.

A nerve at the corner of his hard mouth gave a twitch. 'I suppose that being caught on camera like this will kill the suspicions of any mocking doubters and prove that we are indeed what we appear to be. But from now on both of us must be aware of what we do and what we say even when we believe we have complete privacy.'

'Life in the fast lane,' she named it bitterly.

'*Si,*' he agreed. 'I am used to it—though not to the degree that I feel the need to hide behind closed curtains,' he put in cynically. 'I would have expected that, having a half-sister like Elise and an insight into your half-brother's way of earning his living, you would know all the pitfalls of life in the fast lane.'

At last Rachel lifted her head to look at him. 'Are you implying that I set this up too?' she demanded.

'No,' he denied. 'I am simply advising you to draw on your knowledge gained from both of your siblings and think carefully before you move or speak.'

'It sounded more like a command to me.'

'Call it what you want,' he said. 'But accept that you will not go out without someone with you,' he instructed. 'I will assign one of my own security people to escort you.'

It was only as he said it that Rachel realised she was stuck here in London, in his apartment with nothing to do. Elise was away. Even Mark was away. She didn't know anyone else in the city! While it was very obvious by the way he was dressed that he was not going to hang around here if at all possible and keep her company.

'So I'm to be a prisoner now as well as your…' She severed the rest but they both knew what she had been about to say.

'It cuts both ways, *cara*,' Raffaelle said unsympathetically. 'I had a life and relative freedom with which to live it until you threw yourself at me. Now I have you, a bed and no life to call my own.'

'At least you get to go to work.'

'It is what I do during the day.'

'Well, lucky you.' Rachel handed him back the newspaper, then she curled on her side and tugged the duvet up to her ears. 'I might as well stay right here then, since it's the only place I am useful.'

He laughed. 'Hold that delightful thought until I return.'

Then he was gone. The door closed. He strode down the hallway and out of the apartment, then into the lift. It took him down to the basement where Dino and his limo awaited him. The moment he settled in the rear seat and opened his laptop his business cellphone began ringing and real life settled in. As he concluded his fourth complicated call of the journey, Dino was pulling the car to a stop outside the Villani building. He climbed out and strode in through the doors into familiar surroundings where that other excitement which came a very close second to sex waited to take him over.

Then it came.

'Congratulations, Mr Villani!'

'Congratulations, sir!'

Congratulations resounded from every corner. The curious smiles that accompanied them were due almost entirely to the photograph printed in this morning's paper, he judged.

His smile was mocking but fixed. And even that was wearing thin by the time he hit the top floor of the building.

'Congratulations, Raffaelle,' his secretary greeted him and dumped a whole load of telephone message slips down on his desk.

'What are those?' he asked dubiously.

'Congratulations and invitations, of course.' She grinned. 'I would hazard a guess that these are only the beginning. It looks as if you and Miss Carmichael will be dining out every night for months!'

He gave her them back. 'You deal with them.'

'Me?'

'Filter out the rubbish and sort the rest into some kind of order,' he instructed. 'Then I will look at them.'

'But wouldn't it be more appropriate if Miss Carmichael did it?'

Recalling the woman he had just walked away from brought a gleam to his eyes. 'No. She has better things to do,' he murmured dryly.

Like playing his personal little sex nymph.

CHAPTER EIGHT

THE SEX NYMPH WAS UP, showered and dressed in jeans and a T-shirt by the time Raffaelle entered his office building to a barrage of congratulations.

The sex nymph could not be more prim and polite when his housekeeper introduced herself as Rosa, the chauffeur's wife; apparently both of them travelled everywhere that Raffaelle went.

And the sex nymph had no intention of being anywhere near the bedroom by the time he got back home again.

She had come up with a much more practical way to spend her time.

Over a light breakfast prepared by Rosa, Rachel planned her day with the concentration of a tourist determined to miss nothing out. Only her tour would not consist of historical sites in the city; she was going to trawl the restaurants and food wholesalers specialising in organic produce.

Her nice new security guard arrived conveniently as she was about to leave. His name was Tony and he had the use of a car, which meant far less footwork.

Still, by the time she had been delivered safely back to the apartment long hours later, she was almost dead on her feet.

Raffaelle was crossing the hall towards his study from the living room as she stepped in through the door. Pinstriped jacket gone, shirt sleeves rolled up, tie knot hanging low at his throat and glass slotted between his fingers, he looked deliciously like the successful man just in from work and ready to wind down from his busy day.

Rachel paused, completely held by his sexual pull.

He paused too and looked at her, silky curls ruffled, face still chilled by the cold breeze blowing outside, woollen coat unbuttoned to reveal a white T-shirt with a neckline that scooped low at the front. He took his time taking in every detail with the slow—slow thoroughness of a seasoned connoisseur of beautiful women.

Knowing that she lacked the connoisseur's high standards right now sent Rachel's chin shooting up, blue eyes challenging him to say something derogatory.

'Did you enjoy your day, *mi amore*?' was the sarcastic comment that fell from his lips.

Defences heightened, she reluctantly supposed she should explain where she'd been. 'I went…'

'I know where you have been,' he cut in. 'Tony works for me, not for you.'

'Then, yes—' they could both play with polite sarcasm, she decided '—I had a very enjoyable day, thank you. And you?'

'I had an…interesting day,' he replied, watching her every step as she made herself walk forward. 'I spent it giving polite replies to polite invitations for us to dine with polite people who cannot wait to get a better look at my future wife.'

Recalling the revealing photograph in this morning's paper sent a rush of heat into her cool cheeks.

'Of course you did the wise thing and politely declined those polite invitations?'

'No, I accepted—most of them.'

Rachel pulled to a standstill. 'I hope you're just teasing.'

He took a sip of his drink, every inch of him vibrating with a kind of sardonic challenge that gave her his answer before he shook his dark head.

'The show must go on.'

'But I don't want to meet your friends!' she protested.

'Scared they might see through us?'

'Yes!' she said. 'Can't we just want to—be alone together—as real engaged couples prefer to be?'

'You're mistaking a new betrothal with a new marriage,' he countered. 'Honeymooners want to—be alone together. Newly betrothed couples want to get out there and—show off.'

'But I don't want to show off!'

A satin black eyebrow arched in enquiry. 'You don't think I am good enough to show off?'

'Don't talk rubbish,' she snapped. What woman in her right mind would say he wasn't fit to show off? 'I just don't think *we* are fit to be seen as an intimate couple within a group of your friends!' Stuffing her hands into her coat pockets and hunching her shoulders in self-defence, she went on, 'I presumed we would do—safer things like go out to quiet restaurants or something.'

'A restaurant it is.' He smiled. 'Eight o'clock. We will be meeting my stepsister and several other close friends of mine.'

Rachel's stomach started rolling sickly. 'Tonight?' she squeezed out painfully.

'*Si*,' he confirmed.

'W-why couldn't you be friendless?' she tossed out helplessly.

He just grinned. 'I'm sorry to disappoint you, *cara*, but I am certainly not friendless.'

'But your stepsister of all people. She *knows* we are fakes!'

His mood changed in a flicker. 'Stop playing the scared innocent, Rachel, when we both know you are far from it,' he clipped out. 'This is what you signed up for to save your sister's marriage. And lovers who fall on one other as often as we do are certainly not faking it!'

She pushed her hands through her hair. 'You know what I meant.'

'And you know what I mean when I say—get your act together,' he instructed, 'because we are going out in public tonight and I want the besotted *lover* by my side, not the farmer with a chip on her shoulder a mile wide!'

Rachel stared at him. 'What's that supposed to imply?'

He threw out an impatient hand. 'You compare yourself badly to your more glamorous sister,' he provided. 'You compare me with your ex-lover and hate the fact that I am Italian like him.'

'I do not!' she denied.

'Was he good-looking?' he demanded.

'What has that got to do with anything?' Her eyes went wide in bewilderment.

'Was he—?' he persisted.

'Yes!'

'How old?'

'My age—'

'And what kind of car did he drive?'

She sucked in an angry breath. 'A red Ferrari,' she answered. 'But that wasn't—'

'Great,' he gritted. 'Mine is silver. Is that a bad mark against me or one against him for being too flashy?'

'You're crazy,' she breathed.

Maybe he was. At this precise moment Raffaelle did not know why he was so fired up about a man he probably would not give a second thought to in other circumstances.

'Just go and get ready.' He turned his back on her and strode into his study, wanting to toss his drink to the back of his angry throat but refusing to allow himself the gut soothing pleasure while she was standing there staring at him. 'And I *don't* like flashy, so don't come out dressed in red!' he could not stop himself from adding.

Then he shut the door—*slammed* the damn door!

Rachel shook all the way into the bedroom. She shook as she removed her coat and laid it aside. She had absolutely no idea what all of that had been about and she didn't think that she wanted to know.

Did he hate her—was that it? she immediately questioned. Did he resent her being here so badly that he needed to take chunks out of her to get his own back on her for putting him in this situation in the first place?

Was he locked in his silly study *praying* that she wasn't pregnant with his child?

And he did not want to see the farmer dressed in flashy red when she came out. Her lips gave a quiver. He preferred to see the sleek Elise look-alike because at least he could relate to her and *pretend* she was his type!

Rachel stripped off her clothes and walked into the bathroom, not sure if she wanted to throw things or cry her eyes out.

The tears almost won the moment she stepped beneath the shower spray and she would have let them if he had not chosen that moment to push open the bathroom door and stride fully naked into the shower.

'No, don't stiffen up,' he said as she did exactly that. 'I am here to make you feel better, not worse.'

He drew her back against him, angling both of them so the shower sprayed down her front, then dropped his lips to her ear. 'I came to apologise for being bad-tempered out there.'

'You mean it's just hit you that you have to trail me in front of your friends having ripped my head off,' Rachel said.

'I had a bad day.'

He was tasting her earlobe now. Rachel jerked it away.

'Accepting invitations you had no desire to accept.'

'While thinking of you and that bed I had walked away from.' He chased the earlobe again. 'So I was bad tempered all day and came home more than ready to find you waiting for me. But you were not here; you were out enjoying yourself.'

'Playing the farmer to my heart's content.'

'I like the farmer,' he murmured lustily. 'She is toned and sleek and very sexy. I am also jealous of the ex-lover…'

That shocking confession finally stopped her from trying to pull away from him.

'Impressed by that?' he mocked.

'Yes,' she answered honestly.

'I thought you might be.' His mouth bit gently into the sensitive crook between her shoulder and neck.

Rachel's breathing feathered and she closed her eyes, giving herself up to this when she knew that she shouldn't. Wanting him to want her for herself and not just because she was here for the taking.

He found the soap and used it to paint every inch of her he could reach. Soon she was lost in a scented steam-filled world that shut out everything else.

Afterwards she felt lazy and languid and much too aware of him as her irresistible lover as the two of them moved around between the bathroom, bedroom and dressing room, preparing to go out.

Which had been the object of the exercise in the shower, she reminded herself. Several times he stopped her passing him by just fusing his mouth to hers in a slow clinging kiss and the lazily hooded way in which he watched her shyly lower her eyes and move away quickly only heightened an intimacy that was threatening to take her over completely if she didn't watch out.

She was relieved when he finally left her alone so she could finish getting ready without having him around as such a breathtaking distraction. By the time she joined him in the living room Rachel truly believed she had managed to get herself together—until he looked up from the broadsheet newspaper he was reading while lounging on a sofa and the whole whirlwind of awareness whipped into action again.

She'd chosen to wear a sleek short V-neck dress in dramatic matt black. Elise had donated the dress, claiming that it did not suit her because she didn't have the curves to fill it out.

Well, Rachel had the curves and, the way that Raffaelle was looking at her, he had not missed a single one. Her hair was loose, its curls carefully ironed out so the style was smooth and sleek. As he rose to his feet her blue eyes followed him, defiant yet anxious—just in case she did not look as good as she hoped she did.

But the look reassured her as he came towards her wearing the kind of black lounge suit that yelled couture *homme*. When an Italian male dressed he never ever dressed badly, was Rachel's single dry-mouthed heart pummelling observation.

'Beautiful,' he murmured as he reached her, sending pleasurable shivers chasing up her spine as he bent to brush a caress on her cheek. 'But I prefer the curls.'

'Different woman,' she answered with a small shrug.

His eyes narrowed, all the sensuality hardened out of his mouth. He said nothing for several long seconds and Rachel knew she had just managed to remind him of the real reason why they were together.

Maybe that was a good thing, she decided, as he helped her into the little black satin evening jacket she had brought into the room with her, still without saying anything else. They left the apartment and travelled in the lift down to where Dino waited by the car with the rear passenger door open. She slid in. The door clicked shut. Raffaelle rounded the bonnet and slid in from the other side. His long body folded with crease-free elegance into the seat beside her.

Lean, sleek, supremely sophisticated, she recognised. Crossing one silk-covered knee over the other, she fixed her attention on the partition which separated them from Dino.

Tension fizzed in the silence. Rachel found herself clinging to her little black beaded purse. The car swished along London's busy streets, recently drenched by a heavy downpour of rain. Everything outside the car seemed to glitter and sparkle in the darkness, everything inside the car was shadowed and oddly flat.

Raffaelle wished he knew what he was feeling right now, but he didn't. It was crazy to have been so taken aback by her reminder of what this was all about when they'd done little else but argue about it since they'd first met.

But he had been taken aback by it, stunned by the gut-twisting reminder that none of this was real—that *she* wasn't real.

Not tonight anyway.

She was the sleek look-alike sister of Elise Castle-Savakis, pretending to be a version of Rachel Carmichael that just did not exist. Even the dress was Elise's, classy and stylish and very sexy on Rachel, but he would be prepared to bet it was not of her own taste or choice.

He preferred the other Rachel with the curls and the spark of defiance in her blue eyes.

'Having second thoughts about risking me in there amongst your friends?' she asked suddenly.

Raffaelle blinked, realising that they'd come to a stop outside the restaurant. By the atmosphere inside the car, they'd been here like this for several seconds.

The restaurant was one of the best Italian restaurants in London. It was a place where the rich set ate. It was his kind of place and his kind of life, but neither were hers.

He turned his head to look at her. Barely an hour ago, she had been coming all around him in a breathtaking pulse of intimacy that still circulated in his blood. He looked at her silk-straight hair and her beautiful pearly-white complexion, the heavily accentuated black-lashed blue eyes and the sexy pink-coated mouth.

He could taste them. He could feel those soft pink-coated lips warm against his own whether she was this Rachel or the other Rachel. And if he was sitting here like this, wanting to know where the two Rachels became one, then he'd found it in that mouth and what happened to her when he claimed it.

'I won't embarrass you, if that's what's worrying you,' she stated, fizzing inside with resentment at the analytical way he was looking her over as if he was actually having to give some deep thought to the sarcastic question she had tossed out.

'You sound very sure about that, little farmer girl,' he said huskily.

'Well, I'm not,' she admitted honestly. 'I suppose I should have said I will *try* not to embarrass you.'

Easing his wide shoulders into the corner of the seat, his eyes glittered over her tense face. 'Do you really believe I will care if you do decide to embarrass me?' he asked curiously.

Rachel offered a shrug. 'I don't know you well enough to judge.'

'No, you don't…'

She didn't like the way he had said that, or the way he was looking at her now. Her tension was zinging along just about every nerve ending she had in her body and she wished he would just—

'Are we going to go in there or not?' she flicked out.

'In a minute,' he said smoothly, 'This conversation is just getting interesting…'

'No, it isn't.'

'Because it has nothing to do with whether you are going to embarrass me,' he said ignoring her interruption. 'It is to do with you being scared that I might embarrass you.'

Rachel stared at him. 'Why should you want to do that?'

'My thought exactly,' he said softly. 'Yet you *are* scared that I am going to take you in there, then just leave you to sink or swim.'

Her pink upper lip gave a vulnerable quiver. 'I was thinking more along the lines of being served up along with the main course,' she confessed.

He laughed. It was bad of him. But it was a very low, sexily-amused laugh and Rachel laughed too—one of those tense little sounds that jump up unexpectedly from the throat.

The atmosphere changed in that single moment, spinning the tension into a fine thread that eddied across the gap between them then morphed into something else. He moved so fast that she didn't see him coming, and then it was too late when he had taken arrogant possession of her mouth.

'You've stolen all my lipstick,' she protested when the kiss came to an end.

'I know.' He sat back a little, watching her as she fumbled in her bag for a tissue and her lipstick case. 'Keep on reapplying it, *cara*,' he advised as she reapplied a coating of pink with a decidedly unsteady hand. 'Because I find I like doing it. In fact I do believe I am becoming addicted to the taste.'

She handed him the tissue. 'It looks better on me than it does on you.'

And he grinned, wiping pink from his lips while his eyes tangled with hers. It was no use pretending that they weren't doing something else here, because they were.

Then suddenly he was being serious. 'Listen to me,' he urged. 'I don't want you to be anyone but yourself tonight, okay? I don't care if you want to spend the evening going on about the pros of organic produce. I don't care if you decide to ruffle your hair into curls or you march off to the kitchens to tout the chef for his business—'

'I'm not quite that uncouth!' she cried.

'You are missing the point,' he chided. 'The point being that I don't give a damn if you are just yourself and act like yourself. The only thing I do care about is that you stick to the main story as to how we met and keep in mind that, when we leave here, we go home to my apartment together as a couple, then to bed and to—this.'

Another kiss was on its way to her. 'Don't you dare,' Rachel drew her head back.

But he did dare—quickly, briefly, not enough to steal her lipstick a second time but more than enough to distract her from what he was about to do next.

She felt her left hand being taken. By the time she had the sense to glance down, the fake sapphire ring had been removed and he was already replacing it with one that looked exactly the same.

'W-what have you done that for?' she demanded.

'The fake might have been a good fake, *cara*, but it did not stand a chance of fooling the experts we are about to meet.'

'It fooled you when you saw it.' She was staring at the exact copy now adorning her finger.

'I was too angry to notice it then.'

'It's so—gaudy.' She sighed, staring at the ring as it shimmered and sparkled much more than its predecessor.

'Not to your taste?'

'Not to anyone's taste,' she said ruefully. 'It was only meant to grab Leo's attention… How did you get hold of this one so quickly?'

'I am the kind of man who gets what he wants when he wants it,' he answered with careless conceit.

He went to put the fake ring into his pocket.

'No—' As quick as a flash Rachel plucked it from his hand and pushed it into her beaded purse. 'I'll wear the real one when we are out together, but only then,' she informed him stubbornly. 'Otherwise I'll wear the fake one.'

'If you're afraid of losing it, it is insured—'

But Rachel gave a shake of her head. This had nothing to do with losing the real ring, but more to do with the fear that if she didn't hang on to the fake she would lose touch with reality.

'I will only wear it when we are out,' she repeated.

'And in our bed?' he demanded shortly.

Rachel thought about that for a second or two. 'I won't wear either ring,' she decided.

'Meaning our sexual relationship has nothing to do with the rest of this?'

Unless he was able to fake what was happening there as well. Then she nodded, because the sex was the only truly honest part of this.

He said nothing but just sighed and went to open the car door—then suddenly changed his mind. He turned on her, caught her chin in his fingers, then dipped his head for a third, definite, lipstick-stealing, full-blooded, possessive lover's kiss.

'The sexual part of this relationship does not stay behind in the bedroom, Rachel,' he stated harshly. 'Remember that, while you fix your lipstick again…'

He climbed out of the car then, leaving her sitting there trembling and shaken by the anger which had erupted from him.

What was the matter with him? Why should he care which ring she wore, so long as she didn't make *him* look the cheap fake?

Her lips felt tender and bruised this time as she reapplied the lipstick. He'd walked around the car and was now standing with her door open, waiting for her to join him on the pavement.

It was chilly outside and her satin jacket had not been made to keep the cold out. She shivered. He stepped closer, fitting her beneath his shoulder and curling his hand into her waist.

Gosh, don't we look the picture of romance? she thought dryly as he walked her towards the restaurant.

'Smile,' he instructed as he pushed the door open.

Rachel looked up to find that he was looking down at her. One of those frozen in time moments suddenly grabbed them, locking them inside their own private space.

'Heavens, Raffaelle,' another voice intruded. 'You were out there so long we were about to lay bets as to whether or not you were going to just take her back home again.'

'As you see, Daniella,' he came back smoothly, 'Rachel's manners are so much better than mine…'

He held Rachel's eyes as he said it. He watched her cheeks warm to a blush when she realised what Daniella had meant. Then he took hold of her hand and lifted it to his lips. The engagement ring sparkled as he kissed it. Her soft pink pulsing mouth gave a telling little quiver that shot an injection of heat down to his groin.

Someone else spoke—he did not know who. When he turned, he could barely make sense of the blur of faces all smiling at them.

What the hell was the matter with him? Was he sickening for something to have double-vision like this? It would be the first germ to catch him out since his childhood, he mused grimly, frowning as he looked back at Rachel.

Her face was in perfect focus. He did not like what that discovery was trying to say to him. With a taut shift of his shoulders, he pulled himself together and turned to face his dinner guests again, then switched on his lazy smile.

'Buona sera,' he greeted. 'My apologies for keeping you waiting when I know you are dying to meet my beautiful Rachel…'

CHAPTER NINE

MY BEAUTIFUL Rachel...

And so began the worst evening of his beautiful Rachel's life.

Raffaelle's stepsister did not believe a single word that either of them said to her. The others were more than happy to welcome her into their set, but they too were surprised and curious about this complete stranger who had arrived out of nowhere into Raffaelle's life.

Rachel supposed she should be relieved that Daniella seemed to have kept her suspicions to herself—or maybe she was too scared of Raffaelle to actually say what she thought outright. But she quizzed Rachel mercilessly about Elise.

'How is she?'

'Wonderful, taking a holiday in Florida with her husband and son.'

'You two met through Elise?'

'No, we met at a dinner party given by friends of Leo and Elise.'

Daniella had eyes like bitter chocolate which constantly flicked from Rachel to Raffaelle. 'Both of you were very secretive about this romance.'

'Rachel liked it that way,' her stepbrother answered. '*We* liked it that way. Look at what happened the moment we were seen in public. It turned into a witch-hunt.'

'When a woman throws herself at you in front of a reporter, it tends to have that effect. So does standing naked in a bedroom window.'

Rachel flushed but Raffaelle remained completely unruffled. 'Behaving like a spoiled child who does not like to know she has been left out of a secret is very unappealing,' he responded lightly.

Reducing her to the level of a spoiled child may have silenced Daniella but it did not kill her suspicions about Rachel not being who she claimed she was—as she made very clear the moment she got Rachel alone in the ladies' room.

'I *know* he was seeing Elise Castle because it was me who told him she was married with a small son! So don't try to pull the wool over my eyes, Miss Carmichael. That ring is a fake, just as everything else about you is fake.'

Rachel looked down at the sparkling diamond and sapphire cluster adorning her finger and grimaced. 'I don't want to fight with you, Daniella—'

'Well, I want to fight with you,' Daniella said fiercely. 'I *saw* you throw yourself at Raffaelle the other night. I *saw* his rage. I think you and Elise are trying to blackmail him!'

Apart from the fact that she was so close to the truth it was scary, Rachel had to feel for Daniella if only because she looked and sounded so worried and protective of Raffaelle.

'And you aren't drinking alcohol!' Daniella said suddenly. 'Are you pregnant, is that it? Did you have a fling with him, as well as your sister, and now you're demanding marriage?'

Rachel stared at the other girl as if she had just grown two heads. Was she psychic or what? 'I don't drink.' She iced out the lie with as much calmness as she could. 'And repeat your accusations to Raffaelle, if you dare,' she challenged.

Then she turned and walked out of the ladies' room. Raffaelle took one look at her flushed angry face and stood up before she could sit down.

His arms came around her. 'Problems?' he asked.

Rachel shook her head, aware of the others listening. 'Just a—headache,' she offered as a very weak excuse.

'Then we will leave.'

It was not a suggestion and Rachel did not argue with him. As they made their farewells Daniella came back to the table. One slicing glance at her stepbrother and her chin shot up in defiance.

To make everything feel even worse, a camera flashed as Raffaelle was helping Rachel on with her jacket. He'd lowered his head to kiss the side of her neck in one of those loving displays he'd been putting on all evening.

'What was it with Daniella?' he demanded the moment they were back in the car.

'She knows,' she responded.

'She knows what?'

'Everything,' she answered heavily. 'She thinks I'm blackmailing you over your affair with Elise.'

'You were blackmailing me,' he pointed out dryly.

'She also accused me of being pregnant because I wasn't drinking tonight, and of having a fling with you at the same time you were with Elise.' She grimaced. 'Great reputation you have there, *Signor*, when even your own family can believe you are capable of swinging it with two women at the same time.'

'She's fishing for information, that's all,' he answered coolly. 'And she—cares about me.'

'Lucky you,' Rachel mumbled.

'Do you say that because your family shows so little concern for you?'

That hit her right below the belt. 'My family care,' she insisted.

'Your uncle, maybe,' Raffaelle conceded. 'But even he made the quick getaway once he believed he had established that I was not your heartbreaker from Naples. I could have been lying to him. He did not hang around long enough to put me to the test.'

'He's a busy man.' She shifted tensely on the seat next to him.

'Like your half-sister and -brother are so busy they have not had time to check if I have chopped you into little pieces and dumped you in the Thames?'

'Sh-shut up,' she breathed.

They finished the rest of the journey in silence. As they travelled up in the lift to Rafaelle's apartment, Rachel stared fixedly down at her feet and he—well, she didn't know what he was looking at but she had an itchy feeling it could be her.

Once inside the apartment she headed for one of the spare bedrooms because there was just no way she was going to sleep with him tonight.

He didn't try to stop her, which only stressed her out more. She slept restlessly beneath a navy-blue duvet wearing only her bra and panties, woke up early the next morning and remade the bed, then crept back into the other bedroom to get some fresh clothes before Rosa arrived.

The plum-covered bed was empty and, by the look of it, Raffaelle had enjoyed a restless night too. She glanced at the closed bathroom door to listen if the shower was running, hoping to goodness that he'd already got up and dressed and taken himself off to work and out of the firing line.

'Discovered your sense of fair play, *amore*?' a smooth voice murmured.

She spun around to find him standing in the dressing room doorway wearing only a towel slung low around his hips. It was like being hit by that high wattage charge again.

'I—thought you would have left by now,' she said without thinking.

He just smiled then began walking forward. Rachel started to back away.

'Slept well?' he asked her.

'Yes, thank you.'

'Need any help tying that robe?'

She glanced down, then released a gasp when she saw the robe she had pinched from the other bathroom was hanging open revealingly. It was too big, a man's full-length heavy towelling bathrobe that trailed the floor at her feet and engulfed her hands. She'd thought she'd tied the belt, but the stupid thing had slid undone.

'Go away,' she shook out, trying to fight with the sleeves so she could grab the two ends of the belt.

But Raffaelle Villani wasn't going anywhere. He just kept coming until he was standing right in front of her. Then, while she mumbled out a protest, he pushed her fingers away and calmly cinched the belt around her waist. His fingers brushed the skin of her stomach as he did it. She breathed in sharply. He ignored the revealing breath, finished his task, then calmly turned away, dropping the towel from around his hips, and strode like the arrogant man he was back into the dressing room and closed the door.

It was the same as a slap in the face. She refused to sleep with him and he was showing her that it made little difference to him.

Rachel ran into the bathroom and wished she was dead, because her body was such a quivering mass of frustration that if he'd stripped the robe from her and thrown her to the bed, she would not have stopped him.

Her day was long and she was tired by the time she trailed into the apartment again. Rosa had gone home hours ago. Raffaelle was still out, which allowed her some time for herself to take a long bath behind a firmly locked bathroom door in an effort to relax some of the tension grinding at her every nerve and muscle.

She stayed in the bath longer than she'd meant to. By the time she let herself back into the bedroom she could sense more than hear that Raffaelle was home, though he was not in the bedroom, thank goodness, which gave her a chance to pull her jeans back on and a fresh T-shirt before she heaved in a breath and went looking for him.

He was in the kitchen making himself a sandwich, the jacket to his suit gone, white shirt-sleeves rolled up. He turned at the sound of her step. Her stomach dipped. She found herself running self conscious fingers through her curls.

'*Ciao*,' he said lightly. 'You look—pink.'

'I stayed in the bath too long,' she explained as naturally as she could.

He turned back to what he was doing. 'Want a sandwich?'

Her stomach gave a hungry growl. 'What's in it?'

'Take your pick,' he invited, pointing to the variety of salad things he had already sliced up. 'There's cheese in the fridge, some chicken and ham.'

Choosing the ham because she saw it first, she took over and handed it to him. Then surprised herself by staying there watching as he layered fresh bread with salad stuff.

'Not going to offer to do it for me?' He arched a look at her.

'Not me,' she said. 'I might grow the produce but I can't cook it,' she confessed. 'Ask me to make a sandwich like that and it will fall apart the moment you pick it up.'

'No culinary skills at all, then.'

'Not a single one.'

'Any good with a coffee machine?'

'Hit and miss.' She grimaced. 'I'm an instant coffee girl.'

'Tragic,' he murmured. 'Give it a try anyway.' He nodded to where the coffee machine stood. 'It's loaded and ready to hit the cup like the instant stuff does, only it tastes better.'

'That's an Italian opinion.' She moved across to the machine and fed it a cup as she'd done two days before.

Two days, she then thought suddenly—they felt like years. How had that happened?

'Tony tells me you have been treading the miles again,' he murmured.

She turned to look at him curiously. 'How often does he report in to you?'

The wide shoulders gave a shrug inside expensive white shirting that didn't quite stop the gold of his skin from showing through. 'Each time you stop somewhere.'

'Do you think it's necessary? I mean, I haven't seen a glimpse of a reporter in the two days I've been out and about.'

'Then you would make a lousy detective.' Turning he pointed to the newspaper lying on the table.

Going over to it, Rachel saw a photo of herself sitting at a table in a top Knightsbridge restaurant drinking morning coffee with its famous chef owner. A flush arrived on her cheeks because, not only was she aware that she had not seen the lurking reporter but she'd now realised that the only reason why she had been sitting there at all was because the chef had recognised her and his curiosity had been piqued.

'Where was Tony when this was taken?' she demanded. It was his job after all to stop this from happening.

'He did clear the reporter off, but not before he had managed to take this one photograph. Then the guy waited until you had left the restaurant and went back to quiz the chef.'

The chef had given an interview, getting a plug for his restaurant by happily telling the reporter what Rachel Carmichael did for a living. There was another photograph in a different paper showing Raffaelle kissing her cheek as he helped her on with her jacket.

'What it is to be famous,' she murmured cynically.

'Well, your secret other life is now out,' Raffaelle declared. 'Which means you can stop hiding behind the mask of Elise when we go out.'

'Daniella is going to love it.'

He turned with two loaded plates in his hands. 'I've spoken to Daniella.'

Rachel froze as he put the plates down on the table.

'She sends you her apologies and promises to behave the next time that you meet.'

'She had nothing to apologise to me for,' Rachel said flatly. 'Actually, I could like her despite…'

'Daniella not liking you?'

'Yes,' she said huskily.

He pulled out a chair and sat down on it. 'You can tell her you like her later when we meet up at the theatre—'

'*Theatre*—?' Rachel stared at him. 'I don't want to go to the theatre!'

'Sit down and eat,' he instructed. 'If you are eating for two you must have a good balanced diet.'

Rachel stared slack-jawed at him.

Steady-eyed, Raffaelle just shrugged. 'I'm the fatalist, remember? I work through problems sometimes before they are problems. It is what helps to keep me at the top.'

'You're not short on insufferable arrogance either. You and Daniella should share the same blood.'

He just grinned over the top of his sandwich. 'Tell me why you don't want to go to the theatre,' he instructed.

She pulled out a chair and sat down on it. 'I don't get the opportunity to go often enough to get to like it.'

'Well, that's about to change.'

'What kind of theatre?' she asked dubiously.

'Opera,' he provided. As her jaw dropped again, he said, 'Get used to it because it is the love of my life. Eat.'

Rachel picked up her sandwich. It arrived by instinct at her mouth because her eyes certainly didn't guide it there—they were still looking at him in horrified disbelief.

'I can't believe you want to put me through an *opera*,' she protested.

'We either go to the opera or we stay in and make love…'

And, just like that, their few minutes of near normality disappeared without a trace.

Rachel put down the sandwich. He chewed on his, his eyes gleaming with challenge.

'I'm will *not* be blackmailed into your bed—!' She flew to her feet.

'Then prepare for an evening of Tosca,' he countered coolly. 'Wear something long and—sexy. Oh, and take your sandwich with you, *mi amore*,' he drawled as she went to flounce out of the room. 'The opera starts early and supper will be late.'

She wore a long slender blue gown that faithfully followed her every curve. Raffaelle took one look at her and staked possessive claim with a hand to the indentation of her waist.

'*Mine*,' he declared huskily. 'Make sure you remember it while we are out.'

Sitting for hours beside a man who seemed to take pleasure in playing the deeply besotted lover throughout the interminable though admittedly moving music heightened her senses to such a degree that she had never felt more relieved to walk out into the ice-cold evening air so she could breathe.

They ate supper with a crowd of people including Daniella, who was quieter than the night before and was almost pleasant to Rachel, though Rachel could tell by the glint in the other woman's brown eyes that the pleasantness ran only skin-deep. Daniella was still suspicious and hostile and hungered for the real truth as to what was going on.

Rachel gave Daniella no chance of getting her on her own that evening, staying put in her seat and keeping her attention fixed on everyone else. At least they seemed to accept her at face value—it was difficult not to when the man sitting beside her rarely took his eyes from her face. Tension zinged between them like static. Rachel refused to so much as glance at him, smiling where she thought she should do and trying to ignore the ever increasing pulse of awareness he was making her suffer. She was quizzed about her occupation and it seemed a good time to launch into the benefits of organic farming with an enthusiastic vigour that set such an animated debate going she almost managed to forget Raffaelle was sitting there.

Then he reached out to gently take hold of her chin and turned it so she had no choice but to look at him. His expression was difficult to read, kind of mocking yet deadly serious at the same time.

'You are here with me,' he said huskily.

'I know who I'm with.' She frowned at him.

'Then don't ignore me.'

'I wasn't ignoring you. I was—'

'Smiling at every other man at this table but me.'

The idea that he might be feeling left out and jealous sent a different kind of sting singing through her blood. Her eyes must have showed it because his thumb arrived to rub across her lower lip in an intimate, very sexual proclamation that brought a telling flush to her cheeks.

But she could not pull back or break eye contact. It was too much like being plugged into an electric current again—lit up from the inside and sensually enlivened. He knew it, he built it until her breathing quickened and her eyes darkened. She could feel Daniella watching them. She heard someone else murmur dryly, 'Time to break up the party, I think.'

'Good idea,' he murmured and leant forward to replace the thumb with his mouth in a brief promise of a kiss that brought him smoothly to his feet.

They travelled back to his apartment in absolute silence. They rode the lift in exactly the same way. Rachel kept her eyes fixed on her feet again but refusing to look at him did not ease the sexual pull taking place. They walked along the hallway towards the bedrooms still accompanied by that highly strung clamour of perfect silence.

When they reached the door to his bedroom they paused. Still he said nothing and still she was fighting it until—

'Well—?' he asked softly.

Rachel drew in a tense, sizzling, battling breath, tried to let it out again but found that she couldn't. Her senses were singing out a chant of surrender and in the end she gave in to it, turning to reach for the door handle to his bedroom.

Without saying a single word he followed her inside and closed the door. Now she'd made the decision to come in here she did not go for modesty but just turned to face him and, with the light of a looming sexual battle lighting her blue eyes, she began to undress right there in front of him. His face was deadly serious as he watched her for a few seconds before he began to undress too.

Clothes landed on the floor all around them. Her dress pooled in a slither of blue silk at her feet. It was all part of the battle that they did not break eye contact.

Rachel walked towards the bed on legs that no longer wished to support her. Indeed they preferred to tingle and sting like the rest of her body, making sure they did not give her a moment to change her mind about this.

No chance—no *hope* of a last-minute reprieve. She wanted him so badly she couldn't think beyond the need.

He took up a position on the other side of the bed and the tip of her tongue crept out to curl across her upper lip as she let her eyes glide over him. Big, lean, hard and aroused. Her breasts grew heavy and her nipples peaked, the wall of muscle around her lower stomach contracting as she tried to contain the ache.

She lifted the duvet. He did the same. They slid into the bed together and arrived in the middle of the mattress in a limb-tangling clasp of body contact.

Then he kissed her. No, he punished her for putting them through twenty-four hours of denial.

That night Rachel learned what it was like to be totally taken over, excruciatingly sapped of her will by a man with a magician's touch. He wove sensual spells around every pleasure point. He drove her wild until she cried out. Then he possessed her, deep, tough and ruthlessly, staking claim in this final act of ownership that had her clinging and trembling and sobbing out his name as she tumbled into release.

And so began four hellish weeks trapped inside heaven.

When Raffaelle had said they were to be as if they were glued together, he'd meant it. Wherever his business took him, Rachel went with him, hopping from London to Milan, Paris, Monaco then back to London then Milan again. In one short month she learned what it was like to become a fully paid-up member of the jet set and how it felt to be recognised as the woman who'd managed to pin the very eligible Raffaelle Villani down.

Everywhere they went he took her out into public places—more restaurants, more theatres, nightclubs and private parties—all very select venues where they could be displayed as a couple.

It was almost all glitz and glamour. There were those in his close circle of friends who were the kind of people she could relate to mainly because they were easy to like. Then there were the other kind who hovered on the fringes of it all who would have sold their grandmothers to be included as a member of his inner set.

Then there was the seemingly endless stream of his ex-lovers from all over the world who had no problem with telling her what they used to be to him and thought it fine to discuss the ins and outs of having a lover like him.

'Have they never heard of the word discretion?' she tossed at him after one particularly vocal beauty had seen nothing wrong in singing his sexual praises to Rachel—in front of Raffaelle. 'Or does it stroke your ego to hear someone talk about you as if you were a stallion put out to stud and therefore free to be debated for your sexual prowess?'

'I don't like it,' he denied.

'Then don't smile that smug smile while they list your assets.'

'It is not a smug smile, it is a forbearing one. And you sound like a jealously disapproving wife.'

'No, just a lover who does not think you are so great in bed that you deserve so much attention,' she denounced.

'No—?'

She should have read the intimation in that *no* but she missed it.

'No,' she repeated.

'Maybe you found the Italian heartbreaker and sex tutor of innocents a better lover?'

She turned icy eyes on him. 'If you're fishing for information, then forget it. Unlike your ex-lovers, this one does not kiss and tell.'

He had been fishing for information, Raffaelle acknowledged. She might be the best lover he'd ever enjoyed but he had no clue as to where she placed him on her admittedly short list.

And he'd accused her of being jealous when he knew that was his issue. Jealous, curious, wary of the way she sometimes looked at him as if he was a being from outer space. Their age difference bothered him. Her youth and her beauty and that softer side she had to her that made some of his previous women appear sex-hardened and clinical. Did she see *him* like that: sex-hardened and clinical?

His male friends were drawn to her. He did not like to see

it because he knew exactly what it was about her that drew them. They wanted to experience what he was experiencing. They wanted to know what it felt like to simply touch a woman like Rachel and have her melt softly for them.

And she did melt. It was his only source of male satisfaction. In company, out of company, he touched her and she melted. He *looked* at her and she melted.

'Well, remember that I am the lover who takes you to heaven each night,' he said.

And, like Alonso, Rachel knew that he would break her heart one day.

He obsessed her mind and her body. She hated him sometimes, but her desire for him was stronger than hate. He knew it too and the inner battles she fought with herself turned him on. She watched it happen, watched right up until the moment they reached the lift which would take them into privacy and saw the social face he wore fall away to reveal the hard, dark, sexually intense man.

The lift became her torture chamber. The stinging strikes of his sexual promise flayed her skin. By the time they stepped through his front door she was a minefield of electric impulses, hardly breathing, hyped up and charged beyond anything sane.

Sometimes he would crash into that minefield right there in the hallway. Sometimes he would draw out the agony by making her wait before he unleashed the sensual storm. She learned to live on a high wire of expectation that allowed no respite and little sleep, with him even invading her dreams.

He knew every single sensitive inch of her. Sometimes he would coax her to stretch out on the bed with her arms raised above her and her legs pressed together, then he'd begin a long slow torture that she loved yet hated with equal passion because he would make her come—eventually—with only the lightest stroke of a finger or the gentlest flicker of his tongue.

It was an unashamed act of male domination which left her aching because he never gave in to his own need on these occasions or finished such torments off with an intimate, deep physical joining.

Why did he do that? Even after four weeks with him she still did not have an answer to that question.

And then there were those other times. The times when he allowed her to perform the same slow torment on him. He would lie there with his eyes closed and his long body taut with sexual tension while she indulged her every whim.

Being equals, he called it. She called it dangerous, because it had reached a stage where she could not look at him without seeing him lost in the throes of what he was feeling on those occasions. A big golden man, trembling and vulnerable, a slave to what she could make him feel.

The elixir which kept her rooted in their relationship, wanting—needing more.

And other things began to torment her which were far more disturbing than the constant overwhelming heat of desire. She knew she had fallen in love with him. She could feel it tugging constantly at the vulnerable muscles around her heart. If he touched her those muscles squeezed and quivered. If she let her eyes rest on him, those same muscles dipped into a sinking tingling dive.

But Raffaelle was not in this for love. He wanted her, yes. He still desired her so fiercely that she would have to be a complete idiot not to know that he was content to keep things the way they were right now.

If she had any sense she would be walking away from it. Elise and Leo were back in Chicago. Elise was happy, Leo was happy and keeping his pregnant wife and his son close to him; the crisis in their marriage was over.

All of this should be over now. And, if it wasn't for the

worrying prospect that her period was overdue, she would have no excuse left to call upon which could allow her to stay.

Then it all went so spectacularly pear-shaped that it threw everything they had together into a reeling spin.

They were in Milan when it happened. Raffaelle was tense, distant, preoccupied—busy with an important deal, he said. But Rachel wondered if the stress of waiting to discover if she was pregnant was getting to him too.

He didn't say so—never mentioned it at all and neither did she.

She knew that she needed to buy a pregnancy test. Putting it off any longer was silly when she was almost a whole week late. She was supposed to be going shopping with one of Raffaelle's many cousins but Carlotta had rung up to say she couldn't make it.

On impulse she snatched up her purse and headed out of the apartment. She should have called Tony to get him to drive her, but she didn't want anyone with her to witness what she was going to do.

She caught a cab into the city, then headed for a row of shops that included a pharmacy. Anxiety kept her locked inside her own thoughts as she walked, but the last thing she expected to happen was to be woken from them by a loud screech of brakes as a glossy red open top Ferrari swished to a sudden stop at her side.

The man driving that car did not bother to open the door to climb out but leapt with lithe limbed grace over the door. 'Rachel—*amore*!' he called out.

Shock held her completely frozen, her blue gaze fixed on his familiar handsome face.

'Alonso—?' she gasped in surprise.

'*Si*—!' He laughed, all flashing white teeth, black silk hair and honey-gold beauty. 'Is this not the greatest surprise of your life?'

CHAPTER TEN

HE BEGAN closing the gap between them, a lean muscled six-foot-two inch-Italian encased in the finest silver-grey suit. A man with so much natural charisma and self-belief that it just would not occur to him that he was anything but a welcome sight to her.

So Rachel found herself engulfed by the pair of arms he folded around her, then found herself being kissed on her cheeks and the tip of her nose, then her surprised, still parted mouth.

She tried to pull back but he was not letting her. 'I saw you get out of a cab and I could not believe my eyes!' he exclaimed. 'And look at you,' he murmured, running a teasing set of fingers through the bouncy curls on her head. 'Still my beautiful Rachel.' He kissed her mouth again. 'This has to be the best moment of my day!'

Well, not mine, thought Rachel, still rolling on the shock of seeing him. 'What are you doing here in Milan?'

'I could ask the same thing of you.' He grinned down at her. 'Though I would have to be blind not to know by now that you have captured the heart of Raffaelle Villani, eh? May good fortune always smile upon the bewitching,' he proposed expansively. 'He is totally besotted with you, as I was, of course…'

Across the street, on the shady side, sitting languidly at a lunch table with five business associates, Raffaelle happened to glance outside in time to see Rachel walking by on the sunny side of the street.

A smile warmed him from the inside. She looked beautiful in her simple white top and her short blue skirt which left a pleasurable amount of her long legs bare. And her silky blonde hair was shining in the sunlight, recently cut by an expert so the curls tumbled around her neck and her face like sensual kisses.

It was no wonder other men stopped to admire her as she walked past them, he observed, a smile catching the corners of his mouth as he saw one guy in particular actually spin around to take a second look.

Sorry, but she belongs exclusively to me, he heard himself stake the silent claim. Then he started to frown when another thought hit him. Where was Tony? Where was his cousin Carlotta? Why was Rachel out shopping alone when she knew the rules about going out without protection from the everwatchful press?

The sound of screeching car brakes diverted his attention. A glossy red Ferrari with its top down had pulled to a sudden stop in the street. Its handsome young owner leapt out with lean grace and approached Rachel with his arms thrown open.

She had stopped to stare at him. What took place next lost Raffaelle the power to maintain a grip on his surroundings. The quiet hum of conversation taking place around the lunch table disappeared from his consciousness as he saw her soft pink mouth frame a name.

The man spoke, his gestures expressive, like the rakish smile he delivered as he gathered her into his arms, then kissed her cheeks, her nose and finally, lingeringly, her parted pink mouth.

A mouth that belonged to *him*. A mouth that did not attempt to draw back from the kiss.

So cold he felt frozen now, Raffaelle watched this other man run his fingers through her curls as he talked.

Small, familiar, intimate gestures. Soft parted pink lips that quivered when she spoke back to him.

They knew each other.

His heart hit his gut because it did not take much intelligence to follow the body language and know without a single hint of doubt who the man had to be.

Alonso. The heartbreaker. He was so sure of it he did not even think to question his certainty.

Had they arranged to meet—right here in broad daylight without a care as to who might see them like this?

How long had they been in touch with each other? Each time he had brought her with him here to Milan?

Was she still in love with him?

Dio. While she stood there in his arms, looking up at him like that, was her heart beating too fast and her throat drying up and her blue eyes helplessly drinking him in?

'Raffaelle…'

The sound of his name being spoken finally sank into his consciousness. Turning his head, he received the impression that it was not the first time one of his lunch companions had said his name.

'My apologies,' he said, managing to add a small grimace. 'My attention strayed for a few moments.'

'And why not, when the woman is as beautiful as the one seated in the window?' one of them said smiling.

Seated? Raffaelle turned again to focus on a table by the restaurant's window where indeed a very beautiful woman sat smiling ruefully back at him.

He had not noticed her before this moment.

He had not noticed any other women for a long time—not since Rachel came into his life.

His gaze flicked away from the smiling woman and across the street again.

He was in shock. He knew that. He knew that several important things were happening inside him even as he watched Rachel's other Italian lover fold an arm across her shoulders and guide her towards his car.

Car horns were blaring. The street was alive with impatient car drivers trapped behind Alonso's car.

'One quick coffee, then,' Rachel agreed as he swung open the door and helped her inside.

She should not be doing this. But they were drawing too much attention and getting into Alonso's car seemed the better of two evils if coffee somewhere was the only way she was going to get rid of him.

Alonso joined her in seconds, sliding into the seat beside her and sending her one of his reckless grins as he slipped the car into gear. He drove them away with a panache that completely disregarded the minor chaos he had been causing in the street.

'Like old times, eh?' he laughed at her.

And it was, just like old times, when he had used to sweep up in one fast car or another without a care while he waited for her to scramble in next to him. His handsome carelessness used to excite her then. Now it just scared her witless as she glanced quickly around them as they drove off, hoping she did not see a face she recognised in the street—or worse, a camera flashing.

'Somewhere quiet, Alonso,' she told him quickly. 'I can't afford to be seen with you.'

'Scared of what your rich new fiancé will say?'

You bet I am, Rachel thought. 'I call it respect for his feelings.'

'And a healthy respect for his bank balance too.'

Before she could challenge that last cynical remark, Alonso pulled into one of the less fashionable squares off the main street. Two minutes later they were sitting opposite each other at one of the pavement cafés that lined the square.

Rachel looked at Alonso and saw a man who worked very hard to look, dress, behave like the man he wished he could be but never would be.

And how did she know that? Because she had spent the last month with the genuine article, a man who didn't need to work hard at being exclusive and special, he just simply was. It was she who, like Alonso, had to work hard at playing the part of someone she was not.

The comparison hit her low in her stomach.

As if he could tell what she was thinking, 'You have done very well for yourself,' Alonso said.

Rachel didn't answer, giving her attention to the waiter who had come to their table. 'Espresso,' she told him. 'N-no, I don't want anything else.'

Alonso ordered the same, then casually dismissed the waiter with a flick of a hand. Had he always behaved with this much casual arrogance and she had been too besotted with him to notice?

'What *are* you doing here in Milan?' She repeated her question from earlier.

Sitting back in his seat and crossing a knee over the other, he said, 'I moved here six months ago—to a better position, of course.'

Of course, Rachel acknowledged. Alonso had always been ambitiously upwardly mobile. 'Still selling cars?'

'Super-cars, *cara*,' he corrected dryly. 'They are not merely cars but engineering works of art. But let us talk about you,' he said turning the subject. 'You must be happy with your new lover. What woman would not be?' His mouth turned cynical as his eyes drifted over her. 'No longer the rosy-cheeked innocent up from the country, eh?'

Recalling that innocent young girl Alsono had known last year, with—if not quite straw in her hair as Raffaelle described her—then pretty close to it, made her smile.

'No,' she agreed.

Their coffees arrived then, putting a halt on the conversation while the waiter did his thing. Eventually, Alonso sat forward to catch the hand she'd used to reach for her cup.

'We had a good time, didn't we?' he said softly. 'I missed you when you left me to go home.'

'Did you?' Not so Rachel had noticed.

'Ah, *si*,' he sighed. 'I almost came after you but—life, you know, got in my way…'

Another new conquest had got in his way, he meant.

'And maybe I did you a very great favour,' he added. 'For look where you are today—betrothed to man with more connections in this city than any other that I know of. A man in possession of his own bank! I salute you, *cara*.'

Leaning towards him, Rachel let him lift her fingers to his lips. She let him try to seduce her with the rueful tease glinting in his sensual dark eyes. She even added a smile.

'You know what, Alonso,' she then said softly. 'You were a beautiful charmer last year when I met you, and you are still a beautiful charmer now.' He smiled and kissed her fingertips. 'But why don't you just tell me what it is that you want from me, because I am going to get up and leave here any minute…'

There was a moment of sharpened stillness, then he sat back in his seat and laughed. 'How did you guess?'

Living the part of a rich man's woman had taught her how useful other people believed she could be to them. 'Raffaelle does not need another new car,' she told him. 'He has too many of them already.'

'An introduction to him and his friends could bode well for me in the future, though.'

'Or ruin your career,' Rachel pointed out. 'Raffaelle knows about you and me, *caro*.'

He caught on, which Rachel had known he would do. The smile died from his features, taking with it all the charm and leaving behind only a rueful kind of petulance.

Then it changed. A sudden well-remembered gleam hit his eyes. 'I don't suppose you would enjoy a little light diversion this afternoon with your old lover—for old time's sake before we part again?'

The business side done with, he was back to playing the sexy charmer. Rachel couldn't help it, she laughed. 'No, I would not!' she refused, still bubbling with amusement at his downright audacity.

His lazy smile reappeared and he reached across the table to gently brush her smiling mouth with his thumb. 'Shame,' he murmured. 'We were so good together once, hmm, *carisima*…'

Across the square on the shady side, a camera caught them for posterity as Rachel reached up to close her hand around his so that she could remove his touch from her mouth.

'One day,' she warned him seriously, 'some beautiful creature is going to come into your life and knock down your outrageous conceit.'

'But she will not be you?'

'No.' She'd tried to do that once and had failed, had survived the experience and had now moved on—though to what, she was not certain about.

Still, it was a good feeling to realise that she was completely free of Alonso. So maybe meeting up with him had not been a bad thing to happen in her life right now.

Getting to her feet, '*Ciao*, Alonso,' she murmured softly, then simply turned and walked away from him.

He did not try to stop her. Maybe he'd read the look in her eyes and knew he had lost the power to make her feel anything for him.

Or, more likely, he simply did not care enough to want to stop her. Who knew? It was just a good feeling to know that she no longer cared.

The camera toting paparazzo had already gone, missing the moment that she'd walked away from her old love with no regrets. And, by the time she reached the main street again, Alonso had been pushed right out of her thoughts by more important things.

Buying a pregnancy testing kit took courage, she discovered. She was constantly glancing around her to check if anyone was watching her and she found herself wandering aimlessly around the shops, putting off the evil moment for as long as she could.

Which in the end turned out to be a foolish exercise because, having found the courage to buy the darn thing, she had been back at the apartment for barely two minutes when Raffaelle arrived home unexpectedly, forcing her to shove her purchase into a bedside drawer.

He was in a strange mood, cold and distant and sarcastic as hell when she tried to speak to him. She needed to tell him about her meeting with Alonso, but he just cut her off with a curt, 'Later,' then locked himself away in his study and did not come out again until it was almost time for them to leave for the restaurant where they were meeting his friends for dinner that evening.

His mood had not improved by the time he'd taken a shower and changed his business suit for a more casual version made of fine charcoal-coloured linen. Her simple black halter dress drew no comment—but then why should it when he'd seen her wearing it several times before?

But she was hurt by the sudden loss of his usual attention. Confessions about surprise meetings with old lovers just did not suit the kind of mood he surrounded them with as they left.

He did not look at her. He did not touch her. When she dared to open her mouth and ask what was wrong with him, he ignored the question by turning to say something to Dino who was driving them tonight.

What with his bad mood, the stress of knowing that the pregnancy test was still burning a hole in the bedside drawer, plus the memory of her meeting with Alonso sitting heavy on her conscience, the last person she needed to see as they walked into the restaurant foyer was his stepsister Daniella, who was standing beside a tall, dark, handsome man. The elusive Gino Rossi, Rachel assumed, by the way Daniella was tucked so intimately into his side.

Raffaelle made the introductions with brusque, cool formality that made both her and Gino Rossi's responses wary and brief. After a moment Raffaelle then turned away and centred his attention on the rest of his friends, determined to get through this damn evening before he decided what he was going to do about what he had witnessed today.

In the inside pocket of his jacket, a photograph of Rachel with her lover being cosy across a café table was trying its best to burn a hole into his chest. The fact that she had been too engrossed to notice the paparazzo who took it only fed his simmering rage. It was perhaps fortunate for him that he was close friends with the newspaper owner to whom the freelance reporter had offered to sell the photograph.

He was now assured that the picture of his betrothed being intimate with another man would not appear in the tabloids, but at a cost to his dignity as well as his wallet, plus an invitation to this evening's dinner party, along with a promised exclusive interview about his wonderful life to date.

A life that included details about the lying, cheating, two-timing blonde wearing his ring right now.

He allowed himself a glance at her, standing there looking

paler than usual with an oddly fragile look to her slender stance. A frown cut a dark crease across his brow. Why fragile? Was her conscience pricking her? Did she possess one? Had she spent the afternoon comparing her old lover with her new lover?

Which of them had won the contest?

A curse rattled its way around his throat and he looked away again, wondering when the hell she had got to him so badly that he even considered that damn question?

Dio. Rachel was bad for him. She had been bad for him from the moment he'd set eyes on her. Her type, her *kind,* were poison to a guy like him and maybe it was time that he got himself the cure.

The owner of the newspaper arrived then, like the perfect answer to his thoughts. Tall, blonde, and beautiful, and dressed in rich, dark purple that moulded her long, slender curves, Francesca de Baggio was the kind of woman who answered most men's desires.

Raffaelle went to meet her. They embraced with murmured greetings to each other that showed the intimacy of lovers from eons ago. As his lips brushed her cheeks he smelled her sensuous perfume, felt the smoothness of her skin at her shoulders beneath his palms. As her red lips lingered at the corner of his mouth he waited for the expected tingle to light him up from the inside.

It did not happen.

'*Ciao, mi amore,*' she moved those red lips to whisper softly in his ear. 'The betrothed does not look happy. Have you beaten her soundly?'

Almond-shaped eyes that matched the colour of her dress gleamed up at him with a conspiratorial smile. Anger erupted inside him, fresh anger—*new* anger—leaping on a desire to jump to Rachel's defence.

'You know better than I do how a photograph can misrepresent the truth.'

The almond eyes widened and filled with amusement. How was it he had forgotten that Francesca was in the tabloid business because she loved the trouble it allowed her to cause?

'His name is Alonso Leopardi,' she informed him softly. 'He sells cars for a living and loves them as much as he loves women. He also rents an apartment above the café they were sitting at being so…cosy. Convenient, hmm?'

Raffaelle was hooked like a fish and he knew it. It was perhaps fortunate that Gino and Daniella came up to greet Francesca then, because it saved him from making a bloody fool of himself by letting Francesca see that she'd reeled him in.

Looking round for Rachel, he could see her nowhere. For a tight, thick, blood-curdling second he thought she must have walked out. For a blinding, sickening, sense-drowning moment he actually saw her in his head, making a run for it, grabbing a cab and heading for her heartbreaker in a white-faced urgent adrenalin rush of need.

A clammy sweat broke out all over him. He took a step away from the group of his friends now gathering around Francesca to welcome her into their fold.

Common sense was telling him not to be so stupid. Rachel would not just walk out on him—even if the way he had been behaving tonight was enough in itself to justify her walking out.

He saw her then, right over on the other side of the busy restaurant. She was just stepping into the ladies' room with her blonde head bowed slightly and a slender white hand pushed up against her mouth.

She'd looked pale all evening, he remembered. His mind flipped from hating her to worrying about her. How could he have forgotten the baby they could have made, which might be making its presence felt as she made a quick dash into the Ladies'?

Concern wanted to send his feet in her direction. Only common sense warned him not to make a scene here. Turning back to Francesca, he saw her watching him with an eyebrow arched curiously. Dragging on his social cloak, he forced himself to smile as he walked back to her.

Rachel was fighting the need to be sick in the toilet. The clammy sweat of nausea had flooded over her the moment she'd seen the way Raffaelle had walked into the arms of the beautiful blonde.

'Ex-lovers,' Daniella had whispered to her. 'Don't they look amazing together? He adored her once but she left him for her now ex-husband. We thought he would never get over it—maybe he didn't. He spent the afternoon with her,' she confided with relish. 'I know because Gino told me Raffaelle cancelled a meeting with him to go to her. Now she's here. An interesting development, don't you think?'

Was it? Rachel discovered that she no longer knew anything. Her head was thumping too thickly to think. A month—a month in which she had lived and slept with him, had trailed around Europe with him as his pretend future bride. But what did she really know about Raffaelle, other than he was a fantastic lover and was willing to go to any lengths to protect himself from getting a negative press?

By the time she felt able to rejoin the party, everyone was gathered around a long wooden table. Still fighting down nausea, Rachel found herself having to take the only seat left available between Daniella and another male friend of Raffaelle's, whose name she couldn't recall right now.

Raffaelle was sitting at the other end of the table. The beautiful Francesca was next to him. She had arrived here on her own and Rachel supposed that, given the odd number of men to women, the dinner placements had become muddled.

But it was the first time that Raffaelle was not occupying the seat beside her like a statement of possession.

Had he even noticed that she was not sitting on his other side?

Not that Rachel could tell. His attention was too firmly fixed on his new dining partner. And she was not the only one to notice the change in place settings, or the difference in him. Others kept sending her brief telling glances, then looking down the table at him.

Raffaelle did not notice. He was too busy plying his beautiful companion with wine and food, while Rachel could barely bring herself to swallow a thing. And, to top this whole disaster of an evening, having her handsome fiancé sitting beside her was enough protection to give Daniella's tongue back its sharpened edge.

'How is Elise?' she began innocently enough.

'Fine,' Rachel responded. 'She's still in Chicago with her husband and son.'

'And your...half-brother? The one with the camera? Is he still enjoying playing tricks on the rich and famous?'

How Daniella had managed to discover that Mark was her half-brother Rachel just did not feel like finding out right now. 'Mark is fine,' she answered in the same level tone and tried to change the subject. 'How are your wedding plans coming along?'

'Wonderful.' Daniella smiled happily. 'I'm here in Milan for my dress-fitting. Isn't that dress you're wearing—?' She named a top designer. 'Did Raffaelle buy it for you? How much do you think you have stung him for by now?'

'My dress is not by that particular designer,' Rachel answered quietly, 'and I pay for my own clothes.'

'Well, don't bother buying anything expensive for my wedding, darling, because by the look of it you will not be coming.' Daniella flicked her eyes down the table. 'Knowing Raffaelle as well as I do, I think I can positively predict that you are on your way out and Francesca is definitely on her way back in.'

One short glance down the table was enough for Rachel to

confirm why Daniella felt so very sure about that. If it wasn't enough that he had ignored her all evening, the way he was smiling that oh-so-familiar lazily sensual smile at the beautiful Francesca was the final straw for her.

'You know what, Daniella?' She turned back to her tormentor. 'Watching you marry that poor fool sitting next to you is the last thing on earth that I want to do.' The poor fool heard what she said and turned sharply to look at her. She ignored him. 'So dance on my grave, if that's what turns you on, *darling*,' she invited. 'And, while you're doing it, tell your stepbrother from me that he can have his Francesca with my absolute blessing!'

Then she stood up. The nausea instantly hit her again. She pushed her chair back and walked away. Silence had fallen around the table. How many of them had heard her exit line she did not know and she did not care.

Raffaelle tuned in too late to catch anything but the sight of Rachel's taut back retreating and the uncomfortable silence that followed. Gino was frowning angrily at Daniella. His stepsister had gone very pale. Someone else muttered a soft, '*Dio*.'

And the whole table watched as he came to his feet. Someone touched his hand. It might have been Francesca. He neither knew nor cared.

He strode after Rachel. 'Where the hell do you think you are going?' he raked out, catching hold of her wrist to bring her to a standstill between two tables.

It came out of nowhere, the rise in anger, the sudden swing round. Next thing she knew, she had slapped him full in the face.

A camera flashed.

His eyes lit up bright silver. 'That's tomorrow's trash out of the way,' he gritted, then hauled her up against him and kissed her hard.

The flashes kept on coming. The whole restaurant had

fallen into complete silence to witness Raffaelle Villani fight
with his future bride. By the time he set her mouth free her
lips were burning and her heart was thumping and tears were
hot in her eyes.

'I wish I'd never met you,' she hissed up at him, then
wrenched free of him and walked away.

Outside the air was cool and she shivered. Dino stood
leaning against the car in the car park but he straightened the
moment he saw Raffaelle appear.

'Rachel—'

'Stay away from me.' She started walking away from both
the driver and Raffaelle, her spindly heels clicking on the hard
pathway's surface. Inside she was a mass of muddled feelings,
nausea and the pumping, pounding need to just get right away
from everything.

She managed about ten metres before the car drew up
beside her, at the same time as a figure leapt out of it and a
hard hand arrived around her waist.

She tried to pull free; the hand tightened. 'You know how this
works,' Raffaelle said grimly. 'You decide which way we do it.'

A camera flashed. They both blinked as it happened.
Raffaelle muttered something nasty as his free hand pulled
open the car door. Shivering, Rachel stiffened away from him
and entered the car under her own steam.

The door closed her in. He walked round the car to get in
beside her. With no glass partition in here to give them privacy,
they were forced to hold their tongues, so the silence pulsed
like a third heartbeat between them.

Anger, hostility, a tight sizzling *hatred* that ran dangerously
close to its unrequited flipside flicked at the muscles in
Raffaelle's face and held Rachel's frozen in her own private hell.

If he had not drunk so much wine, keeping up with
Francesca in his attempt to divert her curious attention away

from Rachel, Raffaelle knew he would have kicked Dino out of the car and taken his place, just to give himself something to do and stop himself from wanting to reach out and kill her for making him feel like this.

And—yes, he freely admitted it—he had been happy to give this woman sitting beside him something useful to think about! Did she think she was the only one of them who could play this game of falseness?

Game, falseness; the two words ricocheted around his head as a brutal reminder as to what this relationship was really about.

Rachel sat beside him with her face averted, fingering the ring on her finger and only realising as she felt its duller contours that she was still wearing the daytime fake.

Looking down, she could see that she had forgotten to swap the ring for the real one. So what was that little error trying to tell her?

You can't live a lie and expect it to spin itself into the truth?

They arrived at his apartment still steeped in thick silence. The journey up in the lift was just as cold and reined in. They entered the apartment. Rachel tossed aside her purse and just kept walking. He followed her into the bedroom and shut the door.

She could feel his anger beating into her. She refused to turn and look at him. 'If you want a row, then you're going to have to save it until tomorrow,' she tossed out coldly. 'I'm not—feeling too well, so I'm going to take a shower, then I'm going to bed and I would prefer it if you found somewhere else to sleep.'

Kicking off her shoes, she headed for the bathroom.

'Pleading a headache, *cara*?'

The drawling tone made her wince. 'Yes, actually,' she answered.

'Perhaps even pining for your Italian heartbreaker—?'

What had made him bring up Alonso now of all times? Rachel stopped walking to turn and look at him. He was standing in front of the closed bedroom door, tall, lean, spectacularly arrogant, with that coldly cynical expression lashed to his handsome features that just said it all.

CHAPTER ELEVEN

An icy chill chased down Rachel's spine. 'You know I bumped into Alonso today,' she murmured.

The tense shape of his top lip twisted. 'Is this *bumped into* an English euphemism for recklessly planned to meet with him in broad daylight on a busy street?'

Refusing to take him up on his cold sarcasm, she replied, 'No, it means bumped into by *accident.*'

'And, having spent the afternoon in his company,' Rafaelle said coldly, 'how would you prefer to describe that to me?'

Rachel frowned. 'But I didn't spend the afternoon with him.'

Shifting out of his taut stance, he walked forward, a long-fingered hand sliding into his inner jacket pocket, then smoothly out again. He halted by the bed, placed a photograph down on it.

Rachel glanced at it briefly. So someone *had* seen them together. She looked back at him. 'If you want to say something, Raffaelle,' she challenged. 'Then just come out and say it.'

'You drank coffee with him.'

'Yes.' She nodded.

'You then moved on to his apartment situated above the café.'

'You have photographic evidence of that too?'

He sliced the air with a hand. 'It stands to reason.'

'Does it?'

'*Si*—!' he bit out.

Suddenly all the rage he had been holding in all evening burst to the fore. He took a step towards her. Rachel took a step back. The raking flick of contempt in his eyes as she did so tensed up her trembling spine.

'You can give me a better explanation as to where you did spend the rest of the afternoon before you returned here?' he demanded.

Refusing to let his anger intimidate her, 'Can you explain where you spent *your* afternoon?' she hit back.

'*Scuzi*—?' He had the gall to look shocked!

'And then you could go on to explain how you had the rank bad taste to bring your *afternoon friend* into my company at dinner tonight!'

'Francesca is—'

'An ex-lover of yours, I know.' She said it for him. 'With darling Daniella around, I do tend to find these things out.'

His angry face hardened. 'We were discussing what you did with your afternoon, not what I did with mine.'

'Well, let's just say, for argument's sake, that we both did the same thing!' she threw back. 'As least you were saved the embarrassment of watching me fawn all over Alonso at dinner, whereas I did not warrant that much respect!'

His wide shoulders clenched inside expensive suiting. 'I did nothing with Francesca this afternoon but spend the time negotiating the price for that photograph! She owns the damn newspaper that bought it!'

'So she deals with the dreaded paparazzi?' Rachel's blue eyes lit up with bitter scorn. 'What lovely loyal people you and I surround ourselves with. Maybe we should introduce her to my brother and between them they could happily make a mockery out of both of us in two countries at the same time!'

'None of which explains what you did with your ex-lover,' he grated.

Her stomach was still churning and her heart was beating much too fast. 'I drank coffee with him, then I walked away. End of subject,' she said and turned back to the bathroom.

'It is the end of nothing.' His roughened voice raked over her as he grabbed her shoulder to spin her back round again, his face hard like granite. 'I want to know the truth!' he bit out.

Dizzy and nauseous, maybe she was not going to need to do any test, Rachel thought shakily. 'I've just given you the truth.'

'And your coffee took four hours to consume?'

Rachel made herself look up at him. 'Your negotiations for the photograph took just as long?' she challenged him right back. 'Or was your time spent on a certain *kind* of negotiation?'

He went white, stiffened and let go of her. 'You will not sink me down to your level, Rachel.'

'My *level*?' She stared at him.

'Your propensity to lie, then, without blinking an eye.'

Well, her eyes certainly blinked now and she took an unsteady step backwards. 'I have never lied to you, Raffaelle,' she breathed out unevenly. 'No—think about that,' she insisted when he parted his hard lips to speak. 'We have a relationship built on lies, yes,' she acknowledged. 'But I have never lied to *you*!'

The way his top lip curled really shook her. This, the whole thing they had going between them, suddenly showed itself up for what it really was—a relationship built on sex and disrespect, which had never stood a chance of being anything more than the tacky way it felt to her right now.

'Scoff at me all you want,' she invited. 'But while you're doing it remember that three months ago you wanted my sister. This month you decided that you might as well have me. Next month you will probably put Francesca back into your bed.

The way you are going through them, Raffaelle, there won't be a woman left in Europe you will be able to look at without experiencing *déjà-vu*!'

Rachel spun away then, needing to head fast for the bathroom. But she didn't make it that far. The room began to swim and she pushed a hand up to her head, swaying like a drunk on her spindly heels.

'What—?' she heard him rasp in a mad mix of concern and anger.

'I don't—f-feel well,' she whispered, before everything started to blacken around the edges and his thick curses accompanied his strong arms which caught her as she started to sink to the ground.

Her own piece of *déjà-vu* followed, as she opened her eyes to find herself lying on the bed with him looming over her. The same look was there, the same closed expression.

A flickering clash of their eyes and she knew what he was thinking.

'It might not be,' she whispered across the hand she pressed against her lips.

He opened his mouth to say something, then closed it again—tight. Then he straightened up and she knew he was drawing himself in ready to deal with the worst.

'I will call a doctor—'

The fatalist at work again, she recognised. 'No,' she shook out and, when he paused as he was turning away from her, Rachel heaved out a sigh and slowly sat up. 'Y-you don't need to call a doctor,' she explained. 'I h-have something…' She waved a hand towards the bedside drawer.

Without saying a word, he walked over to the drawer and opened it. Long fingers withdrew the paper bag containing the only purchase she had made that afternoon.

Such a small purchase for something so important, Rachel

thought bleakly as he withdrew what was inside the bag, then just stood looking down at it.

The mood was different now, still tense but thick and heavy. She looked at his profile and saw that the drawbridge had been brought down on his anger and what he was thinking.

'When did you buy this?'

'Today,' she answered. 'Th-this afternoon.'

'I thought we agreed that you would not risk making intimate purchases like this,' he said with super-controlled cool.

A strained little laugh left her throat. 'There was no one I could trust enough to get them to do it for me and I…needed to know.'

'Did you?'

The odd way he said that brought her head up. 'Of course—don't you want to know?'

He did not answer. There was something very peculiar about the way he was standing there, tense and grim.

'If you're concerned that I've given the paparazzi something else about us to feed on, then I was careful,' she assured him. 'In fact,' she said, sliding her feet to the floor, 'you wanted to know what I did with my afternoon. Well, wandering round the shops trying to fool any followers into leaving me alone before I dared to buy the test was it.'

He said nothing. Rachel wished she knew what was going on in his head. Hurt was beginning to prick at her nerve endings. Didn't he think this situation was difficult enough without him standing there resembling a block of stone? Was he scared in case they discovered she was pregnant and that sense of honour he liked to believe he possessed would require him to marry her when he didn't want to?

Standing up, she went to take the package from him. 'I'll go and find out if it's—'

His fingers closed around it. 'No,' he said gruffly.

Rachel just stared at his hard profile.

'We—need to talk first,' he added.

'Talk about what?' she said curtly. 'If I am pregnant we will deal with it like grown-ups. If I'm not pregnant, then I go home.'

'What do you mean, we deal with it like grown-ups?' At last he swung round to look at her. His face was pale and taut.

Rachel sighed. 'If I am pregnant I'm not marrying you, Raffaelle,' she informed him wearily.

'Why not—?'

Why not—? If she dared to do it without risking setting her queasy stomach off again—Rachel would have laughed. 'Because you don't want to marry me?' she threw at him. 'Because I can take care of myself *and* a child! And because I refuse to tie myself to a man who just *loves* to believe the worst of me!' She heaved in a breath. 'Do you want more—?'

'Yes,' he gritted.

She blinked, not expecting that response.

'Okay.' She folded her arms across her shaking body and looked at him coldly. 'You don't trust me. You think I am a liar and a cheat. I give you perhaps a couple of months held in marital captivity before you start questioning if the baby could be some other man's.'

'I am not that twisted!' he defended that last accusation.

She put in a shrug. 'Trapped by a child on purpose, then.'

'We've been through that. I *don't* think that!'

'You've got your old lover already lined up ready to take my place.'

'Francesca was not lined up for anything other than to get that photograph,' he sighed out.

'Well, guess what?' Rachel said. 'I don't believe *you*.'

Now that was a twist in the proceedings, she saw, as he stared at her down the length of his arrogant nose. She made a grab at the package.

This time he let go of it.

On a shivering breath she turned and walked into the bathroom, then closed and locked the door.

By the time she came out again, she was stunned, shaken, totally hollowed out from the inside.

Raffaelle was standing by the window, his body tense inside his well-cut jacket. When he heard the door open he spun round, then went perfectly still.

'Well—?' he said harshly.

Rachel pressed her pale lips together and gave a shake of her head.

Tension sizzled. 'Is that a *no*, as in you are *not* pregnant?' he demanded.

Hands ice-cold and trembling where she clutched them together in front of her, Rachel nodded.

He moved—one of those short, sharp jerks of the body. 'You have to be pregnant,' she thought she heard him mutter beneath his breath. 'Why did you feel sick—why the fainting?' he asked hoarsely.

'W-women's stuff,' she mumbled dully. 'It—it's like that sometimes.' She added a shrug. 'The real thing should h-happen any day now…'

Silence fell, one of those horrible awkward, don't-know-what-to-say-next kind of silences that grabbed at the air and choked it to death.

Rachel couldn't stand it. She was in shock. She wasn't really functioning properly on any level. She'd been so sure that the answer to the test would come out positive, and if she did not find herself something practical to do she knew she was going to embarrass both of them by bursting out crying with sheer disappointment!

With no control at all over her trembling legs, she walked like a drunk towards the dressing room. 'I'll pack,' she whispered.

'What the hell for—?' he raked out.

'Time to call it quits, I think.' She even added a flicker of a wobbly smile.

'No,' he ground out roughly. 'I—don't want you to go.'

White as a sheet, Rachel shook her head. 'It might as well be now than next week—next month—'

'No,' he repeated.

'But there's no reason left for me to stay now!'

His wide shoulders squared. 'Am I not a good enough reason?' he demanded harshly. 'Have our weeks together meant so little to you that you could just decide to leave me like this—?'

Stunned by the harsh husky agony in his tone, Rachel was further shocked to see how pale he looked.

Tears burst to life. 'Raffaelle…' she murmured pleadingly. 'You know we only—'

'No,' he cut in on her yet again. 'Don't say my name like that—don't *look* at me like that.'

'But there is no baby!' She had to say it—*had to!*

'To hell with babies,' he bit out fiercely. 'We can make babies any time! This is about you and me and what *we* want. And *I* want you to stay!'

Was he saying what she thought he was saying? She just stared at him, not daring to trust what her ears were telling her. 'Francesca—'

'Forget about Francesca,' he said impatiently. 'I am blind to Francesca. I am *blind* to any woman who is not you.'

She took a wary step towards him. 'Are you saying that you want me to stay even without a baby—?'

He threw out an angry hand. 'Why do you need me to keep on saying it?' he thrust out. 'I want you to stay…because I want *you* to stay!'

'H-how long?'

'*Dio*, woman,' he breathed savagely. 'What are you trying

to do to me?' His silver-green eyes gave an aggressive flash. 'For ever, okay? I want it all: the love, the ring, the marriage—the whole damn crazy package!'

'Then why are you so angry about it?' she cried out.

He squared his wide shoulders. Pale and tense, 'It would not hurt you, Rachel, to give me some small encouragement to feel happy about loving you,' he pushed out.

Then he turned his back to her and grabbed his nape with long angry fingers. Rachel hovered, wanting to go to him but still too scared to move.

Then, why are *you* scared? she asked herself. He had just said he loved her and she was standing here giving him every impression that she—

She closed the gap between them, running her arms around his waist and pressing herself in close to his rigid back. 'I'm sorry,' she whispered. 'But I've loved you so much and for so long when I *knew* I didn't have the right to feel like this!'

A sound ripped from his throat and he spun in her arms. His eyes were like twin black diamonds, still angry, possessive—real.

'No—w-wait, I need to say this—' she shivered out when she saw what was coming. 'I knew that I had no right to fall in love with you after the way I had hit on you without giving a thought to the trouble I was going to cause! Then w-we thought we had made a baby so I used it as an excuse to stay and—'

'We used it.'

'But it just wasn't fair of me to load you down with my foolish feelings when—No!' she protested. 'I've not—'

Finished…

What a waste of breath, Rachel thought as she fell into the kind of kiss that made words redundant.

By the time he lifted his head again, streaks of desire were burning into his cheekbones. 'Any reason why we cannot continue this…discussion in bed?' he said huskily.

What discussion? Rachel thought dryly as she wound her arms around his neck. 'You want to…talk?' she asked innocently.

His mouth twitched. 'No.'

'You perhaps want to say something about the way you unleashed your charms on another woman tonight?'

He tensed. 'You want me to apologise—'

'I want you to *pay*,' Rachel told him. 'At least you were saved from watching me act like that with Alonso.'

'But I did see.' He grimaced. 'I watched the handsome bastard leap out of his car and take you in his arms. I watched him kiss you as if he had every right to do it, and I saw the adoring expression on your face as you looked up at him!'

'It wasn't adoring, it was shock!' Rachel protested.

'You *let* him kiss you.'

'Italians are always kissing each other.' She dismissed that accusation.

'You let him drive you away in his flashy red car.'

'It was either that or get caught in the street by a snooping reporter.' Then she frowned. 'Where were you when this was happening?'

His sigh was rueful. 'Making a fool of myself over lunch with five important business associates, by just getting up and walking away,' he confessed. 'Then I got the call from Francesca and my day just continued downhill from there.' He ran his fingers through her hair, his eyes hooded. 'When you walked out of the restaurant I thought you were going to go to him.'

Rachel stared at him in blank disbelief. 'Since when have you been so short on ego to *think* such a thing?'

'Since I met you,' he said. 'You have a unique way of eating away at my ego.'

'That's such a lie,' she denounced. 'You've done nothing but bully me and want sex from me since we met!'

'You hit on me, but not because you wanted me. And you taunted me with other lovers.' He shrugged.

'I've had *one* lover before you,' she reminded him. 'My *one* lined up against your many who have trailed themselves past me seems a pretty pathetic comparison to me.'

He touched his tongue to the corner of her sulky mouth. 'I love you,' he murmured. 'Can we forget the others?'

Rachel sighed out a groan because he was right and harking on about old lovers had nothing to do with what they had here. 'Just take me to bed and love me, Raffaelle,' she begged.

He did not need asking twice. Their clothes fell away like rags for jumble. He pulled her against him, lips almost bruising in their intensity, his hands sliding possessively along her slender curves until he found the indentation of her waist, where he gripped and lifted her off the ground.

For a few clamouring seconds when her legs wrapped round him she thought he was going to do it standing right there with no preliminaries. Their mouths were straining and he was on fire, pumped up and ready for her. And she was pretty well much the same.

Then he turned and toppled them on to the duvet. What followed was the kind of fierce, fevered loving that staked absolute possession and claim. He gave her all of him and she took it greedily and gave back the same.

Afterwards they lay spread across the mattress, Rachel nothing more than a slender, soft, boneless creature lying beneath him, still lost in a wonderful, sensual world.

'In all my life,' Rafaelle murmured as he gently kissed her back down to earth again, 'I have never known the power of what you can do to me.'

So, gravely serious, opening her eyes, Rachel smiled at him. 'Hit on, trapped, taken over,' she said approvingly.

His eyes began to glint. 'Now you are asking for trouble,' he warned and climbed over her to land lightly on his feet by the bed.

'I didn't mean it—!' she cried out, sitting up jerkily.

He'd moved to the dressing table; now he was back by the bed. Stretching out beside her, he took hold of her left hand.

'Oh, I forgot,' she said, staring as the fake ring was removed from her finger.

The real one glittered and flashed as he slid it on to her finger. They lay there beside each other while he held up her hand. 'Hit on, trapped and marked as mine for ever,' he said turning her own words back on her with some very satisfied-sounding additions.

Then the fake ring spun in the air as he tossed it carelessly away.

'Did I tell you I love you?' Rachel said softly.

He rose above her, eyes dark and slumberous in his golden face. 'Tell me again,' he commanded.

'Love you,' she obliged and sealed it this time with a warm clinging kiss.

'And you will be my wife?'

Warm, dark, golden, gorgeous—she placed a finger on the thoroughly kissed fullness of his lower lip, loving the very possessive sound of *my wife*.

'Tomorrow.' She nodded gravely.

'Even though you get Daniella as a stepsister-in-law?'

'You get worse from me,' Rachel said. 'You get a fully paid-up member of the paparazzi as your brother-in-law.'

'Stung again—' he sighed '—you are going to have to work very hard to make it worth my while.'

The kiss she laid on his mouth worked very hard to make it worth his while.

'By the way,' she murmured a long time later, flickering innocent blue eyes up to look at him, 'you forgot to use any protection…'

THE GREEK'S VIRGIN

TRISH MOREY

One of the best things about being part of the romance-writing community is that you make such fantastic friends, and friends you can call on in a crisis anywhere around the world for brainstorming, plot-storming or just general laughs, inspiration and support. Here's special thanks to just a few of my favourite romance-writing friends, many published, some yet to be (but who sure as eggs will be one day!), who never fail to help a fellow writer out in a crisis—

The Wipits—Yvonne Lindsay and Bronwyn Jameson.
The Pyrate and Ferret Galz—Anne Gracie,
Kelly Hunter and Holly Cook
SA Galz—Kathy Smart, Anne Oliver,
Sharon Francesca and Linda Brown
and the entire Wet Noodle Posse
(http://www.wetnoodleposse.com)

Without you all, this book would have been written eventually, but it wouldn't have been half as much fun.

Thanks, everyone!

PROLOGUE

Sydney, Australia

BLISS! Life could never get better than this.

Saskia Prentice allowed him to ease her naked body down amongst the soft pillows, her young heart swelling, her lips still humming and swollen from his latest kiss, every cell in her body tingling, plumped and primed in anticipation.

Moonlight stroked against the window, rippling through the silk curtains, turning his skin to satin and illuminating the room in a warm, lunar glow, as if even the heavens approved. And offering just enough light to look up into the dark depths of his eyes as he positioned himself over her. She melted, her body softening even more, as she looked into them.

The eyes of the man she loved.

A moment of crystal-clear clarity pierced the pleasure fog surrounding her as his legs nestled into a welcome place between her own. Not quite eighteen, and already she'd found her soul mate, the one special man on this earth truly destined for her. There was no mistake. He was the one. And they would have years of loving together, years of feeling just like this.

How lucky could one woman get?

Then she stopped thinking and gave herself totally to the

feeling of him pressing against her, wanting to feel him make her his own, wanting to welcome him inside her, compelling him to press harder to unite them and to end this desperate, urgent need…

Their eyes connected briefly as her body began to accept his, as their burning bodies began to meld.

'I love you,' she whispered, putting in words what her heart already knew, her eyelids fluttering closed as she arched against him, urging him to break through that final stinging barrier, urging him to completion.

A second later the bed bucked and all pressure was gone. *He* was gone.

And cold air swept cruelly over the places he'd been.

She opened her eyes, blinking in shock, searching for him. But already he was across the room and dragging on his jeans, throwing on a shirt. And his face was as bleak as the stormiest night, his eyes filled with the darkest savagery.

'Put something on. I'll order you a taxi.'

His voice was coarse and gravelly, and nothing like she'd ever heard before. She looked up at him in horror, feeling suddenly exposed and vulnerable and inadequate all at the same time.

'Alex? What's wrong?'

'Tsou,' he spat roughly, tossing his head back as if he was disgusted with himself. His eyes glinted in the moonlight, hard and cold as granite, as he threw her clothes at her on the bed. 'This was a mistake.'

She curled herself behind them as best she could, shame and humiliation flaming her exposed flesh. Was her innocence so much of a turn-off?

'Did I do something wrong? I'm sorry—'

'Get dressed!' he ordered, his words uncompromising, his voice unrecognisable. *The voice of a stranger.*

'But…' Tears pricked at her eyes as she forced back the lump in her throat and fought her way into her clothes. 'But why?'

In the half-light his face was all dark shadows and tight ridges, his muscled body moving with a tenseness tainted with something that simmered like hatred.

'Just get out!' he roared. 'I don't do virgins!'

CHAPTER ONE

London—Eight years later

SUCCESS! Saskia Prentice breathed in that sweet smell as she approached the boardroom doors, the high of achievement fizzing in her veins.

In less than five minutes it would be official—she'd become editor-in-chief of the business magazine *AlphaBiz*.

And she'd worked so hard for this!

Twelve months of intense and sometimes bitterly fought competition with fellow journalist Carmen Rivers was proof of that. Carmen had made no secret of the fact that she'd do *anything* to ensure she got the job—and, given her rival's reputation, she probably had. But still it had been Saskia who'd consistently filed the best stories from around the globe, producing the most difficult-to-extract business profiles. Just two days ago the chairman had intimated that she'd won, that the job would be hers come today's board meeting.

She'd been waiting on tenterhooks all day, until at last the summons had come. Finally the job would be hers. And finally she'd have the means to rescue her father from his grungy retirement bedsit and get him a place in a decent care facility in the country. She had it all planned—a small cottage for herself close by with a back garden for him to potter around in on the weekends. The generous sign-on bonus, together with the substantially larger pay packet that went with the job, would make all that possible and more.

One hand on the door latch, the other checking her crazy curls were well slicked down and locked into the tight bun at the nape of her neck, she took one last glorious breath, stringing out the extra buzz of adrenaline at the imminent realisation of her dreams. This was her big chance to make the Prentice name really worth something in business circles once again. And this was her opportunity to give her father back something of the pride that had been so ruthlessly stolen from him.

She let go her breath, tapped lightly on the rich timber doors and let herself in.

Muted sunlight streamed in through the large window, momentarily blinding her. She blinked, surprised, as her eyes adjusted to see not the entire board, as she'd been expecting, but just the chairman, sitting near the head of the table, the sunlight framing his silhouette, transforming him to just a blur of dark against the bright light, his expression indiscernible. In spite of the temperature-controlled air, she shivered.

'Ah, Miss Prentice…*Saskia*,' his voice a low rumble, as he gestured her to sit opposite. 'Thank you so much for coming.'

She responded automatically as she blinked into the light, a disturbing feeling of unease creeping along her spine.

Something was wrong.

Sir Rodney Krieg was a bear of a man, with a booming voice, and yet today he sounded almost gentle. Sir Rodney *never* sounded gentle. And where was the board? Why weren't they all present for the announcement?

The chairman huffed out a long sigh that almost sounded defeated. 'You know that when we organised this meeting we were expecting to be able to formalise our plans to appoint you as the new editor-in-chief?'

She nodded, a sudden tightness in her throat rendering her speechless, feeling his words tugging at the threads of her earlier euphoria.

'Well, I'm afraid there's been a slight change of plans.'

'I don't understand.' She squeezed the words out, battling the crushing chill of disappointment suddenly clamping around her heart, yet still refusing to give up on her dreams just yet. Maybe it was just a delay?

Unless they'd given the job to Carmen after all...

'Has the board decided to go with Carmen instead?'

He shook his head, and for one tiny moment she felt relief.

'Or at least,' Sir Rodney continued, 'not yet.'

And her hopes died anew.

But she wasn't about to go down without a fight. She wouldn't give up on everything she'd worked for that easily. Dry-mouthed, she forced herself to respond, anger building inside. 'What do you mean, "not yet"? What happened? Only two days ago you said—'

He held up one hand to silence her. 'It's irregular, I admit, but Carmen has been having a word in the ear of some of the board members, doing some lobbying on her own behalf...'

Saskia froze. So Carmen had got wind of the board's decision and decided to head it off at the pass? It might be an uncharitable thought, but if Carmen was desperate enough for this position, she didn't want to think about the type of *word* she'd been having in the board members' ears.

'...and to cut a long story short,' Sir Rodney continued, 'the board has decided that a decision as to who is going to head the editorial team shouldn't be rushed.'

'It was hardly rushed,' she protested. 'The board has been deliberating on this for the last twelve months.'

'Nevertheless, the board feels that perhaps Carmen has a point. You've been engaged on different projects during that time. Maybe she hasn't had the opportunity to show her full potential after all.'

Saskia might almost have sneered if she hadn't been more concerned at the mental image of her small cottage in the country misting, the fabric of her dreams unravelling faster than she could tie off the ends. What would she tell her father? With only one, maybe two years of time before his increasing frailty rendered him bedridden, he'd been so looking forward to the move out of the city. She couldn't afford any delays to her plans, let alone risk losing this chance altogether.

'So what happens now?' she asked, her spirits at an all-time low. She'd worked so hard for this opportunity and it had just about been in her grasp. To have it pulled from her reach now, when it had been so close, was more than unfair. 'How long will the board take to make a final decision?'

'Ah. That all depends on you—and Carmen, of course.'

She raised an eyebrow. 'What do you mean?'

Sir Rodney actually managed to look enthusiastic. 'You see, the board has decided that the best way to compare your talents is with a head-to-head contest. You'll each be given a subject we've chosen—in this case, extremely successful businessmen who've chosen to live for whatever reason almost completely out of the public eye. Their public appearances are so rare we know hardly anything about the men themselves, while we see their businesses grow in stature every day. So we want you and Carmen to bring in the goods—what makes them tick? What drives them? The one who brings in the best profile within the month gets their story on the cover of our annual special edition, along with the news of their promotion.'

'But Sir Rodney, I've been consistently turning in great profiles all year—'

'Then one more shouldn't present any problem! I'm sorry, Saskia, but this has come from the board. They want you two to slug it out for the position, and that's what you're going to have to do to get it.'

'I see,' she snipped, hoping her subject wasn't too far flung. With this promotion she'd been counting on an end to her incessant traveling, so she could keep an eye on her father's condition. But she took heart from the time frame. This job couldn't take longer than a month. She'd make sure she did it in less. And then the promotion would be hers. Because she *would* deliver the best profile. There was no question of that! This was no more than a short delay to her plans.

'So who have I been assigned?'

Sir Rodney pushed his glasses on as he lifted up a manila folder lying nearby and flicked open the cover, scanning the information contained within.

'One very interesting character, it appears. You've scored a fellow Sydney-sider who now has extensive interests all over the world. Another one of Australia's Greek success stories, apparently.'

Cold needles of dread crawled up her spine. A Greek Australian from Sydney?

Oh, no way. It couldn't be…

There had to be dozens that fitted that description…

There wasn't a chance in the world…

'A fellow by the name of Alexander Koutoufides. Have you heard of him?'

Every organ and muscle inside Saskia seemed to clamp

down tight, squeezing the air from her lungs and the very blood from her veins. *Had she heard of him?* Part of her wanted to laugh hysterically even as the vacuum in her stomach began to fill with the bitter juices of the past.

He was the man she'd so stupidly imagined herself in love with, the same man who had so savagely thrust her from his bed—right before he'd turned around and coldly destroyed her father's business!

Oh, yes—she'd heard of Alexander Koutoufides!

And there was no way in the world that she was going to profile him. Hell, there was no way she was ever meeting that man again, let alone hanging around long enough to play twenty questions.

Sir Rodney hadn't waited for her response, clearly expecting her to answer in the positive. She forced herself to put aside her shock and focus on his words.

'...seems he made a big splash in business circles until about eight years ago, when he suddenly dropped right out of business circles and became almost a recluse, nonetheless quietly expanding his business interests into the northern hemisphere while refusing all requests for interviews...'

She raised one hand, beseeching him to stop. She didn't need to hear any more. 'I'm sorry, Sir Rodney. I really don't think me doing a profile on Alexander Koutoufides is a very good idea.'

He paused, leaning forward in his chair so slowly that it creaked. 'I'm not actually *asking* whether you think this is a good idea. I'm giving you your assignment!'

'No,' she said. 'Not Alex Koutoufides. It's not going to happen.'

He surveyed her, disbelief unbridled in his eyes, before he slapped the folder back down onto the table. 'But, Saskia, why on earth would you dip out of this opportunity when the promotion is at stake?'

'Because I've met Alexander Koutoufides. We…' She licked her lips while she searched for the right words. 'You might say we have history.'

His eyes widened, glinting with delight as he straightened in his chair. 'Excellent!' he announced, his voice back to booming proportions. 'Why didn't you tell me? That should give you a real head start. I hear our Mr Koutoufides is very wary of the press—although, given his celebrity sister and her latest escapades with a certain twenty-something Formula One driver, that's hardly surprising.'

Saskia blinked as the meaning behind his words registered. 'Marla Quartermain is Alex Koutoufides's sister?' She'd seen the articles—they'd been impossible to miss after *AlphaBiz's* sister magazine, *Snap!*, had run a cover spread on the scandal that had blown the affair both sky-high and worldwide. She vaguely remembered he had an older sister, but they'd never met, and not once had she connected the glamorous jet-setter with Alex. 'He sure kept that under wraps.'

'Exactly the way he wanted it, no doubt. It helped that she took her first husband's name—some joker she married aged sixteen, only to divorce him less than a year later. The first of a long string of failed marriages and sad affairs.' He sighed as he rolled his fountain pen between his fingers. 'But this time she's obviously gone too far—Alex must have decided it was time to take control. He was spotted by one of our photographers whisking her out the back entrance of a Sydney hotel. At first he was assumed to be some new love interest, but a little digging turned up the family connection—something infinitely more interesting to all concerned.'

Saskia's mind digested the new information. *AlphaBiz's*

sister magazine had been none too complimentary about the aging party girl, charging her with all manner of celebrity crime. Any brother would want to protect his sister from that kind of exposure.

'Given what *Snap!* published about Marla,' she reasoned, putting voice to her concerns, 'Alex is hardly going to be receptive to a request for a profile from this organisation—even if the two magazines are poles apart.'

Sir Rodney held out his hands in a wide shrug. 'That's where your previous relationship will give you the inside running, wouldn't you say?'

'Not a chance,' she stated, shaking her head defiantly. 'Alex Koutoufides…' She paused, choosing her words carefully—Sir Rodney didn't need to know the whole sordid story. 'Well, more than twenty years ago our fathers were in business together in Sydney, but my father struck a deal that saw him whisk Alex's father's business out from under his feet. Alex never forgave him. Eight years ago Alex destroyed my father's business as payback. He's ruthless and thoroughly without morals, and I dare say he hasn't improved with age. I hate the man with a passion. And I won't profile him.'

'You must be kidding, surely? You have right there the seeds of a brilliant profile!' The chairman peered at her as if he couldn't believe what he was hearing. 'I've never seen you back away from anything or anyone. What are you so afraid of?'

'I'm not afraid! I simply have no desire to ever see that man again.'

'Then consider it your chance to get back at him for what he did!' He slammed his hand on the table. 'Find the dirt on Alexander Koutoufides. He must be hiding something other than that sister of his. Find out what it is.'

She turned on him in a flash. '*AlphaBiz* doesn't do dirt—not in my profiles! Not that it matters, because I won't do it anyway.'

'You'd give up your chance at this promotion?'

'Why does it have to be him? Surely there's someone else I can profile?'

Sir Rodney harrumphed and drew back in his chair. 'I dare say the board won't be impressed, but I suppose if you feel that strongly about it we could possibly come to some arrangement. Perhaps we could swap your assignment for Carmen's?'

So she'd get Carmen's subject and Carmen would profile Alex instead? Saskia choked back her instant irrational objection. Maybe the chairman had a point. Why *not* set Carmen onto Alex? They probably deserved each other. Carmen would be only too eager once she discovered how good-looking he was—the perfect specimen on which to employ her famed horizontal interview techniques. And, let's face it, once she got him there Alex would have no reason to hurl Carmen from his bed—leastways not for the same reason *she'd* been so viciously ejected all those years ago!

Oh, yes, maybe they did deserve each other. She could just see it now… Pictures splashed across her mind's eye, shockingly vivid, staggeringly carnal, frame by slow, pulsating frame…

Carmen with Alex. Carmen on top of Alex, crawling all over him, over his chest, her mouth on his nipples, her hair tickling the firm flesh of his chest. And Alex, flipping her over, finding that tender place between her thighs…

Bile rose sharp and bitter in her throat.

Carmen didn't know the first thing about Alex! Whereas she herself *did* have a head start. She knew what the man was like, and she had a compelling reason, so he might just agree to do it.

Perhaps Sir Rodney was right—maybe this *was* her opportunity to get even with the man who'd destroyed her father's life and humiliated her into the deal? And maybe this was her chance to take Alex Koutoufides down a peg or two in the process.

'Sir Rodney,' she ventured calmly, in a voice that sounded strangely distant, as if separated from logic and reason. 'Maybe I was too hasty…'

He leaned his bulk across the desk in anticipation. 'Then you'll do it? You'll profile Alex Koutoufides?'

She lifted her eyes to meet his and swallowed, still half wondering what the hell she was letting herself in for and why.

For my father, she answered herself in the hammer of her heartbeat.

For revenge…

'I'll do it,' she said before she could change her mind again. 'When do I leave?'

CHAPTER TWO

ALEX KOUTOUFIDES was playing hard to get. Word on the streets in Sydney suggested he'd gone to ground, hoping to sit out the interest in his sister's latest affair. There was probably some logic in that, Saskia acknowledged as she edged quietly along the shadowy strip of sand lining the tiny and exclusive Sydney Harbour cove. Before too long another celebrity scandal was bound to knock Marla Quartermain's latest indiscretion off the front pages. Not that that would let Alex off the hook as far as Saskia was concerned.

But, with no sightings of him since the incident at the hotel, and no record of him leaving the country, Saskia had no option but to follow up on a hunch. Which was precisely why she was here, hugging the vegetation that lined the beach, contemplating the multi-storey beach house alongside.

The same beach house Alex had brought her to eight years before.

Saskia tried to ignore the steel bands tightening around her gut as she scrutinised the outline of the house in the fading sunlight, searching for any signs of life behind the curtain-lined glass walls. She wouldn't let herself think back to that night or she'd never be able to focus on her job. It was just a house, and Alex was just a man—not that it even looked as if he was here.

The garages facing the road high above had all been locked down, and there'd been no answer to her several rings of the gate bell. And she'd found not one reference to the property being owned by Alex or any of his known companies in any of her searches. Maybe it had never even been his.

Yet the strange prickle at the base of her neck told her otherwise, and despite the bad taste in her mouth at the prospect of meeting Alex Koutoufides again the thrill of the chase still set adrenaline pumping around her veins. It might be a long shot, but she'd won her fair share of industry accolades for stories that had resulted from her following up on just such hunches.

Alex obviously didn't want to be found. And if nobody knew about the beach house, then maybe this was the perfect place for him to lie low?

Her eyes scanned the height and breadth of the building, an architectural triumph in timber and glass, its stepped construction clinging to the slope behind as if it was part of it, and its generous balconies extending the living space seawards on every level. And from what she remembered the house was just as magnificent on the inside.

She jumped, swallowing down on a breath as a light came on inside. Because she knew that room. She'd been there, had lain naked across the endless bed while the welcoming sea breeze had stirred the curtains and the sea had played outside on the shoreline below. Even now she could recall the magic promise of that night. And even now she could feel the raw shock of Alex's cruel dismissal…

She squeezed her eyes shut, trying to banish those unwelcome memories. No way would she let herself relive the hurt he'd inflicted so savagely. She'd buried the mistake that had been her infatuation with Alex long ago. She was over it! Besides, right now she had more important things to think about. The house wasn't as empty as it looked. *Somebody* was in residence and she needed to get closer.

She flipped the collar of her dark jacket up, and checked to ensure her crazy hair was safely tucked under her cap— she was taking no chances that her honey-gold curls would give her away in the moonlight—before she looked back behind her, checking she was alone. But this was a private beach, almost impossible to get to, the steep path from the road barely more than a goat track. The shoreline was deserted behind her, the sounds of the wind moving through the leaves and a distant ferry her only companions.

Until the sound of a door sliding open pulled her attention back to the house. There was movement, the curtains pulled back, and she shrugged back into her cover of foliage as a lone figure wearing nothing but a low-slung pair of faded jeans stepped onto the balcony. Breath snagged in her throat. The light might be fading fast, but it couldn't disguise the identity of the owner of the powerful stride that carried him almost arrogantly to the balustrade. Nor could it hide the width of those broad shoulders, or the sculpted perfection of that bare torso as it tapered down to meet his jeans.

She lifted her gaze to his face, knowing she'd already had all the confirmation she needed before she even registered his features. But there was no mistake. She could just make out the stubble shadowing his jaw, his hair damp, as if he'd just showered, glossy and strong, framing his dark features and the chiselled lines of his face.

And inside her hatred simmered alongside satisfaction. She'd found her quarry. She'd found Alex Koutoufides in the flesh!

He shifted position against the railing and shadow and light rippled down his torso, stirring memories and comparisons. *In the flesh, indeed.* He didn't look so different from the way she remembered. His face might be leaner and harder, his chin more determined, as if he didn't make a habit of smiling, but he'd filled out across his shoulders, power underlined in each swell of muscle. Her eyes took all of him in, scanning him for changes, drawn to his chest and dark nipples, then further down, to where a whirl of dark hairs disappeared downwards into the soft denim that hugged close and low over his lean hips.

Those same hips had lain between hers. Those same shoulders had angled broadly above her as he'd positioned himself, preparing to take her…

She shifted, all dry throat and hammering blood, agitated with her body's instinctive feminine reaction and angry with herself for believing she could ever forget what had happened here so many years ago. She would never forget—*mustn't* let herself forget—not after the way he'd used her and abused her and stripped her father's company bare!

Saskia lifted her digital camera and fired off a couple of low-light photographs—just for confirmation. Sir Rodney would be delighted she'd tracked him down so quickly. How ironic that the place Alex had brought her to all those years ago, the place where he'd smashed her youthful dreams of love eternal to smithereens, had now put her in the driver's seat. It brought a smile to her lips as she stashed her camera back in her bag; there was a certain symmetry about it that appealed.

She'd get Alex to co-operate on this profile to give her the best chance to win that promotion, provide her with financial security and the means to take care of her father, or he'd pay for it with the publication of a few salient facts she was certain he would not want to be revealed to the world. Of course, the choice would be his, she thought with a smile. Unlike him, nobody could accuse *her* of being ruthless.

Right now he gazed out to sea like a master surveying his domain, one hand nursing a tumbler, the other angled wide along the brass-railed glass balustrade. Shrouded in shadow, she watched from below. Now all she had to do was watch for a chance to scramble up the hill and wait it out in her car. If he made so much as a move she'd know about it.

He turned his head her way and she shifted instinctively, aiming to get deeper under cover. But she stumbled on something solid behind her—a piece of driftwood. She managed to clamp down on a cry of surprise but momentarily lost her footing, grabbing onto a branch and rattling her cover of leaves while the driftwood skipped away down the thin strip of firm sand, rolling into the sea with a soft plop.

It was good to get some fresh air. The sea breeze on his face felt refreshing. The darkening ripples of the harbour were starting to sparkle as lights went on around the shore. The last few days staying here, with Marla constantly complaining about being cooped up, were really starting to get to him. But what choice did he have? The paparazzi were still swarming all over the Sydney office, waiting for him to put in an appearance, and there was no way he was risking letting them anywhere near Marla—not when they'd done such a great hatchet job on her already. He couldn't even rely on the beach house remaining secret, not now he knew all his records and property transactions were currently being raked over by every two-bit reporter in town, trying to track down where they'd disappeared to. As it was, someone had been leaning on the doorbell just an hour ago. A coincidence? Unlikely.

But they'd be out of here soon. All he was waiting for was the phone call to confirm they'd secured a place for Marla in a place near Lake Tahoe. Once inside the private clinic that doubled as a resort, Marla would be both safe from the press and entertained twenty-four hours a day. Tennis, massage or cosmetic surgery—the choice would be hers. By the time she came out the press would have lost interest. And maybe this time she'd manage to clean up her act for good.

He swirled his glass of soda unenthusiastically. What he'd really like right now was a slug of Laphroaig. The robust single malt would be the perfect accompaniment to the tang of sea air. But he'd made a deal with Marla and the house had been stripped of alcohol—he wouldn't drink if she couldn't. But hopefully tomorrow she'd be on her way. All that remained was to get her through the airport without being noticed.

His eyes scanned the surrounding beach. At least they were safe enough here.

The glass was tipped halfway to his lips when he heard it—the sudden rustle of undergrowth, the splash of something hitting the water. Instantly his eyes returned to the area below the balcony. An intruder? Or simply a possum skittering through the trees, sending debris seawards?

'Alex?' Marla called from inside the house. 'Where are you? What will I need—?'

'Stay there!' he barked over his shoulder. 'I'll be right in.'

He scanned the shoreline one last time before pushing away from the railing and turning for the door, sliding it home with a decided *thud*.

The breath she'd been holding rushed from her lungs. A close call. If the woman inside hadn't called out he'd have been bound to see her, lurking below his balcony. And skulking in the bushes was hardly the professional image she needed to convey if she was to convince him that she wanted a serious interview. She swung her bag over her shoulder and pulled her cap down low and tight. She'd acted on her hunch and she'd found Alex. Now it was time to climb back to the top and, if he wouldn't answer the door, wait him out. He had to come out eventually.

As for the woman? She clamped down on twinge of resentment—because it couldn't be jealousy—not a chance. Besides which, logic insisted it was most likely his sister he was protecting. Although the way he was dressed—or undressed…

She breathed out an irritated sigh. It didn't matter, anyway. It wasn't as if Saskia would have been the only woman Alex had brought here over the years. Whoever the woman was, she was welcome to him.

Carefully she picked her way along the shore. It was darker now, and the overgrown entry to the path was all but invisible in the low light. She was still searching for it when she heard the faint squeak of sand behind her.

There was no time to look around. A steel-like grip bit down on one arm and pulled, hard. She grunted in shock and tried to wrench free, but her feet tangled in her panic and she stumbled, the weight of her assailant behind her forcing her crashing down to the beach.

Breath whooshed out of her as she landed, her face cheek-deep in the sand, grains clinging to her lips and lashes, while behind her one arm was twisted high and tight. Pain bit deep in her shoulder.

'Who are you and what the hell do you want?'

His voice ripped through her like a chainsaw, and fear bloomed like a storm cloud inside her. Was it any relief that she knew her attacker? Hardly. Not when she knew the sort of low acts he was capable of. And not when he was hardly likely to be any more welcoming when he found out who she was.

She winced, her back arching and her head lifting from the sand as her arm was forced higher. 'You're hurting me,' she wheezed.

What the—?

Instantly he let go and eased his weight from her, horrified that he'd brought a woman down—but then he'd had no idea there was a female lurking under the bulky black jacket and cap, and whoever she was, she still had no right to be here. He crouched over her in the sand, not touching her, satisfied he didn't need to use any more force. She was going nowhere fast.

'What are you doing here? This is a private beach.'

She stretched her elbow, as if testing it, before planting it on the sand and using it to spin herself around into a sitting position.

Her jaw thrust up to meet him, and for a moment she was all pouting lips on a mouth that looked as if it wanted to spit hellfire and brimstone. He frowned, trying to make out more of the shadowed features of her face. She angled herself out from behind his cover and let moonlight hit her face, while at the same time she pulled the cap from her hair, letting her honey-gold curls tumble free. And finally those pouting lips turned up in a smile that came nowhere near her eyes.

'Why, I came to see *you*, Alex.'

And it hit him with all the force of a body-blow.

'Theos!' The word exploded from him like a shotgun blast, forcing him back up onto his feet. 'What the hell are *you* doing here?'

'I came to interview you,' she replied calmly, rising to stand in front of him and dust the sand from herself. 'But first I had to find you. Looks like I did.'

Before she'd finished speaking he'd already made a lunge for her shoulder bag and was rifling through the contents.

'Hey!' she protested, fighting him for control of the bag. 'What do you think you're doing?'

But he'd already found her mobile phone and camera and he ignored her, letting her snatch back the bag as a consolation prize. By the time she'd realised he had exactly what he'd been looking for, he already had the camera turned on.

Fury set his blood to a simmer as he scrolled through, finding the pictures of himself she'd taken from under the balcony. *'Vlaka!'* he swore under his breath, cursing himself for relaxing his guard for even just a moment. Just as he'd suspected—this was no innocent visitor! And now that *one* of the vultures had found them, at any moment the entire paparazzi contingent would descend upon them. Marla wasn't safe here any more. None of them were.

He flipped open the cover, popped out the memory card and flicked it low and long over the sea. He watched its trajectory over the water, only satisfied when it landed metres out into the bay.

'You can't do that!'

'I just did.'

He turned back to her, taking his time to really look her over this time—this ghost from the past come to haunt him. Little Saskia Prentice, all grown up. Sure, there were still those same long curls framing that heart-shaped face, the same too-wide mouth and milky complexion surrounding the greenest eyes he'd ever seen—but, from what he could see of the curves under that open zipper jacket, it looked as if the transition from teenager to woman had been good to her. Only the spark of innocence in those eyes was missing. Cold, hard cynicism ran deep in those liquid green depths.

For a moment he wondered—just how much had that been down to him? But he discarded that thought in a blink. No, her job would have knocked that out of her regardless. Nobody could stay an innocent for long in her line of work.

A line of work he abhorred.

'You're a reporter,' he said, pocketing both her phone and her camera in the shirt he'd hastily flung on before leaving the house. He hoped she wouldn't take his words as a compliment. They weren't meant to be. 'I suppose it's hardly surprising someone like you would end up working for the gutter press.'

'I'm a *journalist*,' she emphasised, her eyes now colder, her chest expanding on an angry breath. 'For a business magazine. And now that you've finished tampering with my goods, perhaps you'd care to hand them back?'

'And give you another chance at stealing one of your seedy shots or summoning up your cronies?' He knew exactly what kind of business magazine peddled the shots of the rich and the celebrated. He'd had his fair share of them. He'd seen how they operated—following their prey like vultures, wanting to make a fast buck by exposing someone else's private life. They were parasites, every last one of them.

'How am I supposed to do that? You've dispensed with the memory card, remember?'

'And a reporter would never carry a spare? I don't think so. Leave me your business card and I'll have your goods delivered to you.'

'That's my property! I'm not leaving without it.'

'And right now you're on *my* property, and I don't recall giving you permission to enter it—let alone take photographs you no doubt intend selling to the highest bidder. I'm sick of you parasites following Marla's every move, waiting for any chance to pull her down.'

'I wouldn't do that! Like I said, I work for—'

'Good,' he interrupted, not believing a word. 'Then getting rid of those photos won't present a problem. Now, who told you I was here?'

She looked at him, her hands on her hips, every part of her body taut and ready to snap.

'Nobody told me.'

'Then how did you find me?'

Her lips turned into something resembling a sneer, her eyes sparking resentment. 'Oh, I just thought I'd drop by on the off chance—*for old times' sake*. Surely you haven't forgotten that night? We had *such* fun together.'

Breath hissed through his teeth.

Forgotten that night? Not a chance. Though he'd tried to scrub his mind free of it time and time again, tried to put it behind him, his memory of that night was like a stain, indelibly printed on his psyche. It had been a mistake—an ugly mistake. And now Saskia herself was back, a three dimensional reminder of the mistakes of the past. What a fool he'd been to bring her to this house! And what a hell of a time to discover just how big a mistake it had been.

But, whatever she wanted from him, she was leaving. She was barking up the wrong tree entirely if she thought that what had happened all those years ago gave her an entrée into his private life now.

'I want you gone—now.'

'All I want is one interview.'

'You're wasting your time. My sister isn't giving interviews.'

'I don't want to talk to your sister. It's *you* my magazine is interested in.'

'Sure,' he said, shepherding her back towards the start of the steep path. 'Now, get going before I have to call the police and have you thrown out.'

She shrugged off his arm and stood her ground. 'I'm not going anywhere. Not without a profile on you.'

'And this is how you thought you'd get it? By lurking in the bushes and playing paparazzi?'

'I had to find out if you were here. You wouldn't answer the door.'

'Maybe because I didn't want to talk to anyone.'

'You have to agree to this interview.'

'Forget it. If you really had anything to do with the business world, you'd know I never give interviews or allow profiles.'

'This time you will. I work for *AlphaBiz* magazine—'

'Hang on.' He stilled in the moonlight. 'That's part of the Snapmedia conglomerate, isn't it? That bunch of dirt-raking parasites? I *knew* you were trouble.'

'I'm with *AlphaBiz*! It's a *business* magazine.'

'Closely aligned to *Snap!* magazine. Part of the same gutter press. And don't try and pretend you're anything special. I've seen the family tree.'

'You have to listen—'

'I don't have to listen to anything. Whereas *you* have to go. Right now.' He took a step closer, making it clear he wanted her to turn and leave. 'Goodbye, Miss Prentice. Be sure to watch your footing on the way up.'

She stood her ground, wishing she were taller, wishing she didn't feel so overwhelmed by his size and proximity, wishing his very heat didn't blur her senses and make her lose focus.

'You really don't want me to go, you know.'

'That's where you're wrong.'

'But if you don't agree to a profile I'll still have to turn one in. And I'll be forced to write it my way. Surely you don't want that?'

He scoffed. 'I have no doubt you'd work that way

anyway, whether or not I agree to this fantasy profile you insist you're here for.'

'I'll say how you assaulted me.'

'Go right ahead. You were trespassing—not to mention dressed like a burglar.'

She dragged in a breath, desperate for oxygen, searching for the courage to be able to force the words out. '*Then* I'll tell the world about the sick way you handle your business deals. You can say goodbye to being a recluse with the amount of media scrutiny you're going to get.'

He moved closer, looking down at her with the look of death he knew curdled the blood of any employee who stepped out of line. But she didn't back away. Instead her green eyes flashed up at him as if *she* was the one issuing a challenge. 'Just what the hell are you talking about?'

'I'll turn you from Mister Squeaky-Clean into a business pariah. Just as well you like living life as a recluse. Because you won't be able to show your face in public by the time I'm through with you.'

'You're bluffing!' he stated, even while a sick feeling foamed in his stomach, a festering of the unease he'd felt ever since he'd realised there was someone down below the balcony watching the house.

'You think so? Then watch me walk away. Because personally I can't *wait* to splash the sad truth of how you go about a takeover and exactly how you like to celebrate your victory by totally humiliating the opposition by seducing and then rejecting their innocent daughters.'

CHAPTER THREE

FURY turned his eyes dark and potent. His top lip curled with hatred as Saskia waited for his response. 'So much for having nothing in common with the gutter press. Looks like you can rake muck with the worst of them.'

'I'm not talking about raking muck,' she stated as calmly as she could, belying the fact that her heart was going at a million miles an hour. 'I'm talking about telling the truth, telling it how it was and what you did to me the very day before you destroyed my father's life by smashing his company to pieces.'

His face came down low, his brows twisted, his skin pulled tight over his features—features that spoke of barely reined-in rage. He leaned so close she could feel his breath on her face, feel his heat setting her own blood on fire.

'And what exactly *did* I do to you?'

'You took advantage of me!'

'So you're planning to pretend I raped you?'

'No! I never said that. Although no doubt you'd like to pretend we never had sexual relations at all.'

'We went to bed together, and you were, I seem to recall, more than willing!'

'As were you! Or so I thought.'

He drew back for a moment, his eyes narrowing.

'Is *that* why you're so angry with me? Because I *didn't* actually finish off what I started?'

She blinked, gulping back on a sudden spike of truth.

'Is that to be your threatening headline, then?' he taunted. *'Man refuses to take woman's virginity.* Are you trying to damn me or make me out to be some kind of saint?'

'Whether or not you stopped has nothing to do with it. You got me into bed, remember?'

'No,' he said, brushing her objections aside. 'I don't know how many men would have stopped when it was so willingly offered to them on a plate! You were all but *begging* for it.'

'That's not the point!' she protested, her stomach churning at the crude way he portrayed what had happened that night. Was that what he believed? Was that how he remembered it? It hadn't been like that. Not for her at least.

Suddenly things were too personal, too painful, his words slicing fresh wounds so that she had to battle twice as hard to overcome both the hurt of the old and the pain of the new. And so what that they hadn't actually had sex? It had been damned close, and his rejection had left her feeling violated. He'd used her for whatever sick purpose he'd had in mind, and then he'd hung her out to dry.

'Then what *is* your *precious* point?' Alex demanded.

'If it hadn't been for the takeover,' she managed, her words spilling out in a rush, 'you would never have had me in your bed. It wasn't enough for you to crush my father and his business. You had to humiliate the entire family in the process!'

His eyes flared and burned like a planet in its death throes, and she knew she was right. But there was no victory in his silent confirmation. Instead, the memory of that night ripped sharp and jagged through her senses as if it were yesterday.

She was back in that bed, her feelings as exposed as her flesh. Bewildered, confused and frightened of the man he'd suddenly become. Her feelings slashed to the core as she realised the fool he'd made of her. *The fool she'd made of herself.* She gulped in air, trying to think, to keep control, to suppress the pain of a night that should never have happened.

'You would never publish that.' His words were whispered and intense. 'You have no idea what you'd be opening yourself up to.'

She could hear the steady wire of warning running through his lowered voice, linking his words together like a threat.

'Try me!' she challenged. If he was threatening her he must be afraid—afraid of what she could reveal about him, afraid of what it could do to his business. 'The whole world is going to learn what kind of man you really are. And won't that do your precious sister a whole lot of good? Seeing you dragged through the press just like her! Goodbye, Alex. Sleep tight.'

She turned and he cursed, low and hard under his breath. Damn her! Just when he'd had Marla almost clear. Just when he was trying to keep her away from that gutter press, that same gutter press was about to turn on him. And there was only one way to stop it happening.

He snaked out a hand, imprisoning her arm before she'd taken two paces. 'Wait.'

She looked down at his hand, then over her shoulder at him, her eyes flashing like green crystals, cold and deadly. 'I don't like you touching me.'

He let her go, not wanting to touch her himself but drawn to her at the same time. 'What's to say that even if I agree to this interview you won't publish that rubbish anyway?'

'My word says so.'

'And why on earth would I trust you?'

'Do you really think I want people to know what you did to me back then? Oh, yes, I'll use it if I have to. But you give me this profile and I won't have to reveal to the entire world how much of a bastard you are and how much of a fool I was.'

'Then I'll give you your interview.'

She blinked, slowly, and his eyes were drawn to the arc of her long lashes, sweeping down over her eyes. But not before he'd caught a glint of something inside—success? Or fear?

But when she opened them up whatever he'd glimpsed was gone.

'Fine,' she said, almost as if she was sorry. 'When is a good time to make the arrangements? I'll stay in the background as much as possible, but you will need to allow for some one-on-one question time.'

'Hold on. I said I'd agree to an interview. Nothing more.'

'But—'

'And you've got ten minutes for it. Starting now.'

'No! That's not how I work. I can't be expected to do an entire profile in ten minutes.'

'So how long does a profile take?'

'At least a week. Sometimes more. It depends how co-operative the subject is. I need to see how you work. I need access to your offices.'

'A week? No deal. I won't even be in the country.'

Her eyes hardened into a renewed ice age. 'Then we have nothing more to discuss. It's a profile, or you can look out for what I write in the paper. And I warn you, it will be very, very good. Although perhaps not so good for you.'

The wake from a long-gone ferry slapped lazily up the shore, cicadas buzzed in the dark foliage, and all the while her eyes held his, daring him, challenging him to make the wrong decision.

Why the hell had she had to come back into his life right now? And with a score to settle. She was the last thing he needed.

The mobile in his back pocket beeped three times, and without moving his eyes he reached behind and put it to his ear, knowing instinctively that it was his number one fix-it man, Jake.

'Yes?'

He listened for a few moments, still watching her, satisfied to hear that by this time tomorrow Marla would be safely on her way to the States. Then what he heard made him do a double-take. 'What do you mean, "a diversion"?'

'The airport's still crawling with reporters,' Jake Wetherill argued. 'We can chopper Marla up to Brisbane and exit from there, but there's no guarantee that will be any clearer. But if we could pull something to get the focus onto you—hopefully Marla can slip through unnoticed.'

Alex's eyes narrowed on Saskia. 'A diversion?' he repeated, thinking wild thoughts. It might just work. And it might just help his cause in the process... 'You've got it,' he snapped into the phone, closing it down and slipping it back into his pocket.

Saskia eyed him warily as he allowed himself a thin smile. 'What was that all about?'

'You'd better come with me,' he said, taking her by the wrist. 'You don't have much time to get ready.'

'What do you mean? Get ready for what?'

'I mean you'll get your profile after all.'

She dug her heels into the sand, clearly not trusting him. *Clever girl.*

'What's the catch? What was all that about "a diversion"?'

'There is no catch,' he responded, pulling harder and forcing her feet into a jerky run to keep up with him. 'I'm just making you a deal. You'll get your profile, and in return you'll do something for me.'

'What "something"?'

He stopped, and swung his body towards hers so fast that she almost slapped bodily into him. He looked down and saw eyes that were wide and mistrustful, lips slightly parted, as if he'd caught her unawares and she was trying to catch her breath.

'Did anyone ever tell you that you ask too many questions?'

'I'm a journalist,' she argued, her gaze glued to his unbuttoned shirt, surveying his chest before backing up as if it might bite her. Her eyes drifted up to his face, widening when she saw the way he'd been watching her, waiting for their eyes to connect. 'It's my job.'

'And all I'm doing is giving you the opportunity to do it,' he announced.

'What do you want *me* to do?'

Alex looked down at her, at the moonlight playing on her curls and her body within humming distance of his senses, and for just one crazy moment he felt like sliding a hand around that slender neck and tipping those lips up towards his.

He must be mad to even think it.

Another time, another place—*another woman*—and that question could almost have been an invitation. But not with Saskia. If there was one thing he'd learned from his mistakes over the years it was not to make them again. Saskia had been one hell of a mistake, and he wasn't about to revisit it.

He raised his eyes skyward to break the contact, to break whatever it was she was doing with those damned green eyes of hers, and started pulling her towards the house. 'We leave tomorrow for the States—do you have your passport handy?'

'At my hotel. But the States? Why?'

'Does it matter where you get your profile?'

'No, but…'

'Then I'll send for your things. You're coming with me. You want a week; you've got one. All I'm asking is that you help me let Marla slip through the airport without being noticed.'

'That "diversion" you were talking about, I take it?'

'Got it in one.'

'So what am I expected to do?'

'Just accompany me through the airport. The press are still looking for Marla. I want them to find me strolling casually through the airport and holding hands—with you.'

He let the last two words sink in.

'You and me?' Her eyes flashed cold fire at the same time as her head started to shake from side to side. 'You want them to think there's something going on between us—that, what?—that I'm your *love interest* or something?'

He allowed himself a smile. She'd ejected those two words like missiles, and he knew he'd found the perfect person for the job. Whatever happened tomorrow, whatever he had to do to convince the press that they were a couple, there was no way she'd want to hold him to it afterwards.

'You must be mad!'

'On the contrary. It's the perfect plan. You get to accompany me and get your precious profile, and Marla escapes the country without a peep.'

'It'll never work. I couldn't… I mean, there's no way I could…'

'There's no way you could what, Saskia?' He slid his hand up her arm over her jacket, skimming over her shoulder, curling around her neck, watching her eyelids flutter in reaction as his fingers smoothed over her skin.

'Pretend you care for me? I think we both know that's not true. I think, if you think back, you might recall just how easy it was to care about me.'

Her eyes snapped open, but the rapid jerk of her neck didn't come close to dislodging his hand. 'That was years ago! There's no way I can pretend to like you now—not after what you did to my family. Not now I know what you're capable of. *Not when I hate you with every bone in my body.*'

'And yet you're here,' he soothed, his fingers gently stroking her skin, marvelling at its satin-smooth texture, feeling the rapid pulse of her heartbeat through his skin. 'Don't you find that odd? If you really hated me, why would you take this job?'

'I had no choice! Not if I want any chance at a career and a future. I certainly didn't volunteer to be here.'

'So you had no choice? And that's the only reason you're here?'

Something fleeting skated across her eyes, but still she didn't pull away. Instead she let her gaze focus, its power intensifying as she glared at him. 'No, it's not the only reason,' she hissed, her delivery gift-wrapped in venom. 'Once I knew I was coming I relished the opportunity to do anything I could to pull you down.'

So she really *did* hate him? So much the better. 'Sorry to disappoint you,' he clipped. 'So we have a deal, then—my profile in exchange for your co-operation on this?'

She nodded. Eventually.

'Good. Then, as soon as Marla is safe and your profile is done, you can take yourself back to wherever you came from and file your story.'

'Agreed,' she said.

'Just one condition,' he added.

'And that is?'

'You don't talk to Marla. Tonight or any time. You don't talk to her, and you don't take photos. Got that?'

Her green eyes flared into life again. 'I told you, I'm not here to interview Marla. My business is with you.'

His own regarded her coolly. 'Make sure it is,' he said after a moment, pulling her with him up the steps leading from the shore to the gate that led from the beach to the house. 'Or you won't know what hit you.'

Regardless of what Alex wanted, Marla was there to meet them as soon as they entered the house. 'So there *was* someone out there?' she said, her face a picture of curiosity, but Alex gestured her to stay back with a firm sweep of his free arm.

'It seems we have an uninvited visitor for the night.' Alex tightened his grip on Saskia's arm, his fingers biting into her flesh as if he was worried she was going to make a dash for his sister now she was so close. 'But I want you to keep right away from her. I'm putting her in the guest wing and she's not moving from it.'

'Who is she?'

'Just some reporter.' He spat the word out as if it tasted of bile. 'Nobody you need worry about—'

'I'm a *journalist*,' Saskia interrupted, sick of being talked about in the third person and conscious of how Marla had recoiled at the word he'd used. 'I came here to ask for a profile on Alex. I work for *AlphaBiz* magazine, and my name is—'

'Not important!' Alex interrupted, turning on her savagely, the look in his eyes enough to stop her in her tracks. 'And no matter what she says,' he directed at Marla, 'we're not taking any chances. Don't talk to her. And, whatever you do, don't answer any questions.'

Marla looked at her warily, as if Saskia might bite. Without the sultry make-up she was used to seeing the woman photographed in, Marla looked pale and vulnerable, her eyes wide and innocent, almost naïve.

'So why is she here?'

Alex was already leading her past Marla and towards a flight of stairs. 'She's going to help us get through the airport tomorrow in return for this profile she claims she wants. While we lead the way, Jake will look after you.'

'I don't want Jake,' his sister cried out. 'I hate him. I don't need a babysitter!'

'You'll do what I say!' Alex called back over his shoulder.

'If you expect me to help you both it might pay to stop insulting me,' Saskia hissed, as he frogmarched her up to a mezzanine level facing the sea, letting go of her only once she was safely deposited in a large sitting room.

He closed the door behind them while she rubbed her arm where he'd held her. She took in the rich décor, in coffee and cream colours with soft golden highlights, and guessed the closed curtains must be hiding spectacular views of the harbour. Through an open door she could make out a bedroom, the large bed and enormous pillows reminding her of another bed in this house, another time… She jerked her eyes away, heat filling her cheeks.

He hadn't brought her here to continue where he'd left off. *Besides which, there wasn't a snowball's chance in hell she'd let him.*

'I don't want you leaving these rooms. I'll send up something for you to eat.'

'So I'm to be your prisoner here, in this—' she swung her arms out wide '—gilded cage?'

His eyes were hooded and dark, his delivery deadpan.

'You'll find you have everything you need. There's an *en suite* bathroom off the bedroom. You'll have no need to leave.'

'I need my luggage. And I have a rental car to return. I can't do either of those if I'm stuck here.'

'Give me your keys. I'll have everything taken care of.'

'I don't want someone else poking around in my things! I want to get them.'

'You're not going anywhere. Not until tomorrow. Until then you're going to do everything I say.'

'Do you get off on bossing around women, telling them what they can and cannot do? Even your own sister isn't allowed to decide who she speaks to or who she travels with.'

'Leave my sister out of this!'

'I wouldn't take that kind of treatment if I had a brother. I'm surprised she puts up with it. I'd tell you well and truly where to get off.'

A pointed hand spun close to her face. 'And I said it's none of your concern! You know nothing about it and you will stay out of it. Have you got that?'

She regarded the hand levelly. 'What I've got is that it wouldn't matter if she *did* complain about your interference. You probably wouldn't listen anyway.'

'For someone who claims not to be interested in my sister, you sure seem to be pretty focused on her right now.'

'Don't you think it's a bit hard when you're making me stay in the same damned house as her? It's not as if she's invisible!'

He spun around. 'You're here for one purpose, and one purpose only—to ensure that Marla gets through the airport without the paparazzi getting wind of it. Do that and you get all the time you want to do this profile you claim you need. Otherwise, no deal. Have you got that?'

'Oh, loud and clear,' she replied. 'But don't you forget—

one wrong move on your part and I'll write an exposé that's going to set your business back years.'

His eyes sparked white-hot and his face took on a rigidity that could challenge concrete. For a moment she felt the heated resentment pulsate across the distance from him in rolling waves. And then something else crossed his eyes and he smiled, all tight lips and sardonic pleasure. 'I'm so glad we understand one another. Your things will be delivered later. Until then, goodnight.'

Sydney's international terminal was buzzing when the black stretch limousine pulled up outside the departures gates. Saskia took a deep breath as she waited for the chauffeur to come around and open the door, trying to prepare herself for her role as Alex's love interest. *Love interest?* Ha! After the way he'd treated her last night she'd have more success playing his hate interest. But with any luck nobody would notice them, and she'd get away with little more than having to hold his hand as they walked through the terminal—though even the thought of touching him was abhorrent to her.

Then she stole a glance at the man at her side and swore a silent *No chance* in her brain. If it wasn't enough of a sign-board to get the longest stretch limo in Sydney, nobody could miss a man of Alex's stature and bearing. And if his dark looks, the Hugo Boss jacket, the fine wool sweater and dark trousers weren't enough, he wore power like a magnet, and it drew people's attention from all directions. And wasn't this whole exercise about being noticed? She was wishing for the impossible.

Alex alighted first and turned back, extending one hand towards her, sunglasses obscuring his eyes. 'Ready?' She'd thought she was, but having him waiting for her, holding his hand out to her in invitation, made her hesitate and catch her breath again as she reminded herself exactly why she was playing along with him.

Just for show, she told herself. *Just for my profile and then I'm gone.*

Saskia reached up a hand, doing her best to ignore the warm tingling rush to her skin as he folded his long fingers around hers, the pressure gentle and firm as he led her from the car. A late summer breeze caught at her curls and the silk chiffon layers of her dress as he drew her close alongside, and with only one free hand it was her hair that came off second best. Even in an atmosphere rich with traffic fumes bouncing around the sun-warmed concourse, it was his scent of which she was most aware, his cologne that teased her nostrils, his masculine warmth that curled its way inside her and did unwanted things to her heart-lung function.

She looked around nervously, trying to take her mind off the man at her side while the chauffeur unloaded their luggage onto a trolley. It seemed to be taking an inordinately long time. But that was no doubt for the press's benefit—to given anyone in the airport time to realise exactly who had just descended upon them. Already heads were turning their way, a palpable buzz of conjecture vying with the constant roar of vehicles. She looked back down the approach lane, knowing that a dozen cars back sat Marla, a brunette bob hiding her trademark bleached silver blonde mane, and a burgundy leisure suit dressing down a body usually more scantily clad. Jake was at her side, both of them waiting for Alex and Saskia to draw any unwanted attention from the press and allow them a clear run through check-in to the relative anonymity of the first-class lounge.

'Do you realise just how beautiful you look today?'

His words snapped her head around and up with a jolt, but neither his dark-shaded eyes nor the firm set of his chin added to the effect of the words. Part of the act, she realised, damping down her erratically beating heart. Besides which, she didn't give a damn what he thought. But then his free hand smoothed the hair she'd been unable to rescue from the wind, curving it behind one ear and lingering there, all gentle touch and potent masculinity at the same time, making a mockery of all her efforts at controlling her crazy heart-rate.

She mustn't let him affect her this way! Once upon a long time ago she had, and it had been the biggest mistake of her life. And yet still, in spite of all she'd experienced and all she knew, he had a knack of getting under her skin.

He'd driven her to frustration this morning, making her change twice before despairing of the serviceable suits and blouses she had in her luggage and ordering in a boutique's worth of outfits and shoes for her to choose from. And even then he hadn't trusted her. He'd selected the dress she was wearing—a confection of fitted artistry and floating length, the muted petal print feminine without being girlish. He'd called in hairstylists, who'd transformed her unruly curls into sleek waves. He'd made her into a woman he'd be prepared to be photographed alongside, and she had to admit she liked the effect. She felt good—better than good—she actually felt beautiful. It didn't help that his words mirrored her own thoughts. It helped even less that his touch magnified what she felt tenfold.

She moved to shrink away from his reach, but he stilled her by placing one hand on her shoulder. 'Easy,' he murmured, his mouth so close that his warm breath fanned her face, sending tiny tremors radiating through her. 'We want this to look convincing.' And then he slid his sunglasses from his face, laughing softly, as if sharing some intimacy, looking down at her as if she was the only thing on earth that mattered to him. A panicked feeling of *déjà-vu* clawed at her fragile insides.

She knew those eyes. She knew what they could do and how they could turn on the heat and the desire and the want. She also knew exactly how easily those eyes could turn savage and cold in an instant, slashing through her soul with ruthless efficiency.

I can't do this.

As if on cue his eyes turned hard and resolute, and instantly she knew she'd unconsciously given voice to her thoughts. 'You *have* to do this,' he ordered, snapping her out of her fears as he steered her towards where their luggage was being wheeled into the terminal. 'We have a bargain.'

She blinked, her mind clearing now that it was passengers and luggage and queues that filled her vision rather than his eyes. He was right. She *could* do this. She had to, because she had no choice. But this time she'd make sure she had nothing to fear.

Because knowledge was power. This time it would be different, because she knew exactly what kind of man Alex Koutoufides was. She knew how he could turn on the charm, and she knew how he could so quickly spin that setting to deep freeze.

So there was no way she'd let him get the better of her.

They hadn't taken half a dozen steps inside the terminal when it started—a swelling hubbub of interest and more swivelled heads. Even though first-class check-in was fast and efficient, the attendant the soul of discretion as he checked their bags, by the time they'd received seat allocations and turned towards the departure lounges they'd attracted every eye in the terminal along with a clutch of photographers, both amateur and professional, who had suddenly appeared out of the woodwork.

'Here come the vultures,' Alex said, taking her arm and ignoring the calls starting to come from the photographers to attract his attention. 'Let's go.'

He didn't wait for her agreement, just forged a path through security as the gathering throng formed an honour guard around them.

'How's Marla?' someone called.

'Where is she?' yelled another, thrusting a tiny microphone into his face.

Alex brushed it away, tossing a pointed, 'I was hoping you could tell me,' at them. 'You seem to know everything else about her,' he finished, while he continued to part the sea of reporters and intrigued bystanders in his path as if they weren't there.

Saskia kept up, swept along as much by Alex's powerful aura as his arm around her shoulders. The noise of the incessant questions, the flash of cameras and the closeness of the press was claustrophobic. No wonder he'd wanted to protect Marla from this sort of circus.

Over the sea of heads and raised cameras the promise of the first-class lounge access appeared, and then disappeared behind them as Alex forged on, irrationally forgoing privacy for a public lounge setting at a cosy bar nearby.

What the hell was he thinking? she thought as he pulled her down alongside him, wrapping a possessive arm around her shoulders.

'So who's the lady friend?' one intrepid reporter asked, obviously tiring of getting no answers about Marla and determined to get at least some copy to file and make today's expedition worthwhile. 'It's not often we get to see Australia's most eligible bachelor, let alone with a woman in tow.'

Like a barometer, his comment was indicative of a change

in the mood of the audience and instantly attention switched from Marla to Saskia. Any story was apparently better than none. Alex smiled at her as he turned from the waitress who'd taken his order for the best French champagne.

'No comment,' he said.

The reporters took the bait, focusing now on Saskia, hitting her with a barrage of questions, each indiscernible from the next. Saskia recoiled from the push of people and microphones, everything and everyone in her face, her eyes blinking at the never-ending flash of cameras, her heart thumping like a cornered rabbit, powering an urge to jump up and flee.

Alex held up one hand to quieten the mob while he took her hand in the other. 'Saskia is a good friend, nothing more.'

But the look he shot her for the benefit of the cameras was pure sin, hot with desire and so heavy with lust that even Saskia caught her breath as his eyes triggered an instantaneous feminine rush of hormones inside her. Under her wisp of a bra her breasts tingled, her nipples firmed and peaked, and electricity crackled from their aching tips all the way down to her core. She dredged up a smile in response as she clamped down on muscles suddenly making their unwelcome presence felt, battling to rein in her inner hormones. It was merely part of the act, she reminded herself stiffly, as the cameras went mad amidst more calls for details.

She smiled enigmatically for the cameras. At least she'd soon be out of here—her mission accomplished. Marla and Jake should have made it through to the first-class lounge by now, and thankfully her part in this charade would soon be over, with the press convinced she was some kind of girlfriend and totally unaware that by the time they reported it the big news affair would already be over.

'Maybe we should tell them after all, sweetheart?'

His words pulled her around, aghast. *Sweetheart?* Tell them *what?* Cold chills worked down her back and she knew she couldn't run now if she tried—her spine had turned to jelly, her legs would cave at the first step.

'Alex?' she whispered, looking for him to reassure her that this game was nearly over, even though her gut instinct told her that Alex was hardly the kind of man to suddenly turn from dragon into knight in shining armour.

'I know, I know,' he countered, still holding his other palm up as he nestled closer to her, his leg brushing against hers from hip to knee. Heated. Arousing.

Irritating.

'I know we meant to keep it just between ourselves for a little while longer.'

'Keep what between yourselves, Mr Koutoufides?' Reporters jostled for the best position, sensing a major announcement. 'So the lady's more than just a good friend?'

Saskia felt a roiling wave of panic course through her. What the hell was he playing at? She'd kept her end of the deal. Hadn't she done enough? She forced a smile to her face, leaned into his shoulder, and hissed, 'This isn't what we planned!'

He tugged her closer into the crook of his shoulder and pressed his lips to her hair. 'I know that, darling. But why wait?' He paused while champagne was poured, and ordered another half-dozen bottles so that everyone could join them in a toast.

'Gentlemen,' he announced, pulling Saskia to her feet alongside him. 'I'd like you to be the first to know. The beautiful Miss Prentice has just agreed to become my wife.'

CHAPTER FOUR

THE atmosphere around them descended into pandemonium as cheers from watching travellers vied with even more questions. The pack were pushing and shoving around them, angling for the best photo opportunity, but Saskia was almost oblivious to the noise. White-hot fury blocked out almost everything and everyone—everyone, that was, apart from the smug tycoon standing alongside her.

'Alex!' she said. 'What the—?'

He didn't wait for her to finish. Whatever she'd been going to say, his mouth crushed the words flat. Shock registered in her eyes, in the way she held herself rigid, and in the exclamation he captured in his mouth. He pulled her hard against him to mould her closer, slanting his mouth over hers. It made a good fit even better. Her lips were lush and moist, her taste sweet and strangely welcoming, given her history of antagonism. She might not like to think she was involved in this kiss, but her body sure was, a body clad in little more than fabric less substantial than tissue paper. And underneath that sweet floral print lurked flesh so dangerously womanly he almost wished he was somewhere a whole lot more private.

He growled his appreciation and felt a tremor reverberate

through her in response, melting her curves into even closer contact with him.

His mobile phone sent out a single beep and his lips curved into a smile over hers. Marla and Jake were safe. Which meant he could stop kissing her now, he registered, even as his fingers splayed wide through her hair, keeping her tightly anchored as his mouth continued to take pleasure in hers. The plan had gone well. He'd kept the reporters entertained, no doubt drawing in any reporters hanging back to see what all the commotion was about, and now they had both a story and pictures to keep them happy. It was a win-win situation for everyone—including himself. He hadn't expected to have found diversionary tactics quite so enjoyable. But now he'd done enough.

Besides which, if he didn't stop kissing her soon, he wouldn't be fit to be seen in public.

Reluctantly he wound down the kiss, taking his time, savouring the fresh taste of woman, lush and ripe, in his mouth. He cradled her head in his arms as he ended it, wary that she still might want to tear him to pieces. But for now at least her fight was gone, her lips plump and pink, her cheeks flushed and her breathing fast and furious. She looked up at him with those large green eyes and he saw confusion competing with anger. Any minute now that anger was going to boil over, and he'd have a hard time containing it, but right now she looked stunned, thoroughly kissed and very, very beddable.

Theos!

One look at her and the reaction he'd sought to contain resumed, unabated. He spun her in front of him and wrapped his arms around her slim waist, feeling her slight gasp of shock as he drew her against his firmness as together they faced the press.

'Thank you,' he said, over questions about where they'd met and whether they'd set a date. 'But now you'll have to excuse us. We have a plane to catch. Feel free to stay and enjoy the champagne.'

Somehow Saskia made it to the escalators up to the first class lounge, her anger rising faster than the metal stairs beneath her feet. And once the sliding glass doors behind them had slid shut she wasn't staying silent any more.

'*That* wasn't part of the deal!'

He smiled down at her, even though he was standing one step behind, his arms spread wide on the risers. If he'd wanted to make her feel trapped his body language couldn't have been any clearer. 'The deal was for you to pretend to be my love interest. I'd say we were pretty convincing on that score, wouldn't you?'

She felt herself colouring under the cold perusal of his eyes—eyes that had looked at her with such savage heat just a few minutes ago, eyes that had all but incinerated her clothes from her. And the heat hadn't been restricted to his eyes. Once his mouth had meshed with hers, once his lips had bent hers to their will, temperatures had been rising everywhere. Compelling heat. Tempting heat. Heat that had stroked her senses and massaged her sensibilities. Heat that had curled into her secret places until they ached with longing.

Only when he'd pulled her in front of him and she'd felt the unmistakable evidence of his arousal pressing hard against her, the shocking equivalent of her own body's reaction, had that heat turned sour, curdling the juices of her stomach.

Sickening heat.

What the hell was he trying to prove?

'Those pictures are going to be splashed all over the papers by tomorrow.'

'I know,' he said, as if he was delighted by the prospect. 'The gutter press is nothing if not efficient.'

'Do you really think I want people to see me pictured—*like that*—with you?'

'Right now, I don't care what you want. It was the means to an end, nothing more.'

'So did you *have* to tell them we were engaged? What the hell was *that* all about?'

'I had to keep their interest,' he conceded. 'I didn't want them drifting off before Marla was safe.'

'Well, you sure kept their interest,' she snapped as they stepped off the escalator into the lounge proper, waiting until they'd been welcomed into the inner confines and been shown to a private room before continuing her tirade. 'But there'll be another story soon. It's going to be the shortest engagement in history.'

'Maybe not,' he answered with a smile, gesturing her to sit in one of the deep club chairs or small sofas surrounding a central coffee table.

She gazed around, momentarily losing her train of thought. 'Where's Marla? Didn't you say Marla was safe? I thought they would be here already.'

His eyes narrowed and his whole face seemed to tighten. 'Do you really think I'm letting you anywhere near Marla? It was enough of a risk having you both in the same house last night.'

'But I told you—'

'No,' he said flatly. 'Marla's safe. And you're not getting anywhere near her. We changed the arrangements last night. Jake is taking her on another airline. Right now they're half a terminal away.'

'I told you, I'm not interested in Marla!'

'Then we're all happy. What would you like to drink?'

She threw herself back into the chair. 'You mean you haven't had enough *celebratory champagne*? I think you should explain what you meant before.'

He curved a lazy eyebrow as he gave his order to the waitress. 'Before…?'

'When you said this engagement might not be the shortest engagement in history. What did you mean?'

He shrugged, as if it was of no consequence at all. 'Simply that it might suit us both to keep this "arrangement" going for a little longer—at least while you get your profile done.'

'You're kidding! You must be mad! This is hardly an "arrangement". You made an announcement. You lied to the press.'

'And tomorrow it will be fact. The world will believe we're to be married.'

'No,' she said, shaking her head. 'No way.'

'You'll find a way,' he said, raising his swiftly delivered glass of Scotch to her. 'Or you won't get your precious profile. It's as simple as that.'

'We already *have* an agreement! I've held up my end of the bargain.'

'I'm just extending some of the terms, that's all.'

'You're reneging on the agreement, that's what you're doing.'

'It makes sense for both of us. Although we'll be staying at Lake Tahoe while we're in the States, I do have a fundraiser to attend in New York in a couple of days. You'll no doubt want to be there, to get something for your profile, and if you *are* there, given this publicity, people are naturally going to ask about our engagement. It will be far less embarrassing to both of us if we maintain the image that we're engaged at least while we're to be seen together.'

'You mean maintain the deceit!' It was unthinkable. There was no way she could act like Alex's lover. It had been hard enough today. And what guarantee would she have that he wouldn't pull another stunt like that?' 'I won't do it. I've done what I agreed to do. It's time to hold up your end of the bargain.'

He shrugged. 'That's too bad. Because if you won't do it, you won't be getting your profile.'

Blood pumped so hot and fast through her veins that she could feel it in her temples. 'Damn you! I should have known never to trust you. Knowing what you did to my father, the ruthless way you took over his business and crushed him, I should have realised you'd do anything to twist things your own sick way.'

His expression soured. His glass hit the table, slopping amber liquid over the sides, but he didn't seem to notice. His eyes were fixed on hers, his face filled with fury.

'And your father was such a paragon of business virtue? Don't give me that. He deserved everything he got. He *deserved* to be crushed!'

She stood up, her heart thumping in her chest, her blood pounding, outraged for her father who'd been destroyed by a ruthless takeover, outraged for her father who was now so ill and defenceless.

'How dare you? It's not enough to ruin the man's life and future. Now you have to stick the boot in with insults. Well, I've had enough of you twisting things your way. You can keep your profile, along with your phoney engagement. I'm telling the story I want to tell. You won't have to look for it—it will be everywhere—and it won't be pretty.'

'And what story is this?'

He sat back, his limbs sprawled over the furniture as if he owned it. The resentment was still there, but it was contained. And there was something new she didn't like—a smugness that irritated her bone-deep.

She looked around, aware that she might be making a scene, thankful that even if the noise of their argument escaped from this room the lounge outside was almost deserted, apart from a few travellers sprinkled around, either plugged into earphones, laptops or mobile phones. Then she looked back at Alex. 'I'm going to tell the world what you did—the way you crushed my father, the way you made a fool out of me.'

He only smiled in response, angering her still more, sending her hands clenching into fists, her nails pressing deep into her flesh as she reached boiling point. Her hands itched to let fly. Oh, to wipe that self-satisfied smile right off his face...

'This is a business magazine?' he said at last. 'Your *AlphaBiz*?'

She kicked up her chin. 'That's what I've been trying to tell you.'

'Do you really think the squalid history of your affair with the man you just became engaged to is going to be the stuff for business pages?' He waited a second, watching her, waiting for his words to sink in before he continued. 'On the other hand, maybe you could try to sell it at *Snap!* magazine. I hear they're always in the market for sordid tales. Perhaps they could use it instead of the pages they've got earmarked for Marla or some other poor victim?'

'But we're not really eng...'

Cold, chilling waves washed over her as the cruel implications of what he'd done to her today sank home. She had no story. Nobody would believe her now. Not once they'd seen the pictures of Alex kissing her spread all over the media. Why would someone who'd suffered such a shocking experience line up to marry the perpetrator? She'd be a laughing stock—if it was ever printed at all.

He'd painted her into a corner.

She'd been prepared to walk away from the profile, to walk away from her chances of promotion and a better level of care for her father—but only if she could have Alex Koutoufides's head on a platter. But now she had no chance of retribution if she took that course.

Revenge would have almost been worth the cost of losing everything. But now, if she walked away from this profile, she wouldn't get a thing. No revenge. No settling of old scores for what he'd done to her father. No satisfaction.

And she'd be giving away all chance of getting that promotion and getting the kind of care her father needed.

'You engineered that whole engagement fiasco!'

He barely raised an eyebrow. 'Of course I did. Did you expect to be able to hold the threat of telling what happened in the past over me the entire time?'

She swallowed, trying desperately to think and knowing instinctively that bluff was her only hope right now.

'It doesn't change anything. I'll still show everyone what a calculating animal you are. I'll tell them the truth—that you engineered this engagement to cover Marla's tracks.'

'Who do you think,' Alex persisted, 'is going to believe you? Nobody will take you seriously. Nobody.'

'But what you did to me! I was only seventeen.'

'And yet, if it was such a terrible experience, why would you turn around and be prepared to marry the man who subjected you to this awful experience?'

'You bastard! This engagement is a farce.'

'But the world won't know that.'

'I'll tell them! I'll make them believe me.'

'And risk making yourself look even more of a victim? Everyone will assume we've had a lovers' tiff, and that for whatever reason you're feeling aggrieved and want to get your own back. I admit it will be embarrassing, but it will hardly ruin my career. Yours, on the other hand…'

He raised an eyebrow and casually crossed his legs, brushing off an invisible fleck of nothing. When still she didn't move he said, 'You look like you could do with that drink now. Why don't you sit down?'

'I hate you,' she whispered, her teeth clenched. But she recognised that she had no choice, knew that bluffing was pointless and that if she wanted to use this opportunity to get back at Alex Koutoufides she was going to have to come up with a new way. Because he had her.

She sat down, as he'd suggested, but that didn't mean she was through with telling him how she felt.

'I hate the way you treat people—using them for whatever sick purpose you have, bending them to what you need them to be. I hate the way you destroy people and their dreams without a second glance. I hate the way you think you own the world.'

Without expression he regarded the remaining contents of his glass before tossing it back in one economical slug. 'I think I preferred it when I was kissing you.'

She tried to ignore the swift, sudden zipper of sensation that wrenched up her spine. 'And what's that supposed to mean?'

'It's the only time you haven't been arguing with me.'

For a moment she was frozen into inaction. Of course the kiss hadn't meant anything to him—what the hell had she thought he was going to say anyway?

'In that case,' she snipped, 'remember it fondly. Because silence like that sure as hell won't be happening again.'

Saskia came to and jerked upright, her vague dreams of warmth and comfort dissolving as the black limousine slowed to a crawl and edged onto a driveway. She looked around her as the car idled, its driver waiting for electronic gates to open. Through them she could see tall straight pine trees, spearing into the clear blue sky, and a large stone residence rising behind.

'What is this place? Are we at Lake Tahoe already?'

'So you're finally awake?' he said behind her. 'You have no further need of my shoulder?'

She looked around in horror—was he joking? But the look on his face told her he wasn't. His position, so close, with his arm extended along the back of the seat behind her, told her that the comfortable support she'd felt for her head had been none other than the crook of his shoulder, and that the warmth she'd been dreaming about and relishing had been none other than the body warmth of the man she abhorred more than anyone in the world.

She must have fallen asleep some time on the two hundred miles of Interstate from San Francisco—although it was barely the middle of the day here, and the flight itself had been relaxing. Or would have been relaxing, she admitted, if it hadn't been for the dark cloud of Alex sitting alongside her, ignoring her for the most part, regarding her through guarded eyes for the rest.

And when they'd entered this car they'd sat as far as possible away from each other. Somewhere along the Interstate that had all changed.

'I fell asleep,' she said, immediately feeling a fool as she realised how unnecessary it had been to say that. And just as instantaneously she changed her mind. It had been necessary. He had to be made to know there was no chance she would have used him for support if she'd been conscious.

She looked out of the window to cover her discomfiture—nothing to do with forcing her eyes from his unshaven skin, the dark stubble adding another texture, another dimension to the chiselled character of his face.

'I realise that,' he said, as the car proceeded down the long driveway. 'Do you usually talk in your sleep?'

Her head snapped right back. She was afraid of the unknown, but damned sure she wasn't going to let him know it. 'So what did I say? How much I hate you?'

He shrugged a little, one corner of his mouth rising as he pulled his arm down from the back of the seat and adjusted his shirt. 'No, I don't recall that.'

'Maybe I was just getting to the good bit,' she snapped, refusing to be cowed.

'Maybe,' he said, as if he didn't believe her. 'Ah, here we are.'

The car came to a stop outside the impressive building. Stone, timber and glass combined to form a two-storey masterpiece. 'This will be your home for the next week.'

'I'm staying here?'

'More or less. I'm putting you in the guesthouse on the lake's edge. I thought you'd appreciate the privacy. It's self-contained, with its own study.'

The fact he'd given any consideration to what she might appreciate surprised her. Likewise his knowledge of the place. She'd assumed he'd rented the house as some kind of bolthole. 'This place is yours?'

'It's one of my properties, yes.'

She looked up at the imposing façade of the house. 'You sure don't do modest well, do you?'

'I've earned everything I have.'

'That's one way of looking at it, I guess.'

'That's the *only* way of looking at it.'

She swung her head back round to look at him, letting ice infuse her words so that he could in no way mistake her meaning. 'If it makes you feel better.'

His eyelids stalled halfway over his eyes. 'I'll let Gerard

drive you around. You can settle in, and I'll come and give you a guided tour of where you can and cannot go on the property in, say, two hours from now?'

She almost laughed. So much for his consideration of her needs. She wasn't being offered privacy; she was being locked down in her own quarters. 'You trust me by myself all that time? I must have come up in the world.'

Behind him the door swung open, as if the driver had instinctively known it was time. Cool high country air swept into the car, the fresh smell of woods and lake flushing out the strained atmosphere.

'Two hours,' he said, stepping out.

'I can hardly wait,' she answered, too low for him to hear as the car pulled away from the main house and continued down the driveway through the trees. As they turned a bend, her breath caught in her throat as the brilliant blue of Lake Tahoe, framed by still snow-capped mountains, extended for miles in all directions.

And there, nestled between trees on a small plot of land edged by boulders, sat what had to be the guesthouse. Like a miniature version of the main house, it featured natural stone, timber and glass set to take in the views that extended for the entire three hundred and sixty degrees around.

Without a word Gerard brought her luggage inside as she explored the cottage, and withdrew just as discreetly, stopping only to ask if she required anything more. If he was unused to installing women in the guesthouse, he certainly didn't show it. Although Alex's lady-friends were much more likely to be received in the main house, she decided. It was only untrustworthy visitors such as she obviously was who would have to be locked away in the far corner of the property.

Though what a corner to be stuck in, she thought, as she

completed her exploration of the two-bedroom, two-bathroom cottage, complete with study and, she acknowledged, as her eyes fell thankfully on the communication facilities, a telephone and even internet capability. Perfect to get this profile done as quickly as possible and let her get out of here. And perfect for the calls she should make to home.

Alex had been right about one thing—she did appreciate the privacy. Even if his motives for stashing her here were entirely selfish.

An hour later, showered and changed into fresh clothes, and ready with a portfolio of her best profiles she wanted to show Alex when he arrived, she hung up the phone after her first call, tears in her eyes. Her father had barely been able to talk—the result of a viral infection, his visiting nurse had told her. Although thankfully she believed he was on the mend.

But damn his cold, damp flat! No way should he have to put up with that any longer—she was going to pull out all the stops to see that she made this promotion, and that her father got the care he so badly needed. If only he hadn't been so stubborn about not moving with her into her own tiny flat and cramping her style years ago—maybe she could have prevented all this.

She swiped back her tears and collected her thoughts, preparing herself for her next call, expecting it to be only marginally easier than her first. She heard the extension being picked up an entire country and an ocean away.

'Sir Rodney—'

'Saskia!' His voice was gruff and urgent. 'You're in all the papers! The Board want to know what the Dickens is going on. I told them you didn't get along with Alexander Koutoufides, like you told me, trying to get you a bit of sympathy here. But now all of a sudden you've not only managed to track him down, you've obviously got him eating out of your hand. What are you playing at?'

'Sir Rodney, listen to me. It's not what you think—'

'It's utter madness, that's what I think. I was expecting a profile. Instead we'll be lucky to end up with a wedding invitation. After all the protests you put up about taking on the assignment, you're not doing yourself any favours with the board for this promotion, you understand.'

'Please listen. Alex Koutoufides and I are *not* engaged.'

'What on earth were you thinking? I thought you *wanted* this promotion. What's that? What did you say?'

'I said we're not really engaged. It's all a sham.'

'But the papers all said…'

'You know newspapers,' Saskia replied, irony heavy in her voice. 'Never believe everything you read.'

'Then what's going on?'

'It's a long story,' she said. *And much too painful to relate right now.* 'But I just want you to know that I'm working on the profile and you'll have it on your desk as soon as possible, as agreed.'

'Just as well. Because you know what's at stake if you don't. Carmen's already managed the impossible, and has convinced Drago Maiolo to allow her to do his profile, so you've got a race on your hands if you really do want this job.'

Saskia tried to absorb the news about Carmen's progress philosophically. Carmen's assignment was bound to be less problematic, without the complications of a history angle to work through. Still, she'd hoped for more of an advantage in getting Alex's co-operation—co-operation that now seemed suspiciously weighted his way.

'I do want that job,' she said.

'Then I'm sure I don't have to tell you how important this assignment is to both of you,' the chairman continued. 'Only one of you can get this promotion. I want you to put everything you can into it—anything that might give you an edge over Carmen. Maybe you can use this strange arrangement of yours to your advantage. Do you think this so-called engagement might give you a different perspective? Something you might be able to exploit?'

'No,' she stated emphatically. 'The engagement won't cut it because there *is* no engagement. It won't be referred to in the article. And as far as I'm concerned the sooner it's forgotten, the better.'

'Then what about the Marla angle? Is there anything there worth pursuing, do you think? What is their relationship? What's it like to be a corporate hotshot with an aging wild-child sister? Is he afraid her bad press will impact on his business? The board want you to find out. There's *something* there, given that he kept the relationship quiet for so long.'

She sighed. 'I'm not sure about that line of attack, Sir Rodney. I've met Marla, and she still seems fragile from that awful *Snap!* feature. And I don't even know where she is at the moment. Alex has done everything he can to keep me away from her.'

'Well, you know the situation there. But you really have to pull out all stops with this one. Carmen's after this job, and it looks like she's off and running. If you can capture both Marla and Alex in your profile, you might just get the edge.'

Saskia gritted her teeth and looked up at the ceiling while she considered her response. Damn this sink-or-swim selection process! Sinking wasn't an option any more. Not now she wouldn't be able to take Alex down with her. She needed to swim if she was to secure this promotion—and fast.

But damn it all that she'd drawn the short straw and been assigned Alex Koutoufides! Especially now, if the board was looking to interfere with the way she worked.

She drew in a breath, not liking what she was hearing. 'Are you telling me that's what the board wants in this profile—the Marla angle played up? Because I'm telling you Alex isn't keen—he's put up barriers the whole time.'

'Who's doing this profile?' Sir Rodney demanded. 'You or Alex Koutoufides? If you expect to become editor-in-chief, don't think you're going to get away from making the tough choices and doing the tough asks.'

It wasn't the way she was used to working, and she wasn't about to start now. Not that she was going to discuss that with Sir Rodney when he was already annoyed with her over this whole engagement fiasco. But somehow she was going to have to find a way, find an angle, to make this profile the best she possibly could without compromising her own integrity and still giving her the edge over Carmen.

'I understand,' she said. 'And don't worry. I'll do it. I'll get you the best profile you and the board have ever seen.'

'I'm counting on it!' he grunted, before hanging up.

She put the phone down, her mind still reeling from the last few days' developments, her senses still torn with concern over her father's sudden deterioration, and yet still too sluggish from changing too many time zones too quickly to know how to deal with it all.

If only there was some straightforward way out of this mess!

But she was kidding herself if she thought there was an easy way out. Alex's ridiculous engagement sham had killed her escape route dead. Now there was no way out but to go forward. He'd made sure she had no choice but to do the profile. And now, with Sir Rodney's words about Carmen's progress, she would have to make it better than ever. But there was no way she was going to stoop to using Marla as bait. This profile was about Alex Koutoufides, it had always been about Alex. And that was what she was going to get.

Saskia heard a noise behind her. She turned and saw the man who'd been occupying her thoughts standing in the doorway to the office, his face like thunder, his stance battle-ready. Her stomach plummeted. How long had he been standing there?

And how much had he heard?

CHAPTER FIVE

'YOU lying bitch!' He watched her take one guilty step towards him.

'Alex—'

'You liar,' he said, cutting her protest off, the blood in his veins surging and simmering into a crazy red foam that coloured his vision and crashed in his ears. 'All that garbage about wanting to interview me. All that rubbish about not being interested in Marla. Lies! All of it *lies*!'

'Alex, listen to me—' She took another step, but stopped dead when he started surging towards her.

'I knew it,' he jeered, coming to a stop right in front of her, so close that she had to crane her neck to look up at him. 'I knew you couldn't go on too long without showing what you were really made of. In spite of all your cries of innocence I knew what you were really after.'

'But it's not like that, I promise—'

'Is it any wonder I didn't want you talking to Marla?' he demanded, his index finger pointing damnably into her shoulder. 'You've obviously got the entire article scoped with—who was that?—your boss?'

'This profile is about you. Not Marla.'

'That wasn't your boss?'

She took a step back, then another, backing herself against the timber desk, swaying away from him as he followed her every move.

'It doesn't matter if it was, you have to understand—'

'Oh, don't worry.' He shook his head, the smile on his lips nowhere near reaching his eyes. 'I understand. I understand perfectly. You'll get this profile you agreed to. You're not sure how you'll get access to her, but you'll play the Marla angle up and you'll hand in the best profile ever. Isn't that what you promised?'

'Well, yes. But—'

'But nothing! You've lied from the start. You knew I'd never agree to let you interview Marla. So you thought that if you pretended to be interested in profiling *me* you'd get close enough to get the dirt on Marla. And you might have succeeded. It was a new angle. Nobody had tried getting to Marla via me before. And in spite of all my doubts, in spite of everything that warned me you were lying, I let you into my own home. I let you get close to Marla. And in spite of my trusting you, you let me down.'

'You never trusted me! Right from the start you've treated me like a cheat and a liar.'

He planted an arm either side of her on the desk, enjoying her desperation at her inability to shrink away from him any further.

'And is it any wonder?'

'What? Stop trying to take the higher moral ground, and stop pretending you let me into your home out of the goodness of your heart. You *never* trusted me. You only invited me into your house because you were too scared of what I was going to tell the world if you slammed the door in my face and afraid of what would happen to your business if you didn't!'

Her eyes were sparking green flame, her cheeks flushed, her

chest rising and falling rapidly, but all that mattered right now were those lips. Either fully animated and going at a hundred miles an hour, or lush and pink and warm when they finally stopped. *And he knew exactly how they felt when they did.*

'You're right,' he said.

She blinked. 'What?'

He scanned her face, watching her indignation turn to surprise, her eyes widening, her lips parting slightly, hesitant, uncertain...*waiting.*

He breathed in deep, inhaling the scent of her—a heady mix of one woman's clean individual smell enhanced with some fragrant lotion and all heightened by potent anger, *heightened by passion*—and he felt his own senses respond. He knew that scent. She'd drifted asleep in the car, her head lolling to the side, and he'd moved closer and thrown around his arm to support her. Only to have her nestle into his chest, fitting him as if she was made for it. So soft and trusting. So accepting. So different from how she was normally.

They'd stayed that way for at least an hour, her curves wedged tight and warm against him, her head tucked into the crook of his arm. And when she'd murmured something in her sleep, something indiscernible, he'd turned his face down to hers, thinking at first that she was stirring, and had felt her warm breath brush against his face, her lips so close, her scent so inviting, her body so warm and supple... But she'd still been asleep, her breath a warm promise against his skin, and as for those lips...

Right now he lifted one hand, unable to resist any longer, touching the pads of his fingers to the twin layers of their sculpted perfection.

'I said, you're right. I didn't want you to go public on what you knew.'

Her eyes dipped in one long blink, remaining still while he traced his fingers over the line of her lips, only the telltale flickering of the pulse in her throat betraying her nervousness.

'I didn't want you to go public on what happened between us.'

Her eyes opened and she swallowed, her lips moving under his fingers as the action in her muscles kicked up her chin. 'And now you've seen to it that I can't.' Her voice came across as rough and husky. *Sex with an edge*, he determined with some satisfaction.

He allowed himself a smile as he let his fingers drift lower, following the line of her jaw down to her throat, tracing the back of his hand down over the scoop neck of her knitted top. She shuddered under his touch, but she didn't pull away and neither did she lower her eyes.

'So I have,' he agreed, aware that his own voice had dropped an octave. 'So where does that leave us now?'

Her eyes were wide, the colour of emeralds sparkling back at him.

'It leaves me stuck here with you—trying for a different story entirely.'

'So maybe…' he ventured softly, '…maybe I should help you out with one.'

His eyes were dark seduction, his lips an invitation to desire. And when they touched hers barely, hardly at all, with just the lightest of touches, a switch flicked on inside her that sent her internal thermostat whirling and turned heated anger into a long, slow burn. She shuddered as his lips moved over hers, surprisingly tender, gently coaxing, achingly sweet, and her own lips could not help but accept his invitation.

So different from that kiss in the airport. That had been squeezed from her, stolen, wrenched from her like some trophy.

This kiss was like a dance set to the music of her beating heart, the rhythm slow and magical, mesmerising, evocative.

She felt one hand slide behind her neck, supporting her head as he deepened the kiss, his warm breath blending with his taste, his lips, his tongue seeking entry, gently probing, coupling with hers.

And it was, if the crust of the previous years had cracked and fallen away. It was like coming home. Because she recognised his taste, she recognised his touch. She let her hands do what they wanted, let them skim over his back, reacquainting themselves with familiar territory while his hands did the same, his touch so well-remembered, so cherished, so long missed. She didn't protest when he hoisted her up the short distance onto the desk. She made no sound other than to gasp when he cupped one breast with his hand and rolled one straining nipple between his fingers. She welcomed the way he found his way under her top so that she could feel his hand on her breast without barrier, his skin on hers. Compelling. Undeniable. Electric.

Was it minutes she felt him at her breasts? Or only seconds? Time expanded, each second filled with sensations too many to catalogue, too delicious to bother.

And then his hand was on her leg, shrugging away her skirt, sliding ever upwards, searing a path along skin to the place that wanted him, needed him, ached for him.

And when, like a replay of how his kiss had started, light and gentle and barely there, he touched her, she wanted to cry out with the bittersweet joy of it all. How many times had she dreamed this dream? Finding Alex the way he'd been, so caring and thoughtful and loving?

How many times had she longed for a repeat of just this special touch?

And now her dream had become reality.

This was the Alex she'd known. This was the way he'd made her feel. This was the Alex she loved.

No!

Her eyes snapped open.

Not loved.

Had loved.

This was the Alex who'd betrayed her.

This was the Alex she hated!

And yet she was letting him do this to her! His mouth was on her throat, hot open-mouthed kisses burning her skin, his hand pushing aside her panties, seeking entry…

She pushed hard at his shoulders. 'Alex. No.'

'Oh, yes,' he murmured, barely taking his mouth from her flesh.

She pressed her legs together, trying to stop him. 'No! Stop this.'

He levered his head away far enough to look her in the eyes, but he didn't remove his hand, continuing to gently stroke her in spite of the pressure of her thighs around him, continuing to find the sensitive nub of her femininity, issuing a challenge that he made it hard to overcome.

'Give me one good reason why I should.'

'Because I *hate* you.'

He allowed himself a smile. 'I figured as much. I could tell that by the way you groan every time I do this.' The pad of his thumb circled her, sending sensations shuddering through her, the barrier of her silk underwear no protection. She raised her eyes to the ceiling and dragged in a breath that was too full of the taste of him to fight. '*Now* tell me you want me to stop,' he dared.

'I—want—you—to…' The next word was nothing but a blur.

'I'm not convinced,' he replied with a low laugh, his fingers testing the lace edging of her panties, creeping beneath, undermining her resolve in the most potent way imaginable.

But she couldn't let him. Not now. Not ever. And breathlessly she battled to bring back all the reasons why.

'No,' she breathed, desperate. 'You have to stop.'

'Really? And why would that be?'

'You mean you've forgotten?' she taunted, with a shove at his shoulders, clutching onto the one thing she remembered so vividly from those days gone by. 'Because you "don't *do* virgins"!'

Alex drew back, allowing her enough room to escape from the desk and his confines to straighten her skirt and top, those words of hers jarring in his memory.

He'd told her that, he remembered. Was she still so resentful that he hadn't finished off what he'd started back then that she'd throw his words back in his face like that?

'So is this your idea of payback? Replaying a scene from years ago so it's you that has the upper hand this time?'

Saskia looked blankly at him, her empty stare frustrating him.

'Oh, come on. There has to be some reason why you'd pull a stunt like that. I mean, you're what? Twenty-five or twenty-six. It's not as if you could still be a virgin.'

She turned her face away. Too fast. But not before he'd seen the honest truth slice across her eyes, the hurt…

'Oh, my God,' he said, surprise fuelling an irrational burst of laughter. 'Who would have thought it? You *are*.'

'Don't make me sound like some kind of freak!'

Her voice fractured on the last word and she spun, her arms crossed, towards the wall. He took a step closer. 'I don't think you're a freak. I'm just surprised.' Very surprised, he thought, given her age and the kind of work she did and the people she'd mix with. It didn't seem the kind of work where you'd keep anything intact for too long, whether it was ethics, integrity or virginity.

But, notwithstanding her occupation, he was more surprised that someone as stunning as she was hadn't been seduced plenty of times, let alone once. Surprised and somewhat strangely, given the circumstances, even a bit pleased.

'Saskia?' he said, reaching out a hand to her shoulder.

'Don't touch me!'

She spun around to face him, her green eyes almost too large for her face, her lashes dark with moisture. But she was still coming out fighting.

'What kind of man are you? One moment you're accusing me of lying to you, of being here to drag Marla's name through the papers, and the next you've got me sprawled on the desk, pawing at me like you're some kind of animal.'

Her words sat uncomfortably with him, rankled with him. He didn't understand it either, but he sure as hell wasn't going to admit it.

'You're tired,' he said. 'Tired and emotional. Let's leave the guided tour until tomorrow. Maybe you should take a nap, and I'll have someone bring you dinner from the house a bit later.'

'Don't patronise me,' she spat. 'And don't bother with a meal. I don't want anything from you beyond one business profile. Nothing more.'

He felt a muscle in his jaw pop. 'A little while ago it was clear you wanted much more than that.'

She had the grace to colour at that. 'A little while ago I wasn't thinking. What's *your* excuse?'

* * *

Tahoe usually relaxed him. Even when he was working in his state-of-the-art office the lake and the woods and even the winter snows calmed him. It was a haven from Sydney and the office, but it was also a place from which he could rule his empire away from the day-to-day distractions of office life. It was supposed to relax him. That was the theory.

But he didn't have to look in a mirror right now to know that he was scowling as he walked back along the path to the house. Damn her. And damn his body's reaction. Though who could blame it? She'd been willing. So what was that she'd said about not thinking at the time? Hell, how much thinking was involved in knowing you wanted someone? It wasn't *University Challenge*.

What was it about her that made him want to forget why he shouldn't touch her—and why he shouldn't want to?

The portfolio she'd thrust into his hands before he'd departed slapped against his leg. He lifted it, regarding its burgundy cover critically. Did she really think a collection of her pieces was going to make a difference to anything now? Not a chance.

The morning was crystal clear, the air so chilled from both the elevation and the remnants of the season's snow that her breath turned to fog as she walked along the boulder-strewn shoreline. Saskia hugged her jacket closer around her and wandered out along the timber pier built into the water.

It was early, not long after dawn, but she hadn't been able to stay in bed. Her body clock was out of whack. Before her the lake stretched miles in every direction, the surface of the water almost polished smooth. Two ducks glided effortlessly across the small bay, their wake the only disturbance to the mirror-like finish of the water.

It was beautiful here. The water so clear she could see the rock-strewn sand below, the air so clean it hurt. If it wasn't for Alex she might almost imagine enjoying her stay.

'You're up early.'

She jumped and spun around. A woman stood on the shore, watching her, her hands deeply buried in her jacket pockets, her face framed with the fluffy fur lining of her hood. But she still recognised her immediately.

'Marla. I didn't hear anyone coming.'

The woman walked towards her, her fancy pink western boots clomping as she sashayed up onto the wooden deck. She stood alongside Saskia, took a deep breath and looked around. 'I just love it here,' she said, smiling. 'It's my favourite place in the world.'

'I didn't realise you were staying here.'

'I wasn't supposed to be. Alex had me booked into a clinic nearby, but I refused point-blank to go. I can't stand the kind of people they get in those places. Desperate movie stars, failed musicians—the whole nip and tuck set. *Ugh*. Don't get me wrong—I know I'm far from perfect, and I like a margarita just as much as the next girl—well...' She smiled conspiratorially and a little sadly and conceded, '...maybe just a tad more. But I know that if anyone makes me go to group therapy one more time I'm going to throw up.'

Saskia laughed for the first time in what seemed like for ever, and then looked over her shoulder self-consciously to where the house loomed up on one side. Could anyone see them down here?

'I'm not supposed to have anything to do with you, you know.'

'I know. Alex told me the same thing.' She pulled a manicured hand from a pocket and placed it on Saskia's, her eyes as brilliant a blue as the ice-cold depths of the lake. 'But I get so tired of being told what to do. Don't you?'

Oh, yes, she thought with a vengeance. But I need this profile. Otherwise things might be different.

'He doesn't trust me,' she told Marla by way of explanation. 'He thinks I want to do some sort of exposé on you.'

Marla laughed, throwing her head up high, and putting her hand back in her pocket. 'My brother is the consummate Mediterranean man—even though our mother was a true-blue Australian. He takes after his father and he doesn't trust anyone, let alone anyone from the press. I have to say I've given him fairly good cause to be wary over the past few years. He's probably entitled to a little paranoia.'

'So you're not worried I'm here to get the scoop on you?'

Marla shook her head. 'If you really wanted to interview me I figure you would have found a way before now. I'll risk it. Besides, I wanted to thank you.'

'Whatever for? Helping you get through the airport?'

'Partly. You don't know what a drag it is not to be able to move without cameras being stuck in your face.'

Saskia grimaced, remembering the melee at the airport. 'Oh, I think I have some idea. I'd hate it, I know.'

'But I really wanted to say thanks for whatever it is you're doing to Alex. You've really got under his skin—I expected more of a fight last night over my refusing to go to the clinic, but it's like he's lost focus. For once he's not permanently on my case. Thanks for taking the heat off me for a while.'

Saskia studied the almost perfect reflection of the trees and the mountains in the lake while she mulled over Marla's words. Alex certainly hadn't lacked any focus yesterday when he'd come on to her. Quite the contrary.

'You know he's told the press we're engaged?'

'Oh, God, I know. It's even made it into the papers here. Haven't you seen? I can get some papers sent over to the guesthouse.'

'Thanks all the same,' Saskia replied. 'But I really don't think I want to see them.'

They stood together at the end of the small pier, silently watching the sun lift over the mountains on the eastern side of the lake, until finally Marla sighed. 'I'd better get back before Jake returns from the gym, notices me missing and puts out an APB. That man really is driving me crazy. Will I see you tomorrow morning, before you leave for New York?'

It took a moment for Saskia to make the connection.

'Oh, you mean the fundraiser? Alex mentioned something before our flight here.' She shook her head. 'But I don't know any of the details.'

'He's taking you to show off as his new fiancée—another exercise in calling the press dogs off me. He's determined to take his brotherly obligations seriously, it seems. I guess I ask for it. It must be a real drag having a middle-aged sister who's totally unemployable and who's got no talent other than to get herself photographed in the most embarrassing predicaments with the worst guys she possibly could.'

'Oh, come on. You're too hard on yourself.'

Marla raised her perfectly sculpted eyebrows, but the ironic smile on her face looked genuine enough.

'Thanks. You're sweet, but I'm not too stupid to realise my own failings. Even though the press like to make more of them than they really are.' She looked up sharply. 'Oh, I didn't mean you.'

'I know,' Saskia conceded with a smile, surprised to find she liked Alex's sister so much. She hadn't expected to. With her bad press, and with her brother's rabid defence of her, she hadn't known what to expect.

'I really have to go, but I'll look out for you here tomorrow morning. It's so nice to have another woman to talk to for a change. And, Saskia?'

'Yes?'

'Do you think you could do a favour for me?'

'Sure.' She shrugged. 'If I can. What is it?'

Marla hesitated, her smile sheepish. 'Do you know anything about publishing—I mean book publishing?'

Saskia surveyed the woman suspiciously. 'Well, a little. I did do one writing unit in my business degree and I've got some connections in the industry. Why?'

The older woman had a hopeful expression. 'A friend of mine wrote down some stories—sort of snippets of her life in anecdotes, nothing fancy. I read it, but I really don't know if it's any good. Do you think you could look it over for her? Maybe even pass it on to someone if it's any good?'

Saskia didn't flinch, even though every cell was on red alert. 'For your *friend*?'

Marla nodded, her blue eyes large and pleading. 'She'd really appreciate it. Please? I'll bring it tomorrow morning, same time, if that's okay?'

'I'm not sure,' Saskia offered in response, not falling for that 'friend' story for an instant. 'I don't think Alex would like it.'

'Please?' Marla implored. 'It's so important to her. And he doesn't have to find out. It'll be our little secret. And it would make my friend so happy.'

She looked so hopeful, almost desperate, and Saskia felt for her. It couldn't be easy being Alex's sister, despite her wealth and creature comforts.

'Of course I will,' she relented, watching the other woman's expression turn to delight even while knowing she must be mad to even consider it. Whatever that book contained, it could be pure dynamite in the wrong hands. If Alex so much as got wind of what she was doing she'd be dead meat.

Which meant she'd just have to make sure he didn't.

CHAPTER SIX

ALEX KOUTOUFIDES was not in a good mood. He couldn't blame it on the weather—at thirty-five thousand feet above the clouds the sun shone in a perfect azure sky as the private jet tracked to New York City. And for once he couldn't blame it on Marla. This morning she'd seemed happier than she had in years, her eyes bright and her smile infectious despite being 'locked away', as she put it, with her jailer, Jake. He couldn't even blame it on the fact he had to attend tonight's fundraiser. In the last few years he'd shunned all but the most select invitations to such events, but even the fact he was going to this one wasn't the reason for his deep-seated irritation.

No, the reason he felt so damned uncomfortable had much more to do with a certain file of articles he'd read last night.

He hadn't meant to read them. His intention had been to flick through and find enough evidence to support his prejudices before tossing the portfolio away, satisfied.

But that hadn't happened. His dismissive flick through had become hijacked by the very first article—a profile on Ralph Schneider, a senior member of the board of the World Bank, a man Alex had met on several occasions, and his interest had been piqued. Instead of finding the lightweight fluff he'd expected, he'd found the article in-depth and well researched, business information and facts balanced with a personal take on the man's character that Alex had found himself agreeing with. Somehow she'd meshed those different worlds to build a picture of a giant in business circles—a giant with a heart, and a giant you could trust to do business with.

But then he'd thought maybe Ralph had been an easy target? He was one of the business world's good guys, after all. He'd turned the page to the next profile—this time a billionaire UK property developer with a reputation for big talk and bigger buildings, and with almost celebrity status for his well-publicised charitable donations. Alex's attention had been riveted. He'd had dealings with a branch of this man's conglomerate back in Sydney, and there was no way he'd ever deal with any of his businesses again, after they'd cut corners on the contract and not delivered to specifications. Here was a man who would have tested her powers of perception.

But again Saskia's reporting of his business empire had been excellent, her coverage of the time she'd spent in his offices fascinating—and as for her profile of the man himself? Outwardly generous, she'd acknowledged, but, for all his popular media persona, definitely not a man to be messed with, and perhaps even one with whom to ensure more than ever that contracts were watertight.

It was a brilliant piece of journalism. There was enough in the article to make the property star feel good about himself, but there was plenty of subtext to make anyone dealing with him wary and cautious.

Alex had devoured the balance of the profiles, trying to find fault or a hint of gossip, but even while Saskia had taken measure of her profilees, she'd not touched on their personal lives. If they had mistresses—and he knew at least three of them who were so-called 'happily married' did—there was no mention of it. There was no mention of rumours of sexual preference, no hint of scandal. It was all extremely well researched and balanced.

In the end he'd flung the file away out of sheer frustration.

No wonder he felt sick. He'd accused her of wanting to get close to Marla. Time and time again she'd denied it, and still he hadn't quite believed her. But if the articles in that file were indicative of the kind of profile she intended to do on him, then he'd completely misjudged her from the start.

Theos!

He stole a look at her in the armchair alongside. Her eyes were glued to the window now, although she'd been busy for most of the flight, writing notes, or drafts, or whatever it was she was doing. What would she write about *him*? What would her profile say about *his* character after the way he'd treated her? It was hardly likely to be flattering. Would she stick to business, or would she be tempted to tell it how it really had been? A man who had promised her everything but delivered nothing? A man who had taken advantage and then taken nothing, and in doing so had left humiliation into the bargain? It was hardly the kind of analysis he wanted out there.

He'd rather not think about that right now.

Soon they'd be landing at JFK. Once this weekend was out the way and they were back in Tahoe he'd give her all the time she needed to get her profile done. And then she could go home, back to her life. Leave him to his. Let him get back to the way he liked to live.

But first they'd make tonight convincing. So what that Saskia wasn't interested in Marla's story? Plenty of others were, and the longer he could distract them, the more likely they were to let her go. He felt in his pocket for the object he'd removed from his safe earlier. He could put the profile off for a couple of days, but some things couldn't wait.

'Here—put this on.'

Reluctantly Saskia peeled her eyes from the window and the view of New York City coming into sight as the privately leased jet banked for its landing approach. They'd barely spoken on the way to the airport and through the flight—Alex seemingly locked up in his own thoughts. And if his mood was as dark as the glower on his face, she was glad he wasn't in the mood for conversation.

'What's that?' she asked as she turned, certain she couldn't have heard him properly. Then her eyes registered what he was holding and she plastered herself back against her wide armchair. 'Oh, no,' she said. 'I don't want it.'

'I'm not asking you,' he said impatiently, lifting the offending article towards her as if he was as keen to get rid of it as she was reluctant to take it. 'I'm telling you. You need to put this on. People will expect it.' She was still shaking her head as he continued, 'It'll be the first thing they'll expect to see.'

He was right. She knew it instinctively. But that didn't make the concept any more palatable. Pretending to be engaged to Alex Koutoufides was one thing. Wearing his ring, a concrete symbol of the promise they were supposed to have made to each other, of the vows they would make if this engagement had been anything other than a farce, was another.

Concrete nothing, she thought with derision. Concrete didn't flash and sparkle like these gems did. These diamonds would scream that she belonged to Alex Koutoufides—lock, stock and barrel.

'You don't like it?'

What was not to like? Its design was as masterful as it was spectacular. A large square cut diamond sat atop a two-tone band already filled to overflowing with a river of baguette-cut diamonds, flashing light and colour from hundreds of brilliant-cut faces.

'Does it matter what I think?' she snapped, knowing there was no point getting attached to it anyway. It wasn't as if it was hers to keep.

'No,' he conceded brusquely, his mood obviously not having improved recently. He reached for her hand before she could snatch it away. 'Not in the least.'

She swallowed as he took her hand in his, their palms brushing, his long fingers cradling her wrist. Why was it that just touching him set her temperature rocketing and jolted her heartbeat into double time? Or was she merely remembering the last time he'd touched her—and where he'd touched her—with those hands?

She must be shaking. His fingers suddenly gripped her wrist more securely. Could he feel her erratic pulse with his fingers? Could he tell how frantically her heart was beating right now?

With his right hand he slipped the ring on, gliding the gold and platinum band along her finger until it came to rest—an almost perfect fit. For a second he didn't move, just cupped her hand in his while in between them the ring sparkled and flashed, mocking them both with white fire.

'There,' he said at last, as if that solved everything. He let her go and sat back in his chair, his eyes closed while the plane made its final approach.

She lifted her hand, feeling the unfamiliar weight of the ring. 'How did you know?'

'Know what?' he asked, without opening his eyes or looking at her.

'What size ring to get.'

'I didn't,' he responded, almost as if he were bored. 'It was my mother's.'

Something squeezed tight in her chest. This was *wrong*! This was no quick purchase made on ebay. This was a family heirloom—an heirloom she had no right to be wearing.

'You can't expect me to wear this. Not your mother's!' She made to pull off the ring, but just as quickly he swung himself around and imprisoned both her hands in his.

'You will wear it. It's the ring she wanted me to give to my fiancée.'

'But I'm not—'

He moved closer, putting himself right in her face. 'When we're in public you are. It's expected of you. You might as well start acting like it.'

She tugged her hands out from under his. 'Fine. I can play the lovestruck fiancée. But let's not have a repeat of what happened at the airport. Pretending to be engaged doesn't mean you get to paw me in public.'

He glared at her, his charcoal eyes narrowing. 'If we're going to convince people that we're soon to become a happily married couple I'll do whatever it takes, and you *will* co-operate.'

The small jet bumped its way onto the tarmac and the engines screamed into reverse thrust. She knew just how they felt—having their efforts changed at the whim of someone who cared nothing but demanded all his machinery performed to his will. She felt like screaming too. But she was no machine. She deserved better than this constant frustration.

'I hope you're going to allocate me some time soon, to really get started on this profile. You've already wasted hours on today's flight, when you could have dealt with some questions I need answers for.'

He drew in a breath and let it out slowly. 'Where's the fire?'

Right now, it's boiling my blood! 'The sooner I get this profile done, the sooner I can get out of your hair and the sooner we can abandon this farce of an engagement you dreamed up. Surely that's what you want? But you've done nothing to help me yet.'

'I don't want to fight. Why can't you just enjoy a fun weekend in New York?'

'Fun? Pretending to be your floozy?' Saskia laughed, a laugh born out of frustration. 'I don't even know why you're persisting with this trip. I can't see that Marla is under any particular threat that you need to save her from, and our engagement story is old news by now. What are you even doing here? I can't imagine why they even invited you. I would have thought a fundraiser in New York was the last thing a known recluse would head for.'

'It is,' Alex agreed through gritted teeth, his indigestion getting worse by the minute as the plane came to a halt on the tarmac. 'Which is why it's so charming to have your delightful company.'

Saskia couldn't help but gasp as they entered the Starlight Roof of the Waldorf-Astoria hotel. If the grand marble rotunda in the entry foyer hadn't been impressive enough, the sight of the spacious art deco ballroom filled with tuxedo-clad men and stunningly dressed women stole her breath away. She'd been places in her career, accompanied businessmen and politicians while they went about their business in all manner of occasions and venues, but nothing compared to the rich opulence of this venue, with its two-storey-high windows framed by damask silks, its gilded ceiling and magnificent Austrian crystal chandeliers.

She gave up a silent prayer of thanks for giving in when

Alex had insisted on providing her with a gown for the evening. He'd already pressed upon her a closet full of clothes for their US trip, and she'd chosen from it a cobalt-blue silk pantsuit to wear—classy, but restrained, she'd thought. But this gown he'd had delivered to her room that afternoon, together with a tiara and a note that this was what she would wear for the evening.

The flash of rebellion she'd felt when she received the message had been short-lived once she'd taken a decent look at the over-the-top golden Oscar de la Renta silk taffeta gown and the diamanté studded tiara with it. Until then the cobalt silk suit had been the most gorgeous thing she'd ever seen. Now, looking around the ballroom, she knew that it wouldn't have cut the mustard. Not in this crowd.

It was sheer fantasy. A long, long time ago this would have been her deepest wish—to be seen in a dress such as this, on Alex's arm and wearing his engagement ring.

It was strange. She couldn't wait to get this profile done. She couldn't wait to get away from Alex Koutoufides and go home. But just for tonight she felt like royalty. Tonight she was a princess. And tonight she was here with the most handsome man in the room.

Why not enjoy it?

Alex tugged at her arm, wanting to get their entrance over. He hated events like this, though strangely for once he didn't feel so out of place. With Saskia on his arm, looking a million bucks in the gown he'd chosen from the shortlist Marla had come up with, for the first time since he'd begun attending the annual Baxter Foundation Ball he didn't feel the urge to leave within the first ten minutes. With Saskia to show off, he might even make it to twenty.

Cameras flashed in their faces, increasingly more so as

the reporters realised who they had in their sights. 'Mr Koutoufides,' someone called excitedly, trying to get his attention. 'Have you two set a date yet?'

Alex looked down at his partner who, surprisingly, instead of having to be reminded of her duty, he found beaming up at him, her green eyes sparking happiness and her lush lips turned into such a beautiful smile it completely blindsided him. Her hair was arranged Grecian goddess-style, topped with a tiara, leaving tendrils coiling around her face that he itched to wrap his fingers around to reel her face closer to his lips. If she kept playing the role as well as this he wouldn't make twenty minutes after all—he'd have her out of here and planted in his bed in under five.

As if sensing his hesitation, she placed a hand over his own—the hand bearing the ring he'd given her earlier—and the cameras took no time in focusing in on it as it sparkled and flashed in their lenses.

'As far as I'm concerned,' he said, feeling his own smile broaden, 'the sooner the better.'

Her eyes widened, her smile wavered, but she kept looking up into his eyes in that way she had, as if they were digging into his very soul, until he wondered once again if he hadn't done the very worst thing he possibly could by insisting she accompany him tonight.

And then the music started, and inspiration wiped out any regrets. Why bother thinking about the mistakes he'd made? Why think about who she was and what her father had done? Why bother beating himself up over things he couldn't change, things that could never be repaired, when instead he could simply take this woman into his arms and hold her close?

'Dance with me,' he said, taking her hand, already leading her to the dance floor. And silently she acquiesced, letting him lead her, letting him fold her into his arms as he drew her close and started moving to the music of the ten-piece orchestra.

She found her space in his arms as if it had been made for her, moulding to his body, moving with him like liquid warmth, and yet still turning him rock-hard.

He inhaled her scent, devoured it, letting it feed into his senses like a drug. Class and sweetness and lush, ripe woman combining in one package to make the ultimate aphrodisiac.

That number ended, the next began, and even the next after that. But still he didn't relinquish her. He kept her wrapped in the circle of his arms, drawing her even closer with every movement, until they were so close she rested her head at his neck. Their bodies were pressed together from head to toe, moving to the beat, moving with each other, until they were moving more to the primitive rhythm of their own bodies than the music of the orchestra.

Saskia didn't want it to end. She was barely conscious of the changes in the music, hardly registered when one number merged into the next, and then the next. If this was pretending to be Alex's fiancée, she'd volunteer for the job permanently. No pressure, no arguments, just the magic feeling of her body pressed up against his, the tang of his masculine scent winding its way through her, the feel of his arms around her, his hands on her—possessive, commanding, intoxicating.

The way he used to feel.

She could stay this way all night if he wanted…

'Saskia Prentice! I don't believe it.'

The familiar cultured girls' school tones knifed into her consciousness. She unpeeled herself from Alex in an instant, breathless and gasping, feeling the heat from every part of her body transfer to her exposed flesh.

'It *is* you! Wow, don't you look sensational?'

Saskia reluctantly blinked the last of her dreams away and plastered a smile to a face so obviously burning with embarrassment that not even the subtle lighting over the dance floor could save her.

'Carmen.' Quickly she recovered enough from her embarrassment to make the introductions. 'I didn't expect to see you here.'

Carmen smiled knowingly and took Saskia's arm, skilfully flashing the diamond lights of the engagement ring as she negotiated them away from the dance floor while raking her eyes over Saskia's dress in such a way that she could almost see the dollar signs ticking over. Not that Carmen's own gown was any slouch, wrapping her slim figure in form-fitting backless silver satin.

'Drago's just gone to get us some champagne. I'm here working tonight—just like you.' Her words might have been intended for Saskia, but her attention was now one hundred percent focused on the man at her side. 'Or maybe not like you,' she said with a soft laugh that made the ends of her sleek black bob sway with her glittering diamond drop earrings. 'I hear congratulations are in order? I didn't quite believe it before, but seeing the size of those rocks on Saskia's finger, and the way the groom-to-be looks at his betrothed, maybe there's some truth to it after all.'

Carmen raised one perfectly manicured diamante-studded fingernail and pressed it to Alex's chest. 'So this is the great Alexander Koutoufides,' she whispered huskily. '*Lucky* Saskia. Who says you can't combine business with pleasure? *I* always try to.' Her smile was too wide, her eyes sharp and pointedly bright, and even the provocative tilt of her body combined to suggest an offer.

Saskia couldn't ignore the blatant messages Carmen was putting out, even though she knew the woman too well to be surprised—if marriage didn't render a man off-limits, then a mere engagement would hardly register. No doubt she'd have a field day if she thought there was anything false about their engagement. She'd be all over Alex like a rash. Just thinking about it had Saskia's hackles rising.

Frustration, she told herself. She was frustrated at the interruption, frustrated at having her rival reminding her of the task at hand, and frustrated at being ignored by the both of them.

She was definitely not jealous. Why would she be? She had no designs on Alex Koutoufides.

Alex smiled in return as he lifted one hand and snared Carmen's, holding it closely between them before touching his lips to her fingers and taking an age to lower it to her side. Saskia knew, because she was counting the seconds.

'You're colleagues, then?' he asked, his full attention focused on Carmen's smiling face, on her delight at his gallant gesture.

'We are. Or rather we *were*. I assume we won't be seeing much of Saskia any more, though, now that she has such a handsome man to keep her busy? Such a shame. I was really looking forward to this competition. But I guess this means she's out of the race?'

'Actually, I'm still very much *in* the race,' Saskia stressed, sick of being excluded from the private exchange going on in front of her and silently cursing the arrangement that was threatening to railroad her chances of success. But she was stuck. She wasn't about to explain to Carmen the nature of her arrangement with Alex. The board were aware of the situation, and that was all that mattered. 'Our engagement changes nothing—'

'What competition?' interrupted Alex.

Carmen smiled up at him. 'Hasn't she told you? The editor-in-chief's position is up for grabs, and we're both in the running for it. Whoever turns in the best profile from our latest assignments gets the job.'

Finally he dragged his gaze from Carmen's and looked down into hers. His eyes were seemingly expressionless, and yet still she could feel them scanning for the truth, searching for answers. She blinked a silent affirmation when in reality she wanted to yell at him, wanted him to know *that* was why she was so desperate to get this damn profile started.

'I've been assigned Drago Maiolo,' Carmen continued, oblivious to the exchange. 'Ah, speaking of whom…'

A squat greying gentleman joined the party, his heavy-lidded eyes flicking over them, cooling as they passed over Alex but warming considerably when he came to Saskia. He handed Carmen her glass and immediately conceded his own to Saskia.

'I see you've found your friends.' His voice was almost as thick as his features, and it seemed to rumble up from below like an approaching roll of thunder.

Carmen smiled her thanks and nestled into his arm on a shrug of innocence. 'Drago told me Alex would be here. I figured you might be too.'

'How did he know?' Saskia asked.

'Alex is *always* here,' Drago replied, answering for her. 'He's been the major benefactor of the Baxter Foundation for years. Isn't that right, Alex?'

'Alex?' Saskia asked, looking for confirmation.

'How are things?' he directed to Drago, without answering either question, tension obvious in the firm set of his jaw.

'Never better. Especially now I have Carmen here to brighten up my nights. I usually have no time for newspaper people, but this woman is something different. I had no idea an interview could be so…stimulating.'

Drago and Carmen both laughed, even while Carmen

squirmed and redirected one roaming hand from low behind her. 'Drago's been most co-operative,' she conceded. 'It's going to be a fabulous profile.'

'It had better be,' Alex replied. 'Or you won't stand a chance of that promotion. I've seen the work Saskia does and it's excellent. And now, if you'll excuse us, I've just seen someone I really should talk to before the speeches get underway.'

He ignored Saskia's open-mouthed response as he steered her away from the couple, leading her up the stairs to the balcony above. She didn't know who was the more dumbfounded—Carmen, at being so thoroughly and cleanly put in her place, or herself, at first learning that Alex was the foundation's major benefactor and then hearing him actually defend her.

She looked around as he backed her into a quiet place overlooking the ballroom from behind a screen of potted palms.

'What are we doing here? I thought you said you wanted to talk to someone.'

'I do. I want to talk to you.'

Saskia recovered in an instant. 'Good, because I want to talk to you too. Did you really read those profiles I gave you?'

His lips curved into a thin smile. 'Did you think I'd made up what I said?'

She blinked. 'But you stood up for me.'

He shrugged, as if he hadn't given it any thought. 'I needed a line to throw her so we could get away. I think it worked quite well.'

'Of course' she said, feeling suddenly deflated that his support had meant so much to her and desperate to change the topic. 'So why didn't you tell me you were the foundation's major benefactor?'

'You didn't ask.'

'But—'

'No. You tell me about this "competition" first.'

She raised her glass in irritation. 'It's like Carmen said. The one who turns in the best profile gets the promotion. They picked two businessmen nobody had managed to interview in more than a decade, and they assigned us one each.'

'Are you sure she's such a threat? She doesn't look it.'

'Don't be taken in by Carmen's appearance. She's got an MBA from Harvard and a cold barracuda mind to go with those curves. She's out to win. And, given the way Drago seems so accommodating, she's already got his full co-operation.'

'It looks like she's got one hell of a lot more than that.'

She looked up at him, remembering the way his lips had lingered over Carmen's fingers and how he'd taken his own good time releasing her. 'That could have been you, you know.'

He blinked into the pause. 'You mean you would have profiled Drago and I would have enjoyed the company of the vivacious Carmen?'

She did her best to ignore the 'enjoyed' part of his comment. 'It might have been easier for everyone. It certainly would have been easier for me.'

'You're forgetting something. You know why I agreed to this profile. You blackmailed me—remember? Said you'd go public on what happened eight years ago if I didn't go along with you. I doubt if even the very come-hither Carmen could have come up with something as creative as that.'

Saskia shrugged. 'Given the way Carmen fills that silver gown, she probably wouldn't have needed to. Creativity would have been the last thing on your mind.'

This time he smiled, lifting a hand and catching one looping tendril, winding it around his fingers, letting it slip through, winding it again. Her scalp tingled from the contact.

That much made sense—but why was it her breasts were suddenly straining, her nipples peaking? And why could she feel heat pooling inside, way down deep?

'I take your point,' he acknowledged, his voice unexpectedly husky, his eyes dark like a moonless night sky, the reflection from the chandeliers like the stars. 'But would you really rather I had Carmen? That wouldn't bother you?'

She swallowed as his face dipped lower, his eyes intent on her mouth. On her lips. And he could be doing this with Carmen? Oh, yes, it would bother her!

Was that what he was trying to prove right now?

'Of course not,' she lied, twisting away so that she tugged her hair from his fingers, carefully ensuring she avoided his eyes at the same time. What did he think—that she was jealous? Not a chance! She leaned her arms on the railing, looking out over the sea of brilliantly dressed guests in the ballroom below.

'If you say so,' he said. 'Although I for one am very pleased you ended up with me.'

Her heart did a slow roll and she turned her face up to meet his again. 'And why is that?'

'Because you'd be wasted on Drago. I didn't save your virginity for the likes of him.'

Shock rooted her to the spot as white-hot fury infused her veins, and only the fact they were in one of the top function rooms in the world, surrounded by the cream of society, stopped her from flinging the contents of her glass in his face.

'How dare you? I can't believe you just said that.'

'Why? You'd rather throw it away on someone like him?'

'How dare you pretend that you somehow "saved" me by what you did, and that that gives you the right to decide whom I make love to. It has nothing to do with you.'

Alex whirled around, pinning her between his body and the balustrade, his face close to her own. 'Now, that's where you're wrong. It has *everything* to do with me. I could have taken all you offered that night, I could have pushed my way into you. I could have deflowered you and used you and discarded you when I'd had enough. But I didn't. I let you go. But not so you could throw it away on some lecherous businessman old enough to be your grandfather.'

'Who says I would have thrown it away on him?'

'It doesn't matter. Whether you threw it or whether he demanded it as payment for his profile, it amounts to the same thing. A total waste.'

Her chest heaving, her temperature off the wall, and her body reacting to his coarse words as if she'd been shot with hormones, she spun around in his arms until she could rest against the balustrade and not be forced to look into those deep, dark eyes. 'I can't believe we're having this conversation.'

But turning around proved a big mistake. He moved closer behind her, so she could feel his warm breath on her ear, feel his body press full length against hers, wedging her tight against the balustrade. She gasped. He was aroused, and his hand snared her waist, dragging her even closer into contact with him, the sensation even through layers of fabric still shockingly intimate, irresistibly carnal.

'So tell me,' he urged, his voice low and thick in her ear, 'what would you rather be doing?'

Every part of her wanted to lean back into his heated strength. Even now her back ached to arch, ached to send that low part of her in motion against him, ached to feel his length caress her. What was he doing to her? Turning her wanton and reckless at the first hint of sex?

Purposefully she fought the battle going on inside her,

battled to quell the swelling of her breasts and nipples and secret places. Battled to suppress the need.

'I want…' she whispered.

'Yes?' he murmured, the tip of his tongue tracing the line of her ear.

'To get this profile done and go home.'

He stilled, and she could feel the disbelief blow holes in his sexual energy. 'The profile?'

'That's why I'm here, after all. Nothing more.'

He let go his hold on her and she slipped out of his reach, covering her relief at her escape by smoothing her skirts.

'So how important is it, this competition? Do you want to win?'

'Of course I want to win!' *I have to win.* 'Why else do you think I bothered to track you down? It certainly wasn't to chew over the fat and talk about old times.'

Why else indeed? He looked intently at her. She must really need this promotion desperately to go to the trouble she had, to risk another encounter with him. And, dammit, why had she walked back into his life? He didn't need reminders of the past. He didn't need the risk to his present. So why the hell couldn't he just leave her alone? 'What's so important?'

Saskia looked back over the crowd below—couples moving on the jam-packed dance floor, small groups gathered around the fringe, talking and laughing. 'What do you care? Isn't it enough that I want this promotion?'

'No, it's not enough.' He was angry now. Angry at all the old emotions she'd brought up. Angry that he couldn't forget them. 'What would make you desperate enough to come looking for me after what happened between us? You must have known the sparks would fly. So what is it that you want—the honour, the prestige?'

She shook her head as she leaned out over the highly polished brass railing. 'No, it's not the prestige.'

'Then it must be money. How much do you need? I can give you money.'

The words were out before he even realised, before he even knew that he meant them. But money was something he could do. Easily. He had more than enough for himself, and if it meant getting rid of her any faster then it would be money well spent.

She looked up at him, her green eyes filled with disbelief. 'You'd do that? You'd give me money?'

Hell, yes, if it meant getting her out of his hair and his life back to normal.

'How much do you need?'

She shook her head.

'I don't want your money. I'm expecting to win this competition. All I need is your co-operation so I can make this profile the best it can be.'

'And if you don't win?'

'I'm going to win.'

'Don't be so stubborn. If it's money you need, I can give it to you.'

'And why would you do that? Why would you suddenly want to give money to the woman you've accused of being the lowest of the low, somebody stalking your sister to get the goods to plaster all over the nearest gossip rag?'

'What was I expected to think, finding you sneaking around taking photographs outside my home at the same time the paparazzi were clamouring for Marla's blood?' He swiped a hand back through his hair. Damn! He was supposed to be trying to convince her to take the money and go, not rehash every problem they already had. 'Look, why not let me help you? Consider it compensation for past transgressions, if you like.'

Her face moved beyond shock to anger in an instant, her green eyes vivid, narrowed in accusation.

'You want to give me *money* because you threw me out of your bed before smashing apart my father's existence? What are you looking for—absolution? Do you think you can pay me off for what you did? That money somehow makes it better? You don't even know how much I need. One hundred thousand dollars? Five hundred? How about one million? How much are you prepared to fork out to assuage your guilt?'

'That's enough!'

'No amount would be enough!' she remonstrated, thankful for the cover of music but still trying to keep her voice low. 'I was seventeen years old, bowled over by the attentions of the best-looking man I'd ever seen. He made me feel like a princess. For weeks he treated me like his queen—and it was all such an outright lie. In one awful night he smashed my hopes and dreams. The next day he smashed my father's. He made a fool out of us both. *Totally humiliated us both.* And now he thinks he can pay me off for what he did with cold, hard cash? Not a chance.'

'Your father deserved everything he got!'

'So you say. Because he ruined your own family's business more than twenty years before. What a nerve! But you sure made him pay for that. What I don't understand is what I did to deserve it too.'

He looked away, his teeth clenched, blood pounding in his head, feeling his hatred for her father pulse through him like a living thing. Feeling hatred for the man he'd been becoming loom up like a gigantic shadow over his life. But what could he say? She was right. She'd done nothing to deserve it.

'It could have been worse,' he bit out at last.

'You think? How the hell could it have been any worse?'

'I could have finished off what I started. I could have made love to you that night after all.'

CHAPTER SEVEN

A THUNDERBOLT of silence followed his remark. Finally she could speak. 'You're right,' Saskia said, but all the while her heart was screaming, *Liar*. 'Thank God I was spared that.'

The look in his eyes, shuttered and bleak, was satisfaction indeed. He glanced down at his watch.

'There are speeches coming up. And then we're leaving,' he announced.

'Already? And just when we're having so much fun.'

Scowling, Alex escorted her down the stairs, Saskia heading for the refuge of the ladies' lounge while he sought out the event's organisers.

The lounge was like a sanctuary inside, the velvet wallpaper, luxurious drapes and deep tub chairs making the room feel more like a sitting room than a bathroom.

She stood at the basins, holding a damp cloth to her heated face. What was it about that man? Lulling her into a false sense of security one minute, digging deep under her skin the next?

The door behind her swung open and she caught the flash of silver satin in the mirror. Saskia let her eyes fall shut and suppressed a groan. The last person she really wanted to see right now was Carmen. Her sanctuary had suddenly turned to hell.

'Things getting a little heated between you two lovers then?' she enquired.

'I've just got something in my eye,' Saskia responded, dabbing the cloth under her lowered eyelashes, uncomfortable with the thought that Carmen had been watching them. She pulled the fabric away, glancing down at the cloth. 'There,' she said smiling, *pretending*, before screwing it into a ball and tossing it into the waste. She turned around as if she was about to leave. 'Are you enjoying the ball? Alex said the speeches are about to begin. I must join him.'

'You're not going to win, you know. This job is going to be mine.' Carmen's face was set into a mask so tightly bound with loathing that Saskia felt the first stirrings of fear. They'd never been what she'd call friends, but this naked anger was something new. Something frightening.

'You seem pretty sure of yourself,' Saskia replied calmly, trying to avoid a slanging match and wishing Carmen would move away from the door so she could escape. 'Good luck with your profile, in that case.'

'So how did you do it?' Carmen asked, not moving an inch.

'How did I do what, exactly?'

'Get Alex to agree to marry you. I thought he'd be the last guy you'd want to get hooked up with after the way he wiped your father's company off the face of the earth.'

Saskia did a double take. 'You know about that? How the hell—?'

Carmen smiled—if you could call the way her lips thinned and curved nastily a smile. 'I do thorough research. It's a particular skill of mine. Or one of them.' She tilted her head, her eyes glinting dangerously even in the subdued lighting. 'Did you think I'd leave it to chance who we were assigned to profile? Who do you think suggested the subjects?'

Saskia laughed. 'You can't be serious. The board would hardly let *you* choose them.'

'Oh, it wasn't that hard,' she boasted, feigning interest in her long scarlet nails. 'A word in an ear here, a hint in another ear there. Pretty soon they get together to discuss things, and *voila!* They're all in agreement. Suddenly it's all their idea. Only you want to ruin it all. You weren't supposed to like the guy, let alone marry him.'

She smiled again, and Saskia imagined it must be how a shark looked before it headed in for the kill.

'But now that too is working in my favour. Already the board is thinking you're not such a good prospect, given you'll be doing the maternity thing before too long. If, indeed, you're not already…'

She let her eyes settle on Saskia's abdomen like an accusation, leaving her words to hang there, letting them drip their poisoned content down slowly.

'Is there already a bastard child of Alexander Koutoufides festering inside you?'

Saskia prayed for strength. Because if she didn't she might just slap the other woman right here, right now. 'Don't you think that's a little unlikely? We've been together barely a week, after all.'

'Enough time to become engaged, however. Tell me, what's he like in bed? Drago is enthusiastic, if nothing else, but he lacks a certain—*finesse*. I'll wager that Alex lacks nothing.'

'Who says I've slept with him?'

'Come on—you're getting married. No man in Alex's position would agree to such a thing without testing the merchandise.'

'And if I told you there was no engagement? That there will be no marriage?'

'Then I'd think you were clutching at straws. And that you were so very, very sad. Because that would mean you'll soon be without a job *and* a man.' She sighed theatrically. 'In that case, enjoy him now, while you can.'

Saskia reefed in a deep breath, trying to quell the mounting sickness inside her. 'You must want this job awfully desperately if you're prepared to lie and cheat to get it.'

'Oh, yes,' Carmen agreed brightly, not even making a pretence at disagreeing with Saskia's summing up. 'And I'm going to get it too.'

Saskia had heard enough. She gathered up her skirts in both hands and drove a straight line for the door, forcing Carmen to back off at the last moment as she soared past, leaving her parting words in her wake.

'Just don't count on it.'

'You missed the speeches.'

Alex slipped her wrap around her shoulders and she grunted her thanks. If he thought she must still be angry from their argument he didn't say anything, and she was glad he didn't pursue it. She was too tightly wound from her run-in with Carmen to make sense right now.

From across the foyer Drago waved and caught her eye, gesturing as if he wanted to talk. Alex steered her purposefully towards the door regardless. 'Come on,' he said.

'Drago—' she said, gesturing to her right in case he hadn't seen.

'I saw him,' he replied, and just kept going, directing her towards the doorman and a line of waiting limousines. The doorman pulled open the rear passenger door for them and waited for her to gather her skirts and climb in.

'Why do I get the impression you're not too fond of Drago?'

'Who says I'm not?' he rejoined, following her in, all lean grace and fluid movement.

The car drove away, and something about the way he'd answered piqued her interest.

'And yet you obviously have so much in common. Both of you hold status as business success stories who prefer to live life out of the public eye. And both of you share the Baxter Foundation in common.'

His jaw twitched markedly as he settled alongside her. 'Hasn't it occurred to you yet? Some people stay out of the public eye because they're naturally private people. Others simply can't stand up to public scrutiny.'

The meaning behind his words was more than clear. 'You're suggesting Drago is into something shady?'

Dark eyes collided with hers. 'I've done business with him in the past. And on the basis of that experience I would never choose to do business with him again.'

'Surely you're not suggesting there's anything underhand about Drago's business interests?'

The look he gave her was intentionally non-committal. 'Just be glad you're not the one doing his profile.'

He settled back into his seat, very relieved again that it wasn't Saskia who'd drawn the Drago Maiolo assignment. Just the thought of those squat diamond-encrusted and nicotine stained fingers anywhere near the sweet curves of Saskia thickened his breathing to growling point. She was still a virgin. Much too good for the likes of Drago.

Hell, she was far too good for anyone. And, no matter who her father was or what he had done, after the way Alex had treated her once before, he included himself in that number.

But that didn't make him stop wanting her.

She'd fitted into his arms tonight as if she was made for

him, her head tucked under his chin, her body pressed within a heartbeat of his, and no longer was she the teenage goddess-in-waiting who had been so hard to walk away from back then. Now she was the real deal, her body rich with the power of her femininity, ripe and lush. *Ready.*

Even now her scent worked its way across the space between them, calling out to him, tempting him. Even now the jade-green colour of her eyes was the colour he saw when he closed his own eyes. Even now, separated by several feet of the finest leather upholstery…

Damn it!

Even now she was making him hard!

'So which one are you?' she asked softly from across the car, cutting into his thoughts.

He turned away from the window and the unseen passing parade of Manhattan buildings. 'What do you mean?'

'Are you merely a naturally private person?' she continued. 'Or is there something you're trying to hide?'

He looked across at her. 'What do you think?' he challenged.

She looked at him for a moment, her features still, her eyes assessing, her lips slightly parted. 'I know you weren't always so media-shy. Something must have happened that made you go low-profile.'

He didn't like the direction this conversation was taking. She wouldn't like it if he went there. 'You're forgetting about Marla. Don't you think one headliner in any family is enough?'

She stared at him. 'Maybe,' she said, as if she'd already written off that possibility. 'Or maybe there's something else you're trying to hide. Why did you drop off the face of the earth like you did?'

Moments expanded into seconds. Seconds expanded into for ever. And a muscle in his jaw worked through it all. Should he tell her that it all went back to that night? That he'd seen what he was becoming, what he was turning into, and he'd run the other way?

Then the car pulled into the drive-through at their hotel, her door was pulled open, a bubble of sounds and light invaded their uncomfortable silence, and the moment was gone.

'I'll co-operate with you on the profile,' he said at last as they exited the car. 'And I'll give you all the time you need to give you the best chance of winning. But there's something I need in return.'

'What is it?' she asked, almost too enthusiastically. If Carmen was going to undermine her every attempt to win this job she was going to need Alex's full co-operation. That would be worth almost anything.

'I want your guarantee that you'll leave Marla out of it. I don't want you having anything to do with her and I don't want her mentioned. Understand?'

She was about to agree unreservedly before she remembered the notebook she had stashed in her luggage—the notebook she'd promised to read. It was a promise she'd made to the woman that she wasn't about to break, no matter what Alex demanded. Besides, it wasn't as if she was about to include anything from it in her profile. Alex might doubt it, but her sense of ethics went a little deeper than that. 'This has always been about you, not Marla. I intend leaving her right out of the profile.'

His eyes drilled into her, as if he were digging into her very soul for the truth.

'Just keep it that way,' was all he said.

It was only when she was alone in her plush suite and getting ready for bed that she realised he'd never answered her question. Why was that? What *had* provoked Alex Koutoufides's sudden departure from public view? What was he trying to hide, and why?

Saskia shrugged as she rehung tonight's gorgeous gown. Did it matter? At least she'd secured his co-operation. Tomorrow she could really start work. She'd assemble the additional reports she needed, she'd have her questions ready, and by the sounds of it he might even let her into the house to watch him at work in his study, managing his empire from half a world away.

Until then she had another job to do. She pulled the fluffy white hotel robe around her and flopped onto the wide bed, propping a pillow under her chest and picking up the red notebook. Her reviewing it obviously meant so much to Marla, but she really wasn't relishing the prospect. Even with a celebrity name behind it, the writing would still have to stand on its own merits, and the chance of publication was a long shot. Hopefully Marla understood that.

Reluctantly she contemplated the cover, where Marla had penned the working title *From the Inside*, expecting to be able to offer nothing more than an honest yet encouraging critique—something she hoped wouldn't crush the woman's hopes and dreams in the process. It was obvious she needed something in her life to make her feel worthwhile. Maybe writing was it.

Saskia turned the cover and started to read.

About a young girl finding her place in the world—a young girl whose perfect, cherished life changed when she encountered sex at the age of fifteen, at the hands of a much older man, a young girl who discovered how much she enjoyed the act and yearned to learn more, who *set out* to learn more.

It told the story of the impact when her parents died in a

horrific boating fire at sea, and how she'd lurched into her marriages. It relived the short-lived bliss and the disasters they'd became. It told of her endless flirtation with celebrity. It covered everything: her slide into drug and alcohol dependency, her time behind the walls drying out, having therapy, thinking she was sane, knowing she must be mad.

It told of a woman who needed to heal herself. A woman who had recognised that it was time to grow up.

The prose wasn't perfect. It was raw, and needed editing and organisation, but the account pulled no punches. It was brutally honest, and it didn't make the author out to be anything more than what she was, but it was funny and gritty and poignant at the same time, and touching beyond belief.

Hours after she'd started, and with tears in her eyes, Saskia closed the notebook. Marla was a remarkable woman. She'd claimed she had no talents, but the woman who'd written this was gifted and insightful and deserved to be given the chance to succeed. If Saskia could do anything to help her, she would. And while she was in New York she had the perfect opportunity—she knew just the person. A former colleague from her magazine now worked in editorial for a publishing house, and lived not far from here. She'd be doing her a favour and getting Marla a second opinion.

In a fizz of excitement she'd reached for the phone at her bedside before she noticed the time. It wasn't long till dawn. She snuggled into bed and snapped off the light, feeling better than she'd felt in ages. She'd call after she'd snatched a few hours' sleep.

Alex was pounding on her door when she raced out of the lift shortly before noon.

'I'm here,' Saskia said breathlessly.

'Where the hell have you been?' he demanded, as she used her room key to unlock the door and pushed it open. 'I've been calling for ages.'

'Nowhere special. I just…went out for a walk.'

'Our car will be here in ten minutes.' His words trailed her into the room.

'It's okay. I'm just about packed.' She didn't bother to take off her jacket even though she felt as if she was burning up after running back. Instead she just threw her purse on a chair and grabbed the last of her toiletries from the bathroom. She zipped them into a bag and turned straight into a wall. The wall of his chest. His hands went to her shoulders, anchoring her before she could step away.

'What's the rush?'

'You said the car—'

'There's time.' He touched a hand to her chin, lifting it so her eyes had no choice but to collide with his. 'Your face is pink.'

She knew full well that her colour couldn't only be attributed to her race to get back. A large dollop of it was relief at completing her task this morning. Her former colleague had been as keen to see Marla's story as she'd expected. Her excitement at reading the first chapter had mirrored Saskia's own, and right now she couldn't wait to get back to Tahoe and let Marla know an editor was considering her work.

As for the rest of her colour? It was due entirely to the way he was making her feel right now, pressed so close to her, his fingers adding an electric thrum to her overheated skin. 'I ran,' she said, when she'd located the thin thread of her voice at last. 'A few blocks. That's all.'

'Maybe you should calm down a little.'

His voice had a husky quality that didn't fit with a rush to the car. Where was his urgency? Where was the panic she'd seen when she'd found him pounding on her door?

She laughed, a half-hearted attempt that sounded as pitiable as it felt. How the hell was she supposed to calm down with him standing over her—touching her?

'Thanks. I will. Now…if you'll excuse me…I'll finish my packing.'

This time he let her go, standing in the doorway, one arm behind his neck, as she stashed the toiletries bag and locked down her luggage.

'I'm ready,' she said, her senses reeling once more from experiencing the let-down after a close encounter with Alex: the sensual build-up, the pull of his body on hers, only to be let go, to be spun out like wreckage from a hurricane, thrown out to crash wherever it landed. It was crazy. How could he have this effect on her when she didn't want anything to do with him?

He pushed himself away from the door to follow her. 'Before we go,' he started, 'last night I offered you money. You objected then, but maybe overnight you thought about it. Maybe you re-considered. I want you to know my offer is still open.'

She closed her eyes for a second, breathing in deep. She'd said too much last night, way too much. She'd reacted too violently to his offer of money and she'd made it sound as if her pain was still raw, that it still mattered.

But it didn't matter any more! She was over it. And if it wasn't for Alex, scraping back the intervening years, peeling back time as if he was ripping off a thick scab and revealing the wound, raw and stinging and deep, the past would have stayed safely where she'd buried it.

'No,' she said at last, slinging the strap of her purse over her shoulder. 'You should never have offered me money.

Especially not for the reason you did. But let's not talk about it any more. It's in the past. Let it stay there.'

He took a step closer, bridging the gap between them. 'Saskia, think about it. You could forget all about this bizarre contest.' He reached out a hand to her arm. 'You could leave now.'

She reeled back. 'Don't touch me!'

A muscle twitched in his cheek, his eyes turned hard as steel.

'You'll never forgive me for what happened, will you?'

'Why should I?' she insisted. 'You can't buy me off. It simply should never have happened in the first place.'

His dark eyes glinted, his jaw square. 'I had my reasons.'

'What? Now you're telling me you had *reasons*? You really have a nerve. I have no idea what kind of sick reasons you think would excuse the way you acted, and I really don't want to know.'

'No,' he muttered, trying to control his anger-coated breathing as she marched out of the room ahead of him. 'I don't imagine you do.'

Marla must have been anxious for news. She was already waiting for her early the next morning, when Saskia took a walk along the lake's edge. Her jeans and thick sweater were keeping out the early-morning chill, although she was already regretting not tying her hair back against the breeze that whipped her curls around her face and turned them to stinging tendrils.

'How was the ball?' Marla asked, a nervous excitement in her smile.

Saskia nodded. 'It was entertaining in places.'

'Good,' she said brightly, and Saskia could see that for all her anxiousness she was too afraid to ask.

'Marla, about that writing…'

'Yes?'

'I know it was yours.'

The older woman looked contrite and laced an arm through Saskia's as they walked out onto the pier. 'Oh, I'm sorry. I thought you might say no if you knew it was mine. And I did so want your opinion on it.' She looked up at Saskia, hope in her eyes. 'So…did you get a chance to read it? What did you think?'

Saskia smiled. The older woman's enthusiasm was infectious. 'Well, first of all, you know how hard it is to get work published, don't you? Some people struggle for years and years and never make it.'

Marla's face dropped. 'Are you saying it was no good, then?'

'No. I thought it was very good.'

'Really? You really did?'

She laughed. 'I really did.'

Still with their arms entwined, Marla clapped her gloved hands together and jumped up and down. 'That's fantastic. So where's the problem?'

'I just don't want you to get your hopes up too high. I've left the book with an editor friend of mine in New York. She was very interested, but it still doesn't mean—'

'You've got an editor reading it? My book?' Marla pulled her arms free and slapped both hands over her mouth. 'That's so fantastic. Oh, Saskia, thank you so, so much!'

She threw her arms around the younger woman and hugged her tight.

'It's great news,' Saskia agreed. 'But don't be too disappointed if they can't use it—okay? There are plenty more publishers out there after all. I'm sure there's one for you somewhere—it might just take a while.'

'Oh, my, I just can't believe it,' Marla said, giving Saskia another squeeze. 'I'm so glad you came. This is the best news I've ever had.'

They walked along the shore, talking companionably, Marla pumping her for comments on various parts of her story, and all the while the wind was picking up. Getting more frustrated with herself for not tying it back, Saskia pushed her hair off her face one more time. 'This hair is driving me crazy.'

Marla looked up at her. 'I love your hair. Those curls make it look so alive, and I just love the colour.' She pulled back the hood of her jacket and ran a hand over her own silvery blonde mane. 'Do you think that colour would suit me? I think it's time I had a change.'

Saskia smiled, recognising immediately that the warmer colour would suit Marla's skin tones perfectly. 'I think it would look great.'

'You wouldn't mind if I tried?'

'Why should I mind? I think you'd look sensational.'

They talked for a while together, about hairstyles and colours, and families, getting to know more about each other, building an easy camaraderie. Until a voice called out through the pines.

'Marla!'

She spun around. 'Oh, God, I've been too long. That's Jake, looking for me. That guy is driving me totally crazy, you know. I'd better run.' She kissed Saskia quickly on the cheek, gave more hurried thanks, and headed off quickly for the house.

Finally Saskia had a chance to get some much needed work done. Alex had been true to his word and had invited her into his large state-of-the-art office, complete with computers, fax and even teleconferencing facilities. 'Wow,' she said, contemplating the screen and taking some shots with the digital camera he'd finally conceded she might need to do her job. 'What a set-up. You've got everything you need to do business anywhere in the world right here.'

'That's the idea. Now that my portfolio is spread so widely, I can't be in every place at once. This is the next best thing.'

He pulled some files out of an oak filing cabinet while she looked at the photographs on his desk. There was one very old one of his family alongside a fishing boat. She picked it up and smiled. Alex must have been around ten or so, his arms crossed and his stance wide, as if he was the boss, but his smile was cheeky as he looked into the camera. Marla stood alongside, looking like a young colt, not that much taller for her years, but all long legs, unbridled energy and classic beauty, even though she must have been just a young teenager. His parents stood behind, his olive-skinned father with an arm around his fair mother's shoulders. Marla's story mentioned they'd died in a boating accident. Had it been that same boat they'd died on?

'My parents,' Alex said softly, pulling the photo from her hands and placing it back on his wide desk.

'How old were you when they died?'

He sighed, at the same time dropping a stack of glossy reports and financial statements on the desk before turning to look out through the large windows into the distance. 'Fourteen.'

'That's so not fair. My mother died when I was still too little to remember her. I can't imagine what it would have been like to have lost her as a teenager.'

He looked over his shoulder at her. 'What happened to her?'

'Breast cancer, apparently. She was too scared to see the doctors, and by the time she did it was too late. But I was a baby, so I don't have any memories of her at all. I think in some ways that's easier. I can't imagine losing both of my parents in such a horrific accident, though. That must have been devastating.'

He turned around completely, his brows drawn together. 'You know how my parents died? How is that? I don't remember telling you.'

She swallowed, suddenly guilty because it had been Marla's memoirs that had filled in the details for her. 'I must have read it somewhere. In my background notes, maybe.'

He considered her answer for a while, his eyes holding hers, locked in the past, swirling with pain. 'Sometimes I think they really died after the takeover. It broke them, you know.' Then he seemed to snap back to the present. He grunted and sat down opposite her. 'If you want this profile, we should get started. Here's what I've got for you to look at already…'

They were still in his office hours later, when the call came through. The late afternoon sun slanted through the long windows and a fresh breeze stirred the curtains, making one think of closing up windows and doors—that the best part of the day would soon be over.

Alex listened for a moment before handing the receiver over. 'It's for you, from London,' he said. 'A Rodney Krieg?'

She accepted the phone while Alex pushed back in his chair, his arms behind his head, his feet crossed on the desk. 'Sir Rodney? I didn't expect to hear from you so soon.'

'Saskia, my dear.' Sir Rodney's gruff voice churned down the line. 'How are you getting on over there?'

'Great. The profile's going really well.' She nodded at Alex. 'I've got Alex's full co-operation—I should be finished within the week.'

'Ah…' blustered the voice at the other end. 'About that profile…'

A cold shiver of trepidation shimmied its way down her

spine. 'What about it?' she asked, her voice tight with concern. 'Is there a problem?'

Alex leaned forward in his chair and she swivelled her own away, so she didn't have to look at him. She didn't need him in on this conversation.

'Well, it's just that the board's more than a little concerned...'

Trepidation gave way to dread.

'About what?'

'There's some talk that you might be going to withdraw from the contest.'

'Why would I do that? I've been working towards this job for at least the last twelve months. Why would I suddenly give it all up?'

'You might if you were worried about taking on such a demanding role in London when you're thinking about settling down and starting a family somewhere else. This is a demanding role. It's no place for a part-time employee or commuter. I expect you realise that. Now in this day and age we can hardly discriminate against you on such grounds—that wouldn't be right at all, of course. But we can ask if you seriously want to proceed to with this application or not—and if not, then it might be wiser to withdraw.'

Her heart skipped a beat. She couldn't be hearing this.

'No, no, Sir Rodney. I explained all that. There is not going to be any marriage. This engagement isn't real. It's just for show—just a diversion for the press to get the focus off Marla. Obviously it must be working, or the board wouldn't be thinking it's real.'

'Now, now,' he soothed, with no conviction at all. 'I know that's what you told me. But you're forgetting one thing. Carmen saw you together at that Baxter Foundation night, looking very much the part, and now the papers are reporting

Alex as saying you're going to be married as soon as possible.
There's even some talk that a family might not be too far distant.'

Saskia's blood froze. There was no mistaking where those
whispers would have come from. 'Did that come from
Carmen? Because she's told me she'll do anything to win that
promotion. Can't you see what she's doing?'

'Does it really matter where it came from when it only
serves to verify what the board already suspects?'

'Of course it matters! Please believe me, Sir Rodney, there
will be no wedding! I told you, it's not a real engagement.'

'I'm sorry, Saskia.' Sir Rodney was sounding impatient. 'I
know how much this promotion means to you, and I know
how hard you've worked, but the board is having trouble accepting that this engagement to a man like Alex Koutoufides
can be anything but real—it doesn't make sense. They don't
want to find out after they've made a decision that you've
decided you're no longer available for the job. This role is too
important.'

'But I wouldn't!'

'Besides which, Carmen has already handed in a preliminary
report. It's excellent—just what we're after. Frankly, the board
are wondering if there's any point proceeding with the contest.'

'But Sir Rodney…'

There was a moment's hesitation. 'I'm sorry, Saskia. It
might be for the best if you get notice of your withdrawal into
the board sooner rather than later.'

Saskia held the phone to her ear even after the final click
had signalled he was gone. Because even just holding it felt
as if she wasn't giving up on her dream. Once she put down
that phone it would be like acknowledging her chances were
dead. And they couldn't be dead.

She'd done everything she could possibly do for this job—

she'd agreed to profile the person she detested more than anyone in the world, the person who'd destroyed her family and whom she held responsible for setting her father on his decline to despair and illness. She hadn't wanted to profile Alex, but she'd agreed because it was the only way that would ensure she had the means of providing the kind of care her father needed and deserved. That or she'd drag him down in the process.

She'd done everything she possibly could, and it was still not enough. Once again her hopes and dreams had been thwarted.

And it was all down to one man.

The man sitting opposite her right now.

Alexander Koutoufides!

She took a deep breath and turned her chair back round, replacing the long-dead receiver, finally acknowledging what she'd known all along—there was no lifeline. No lifeline, no white knight to ride out on a charger and save her, no fairies at the bottom of the garden. This was real life, and if she needed saving she was going to have to do it herself.

'What's wrong?' he asked from across the desk. 'What's happened?'

She lifted her eyes to meet his, momentarily taken aback at the level of concern she saw there—but only momentarily. He didn't mean it. He didn't care about her or her job, and least of all her father. He'd used her once again and this was the result. Another disaster. Another nightmare. And all at the hands of Alex Koutoufides. Oh, Carmen Rivers might have taken advantage of the situation, but it had been manufactured by this one man.

She stood—unable to sit, unable to control the buzzing forces that screamed for release inside her, unable to control the trembling fury that possessed every muscle.

'You bastard!' she seethed. 'You total bastard. If you hadn't insisted on all this engagement garbage—if you hadn't told every reporter going that you couldn't wait to get married—'

'Hey,' he said coming around the desk towards her. 'What am I supposed to have done?'

'I'm out of the running for the promotion. The board has decided that it can't give me the position—regardless of the profile I turn in—because it wouldn't be fair to the magazine or to *our marriage*.'

'I thought you'd already explained what was going on.'

'I had! And I thought he finally believed me. But you had to insist on taking me to New York. You insisted on me wearing a fortune in your mother's diamonds to flash in front of everyone, including the one person I was competing with for the position. And then you had to tell the press that we were getting married as soon as possible. Now there's no chance I can get that job. It doesn't matter what I do, or how this profile turns out, they won't give it to me. And it's all your fault!'

'But they can't do that, surely? Whether or not you're married is irrelevant. They can't discriminate against you on those grounds.'

'They're not! They're expecting me to withdraw. Especially now Carmen has already given them a teaser of *her* profile. They're not even interested in anything I might present.'

Her chest heaving, her breathing ragged, she battled to control her thoughts. There had to be an answer. There just had to be.

He rounded the desk towards her and she spun away as he spoke. 'Maybe things aren't as bad as you think?'

'You have no idea how bad!' That job should have been hers. The chance to see her father was cared for decently—it had been within her grasp. She'd fought so hard for it. She'd more than paid the price. Only to have success snatched cruelly and bitterly from her. 'You have no idea what you've done or what you've cost me. You ruined my life eight years ago and you've ruined it all over again. You couldn't have ruined it more thoroughly if you'd tried.'

She felt a hand on her shoulder and spun back round, lashing out with her hands, wanting to beat her fists against his chest, wanting to strike him and pound him and hurt him so that he'd know something of what she was feeling. Something of the pain. Something of the despair.

'I hate you Alex Koutoufides. I hate you to hell and back!'

She couldn't see him, but still she struck out. Tears distorted her vision and anguish distorted her mind, but still she pounded away. Only the pain was focused, sharp and deep and burning hot. And the pain tore through everything, savagely slicing open old wounds, jaggedly ripping through her heart, fuelling her beating muscles, screaming out the truth.

She'd failed.

She'd been so close to succeeding, so close to success that she'd been able to taste it, and yet still she'd failed. Now she would have nothing to offer her father. Now there would be nothing she could do for him. Nothing.

There was no point any more. There was no reason to fight any more. Everything she'd battled for, everything she'd held precious, was worth nothing. And now she had nothing left to lose. There was nothing left to fight for.

She was like a hurricane in his arms, unpredictable, unstoppable, a powerhouse of energy and emotion that had to spin itself out. All he could do was hold her, let herself work it out of her system and take it out on him.

Except he couldn't wait.

She was in his arms, passionate, desperate, and he was passionate and desperate enough to take advantage of it. How could he resist the erratic pounding of her heart, the frantic rise and fall of her breasts, her scent, and the sweet press of her feminine curves so close to his own? Why should he even bother?

He dropped his head, pressed his mouth to the top of her head, burying his lips in her mussed hair, inhaling the warm scent of woman—this one special woman.

Her breathing caught and she stilled her fight momentarily, giving him a chance to reach a hand under her chin and turn her face up to meet his. Her eyes were cloudy and damp, but warm, like the sky after a tropical storm, her lips moist and pink and slightly parted.

He shook his head. What the hell was he thinking? But then, what did it matter anyway? These thoughts skipped through his brain before he decided that thinking was surplus to requirements and dipped his mouth to hers because it seemed like the most natural thing in the world.

The most obvious thing.

The most inevitable thing.

Her breath caught and she froze, fought for an instant, and then relaxed as his mouth refused to let go of hers. She tasted of that storm and its aftermath, of maelstrom giving way to peace, of tempest followed by calm. And her lips moved under his. And as they did her body changed again, her breathing quickening, her energy returning, so that he could feel it as a living, pulsing force.

And soon the storm was back.

She was giving as good as she got, her lips demanding more, her tongue seeking his own. Her arms found purchase around his body and she pressed herself up against him, so close it was as if she wanted to be part of him, and he ached to make her so. Then she forced her hands up between their bodies, her nails raking against his shirt, unzipping his desire, before pulling his mouth down on hers again. Did she realise what she was doing to him? Did she have any idea what her body was inviting?

'*Sto thiavolo,*' he murmured against her ear, her answering shudder feeding into his wants and desires. To hell with it, indeed. The rush of blood through his veins told him he was going there for sure.

She wasn't asking him to stop, and somehow he knew he was no longer capable of it anyway.

'What are you doing?' she asked, her voice thick with need, as he swung her into his arms and carried her through a short passageway to a sprawling bedroom.

He pressed his lips to her forehead and let them linger, sampling her sweetness, tasting her desire. Then he drew back and lost himself in her green, green eyes.

'Something I should have done a long time ago.'

CHAPTER EIGHT

LIFE didn't come with second chances, let alone third. Alex knew that. All his life he'd taken his opportunities when and wherever they appeared and not relied on waiting for a second chance to come around. He'd clawed his way back from having nothing because of it. He'd built his success around it. And in the unlikely event that he'd missed an opportunity he'd lived with the consequences.

He'd had his chance with Saskia Prentice eight years ago. He'd had it and he'd blown it, and he had been happy to live with the consequences. Well, maybe not happy, but resigned. He knew the way he'd treated her back then had been a mistake, he knew what he'd lost before it had been gained, but then this was the price he'd had to pay.

But now life was giving him a second chance. And what with second chances coming around so rarely, no way was he going to mess this up.

It was like a gift from the gods. He laid her down on the bed, intending to shrug off his clothes before he joined her, but one look into her large green eyes and he knew that his place was there, alongside her, right now. He took the time to lever off no more than his shoes before he lowered himself, fully clothed, gathering her close. *'Agape mou,'* he told her, because right at this moment the English language didn't seem large enough to describe what he felt. 'You're so beautiful,' he said, echoing what his eyes had already told her. Then it was the turn of his lips and his hands to prove it.

The sun moved lower in the sky, the breeze carried more of a chill, but inside the room temperatures were soaring exponentially with need. He wanted to feel every part of her, to taste every part of her, all at once.

And she was hungry too—her hands reaching out for him, reefing out his shirt, seeking out his skin. And knowing she wanted him only ramped up his own need tenfold.

She was a virgin. He'd had the opportunity before to accept her gift eight years ago and he'd blown it. And yet here she was, still entrusting him with the heady responsibility of showing her the full magic of being a woman, and the supreme power of what she could do to a man.

And that was a gift indeed. A gift he wasn't about to turn away again. Not when he could have his fill of her and get her out of his system at the same time. Because if he had her he wouldn't crave her any more. It was worth making love to her simply for that.

His hands moved over her, hot and hungry, falling on her breasts, unpeeling clothes and lace and anything that got in the way of his need and his purpose. He cupped her breasts in his hands. He suckled her nipples, one after the other, feeling her body arch underneath him as she cried out in torturous pleasure, and she wrenched off his shirt, clamping him to her, demanding more.

He dispensed with his own jeans, then with her trousers, peeling them from her like a second skin, revealing the pearl-like skin of her long legs to his hungry gaze.

He ran his hands up their length as his kiss preceded them.

They were smooth legs, firm legs. Legs made to wrap around a man and draw him in close.

And right now he was that man.

His hands reached the top of her thighs, toying with the band of her silk panties, while her hands reached his head, her fingers raking through his hair, tugging, insistent.

'Alex,' she cried.

But he wasn't through with her yet. She hadn't felt all he could make her feel. He pressed his face against her and breathed in her rich feminine desire, a scent made just for him, just for this time. A scent that filled every remaining part of his mind and body with need.

He stripped away the underwear in an instant, parting her tenderly with his fingers, dipping his tongue and circling the lush pink bud within, dipping his tongue further and tasting her honeyed sweetness.

She cried out again, her hands clutching at his head, then pounding at her pillow as she bucked, then back again as he anchored her to her mouth, drawing out the sweetness, teasing out the pleasure.

'Please…' she pleaded.

He wanted to please her. He wanted to show her how good it could be. How good it *should* be. But it was so hard not to be waylaid by how perfect she was. He lifted his head and touched her gently with his fingers, feeling the liquid heat welcome him. He raised his eyes and watched her face as his fingers stroked her entrance and then entered her, first one and then another, feeling her tight silken heat envelop them, tugging, insistent, inviting, as his thumb continued to circle that tight bud.

'Alex!'

He wanted to take his time. He meant to. He knew she was

a virgin and he should go slowly. He knew he should take his time and make it as wonderful for her as he knew it was going to be for him. But the desperate edge to her voice, the keening note it contained, was his undoing.

Driven by need, compelled by desire, he moved between her thighs, spreading them wide, remembering only at the last instant to take precautions. He fumbled with the details. Any delay now was far too long. He'd waited eight long years as it was.

And then he was there. She held onto him, her arms entwined around his neck, her mouth working with his, welcoming his tongue inside as she would soon welcome him.

And he entered her, smoothly, cleanly, in one swift, painless thrust that took both her breath and her virginity away. And as she gripped him with new-found muscles that held him tight and dared him to go deeper, he heard in his heartbeat a distant echo of a former time. It made no sense, its rhythm drowned out by the force of what was happening between them, the power of his thrusts, the magic receptiveness of her body, tilting, angling to receive him even deeper. And deeper.

He was lost, her power taking him where it wanted, drawing him over the edge even as it took her. She stilled and came apart in his arms, her muscles contracting all around him like firecrackers until he had nowhere to go but to explode in the aftermath.

And it was only in the quietening minutes after that his heartbeat settled down once again into a steady rhythm that he could recognise. He listened to the beat, his limbs heavy in his post-sex state. He listened to what it told him. And it approved of his choice of bed partner. With her wild hair and lush curves and her too-wide mouth, she was a woman to hold onto, a woman you could love.

Theos! His body tensed, his spine chilled and his senses went from drowsy to red alert.

Where the hell had *that* come from? He couldn't love her. It would never happen. This was an exercise in taking what she'd offered, in getting her out of his system. Nothing more.

He shifted to one side, wanting suddenly to get away, yet strangely moved when she followed him, nestling in close. He looked at her, her eyes closed, her hair spread on the pillow like some coiled mantilla, a spiral curl of it falling over her cheek. Unable to resist, he lifted a hand, smoothing it back from her face, and her eyelids fluttered open.

Green eyes greeted him, moisture laden green eyes, and an unexpected guilt bit deep.

'Did I hurt you?'

Suddenly he realised that it mattered. That he didn't want to make her cry. And that made him even more unsettled.

'No,' she said. 'Were you supposed to?'

'I'm glad,' he said, more brusquely than he'd needed, avoiding the issue altogether. He didn't want to know why she was crying. He didn't want to muddy the waters any more when he didn't understand why sex should suddenly felt like something else entirely. But he wouldn't have to think about it for long—not if he could get her out of here quickly.

'I'm taking you to England tomorrow,' he said, his hand unable to resist sweeping gently along the dips and curves of her body even while planning his escape route

'England?' It was hard to think with him doing that, stirring her flesh all over again. Saskia had thought it couldn't be any better than that first time, but the way he had her feeling already made her think otherwise. But a trip to England? If they were anywhere near London she might have a chance to visit her father. 'Do you have business there?'

'No. We both do. I'm taking you to see Sir Rodney and the

board. I'm going to tell them the truth. I'm going to make them believe there never was an engagement.'

Something inside her chilled and set.

'You'd do that for me?' she asked. It was more than she'd ever expected from him, and yet still it was hard to sound excited about it.

'That promotion means so much to you. And it's because of me that you run the risk of losing it. It's the only thing I can do.'

It's not the only thing you can do, she wanted to argue. You could… What? What did she expect him to do? Admit his undying love for her? Marry her? On the strength of one hasty if spectacular sexual encounter? She didn't want that herself.

Did she?

But, no, she was no naïve teenager any more—and now she was no naïve virgin. She'd shed a tear as she'd waved one part of her life behind, even as she'd embraced the new. Because how could she feel the same and yet feel so different at the same time?

Right now it was too hard to think—much too hard to think. Especially when his mouth was weaving its magic on her skin and his hands were moving hot and heavy over her flesh. And when he entered her again she forgot all thoughts anyway.

He flipped her over in his arms until she was sitting astride him, his hands curving from her hips to her waist and up higher, till he took both breasts in his hands, cherishing them, taking pleasure in them, celebrating their fullness, his thumbs rolling the pebbled peaks of her nipples between them.

And then he moved inside her and she gasped, her back arching. The feeling was different, fuller, deeper than anything before, and pleasure roiled within her. Pleasure and aching heat. He moved again, his hands on her hips, guiding her along his length till she was almost at his limit and then letting her fill herself with him again. He let her find the rhythm, sometimes achingly slow, sometimes descending like a woman possessed. As she must be. Possessed by him.

Absorbing him.

Loving him.

It was back, she realised on a gasp, and worse than before. She'd been but a teenager, totally inexperienced in the world, when she'd first fallen in love. Now she should know better than to fall in love with a man like Alex Koutoufides. But that still didn't stop her.

Damn her, but she loved him. She wanted him. Every part of him.

And it frightened her, this new knowledge of loving him, of new experiences and new sensations. Of his hard length even now swelling inside her, and how much power she held over him. She watched the sweat break out on his brow as he searched for control even while she battled to retain hers against the mounting forces that felt as if they were trying to split her apart. With a sudden cry he grabbed for her hips, flipping her underneath him and lunging into her, each time bringing her closer and closer to that shattering conclusion she craved, taking her there in one final thrust and going with her into that gasping, yawning chasm of release.

Saskia felt a mounting sickness inside her. After a night of making love and a morning spent waking up to it, he'd organised a jet to take them to London. They had finally touched down in the evening, too late for anything but a late dinner in the plush hotel restaurant. An appointment had been requested with Sir Rodney first thing in the morning and if all went well there Saskia planned to visit with her father later in the afternoon. Hopefully the news would be good.

Now, Saskia toyed with her wine glass, turning the stem between her fingers, looking absently out of the large picture windows overlooking Regents Park while she waited for Alex to return from making a call. If she received this promotion she'd be based near London permanently, her time primarily taken up with her new role with the magazine, her weekends taken up with caring for her father. And whatever was happening here between her and Alex would be over.

Thank goodness.

How she'd managed to even look at herself in the mirror this morning she didn't know. She'd thrown herself upon him like a desperate virgin incensed that he'd rejected her once before. She'd fallen for the man who'd destroyed her father's life.

How could she even face her father after that?

Cramps squeezed what little she'd eaten into a tight ball inside her.

Thank God this would soon be over. Alex had been tense all day. He wanted her gone just as much as she needed to flee. Why else would he be pursuing any chance to help her win her job? He was pulling out all the stops to ensure she had a chance for this promotion.

Alex returned to the table and smiled tensely down at her, apologising for taking so long as he lifted a bottle of champagne from the ice bucket and filled both their glasses. And in spite of the churning in her tummy she couldn't help an uneasy smile back. Because right this minute it didn't matter if he didn't want her beyond tonight. Already muscles she'd thought well spent made themselves felt, making their interest clear to her in a way that brought heat and colour to her cheeks. She had this night to look forward to—why spoil it?

He picked up his flute and slanted it towards her. 'It's confirmed. We meet Sir Rodney at eleven. Here's to a successful outcome. Here's to getting what you want.'

They touched glasses, the expensive tink of crystal against crystal a total contrast to the sensation of her stomach crunching into more knots.

How could she get what she really wanted when she didn't know what she wanted herself?

She sipped from her glass, tiny beads sparkling in the fine wine, her heart strangely heavy.

'Would you like to do something after the meeting? Maybe take in a river cruise or visit a gallery?'

'Thanks,' she said, 'but I've got plans for the afternoon already.'

Surprise gave way to a resigned shrug. 'I see.' He picked up his glass. 'What have you arranged?'

She took a deep breath. 'I'm visiting with my father.'

His glass stilled at his mouth, mid swallow, before slowly he replaced it on the table. 'Your father lives here? In London? When did that happen?'

Her eyes challenged him. 'Where did you think he lived? Still back in Sydney? He came with me when I got my scholarship to the London School of Economics. Did you really think I'd leave him alone in Sydney after everything that had happened? He couldn't wait to get away and make a fresh start.'

'And has he?' Alex demanded, his tone suddenly aggressive. 'What kind of "fresh start" has he made?'

Saskia twisted her serviette in her lap. He had tried—at least in those first years. He'd started out in a new country with determination and a whole new zest for living. But when proposal after proposal for new businesses had been knocked back, with partners pulling out at the last minute, finance continually declined, then so had he. His dreams to start another business curtailed, he'd searched for employment. But jobs for aging executives with experience half a world away were thin on the ground. Soon he hadn't even been trying, and it had been only then that she'd found him spending more time with the betting pages than the employment guide. Before long she had discovered he'd gambled what little they'd had left clean away, and the debts were already mounting.

'These last few years,' she admitted, 'it's been hard.'

'*Life's* hard.'

Her sadness evaporated in an instant, incinerated in the harshness of his pronouncement. 'I certainly didn't expect any sympathy from you! Not after you'd done your bit—pulling the company out from under his feet the way you did.'

'In exactly the same way he ruined *my* father's business. If he could dish it out, you'd think he might have been able to take it.'

She stood up to go, placing her napkin on the table. 'I really don't want to sit here and listen to this.'

Alex snared her wrist in one hand. 'Sit down,' he snapped. Then, softer, 'Please. I shouldn't have said anything. Let's not argue tonight.'

She stood there, torn between leaving his man with a hatred for her father she couldn't understand—a man she shouldn't be with, not if loyalty to her father meant anything. And yet the very thought of walking away from Alex right now almost ripped her in two.

In the end it was only the thought that she would have to leave him anyway, and soon, that allowed her to sit down. That and the fact she still needed his help tomorrow with the board if she was going to be able to help her father at all. But soon enough she'd never see Alex again. Soon enough he'd be gone from her life. What was one more night of passion to steal before then?

A tense meal stretched into tense coffee, stretched into a tense journey to the penthouse suite. Alex hadn't even made a pretence of booking two rooms for them this trip, and both of them knew what was in store.

Inside the suite's welcoming lobby he pulled her straight into his arms. She came reluctantly, like a piece of board, all angles and stiffness and attitude. And then his mouth met hers and he felt the resistance drain out of her, her lips parting and welcoming, his tongue meeting hers, tasting and duelling. And somewhere in the midst of it their mutual resentment gave way to mutual desperate need, and clothes were tackled, peeled off, shucked. He manoeuvred her through to the magnificent bedroom and they hit the four-poster bed, a frenzy of entwined lips and tangled limbs and frantic grabs for air. He barely had time to sheath himself before he was inside her, driving, thrusting, seeking that place that wiped all others away, finding it in her and spinning them both over the abyss.

For a while they lay gasping together, their bodies humming, their senses slowly returning to something approaching normality. 'Stay there,' he said, kissing her forehead before easing away, padding to the bathroom and turning on the gold-plated taps over the large oval-shaped bathtub. A bottle of hotel bubble bath followed. When he came back he found her wrapped in a fluffy robe at the dressing table, removing her jewellery.

He growled and caught hold of her and spun her towards him, taking hold of the tied ends of the robe and unlooping them. He let the sides fall open, exposing a long window of shimmering skin, of womanly curves and golden blonde curls, and he felt himself start to get hard all over again.

She watched him with those green, green eyes, watched him drink her in, watched him take his fill of her and smile. And he saw sadness in those green eyes, mixed in with her desire. And he saw his own desire reflected back at him.

And then he buried his mouth on her neck, where her pulse jumped ragged for him. 'I'm running a bath for us,' he said. 'So you won't be needing this.' He let the robe drop from her shoulders, leaving her naked in his arms, his hands scanning her surface, cherishing every dip, memorising every curve.

'You go ahead,' he said at last, while he knew he was still capable of letting her go. 'I'll get us a drink.'

Still he turned to watch her go across the carpet, the gentle sway of her hips like a seduction in itself. He breathed in a groan and threw his head back, reefing his hands through his hair. She was going to walk out of his life the same way she'd just walked to the bathroom.

Eight years after he'd sent her packing, he was about to lose her again. And he was doing his utmost to ensure it happened.

Eight years ago he'd been sure about his decision. Now he didn't know what to think.

But he couldn't let her just walk out of his life as if she'd never been there. He'd been given a second chance—a second chance to get things right, not merely a second chance to make love to her. What the hell was wrong with him? Why hadn't he been able to see that before?

He *would* make things right. For both of them. Starting now.

She didn't have to take that job. Whatever it was that meant so much to her about it, he'd give her that tenfold. She didn't want his money, she'd made that clear, but he could make up for what had happened in the past with more than mere cash. She could come and live with him. She wouldn't need to scrimp and worry about money again. They could pretend the past had never happened. They could start afresh.

And he'd take care of her.

Starting tonight.

A bottle of champagne stood chilling in a crystal ice bucket on a silver tray, two crystal flutes alongside. He popped the cork on the champagne, filling the flutes only halfway. He'd just picked up the bottle and glasses when a flashing light caught his eye. Someone had left a message while they were out.

He almost didn't bother picking it up, but if Sir Rodney and his cronies had changed the appointment time they would be better off finding out tonight, before the two of them embarked on what he expected would be another long night of sex. It wouldn't do to be late for the meeting, even though now his own agenda had taken a slight change of direction. If he played his cards right tonight, Saskia would no longer have to plead for a chance at this promotion. She'd be handing in her resignation. He put the bottle down and picked up the receiver, pressing the message bank button as he happily contemplated tomorrow's meeting.

'Saskia!'

He blinked as he recognised the voice, a prickly suspicion crawling through him, congealing in his gut. Why the hell would Marla be calling Saskia? He focused on the message she'd left.

'I have such exciting news. They've made an offer on my memoirs. They recommended I get an agent straight away, so I need your help. When are you back? Call me when you get a chance. I can't believe it—they're going to publish my book! And I owe it all to you!'

CHAPTER NINE

THE bath was liquid heaven, the bubbles up to her chin, the spa jets gently massaging muscles sore in places from abilities she had never dreamed possible. She closed her eyes and let her head loll back against the rim. But she wasn't about to go to sleep. Not a chance. Soon Alex would join her, and another chapter in her sexual awakening would begin. And in the slippery oil-scented water she was very much looking forward to this particular chapter.

Tonight she wouldn't think about anything but what he would teach her and what she would learn. Tomorrow there would be time enough for recriminations.

Saskia sensed rather than heard the door open. She opened her eyes and looked around, expecting him to be still naked, expecting him to join her. But he was wearing jeans and a buttoned shirt, and the look on his face was dark thunder. She frowned, lifting herself a little higher in the water.

'Alex?'

'You bitch,' he snarled. 'How the hell did you think you'd get away with it?'

She sat right up now, turning around to face him, ignoring the sluice of water and the slide of bubbles from her skin. 'Alex, what's wrong?'

'All the time you demanded to be trusted. All the time you pretended to be something you're not. All that crap about a profile. All that rubbish about suddenly not being in the running for the promotion. It was all one big con. There never was any promotion. There never was any competition. It was all one big cover-up for what you were really doing.'

'I don't understand.' She pushed herself up and out of the bath, securing one of the enormous bath sheets around her while he continued to stand like some gunslinger looking to shoot her down. 'What are you talking about?'

'Marla's memoirs are what I'm talking about!'

Fear sent shivers down her spine. He'd been bound to find out some time, but why now? Why now, before Marla had had a chance to speak to him about it herself? 'How did you find out?'

His lips turned into a sneer. 'And you're in so deep you can't even deny it.'

She shook her head, grabbed another smaller towel to wipe away the foam that still clung to her shoulders and hair. 'Why should I deny it? She asked me to read them.'

He grabbed the towel and whipped it out of her reach, forcing her to focus on him and him alone. 'You're lying! You've been stalking her from the start.'

'You don't know what you're talking about. Marla asked me to read them. So I did, and they were good. And I passed them onto a friend of mine who works for a publisher in New York. Like Marla also asked me to do.'

'I told you to stay away from her!'

'And I did. She sought *me* out. I didn't go looking for her.'

'You're lying.'

'It's the truth! Don't blame me. Blame yourself. Marla and

I might have been confined to different cell blocks, but you were the one who had us living in the same prison compound.'

'You promised me in New York that you'd stay away from her.'

'No! I promised you that this profile would be about you!' she reminded him. 'Besides, I'd already told Marla I'd read her manuscript, and I wasn't about to break a promise I'd made to her.'

'You didn't tell me.'

'Why the hell should I? I knew what you'd say, how you'd react. So did Marla. But she pleaded with me to read it and I did.' She glared up at him, waiting for the next explosion. 'So what's happened?' she asked. Sick of being confined to the bathroom, she shoved past him and made her way to the dressing room, needing the security of clothes. She couldn't hold this conversation wearing only a towel.

'Did Marla call?'

'She left you a message,' he responded, following her. 'Some sleazy publisher has offered her a contract to publish them.'

She spun around, her hands full of clothes, the significance of his message overshadowing his insult. 'They want to make her an offer? But that's great news. She must be so excited. Surely you can see how wonderful an opportunity this is for her?'

'What I can see,' Alex said, coming towards her so fast he seemed to rise up like a mountain over her, 'is that you've succeeded in getting my sister to splash the sordid details of her entire life to the papers.'

'This isn't the papers, and it's not about sordid details. If what you say is true, and I hope it is for her sake, then it's a book deal. She's actually scored the heady achievement of selling her first book. Do you have any idea how rare it is to have your first book published?'

'Sleaze will always find a market.'

'How *dare* you say that? This is your sister's writing we're talking about. And if you bothered to read it you'd see it's an amazingly well-written account of one person's life and her struggle to find herself. *In her words*. Noone else's. And it's funny and witty and touching and wise. Did you know your sister was so talented? I doubt it. I bet you didn't even know your sister was a writer.'

His eyes slid away and she knew she'd hit a raw nerve.

'Marla's a gifted writer,' she continued, 'and now she might even have the start of a career. Don't you want that for her? Don't you want her to have a real life? Or are you so determined to keep up this big brother act, keep her locked away, that you can't even see what's good for her any more? Can't you see that's why she breaks out? Because she wants freedom—not to be treated like a child!'

'She needs my support.'

'No, she needs her freedom. You keep her locked away in a gilded prison. No wonder when she breaks out she seeks every bit of attention she can find. You've got her so locked away she doesn't even know who she is.'

'And you think *you* know what's good for her?' His face was severe, his mouth twisted, and Saskia knew she'd hurt him.

'Look, I know you care for her. She's your sister and you love her. But maybe you should back off a bit. Maybe you should give her a bit more responsibility and freedom. I know she wants it.'

'And splattering her life in print is the way to do it? Why couldn't you leave her alone? I told you to leave her alone!'

'Alex, listen—'

'Marla was fine until your family came along. What business do you have in trying to ruin her life? Don't you think your father's done enough to her already?'

His words shocked her into silence, and he stood over her, his chest heaving, the words hanging between them like a damnation. Why should he hold such deep-seated hatred for her father? Sure, their families had history, but so did just about every other family engaged in business in Sydney. It was an occupational hazard.

'Look, we both know my father took over your family's business. And I know it must have been difficult for your family. But it was such a long time ago. Maybe it's time you got over it.'

He laughed—the sound of the devil, evil and poisoned with acrimony—and fear flared out from her spine. 'I'm not talking about the takeover,' he sneered, his face now only inches from her own.

Dread rooted her to the spot. But if it wasn't the takeover… 'Then, what?'

'I'm talking about when your father raped my sister!'

Cold shock drenched through her, dousing her in disbelief. She was unable to speak, unable to respond, the shaking of her head the only movement she was capable of.

'You don't believe me? You don't believe your precious father could do such a thing?'

'No,' she protested. It was too revolting, too ugly to have any measure of truth. Dear God, not her father. It was a lie. It had to be.

'Believe it,' he said. 'Your dear sweet father wasn't content to strip my father's business bare. He decided to strip Marla of her virginity as well.'

'No! It can't be possible.'

'More than possible. It happened. And your father waved the fact he'd stolen Marla's virginity in front of my father like a trophy.'

'It can't be true.'

'She was *fifteen* years old!'

Every revelation was worse than the one before. She cowered before him, reeling from his accusations as if they were body blows. Marla had been a teenager—little more than a child. It couldn't be true. It just couldn't.

Until she remembered the memoirs—how Marla had lost her virginity at the age of fifteen—to a much older man.

Could that man have been Saskia's own father?

Could he have acted that way? Her own father? How could he have done it? Surely he could never have committed such a horrendous act, only then to turn around and flaunt the fact in front of Marla's father? It would have destroyed them.

But then, it *had* destroyed them, hadn't it?

What had Alex told her? His parents had never recovered from the shock of the takeover. Only now she could see that it hadn't been the takeover that had destroyed them, it had been despair at what had happened to their young daughter.

Why else would Alex hate her father so much? He must know it was true. And so far nothing else made sense. Nothing else fitted.

She'd always known her father had prided himself on his ruthless business skills, but she'd never seen him in that light. Saskia must have been only about one year old at the time, and to her as a child her father had been her gruff teddy bear, who'd sent her into fits of laughter by teasing her with his whiskers when wishing her goodnight.

How could the same man who had tickled her and kissed her goodnight do something so hideous to someone else's daughter? She shuddered. Had he kissed her goodnight after what he'd done to Marla? Oh, God, she hoped not.

With a cry of grief and disgust she bolted for the bathroom, losing what little she'd managed to eat of her Michelin three-star meal.

He stalked up behind her, throwing her a towel that she grabbed hold of and clutched to her mouth. 'I know,' he said, his voice hard and remorseless. 'It turns my stomach too.'

She was shaking, her body too weak to stand, her breathing ragged. 'Alex,' she croaked. 'I had no idea. I didn't know.'

'So now you do. And now you know why I didn't want you having anything to do with Marla from the start.'

'You were protecting me from discovering what my father had done.'

'I was protecting *her*! This was always about Marla, about keeping her safe.'

Oh no, she suddenly thought. *Marla*. The woman had trusted her, had sought out her help. She looked up at him, 'Does she know? I mean, about me... I mean...'

'That you're *his* daughter? Of course she doesn't! Why the hell else would she have anything to do with you?'

'I don't know what to say,' she said, blotting her face on the towel, wishing it could soak up the horror, wishing it could mop up the past.

'Then do me a favour and don't say anything.' His face had moved beyond fury. The heat had dispersed and now it was ice that met her gaze—cold, unforgiving ice that chilled her heart and soul.

'You know, I actually believed we could forget the past because I thought you were different. For a while there you had me so taken with sleeping with you I even forgot who your father was.' He laughed, this time a self-deprecating sound that smacked of how much of a fool he thought he'd been. 'But you're no different than he is—preying on the naïve and vulnerable for your own sick purpose. Now I can see you're truly your father's daughter. You two really deserve each other.'

He disappeared once more into the suite. A few seconds later she heard him talking, barking orders into the phone.

She stood, still shaky, and washed her face, shocked at how pale her skin looked in the mirror. She saw movement behind her and turned. Alex had his leather briefcase and suit bag in his hands, and her heart—something she hadn't thought could get any lower—took a dive.

'You're leaving?'

'I'm moving to another suite. I'll be flying back first thing tomorrow. I'll ship over anything you left.'

'What about tomorrow morning's meeting?'

'Oh, come on, Saskia. Enough's enough. You don't expect me to believe that rubbish still. You've got what you wanted. You've already got Marla bending over backwards to spill her guts to the tabloids, or wherever else you want her to, even if I do manage to get that manuscript back. You don't have to convince me now. It's too late.'

She thought she saw something move across his eyes—a sad look, almost of regret—but it was fleeting and too quickly blinked away. And too easily misinterpreted, she thought, knowing that looking for something in his eyes, hoping for it, would not make it so.

Like he said, it was too late.

And it was no wonder he didn't want anything to do with her. She was a constant reminder of what her father had done.

'Oh, and when you see your father tomorrow…'

She waited a few seconds, then, 'Yes?'

'Let him know that he's the only man I ever felt like murdering. Tell him that under the circumstances he ended up getting off lightly.'

Saskia closed her eyes against the bitterness of his parting jibe, and by the time she'd opened them he'd gone. Seconds later she heard the cushioned thunk of the suite's solid front door closing.

He was gone.

Again.

For the second time in her life he was casting her aside. And for the second time in her life she felt as if her insides had been ripped out of her body, shredded into ribbons and hung out to dry.

CHAPTER TEN

THE meeting with Sir Rodney and the board had gone as well as could be expected. At least that was what Saskia told herself, trying to find some positive angle as she stood outside the Snapmedia building, wrapping her coat more tightly around her and battling back tears under the grey, sleet-threatening sky.

Because, in all seriousness, what had she expected? The board were bound to have been unimpressed with the fact that the man who'd insisted they all get together for a meeting to convince them their engagement had been a farce from the start hadn't even bothered to show up.

If she'd slept last night, if she hadn't lain awake in the empty suite, being tormented by the awful knowledge that her father was not the man she thought he was, that he was suddenly a stranger, then she might have been able to argue her case. But she'd been shattered by both the news and her sleepless night, and part of her wondered if she'd even wanted to fight anyway.

In the end the board had conceded that if she could get her profile in within the week there was a slim chance she might still be considered for the position, but it would have to stack up against Carmen's excellent in-depth report.

She'd almost laughed in their faces. How could she turn in a profile when her subject had just walked out on her? She didn't stand a chance. But then, why did she even need a chance?

Why did she need this job to pay for a house for her father when right now she wasn't even sure she ever wanted to see him again?

She sniffed against the heavy cold air, blinking away the tears from her scratchy eyes as engaged cab after engaged cab cruised past. Of course she wanted to see him—he was her father, after all. The only father she'd ever have. And he was old and frail, and he had no one else to take care of him, and she had no one else to take care of.

But if it were true…

If he'd committed such an unforgivable act…

Oh, where *were* all the empty cabs in London?

She rubbed her hands together, wishing she'd worn gloves and suddenly missing Alex, with his limousines and jets on tap. He turned travel into an art form, not this battle for survival.

Finally she managed to coax a black cab to the kerb. She pulled open the back door and jumped inside.

'Where to, luv?' asked the driver.

It was warm in the cab, much warmer than outside, and it took her a moment to register that she needed to make a decision—now.

She took a deep breath and gave him her father's address.

Twenty minutes and half a lifetime of dread later the taxi pulled up opposite her father's dingy block of flats.

He's an old man, she told herself as she climbed the stairs to the second floor.

He was still the same old man she'd spoken to a week ago.

And, whatever else he'd done, he was still her father. But it was hard to convince herself of that—so hard to feel warm for the man who'd tucked her in at night at the same time. God only knew what else had been happening.

It was after the third time she'd knocked that she started regretting the fact she hadn't let him know she was coming. But then she hadn't known what she was going to say. And what *could* she say?—*Hi, Dad, what was it like to have sex with Alex Koutoufides's sister?*

Maybe it was just as well he wasn't home. Maybe she wasn't ready for this. But then, where was he? The last time she'd rung he'd been too ill to leave the flat.

The door of the adjoining flat opened and a woman peered out.

'Mrs Sharpe,' Saskia said, relieved to see the neighbour. 'I've come to visit my father, but he's not answering. Do you know where he might be?'

Enid Sharpe's face creased into wrinkles deep enough for caverns and her bird-like frame shuffled out through the door towards her. 'Oh, Saskia, my luvvy, haven't you heard?'

Alex was in a foul mood by the time he got back to Tahoe, and it didn't help matters when Marla came outside to meet the car, the smile on her face broader than he'd seen in years. She rushed up to kiss him on the cheek, and then looked around the car, puzzled.

'Where's Saskia?'

'London,' he snapped, snatching up his bags from the boot of the car himself, before the driver could collect them.

'But why? When's she coming back?'

'She won't be,' he said, noticing Jake standing by the door, waiting. He nodded. 'Jake.'

'Good to have you back, boss.'

You won't think that when I'm done with you. 'Meet me in

my office,' he told him. They had a few matters to discuss con-
cerning Marla's secret liaisons. 'Fifteen minutes.'

Marla trailed him through to the massive timber-beamed
living area. 'But…'

He turned around alongside the stone fireplace, ready to
snap her head off, and then something struck him as different about her. 'What have you done to yourself?' he asked.
'You look different.'

She reached a tentative hand to her hair and shrugged. 'I
coloured it, that's all. Do you like it?'

What was not to like? It was honey-gold, just the way he
liked it. Just like… He growled, clamping down on the thought.

'I got your message,' he said. 'I know about the book.'

She blinked. 'Oh?'

'And I want you to know I'll do everything I can to get it back.'

'What do you mean?' Her hands clutched his arm. 'They
want to buy it. It's going to be published.'

'Not if I can help it.'

'No! You don't understand. Saskia said—'

He shrugged off her hands. 'I don't care what Saskia said!'

She stood watching him, her breathing fast and furious.
'How did you find out? I left that message for Saskia, and she
wouldn't have told you. I asked for Saskia's room…' Her eyes
suddenly widened. 'You two shared a room. You slept with
her, didn't you?'

Alex swung his bags around and resumed walking past the
fireplace towards the master bedroom wing.

'You slept with Saskia. I *knew* you would. It was obvious
you wanted to. Is that why she hasn't returned my calls? But
what did you say to her? What did you do to her to make her
stay in London?'

He spun around, incensed at what his sister was saying—

doubly incensed at what she'd perceived. 'I told her from the very beginning to stay away from you. But she couldn't, could she? She pretended to be here to interview me, when all along she was angling to get the dirt on you. I trusted her to keep away from you, and she couldn't.'

'You've never trusted anybody in your life!'

'She told me she was here to do my profile.'

'And she was.'

'Then how did she end up selling *your* story?'

'Because I sought her out! I saw her walking along the lake shore in the early morning and I went down to talk to her. I liked her. It was nice to talk to another woman for a change, and that's when I asked if she'd be willing to read my manuscript.'

'I'm sure that's how it was.'

'She told me you wouldn't like it. I had to beg her to read it. I even had to pretend it was written by someone else. She didn't believe me for a minute, though. And I know she was thinking it was going to be hopeless, and she really didn't want to know, but I was desperate. I made her take it.'

Alex looked at his sister, weighing up her words. Marla had done plenty of things in her time that he didn't like, but she'd never lied to him. And wasn't that exactly what Saskia had told him—that Marla had sought her out?

But so what? It didn't matter in the scheme of things. She was still who she was. Nothing would ever change that.

'It doesn't change the fact that you have to pull that manuscript. We have to get it back.'

Marla crossed her arms and stamped her heel down hard. 'What if I don't want to?'

'Then it's getting pulled anyway. You know I'm only doing what's best for you.'

'No, you're not. How can you know what's best for me?

Have you ever *asked* me what I'd like? And, given the way you've obviously treated Saskia over this, you don't even know what's best for you. How can you possibly think you're any judge of what might be good for someone else?'

Alex sighed and raked the fingers of one hand through his hair. He was tired and hungry and he'd had enough of women lately—especially women who couldn't see what was obvious and yet imagined all sorts of other things. But maybe he'd come on too strong all the same. There was no point taking out his frustrations over what had happened with Saskia on Marla.

'Look, I just want you to be happy, okay?'

'Fine. That makes two of us.'

'Then there's no point publishing a whole lot of stuff that's going to hit the fan big time.'

'How do you know that's going to happen? You haven't even read it.'

'Come on, Marla. Since when has anyone published anything about you that hasn't caused trouble?'

'But *I* wrote this. Don't you even trust me to get it right?'

'This isn't about trust—'

'Yes, it is! I'm nearly forty years old, and still you don't trust me to tell my story my way and not screw it up. If you just talked to Saskia—'

'*No!* I will not be talking to Saskia—and if you know what's good for you, neither will you.'

'And yet it was okay for you to sleep with her?'

Breath hissed through his teeth. 'You don't understand. You don't know what kind of person she is.'

'I know she's not the gutter press you'd like to make her out to be.'

'It's not just what she is; it's *who* she is.'

'Because she's Victor Prentice's daughter?'

With his brain still fogged from too much travel and too little sleep he had to take a second to assimilate what she'd just said.

'You knew?'

'Of course I knew! I mean, not straight away, but it wasn't too hard to work out—not with her photo and her name plastered all over every paper in town.'

'But her father…'

'You don't have to remind me who her father is or what her father did! I was there—remember?'

'You were only fifteen!'

'And you were only twelve! What could you have really known about it at the time? I wish you'd never found out. I wish Dad had never said anything to you.'

'I knew something was going on even before he did. So many hushed conversations. So many tears. And when I found out he'd raped you I wanted to kill him. I swore I'd have my revenge for what he did.'

She looked at him open-mouthed. 'What did you just say? He *raped* me? Is that what you've believed all these years?'

'He took your virginity. You were only a teenager. What would you call it?'

'I'd call it sex. I'd call it satisfying a mutual need.'

'Tsou!' The word exploded from him as he reeled away. When he turned he was pointing his finger at her like an accusation. 'He was old enough to be your father! Why would you feel any such need with *him*? How would you even know what you needed?'

She shrugged. 'Who can explain attraction? He was older, and I thought he was so dashing and powerful. I was drawn to him, and curious about sex. And he was so lonely and sad—with no wife and a tiny child. I guess I felt sorry for him.'

'But why would you agree to do such a thing?'

'I didn't agree. *He* did.'

She gave him time to let the words sink in—time that he desperately needed to make sense of it all.

'But that would mean…'

'Exactly,' she said. 'I *asked* him to make love to me. I chose him to show me what it was to be a woman. I know what he did was wrong, and so did he, but I begged him—even forced myself on him, if you must know.' She tilted her head, her brow furrowed slightly. 'Is this why you've been so against Saskia from the start? It wasn't just that she was a journalist? It was because she was Victor's daughter? How could you possibly hold that against her, when she was still in nappies at the time?'

He reached his arms up, pushing his neck back against his knotted fingers. 'It doesn't matter. He still had sex with you. He had no right—'

'Forget about Victor! You have to let this hatred go, Alex! It's history. Besides, Victor's little more than a broken man now. He's frail, and needs constant help.' She stopped when she saw his double-take. 'You mean you didn't know? Didn't you speak to Saskia at all while you had her here? Or were you too busy angling her into your bed? Why else do you think she's so desperate for this promotion of hers? It's the only way she's going to be able to afford decent care for him.'

'*Theos!*' he said, closing his eyes as he spun around, feeling suddenly ill. He couldn't have managed this more badly if he'd tried.

'What have you done?' Marla came closer, put a hand to his arm. 'Didn't you go over there to help her? What happened?'

He looked down at his sister, but he saw nothing but the pain on Saskia's face—the pain he'd savagely inflicted when he'd accused her father of committing the most hideous of crimes, of raping his sister. He heard Marla's rapid intake of breath, registered her shocked withdrawal.

'Oh, my God! You didn't tell her… Please say you didn't tell her that…?'

He shook his head. He couldn't deny it. Just as he couldn't deny he'd sent her packing for the second time. He'd used her and insulted her and then thrown her to the wolves, discarding her like a piece of dirt. And he'd felt so righteous. In spite of everything there had been moments in that hotel room in London when he'd wanted to keep her, wanted to have her in his bed and by his side, when he hadn't wanted to let her go. But at the last minute he'd been saved from those weak urges by hearing Marla's news and proving he'd been right not to trust Saskia all along.

What the hell had he done?

Alex stood in his study, his hands in his pockets, gazing unseeingly out of the floor-to-ceiling cedar-framed windows. He knew what the view looked like from here. He knew every tree and boulder leading down to the lake. He knew every mountain rising on the far distant shore.

So why today did everything look so different?

The morning was sharp and crisp, the lake water so still and clear he could see right down into the boulder strewn shallows. He'd given up on sleep and spent most of the night in his study, catching up on business he'd neglected over the last few days.

But his mind hadn't been on business either.

Sleep eluded him. Business escaped him. Only one thing stood as stark and clear as the towering pines that framed his view. Only one thing accounted for the sick feeling in his empty stomach.

He'd been wrong.

Totally, completely, unforgivably wrong.

And that was just about his sister.

For years he'd thought he was protecting her, wrapping her up in cotton wool, trying to keep her safe and wondering why she'd escape his protective custody at every opportunity. Who could blame her? He'd never trusted her. He'd never let her find her own way. He'd taken her mistakes as signals that he should make all the decisions, not that she just needed the space and time to learn.

It was a wonder she still deigned to call him her brother.

But if he'd done wrong by Marla, his own sister, then what he'd done to Saskia was one thousand times worse.

He'd misjudged her, he'd mistrusted her, he'd damned her to hell—a hell that he himself had crafted for her—and then he'd left her there to rot.

Hell, if he ran his business this way he'd be bankrupt in a minute.

And wasn't that word appropriate?

Bankrupt.

Morally and ethically, when it came to Saskia, he lacked the most basic resources. He'd misjudged her from the start because of who she was and what she reminded him of. He'd misjudged her motives, he'd mistrusted her, he'd refused to believe her. And when he'd learned about Marla selling her memoirs all his vile prejudices had thrown a party and celebrated. He'd been right all along!

And yet he'd been so wrong.

He'd taken the moral high ground, thinking that ground was solid, not realising how thin a crust he was standing on.

And that crust had crumbled into chalk dust when he'd learned the truth about her.

She hadn't lied to him. She hadn't betrayed his trust. She'd recognised things about his relationship with his sister that he'd been blind to, that he hadn't wanted to hear. And she'd come here, dealing with the one person she'd never wanted to see in her life again, not for personal gain but to ensure she could care for her father.

What a damned fool he was! He fisted his hands to his forehead as the trees, the lake, the mountains all faded away before him. All he could see was her body slumped on the bathroom floor, her hand clutching a towel to her face, her eyes large and fearful like a wounded animal's. He'd dumped the news of what her father had done to his sister like a victory. It had been his *pièce de résistance* and he'd made the most of it, twisting it like a long, sharp-bladed knife in deep.

He'd trashed her father. He'd trashed her career by not staying to support her in front of her board. He'd trashed her life. And then he'd coldly walked away.

He'd had his second chance with her. He'd had a chance to put things between them to rights. And for a brief time he'd thought he could—that they might even have a life together, a future.

But he'd blown his precious chance sky-high.

Now there was no hope.

Saskia squirmed to wakefulness in the vinyl chair, its wooden arms cutting into her legs where they tucked under her. She opened her eyes and looked over at her father, hoping to see some improvement. Her heart sank as rapidly as it had risen.

No change.

After three days at his bedside she knew what to look for. After three days she was beginning to wonder if the coma that had claimed him after his inoperable brain stem haemorrhage was ever going to let him go. Would he ever be able to breathe without that tube down his throat and a machine to fill his chest with air?

'It could be five days before he wakes up,' the doctors had warned her. 'Or it could be five months. And even then…'

She clamped her eyes shut, trying to keep back the glum prognosis they'd issued, but the painful truth seeped through. She had to be ready, they'd told her. Even if he woke up he'd need months, maybe even years of rehabilitation. And that was the up side.

She didn't want to think about any of it. She'd already tied herself up in knots thinking, but right now what was the alternative? Trawling over the train wreck of the last couple of weeks with Alex? Not likely. There was no joy down that path. Only self-recrimination. Because for the second time in her life she'd offered herself to the man she'd fancied herself in love with. And for the second time she'd been discarded like something stinking stuck to his shoe.

But how utterly stupid of her was it that it had been the same man both times?

Hadn't she learned *anything* the first time around?

Saskia looked over at her father. The machine alongside him was ensuring the constant rise and fall of his chest, keeping him alive until such time as he could breathe on his own again. She looked at his creased sunken cheeks and his closed eyes as he slept, and he just looked like an old man.

When she'd gone to see him at the flat she'd been sick to the stomach over how she would greet him. What would she say? How could she believe what Alex had told her was true, and that her own father was capable of such an act? Because she was so very scared it was.

But now he was lying there in a coma, critically ill, possibly dying. Now only one fact mattered.

He was her father.

The only father she had.

And, God forgive her, she still loved him.

Tears slid down her cheeks. So what kind of person did that make her? Maybe Alex had been right. Maybe she truly was her father's daughter.

The door swung open and a nurse bustled into the room, flashing her a compassionate smile as she breezed by to check her patient's vitals. 'Beautiful day outside, Miss Prentice, but they're predicting it'll rain later. Maybe you should grab a cup of tea and get some fresh air while you can?'

Saskia stretched, and eased her feet into her shoes.

'Maybe you're right,' she agreed, swiping away at her own precipitation. There was precious little she could do here.

It was dark when she made it back to her tiny one-bedroom flat, bone-weary and wanting nothing more taxing than to lose herself in a long hot bath. She'd been at the hospital for five and a half days, refusing to go further than the gardens outside, refusing to leave her father's side for any length of time. He had nobody else—what if he woke up?

But the doctors were right. It was time to go home.

She swung the door open and let herself inside, snapping on the light. A neat pile of mail sat on the dresser and she gave silent thanks—as usual, her landlady had been keeping an eye on the place while she'd been away. Then she turned to see an untidier stack of boxes filling one half of her living room.

She looked at them, blinking as she moved closer, checking for the forwarding address.

Tahoe. That explained it. Alex had said he'd send her things. But why so many? She'd left barely anything there. And what she had left she really didn't care if she never saw again.

She slit through the tape on the first box and peeled back the flaps. Clothes. The outfits he'd bought her in Sydney—the boutique full of clothes he'd had delivered so she could look the part of his fiancée. Clothes she'd never considered hers. The beautiful silk-chiffon dress she'd worn at the airport that first day ran through her fingers. The ballgown she'd worn in New York was folded like treasure, and everything else was in between. There were clothes she'd never worn, and shoes and bags and underwear.

She sat back on her heels and contemplated it all, absorbing the shock of her discoveries, trying to come to terms with the sheer cold-bloodedness of it all. She began to laugh.

It was funny, really. They'd never been her clothes, but he'd cleared the cupboards and sent everything to her as if they were. There was a box of ballgowns here! A boutique in a box there! 'Here a box, there a box,' she cried, whooping with laughter as an old nursery rhyme came to mind. 'Everywhere a box, box.'

She laughed and laughed, unable to stop the hysteria welling up inside. He'd dispensed with every trace of anything she might have breathed on, let alone touched. He'd wiped her existence from his life as if she'd never been there, and he'd bundled up and sent her the crumbs, so she would know just how little he wanted to be reminded of her.

It was too funny for words. Because what made Alex think for a moment that she wanted to be reminded of *him*?

And she kept on laughing, the tears streaming down her face, unable to recall later, when she'd dragged herself off to bed, just when it was that her laughter had given way to tears.

* * *

Twenty-four hours later she was functioning again. If you could call it that. The doorbell rang and she pulled her still wet hair into a ponytail, calling out that she was coming. The charity group she'd called to take away the boxes obviously hadn't wasted any time—but that was good. The sooner they were gone, the sooner she would be rid of the physical reminders of her time with Alex. The memories she knew would take longer.

She pulled open the door wide to let them in, and froze.

'Hello, Saskia.'

CHAPTER ELEVEN

SHE blinked, took a breath, but when she opened her eyes again it was still Alex standing on her threshold—and it was still an angry knot that was tangling up and pulling tight inside her.

'What are you doing here?'

'I came to see you.' She noticed the tight lines around his jaw, the lines between his brows. She took in the creases in his chambray shirt and the slight slump to his shoulders. He looked tired, maybe a little shattered. Even so, he looked a darned sight better than she knew she did.

'Aren't you going to ask me in?'

'Why should I?'

'Because we have to talk.'

She shook her head. 'I don't think so. I don't think there's anything left to say.'

Two men, one middle-aged and wearing overalls and one in his twenties in baggy jeans and a sloppy T-shirt, appeared behind Alex's shoulder, trying to get her attention. 'You got a pick-up for Charity Central, luv?'

'That's right,' she said. 'Just through here.'

Alex didn't move out of the way, she noticed with irritation. Instead he moved inside the room to let them pass.

She indicated the boxes with a sweep of her hand. 'All of these.'

Alex looked at the boxes and then back at her as the first box was lugged into strong arms and disappeared out through the door. 'Hang on a minute,' he protested. 'Aren't these…?'

She nodded. 'The very same.'

'Those clothes cost a fortune.'

'Your fortune,' she said. 'Not mine. But if you want them…'

The older man stopped midway to the door. 'So are they going or staying?'

'They're going.'

'They're staying.'

They spoke together.

The man huffed and put the box down, tapping his returning assistant on the arm to stop him picking up the next box. He drummed his fingers on the top of one box. 'So what's it to be, guv?' he said, deferring to Alex.

'I bought them for you,' he told Saskia accusingly.

'You bought them for your fake fiancée,' she replied, 'who is now surplus to requirements. As are these clothes. If I don't want them, and you don't want them, charity seems the perfect solution.'

'Fine,' Alex said, as if he was speaking through gritted teeth. 'Take them away.'

The man looked from one to the other and then nodded at his colleague. In three trips they'd cleared the living room, smiled their brief thanks and disappeared, before either of them could change their minds.

Saskia breathed a sigh of relief as she boiled the kettle for a long-deserved cup of tea. The boxes were gone. If only Alex, still occupying her living room as if he belonged there, could be dispensed with so easily.

'What was that all about?' he demanded, coming up behind her.

'This is my home,' she warned him, spinning around. 'You might rule the roost in your own fleet of houses and hotel rooms, but here, in this flat, what I say goes. Have you got that?'

She knew her voice sounded thready and weak. Hell, she *felt* thready and weak. But she couldn't just let him take control. 'Besides which,' she said, 'I don't actually remember inviting you in.'

His eyelids dipped, almost as if he was shutting out her protest. 'Nevertheless, I'm here.'

She turned to look at him, saw the hurt and ache that coursed through his eyes and suddenly wished she hadn't. What right did he have to want sympathy? After everything he'd done?

She turned back towards the bench, squeezing out her teabag, twisting it around a spoon to wring it out, and finally dropping it in the bin, all her actions running comfortingly on autopilot. Then she stirred in a heaped teaspoon full of sugar, just for good measure. Right now she could do with all the fortification she could get.

'What if I don't want you here? Did you consider that?'

'Oh, yes. I considered that.'

'And?'

'It wasn't an option.'

She laughed, feeling the lingering hysteria of the night before revisiting her. Only now that hysteria wanted to be magnified by his presence. 'Now, that sounds like the great Alexander Koutoufides.'

'No!' he said, grabbing her arm and sending boiling liquid sloshing over the rim floorwards, thankfully not over her.

She looked down at his hand, then up at him. 'Let me go.'

'I didn't come here to argue with you.'

'Then why *are* you here, Alex? What could you possibly want after all that's happened?'

He looked at her, and the longer he did so the more she wished she'd never let him in.

'I came to tell you I was sorry.'

She drank in a deep breath, plastering a thin smile to her face. 'Well, that makes up for just about everything, then.'

She forced herself to take a sip of her tea, knowing it was still too hot but needing something to do. Something that didn't involve interaction with him. And yet, even scalding hot, her tea was no competition for the heat generated by his presence.

'Marla told me she pursued you about getting her memoirs published. She said you didn't come after her at all.'

She barely threw him a glance. 'Oh, and isn't that what I'd told you already? I had the distinct impression you didn't believe me.'

Her accusation hung heavy in the air, but even though his head was bowed his eyes still held hers.

'I realise you don't have to make this easy for me, but I am trying to apologise.'

'Of course. Apology accepted,' she said brightly, clearly throwing him off balance. 'Now, if there's nothing more…' She gestured to the door.

'Dammit, Saskia! Of course there's more—lots more.' He wheeled away, forcing hands rigid like claws through his hair. When he spun back he was holding out his hands almost in supplication. 'I left London because I thought you'd betrayed my trust. I thought you'd gone behind my back to get whatever dirt you could on my sister. And when I spoke to Marla and found out how wrong I was, do you know how bad I felt?'

'No,' she said frankly. 'I have no idea.'

'I'd not only accused you of a lie,' he continued, ignoring her snippy reply, 'I'd abandoned you to face your boss and your board alone for probably the most important meeting of your career. How bad was it?'

'Oh, it was just peachy,' she told him. 'And they were good enough to give me a few days to get my profile in. Only problem was, my subject had walked out on me.' She shrugged as she took a sip of her sweet tea. *'C'est la vie.'*

'You'll get that job, if you still want it, with or without my profile.'

She looked up at him. 'How sweet of you to say so.' Then, just as his eyes were starting to relax and warm, she held one hand up and waved it in the air. 'But I don't care any more. I've decided to let Carmen have the job. She wants it so badly—frankly she must do, to have poured herself all over Drago the way she did—and she'll be good at it, I know.'

'Saskia, Carmen won't be needing that job.'

'What do you mean?'

'You haven't been listening to the news today? Drago Maiolo had a heart attack and drove his Ferrari through a barricade and over a cliff.'

'Oh God, that's awful. But what's that got to do with Carmen?'

'Carmen was in the car alongside him. She didn't stand a chance.'

It was too much. When would it all stop? She squeezed her eyes shut and swayed, letting herself slump into a chair. No matter how much Carmen had done to hurt her, nobody deserved to die like that.

'I'm sorry,' he told her. 'There was no easy way to say it. But don't you see? Now that job can be yours.'

She rested her forehead against her hand. 'And don't *you* see? I don't want that job!'

'But I thought you needed it for your father.'

She looked up at him, blinking blindly, her stomach yawning open into a whirlpool, sucking her down further into that dark, fetid, bottomless place.

'I know all about it,' he explained. 'Marla told me he was sick. She said you need money to fund his care. And she told me more—'

From somewhere she dredged the energy to stand. 'And now I'm supposed to believe you suddenly care about my father?' Her voice was accusing, though her senses were still reeling as she swiped up her barely touched cup and transferred it to the sink.

'Listen to me,' he urged. 'I spoke to Marla. What I said in that hotel—'

She spun round, ignoring him, cutting him off. 'I'm awfully sorry to have to tell you I didn't get to pass on your message.'

'Message?'

'About how much you'd always wanted him dead.'

'*Theos!* Saskia, I never should have said that. I lashed out at you. I didn't mean—'

'Of course you meant it! You meant every word. And all the time we were together, all the time you were making love to me, you still hated my father so much you wanted him dead. How you must have hated having anything to do with *me*, the daughter of the man you hated so deeply. Frankly, I'm surprised you could bear to touch me.'

'It wasn't like that.'

She held up a hand to silence him, her smile thin. 'Don't worry. It doesn't matter. What does matter is that you got your wish.'

Silence hung over the small kitchen like a shroud.

'What are you talking about?'

'Didn't you know? My father died yesterday.'

All of a sudden the dark circles around eyes almost too large in the unearthly pallor of her skin of her face made sense.

Victor Prentice was dead.

'Saskia,' he said, automatically reaching out for her, thinking back to when his own parents had died, remembering the awful sense of loss, knowing how terrible she must be feeling without him having unceremoniously dumped the news of Carmen's death on her as well.

Clumsily she darted out of his reach across the kitchen, putting the dining table between them and crossing her arms defensively in front of her. 'Don't you dare touch me!'

'Saskia…'

'And please don't insult my intelligence by pretending you're sorry! You wanted him dead all along. You must be so relieved he's finally out of the way.'

'No. I'm not going to pretend I ever liked or respected your father,' he said honestly, 'but I was wrong about him. And I was wrong to tell you what I did. I hurt you, and I shouldn't have.'

She blinked, her green eyes glossy and as hard as jade. 'What do you care about me anyway? I never meant more to you than a means of revenge—somebody you could thoroughly humiliate in order to satisfy your own personal need for vengeance.'

'That's not true,' he argued. 'The last thing I ever wanted was to humiliate you.'

Her eyes looked bigger than ever. Brilliant green pools of disbelief.

'And you don't think you did? I don't believe you. You led

me on, you took me out and made me feel like a princess—and I did—I've never felt so special in my life. And once you'd got me in the palm of your hand—*whammo*—you not only pulled the rug out from under my feet, you did it when I was at my most vulnerable, when I was naked in your bed. Don't you have any concept of how humiliating that was?'

He bowed his head, knowing every word of what she said was true. 'Believe me, I didn't want that.'

'Then what the hell did you think you were doing? Don't you remember how you used me? Oh, my—' She stopped, clamping one hand over her mouth. 'Why didn't I see it before? All this time I thought you just wanted to humiliate my family because of what my father had done in ruining your father's business. But you had an even better reason. You took me to bed because you were replaying what my father had done to your sister. As if what he did wasn't bad enough, you had to repeat the act! What kind of monster does that make you?'

'Listen, Saskia—' He moved in closer.

She moved back, every movement strained and wary, screaming muscles on red alert.

'That was why you took me to bed, wasn't it? You were performing the ultimate revenge. You took me to bed—purely to get back at my father for what he'd done to Marla!'

He stood motionless. 'It's true. I was going to take your virginity just as your father had taken Marla's. But I couldn't do it. I couldn't go through with it. That's why I stopped.'

'You didn't stop! You threw me out of bed.'

'Because I didn't want to hurt you.'

'Don't give me that. You threw me out of bed because you're a cold-hearted bastard. You don't care about anything or anyone apart from your own sister, who doesn't even want your help. And you're too arrogant and full of yourself to realise it.'

'No! Don't you see? If I'd been the cold-hearted bastard you accuse me of being, I wouldn't have thrown you out of bed. I would have stayed there, forced my way into you and finished the deed!'

'But you told me—'

Oh, yes, he remembered only too well what he'd told her that night. Hadn't she reminded him of it only recently? 'I didn't throw you out of bed because you were a virgin.'

She swallowed, her throat scratchy and dry. 'Then…why?'

'Because I couldn't do what I'd planned to. I'd worked it all out like a military operation. I had your father's business in striking distance and I had you exactly where I wanted. I had *everything* I wanted, all lined up like ducks in a row.'

'I trusted you!'

'I know. But you have to listen,' he implored. 'Because all the time I was with you—taking you out to dinner or the movies or dancing, supposedly getting you ripe for the picking so I could reap my revenge—I started to care for you. I wasn't expecting to. It was the last thing I wanted. But you were bright and fun and so beautiful, and it was no hardship to be with you. You were easy to like. But I had the memory of what your father had done to Marla and I had a goal—and I was determined that *nothing* was going to keep me from that.'

He paused, looking at her face, at the pain of the past merging with the pain of her recent loss, and he wished he could rewrite the past to make the present somehow more tolerable for her.

'I had it all planned,' he continued. 'I took you to the beach house. There'd be no interruptions—nobody would know we were there because I never took anyone there. And, just like I'd planned, you were ready for me. When I asked you to make love to me you came willingly. You let me take off your clothes and lie you down amongst the pillows.' He held up one hand, his index finger and thumb a bare millimetre apart. 'I was *this* close to taking what I wanted. I was *this* close to exacting my revenge.' He sighed.

'What happened? What changed your mind?'

'It was something you said that suddenly made me realise what kind of person I was becoming. All of a sudden I understood what I'd been doing ever since I was twelve years old and clawing my way up the ladder to get back everything my parents had lost and more. I'd never realised it for all those years, but you made me see just how far I'd sunk.'

'And that's why you dropped out of business society? It wasn't Marla?'

'No. It wasn't Marla. It was me, and the man I'd made myself into. And it was an ugly revelation. You made me realise that in seeking my revenge, in becoming a ruthless businessman and committing the same atrocious act your father had, I was turning into the very man I hated most in the world. I was so ashamed that from then on I knew I had to live a different life. I could still be successful, but I didn't need the ruthless tactics. I didn't need to be front-page news. I chose to hide away. Just like you guessed while we were in New York I had things I never wanted anyone to know, because it was hard enough facing them myself.'

He moved closer, and this time she didn't back away. He reached for her hands, cradling them in his own. 'Don't you understand? I knew I was going to hurt you, whatever I did that night, and I knew you would hate me. But I figured that at least I wouldn't rob you of everything. At least you'd still have something to offer someone else. Someone who might even deserve it—God knows, I didn't.'

She swallowed, the action pulling his attention to her lips and the long smooth ride of her throat. 'What was it I said?'

He smiled weakly, remembering the way she'd lain under him, her eyes so full of trust, her arms wrapped so tightly around his neck, her body so welcoming. 'You told me you loved me.'

Silence followed his words, allowing the sounds of the ticking mantel clock to fill the void, unnaturally loud in the ensuing silence.

'I thought I did back then,' she said softly at last, her voice barely more than a whisper, her use of the past tense slicing through his flesh like a scythe. 'I thought I was the luckiest woman on earth.'

He reached out, putting a hand to her hair, still damp and fresh from her shower, resting his forearm on her shoulder. Her scent, fresh and unadulterated, wove its way through him—the scent he'd missed so much since he'd walked out of their hotel suite days ago. He inhaled it, drinking her in, worried that this might well be the last time.

'Saskia, I'm so sorry.' Sorry for what he'd done. Sorry for what her words revealed. She *had* loved him—in the past. Was there no chance of rekindling that love? Was there no hope at all for their future now?

'You were so angry with me that night. I don't think I've ever been more afraid.'

He toyed with the loose spiral ends of her hair, running them through his fingers. 'I know. You bore the brunt of it, but I was furious with *me*—disgusted for letting myself sink to such depths. I'd been so completely blindsided by my desperate need for revenge that I couldn't see what was in front of me—that I cared for you and that it meant something that you loved me. But I knew that I'd just ruined whatever chance I might have had with you. I knew I had to find a reason to throw you out of my bed and that it had to be one that would make you hate me for what I had done. Can you ever forgive me?'

'It's okay,' she said, closing her eyes to his ministrations as two fat tears rolled down her cheeks. 'Under the circumstances, I guess I should thank you for sparing me the same fate as your sister.'

Her words speared into his conscience. He touched the other hand to her cheek, brushing the tears away, feeling her tremble and feeling his own guilt build up by another layer. 'It's not okay. Because I never should have had you in my bed. Not for the reasons I used. I got it all wrong. Your father never raped my sister.'

Her eyes widened and she leaned back away from him. His hand was still on her shoulder. She anchored a hand on his forearm as if to steady herself.

'What did you say?'

'I spoke to Marla. It wasn't how I thought.'

'What do you mean? Are you saying they didn't have sex?'

He took a moment to steady her. 'They did, and she *was* only fifteen, but Marla insists it was hardly forced. In fact she maintains that he was reluctant but she pursued him—that she all but threw herself at him.'

Saskia sniffed, and touched the back of her hand to her nose.

'But what about him flaunting the fact he'd taken her virginity in front of your parents like you told me? Was that not true either?'

Alex sighed. 'That much he *did* do. He told my father he'd taken Marla's virginity as part of the deal.'

'But why would he do that?'

Alex ground his teeth together. 'Apparently he wasn't proud of what he'd done, but there was no way he wanted the truth to come out. He let my parents think he'd stolen her virginity so that they would hate him and not turn against her. In his own way, it seems he was protecting her.'

She blinked her haunted eyes, and he could see how much effort she was putting into holding herself together, but there were at least the beginnings of something like hope in her features.

'So you're saying my father was never a rapist?'

'No,' he said quietly. 'And I wish I could take back all those ugly words I hurled at you. I wish I could have saved you that. I was so wrong.'

'You thought you were avenging your sister. I can't imagine anyone going to such lengths for *me*.'

I would, he thought. *If only I had a chance.*

Saskia took a deep breath and moved across the kitchen, wiping her face with her hands. 'I should thank you for coming and explaining everything. Especially for what you just told me. I appreciate you coming so far to clear it up.'

He froze. She was dismissing him. And he hadn't finished what he'd come here to tell her. But she was still raw from her father's death, and she'd had enough to assimilate for one day.

'Then I'll go,' he said.

Saskia tied her ponytail with a black satin ribbon and stood back to survey her reflection, tugging on the hem of her black jacket. The dark circles were still there under her eyes. Make-up had made them less obvious, and lipstick had given her face some much needed colour, but overall... She grimaced. How was she expected to sleep anyway? She would have to do as she was. It was hardly a fashion parade after all.

She glanced at her watch and took a deep breath. It was time. In a strange way she was looking forward to the funeral. These last two days she'd done a lot of thinking about her father—missing him dreadfully, contemplating life without him, but thankful also that he had been spared possibly months in a coma. At least the end, when it had come, had come blessedly quickly.

And the funeral would be some kind of closure. She knew now how it must have been with Marla and her father—a pretty young girl, a lonely man missing his wife. It hadn't been the right thing, but thank heavens it wasn't as bad as she'd first feared. At least now she knew.

She gathered up her handbag and keys and pulled open the door to meet the gloomy grey day, heading out to meet the cab that would be here any minute.

'Can I offer you a lift?'

She took a step back. The dark-suited figure leaning against the sleek black Jaguar was the last thing she'd been expecting to see outside her door.

'What are you doing here? I thought you'd gone.'

He *had* gone. She'd sent him away herself, and he had left as smoothly as the chiffon dress she'd sent to charity had slipped through her fingers. He'd done what he'd come for. He'd made his apologies and given her plenty to think about.

Surely he should already be back ruling his empire from Sydney, or Tahoe, or wherever it was that he was based right now? Why was he still hanging around here?

'I came to take you to the funeral.'

'I don't think so,' she said, knowing she wasn't strong enough today to deal with both the loss of her father and Alex's presence. 'You spent your entire life hating my father. Do you think there's a chance in hell I'd let you take me to his funeral?'

He straightened and looked her in the eyes, his charcoal gaze steady and direct.

'I told you why I felt that way. And I told you I was wrong.'

'Yes,' she agreed. 'You were wrong.'

'But my being here today has nothing to do with how I felt about your father. This has everything to do with how I feel about you.'

She was too tired to work out what he meant. Instead she looked up and down the street. 'I've ordered a cab.'

'And I've sent it away.'

'You did what?' She shook her head and dived into her purse for her keys. 'Then maybe I'll take my car after all.'

'You shouldn't drive—not today. Do you have someone else to take you?'

Her sideways look told him everything he needed to know. There was no one else. She was alone. And she'd had no intention of driving.

'Then I'll take you,' he decided.

'You might have asked if you could come.'

'And you would have let me?'

'No.'

Ten minutes later he pulled into a parking space outside the small funeral chapel and killed the engine. She made no move to get out of the car.

'You'll feel better once it's over.'

She looked at him, her eyes so filled with grief and despair he just wanted to take her in his arms and hold her. But instead he took her hand and squeezed it gently. 'Come on,' he said.

There were few in attendance. Enid Sharpe from next door, his visiting nurse and a couple of old cronies he'd played bridge with. Throughout the brief ceremony she held herself together, the strain etched in lines around her eyes and mouth as she contemplated the flower strewn coffin bearing her father.

Bearing the man Alex had hated for almost a quarter of a century. And all for what? A pointless exercise in revenge for something that had never happened. And now what did he have to show for all that hate? What had it produced but more problems? Marla had been so right. It was time to let it go.

At the end of the service he felt Saskia's hand slip into his, and he looked down into the green pools of her eyes. 'Thank you for bringing me,' she said, before Enid came up to give her a hug.

Afterwards they stayed only long enough for a cup of tea, exchanging small talk with the minister.

She slumped back in her seat when he got her into the car, her head tipped back, her eyes closed. 'Thank God that's over,' she said on a sigh.

She looked exhausted, and from the way her black suit bagged around her he suspected it was days since she'd eaten properly. She was just about asleep before they made it back to her flat. He carried her in, despite her protests.

'Would you like me to run you a bath?' he asked.

She shook her head. 'No, just bed,' she muttered sleepily, her arms around his neck, her face nestled into his chest.

He carried her to her room and pulled back the covers, placing her gently down. He slid off her shoes and peeled away the baggy suit without protest from her, shocked at how much flesh had wasted from her bones. She shivered, and he tucked the blankets closer around her.

'So cold,' she whispered, trembling.

He couldn't leave her like that. He pulled off his own shoes and stripped off his suit in a moment, joining her in the bed, collecting her into his arms and wrapping himself around her. She clung to him and cuddled closer, her head resting on his shoulder, her legs scissored between his, and he willed his heat into her, feeling her trembling gradually subside and her breathing steady as she drifted towards sleep.

He kissed her hair, breathed in the sweet scent of her and tucked her closer.

'I love you,' he said. *'Agape mou.'*

CHAPTER TWELVE

SASKIA woke up feeling better than she had for days. She must have slept for hours, filled with dreams of warmth and loving. And then she remembered. *Alex.* She spun around, but she was alone and her heart pitched south. He'd been so good to her yesterday, so gentle and understanding. Surely he couldn't have left? But why had he been here in the first place? He'd made his apologies. What could he still want with her now?

Her bedroom door swung open. 'Perfect timing.' Alex smiled at her as he came around the door, still wearing the dark suit trousers and white shirt of yesterday, but with the sleeves rolled up and the buttons left undone, exposing a tantalising glimpse of firm olive-skinned torso. But right now it was the tray he was carrying that snagged her attention, piled high with plates and cups and from which the most heavenly smells were coming. 'Are you hungry?'

She took another long look at that patch of skin, and the whirl of hairs that disappeared down into his trousers. He looked good enough to eat himself, but her stomach was sounding a definite protest. 'Famished,' she said, surprised at how true it was. She hadn't felt like eating for days, and suddenly her body seemed to want to make up for it.

'You go wash up,' he said. 'I'll get the coffee.'

She skipped out of bed, grabbing her robe and making for the bathroom, horrified at her reflection. Hair everywhere, and yesterday's make-up sliding wherever, but at least her eyes didn't look so hollow any more. She rinsed her face and attacked her curls with a comb.

'Back into bed,' he ordered when she reappeared, and she didn't think to argue, too busy contemplating the plates piled with eggs, bacon and tomatoes, the racks of toast and dishes of butter and jam.

He loaded up a plate and handed it to her, and it was all she could do not to inhale it all in one delicious whoosh.

'Oh, my,' she said, sipping on a coffee as she leaned back against her headboard. 'That was wonderful.'

'You've had enough?'

'Hold the dessert,' she joked as she patted her tummy. 'Seriously, thank you,' she said. 'Not just for breakfast, but for everything you did for me yesterday. I was so tired last night, so cold, and you kept me warm and safe. And I didn't think I wanted you at the funeral but I'm glad you were there.'

He topped up her coffee and set the plates aside. 'It was important for me too. I carried around that hatred for so long—too long—it was time to let it go. I'd been so wrong about everything, so damned stupid, but all along he was your father, and he'd made a beautiful daughter in you. How could I hate him?'

She smiled, tears springing into her eyes. 'Oh, hell,' she said, reaching for a box of tissues. 'I thought I was done with the tears.'

He laughed softly, moving closer, taking the tissue and touching it gently to her eyes, soaking up the moisture. She blinked her eyes open, studying his eyes, so close to her own.

'Why are you still here?'

He leaned back, his charcoal eyes so desperately focused on hers she could feel the communication between them. 'There's something I have to ask you. I want to know if you can ever forgive me for what I did and for all the hurt I've caused you.'

'You've apologised already.'

'No,' he said. 'That wasn't enough. I need to know if you forgive me, because only then can we really put what's happened behind us.'

She hesitated. 'And that's important because…?'

'Because then we have a chance at a future together. If you want one. Because I love you, Saskia. God knows I don't deserve you, but I don't want to spend my future apart from you.'

'You love me?' She blinked, remembering those words from a dream, warm and loving and happy. But this was far better than the foggy memory of a distant dream. Far better. This was real.

He smiled. 'I love you. It took me a long time to realise it—much too long. But I want to spend my life loving you, if you'll have me.'

'You love me,' she said again, in awe and wonder, her lips curling at the sound of the words, at their taste on her tongue, at the way they fed her soul.

He laughed, a rich, deep sound that radiated warmth. 'Can I take it you don't mind, then?'

'Don't mind? Do you know how long I've waited to hear those words from you?'

'And do you know how much I've missed hearing those words from you? You said it to me once. But I'll understand if you can never bring yourself to say it to me again.'

'Oh, Alex.' She shook her head. 'I tried not to,' she said. 'I really tried to stop loving you. For so long I told myself I hated you, that I couldn't possibly love you. But, damn you, I've always loved you, Alex Koutoufides. I never stopped loving you, and I never stopped hoping one day that I'd hear you say those words to me. Of course I love you.'

'Saskia,' he said, pulling her into his arms. 'You don't know how good it is to hear that from you. Because I love you so very much. And I have so much to make up for.'

And he kissed her, a kiss so achingly sweet and full of love it moved her soul. This was the man she was destined to be with. This was her mate. This was her destiny. All those years ago, as a seventeen-year-old young woman, she'd known it. And all these years later it was finally coming to pass.

His kiss told her how much he loved her and how much he wanted her. His hands moved over her, his touch like worship, cherishing her, seducing her, setting her body alight while her hands pushed their way under his shirt, desperate to get closer, itching to feel more of the muscled wall of his chest.

'About that dessert…' he whispered, his breathing already choppy as he ripped off his shirt and tugged at the ties of her robe.

'Bring it on.' She chuckled as she dragged him back down to her lips. 'Didn't I tell you I was famished?'

EPILOGUE

BLISS. Life could never get better than this.

Saskia paused as she looked out onto the enclosed patio of their Tahoe home, watching Alex cradle the tiny bundle that was his month-old daughter on his jeans-covered legs.

Their daughter.

The daughter they'd made together in an act of love.

He looked down at baby Sophie so adoringly that she sucked in a lungful of pure happiness. She loved him so much. Even now she got a thrill thinking of her name aligned with his. Even after a year of marriage the wonder was still there.

And tiny Sophie's arrival had magnified that wonder tenfold.

She picked up two of the salads the housekeeper had prepared earlier and stepped out onto the deck, placing them on the table, watching his face light up with warmth as he welcomed her approach.

'What time are our visitors arriving?'

'Any minute now. I hope you've got the champagne chilling. Marla told me they've got an announcement to make.'

He looked up quickly, still with Sophie's tiny hands clinging to his fingers, as Saskia sat down in the chair alongside. 'Are you thinking what I'm thinking?'

She nodded. 'Oh, yes. Jake's the one. They've been

together a good while now, and he's good for her. He's solid and loyal, and she'll need that stability—especially now she's going to be doing this book tour. It's obvious they've been crazy about each other for ages, despite all her protests to the contrary. I'm glad they're planning on making it official.'

'She's so different now,' he said, gazing back into his baby's big dark eyes. 'So much more self-assured. The book's success has been amazing.'

'I think Marla's found herself. She has her own career now, with her writing. You know she's picked up another national monthly column? She actually feels like she's making her own way in the world, and she's loving it.'

'And you're responsible for that.'

She shook her head. 'No, Marla is. She's the one who took control of her life. All we had to do was help her make it happen. And you letting go the reins had as much to do with it as I did.'

He looked at her with equal measures of respect and love. 'You will never stop astounding me, you know. I think I might just love you, Mrs Koutoufides.'

'I think I might just love you back, Mr Koutoufides.'

He snaked an arm around her neck and pulled her in, kissing her over the squirming baby below. 'So, what's next for your own career? Have you given Marla's offer any more thought?'

She nodded. 'I'm going to tell her today. I'll take on her press work—it should be fun—and I'll fit in my own freelance articles when I get a chance. It should be the perfect stay-at-home job.'

'You don't miss *AlphaBiz*?' he asked, when finally he let her go.

She smiled, and touched a finger to the baby-soft curls adorning Sophie's head. 'What kind of a question is that? No. I wasn't happy with the way they seemed to be going anyway—increasingly chasing the celebrity angle. I don't want to write that way. Besides,' she said, smiling into the dark eyes of her young child, 'why would I rather be seeking out crusty old businessmen to interview when I can have the best of both worlds—doing freelance work and looking after this little one and her father?'

He scowled. 'Crusty old businessmen, eh?'

'Present company excluded,' she added with a grin. 'Anyone as gorgeously talented and virile as you can't be too crusty.'

He pulled her close again, measuring the ripe sway of her breasts in his free hand. 'Maybe later on I might be able to convince you just how virile and uncrusty I am.'

'I warn you now,' she said, already feeling her body awaken and stir at his sensual caress, 'I might take some convincing.'

He growled and pulled her close, and they shared a kiss so deep and rich with promise that it was only the plaintive cry of the child on his lap that broke it off. He turned his attentions back to his child, scooping her up into his arms, kissing her softly on the forehead.

'Was I neglecting you, sweetheart?'

Her cries stilled, her eyes locking onto her father's, her tiny mouth stretching into a wide, gummy smile.

'She smiled at me!' He looked at Saskia. 'Look at that! They said she wouldn't do that until at she was at least six weeks old.'

'Of course she smiled at you,' she responded, stroking the downy dark hair of little Sophie. 'How could she resist? I never could.'

He beamed back at her. 'And, when it comes to the women in my life, that's just the way I like it.'

He contemplated the child in his arms again, and breathed in deep as he looked back at the woman he loved. 'I love you,

Saskia, for your warmth and your beauty and for giving me this child. But most of all for your forgiveness and your love. You've made me the happiest man in the entire world.'

She wrapped her arms around both the man she loved and the tiny baby cradled in his arms, feeling the love radiating out from him and breathing in the magic scent of pure one hundred per cent male mixed with the sweet, innocent smell of a newborn.

It was a mix that moved her like no other.

It was love she could sense.

It was intoxicating.

It was simply…

Bliss.

AT THE GREEK
BOSS'S BIDDING

JANE PORTER

For two of my favourite heroes, my brothers
Dr Thomas W Porter and Robert George Porter.

PROLOGUE

THE helicopter slammed against the rocky incline of the mountain thick with drifts of snow.

Glass shattered, metal crunched and red flames shot from the engine, turning what Kristian Koumantaros knew was glacial white into a shimmering dance of fire and ice.

Unable to see, he struggled with his seatbelt. The helicopter tilted, sliding a few feet. Fire burned everywhere as the heat surgéd, surrounding him. Kristian tugged his seatbelt again. The clip was jammed.

The smoke seared his lungs, blistering each breath.

Life and death, he thought woozily. Life and death came down to this. And life-and-death decisions were often no different than any other decisions. You did what you had to do and the consequences be damned.

Kristian had done what he had to do and the consequences damned him.

As the roar of the fire grew louder, the helicopter shifted again, the snow giving way.

My God. Kristian threw his arms out, and yet there was nothing to grab, and they were sent tumbling down the mountain face. Another avalanche, he thought, deafened by the endless roar—

And then nothing.

CHAPTER ONE

"*OHI.* No." The deep rough voice could be none other than Kristian Koumantaros himself. "Not interested. Tell her to go away."

Standing in the hall outside the library, Elizabeth Hatchet drew a deep breath, strengthening her resolve. This was not going to be easy, but then nothing about Kristian Koumantaros's case had been easy. Not the accident, not the rehab, not the location of his estate.

It had taken her two days to get here from London—a flight from London to Athens, an endless drive from Athens to Sparta, and finally a bone-jarring cart and donkey trip halfway up the ridiculously inaccessible mountain.

Why anybody, much less a man who couldn't walk and couldn't see, would want to live in a former monastery built on a rocky crag on a slope of Taygetos, the highest mountain in the Peloponnese, was beyond her. But now that she was here, she wasn't going to go away.

"*Kyrios.*" Another voice sounded from within the library and Elizabeth recognized the voice as the Greek servant who'd met her at the door. "She's traveled a long way—"

"I've had it with the bloody help from First Class Rehab. First Class, my ass."

Elizabeth closed her eyes and exhaled slowly, counting to ten as she did so.

She'd been told by her Athens staff that it was a long trip to the former monastery.

She'd been warned that reaching rugged Taygetos, with its severe landscape but breathtaking vistas, was nearly as exhausting as caring for Mr. Koumantaros.

Her staff had counseled that traveling up this spectacular mountain with its ancient Byzantine ruins would seem at turns mythical as well as impossible, but Elizabeth, climbing into the donkey cart, had thought she'd been prepared. She'd thought she knew what she was getting into.

Just like she'd thought she knew what she was getting into when she agreed to provide Mr. Koumantaros's home health care after he was released from the French hospital.

In both cases she had been wrong.

The painfully slow, bumpy ride had left her woozy, with a queasy stomach and a pounding headache.

Attempting to rehabilitate Mr. Koumantaros had made her suffer far worse. Quite bluntly, he'd nearly bankrupted her company.

Elizabeth tensed at the sound of glass breaking, followed by a string of select and exceptionally colorful Greek curses.

"*Kyrios,* it's just a glass. It can be replaced."

"I hate this, Pano. Hate everything about this—"

"I know, *kyrios.*" Pano's voice dropped low, and Elizabeth couldn't hear much of what was said, but apparently it had the effect of calming Mr. Koumantaros.

Elizabeth wasn't soothed.

Kristian Koumantaros might be fabulously wealthy and able to afford an eccentric and reclusive lifestyle in the Peloponnese, but that didn't excuse his behavior. And his behavior was nothing short of self-absorbed and self-destructive.

She was here because Kristian Koumantaros couldn't keep a nurse, and he couldn't keep a nurse because he couldn't keep his temper.

The voices in the library were growing louder again. Elizabeth, fluent in Greek, listened as they discussed her.

Mr. Koumantaros didn't want her here.

Pano, the elderly butler, was attempting to convince that Mr. Koumantaros it wouldn't be polite to send the nurse away without seeing her.

Mr. Koumantaros said he didn't care about being polite.

Elizabeth's mouth curved wryly as the butler urged Mr. Koumantaros to at least offer her some refreshment.

Her wry smile disappeared as she heard Mr. Koumantaros answer that as most nurses from First Class Rehab were large women Ms. Hatchet could probably benefit from passing on an afternoon snack.

"Kyrios," Pano persisted, "she's brought a suitcase. Luggage. Ms. Hatchet intends to stay."

"Stay?" Koumantaros roared.

"Yes, *kyrios.*" The elderly Greek's tone couldn't have been any more apologetic, but his words had the effect of sending Kristian into another litany of curses.

"For God's sake, Pano, leave the damn glass alone and dispense with her. Throw her a bone. Get her a donkey. I don't care. Just do it. *Now.*"

"But she's traveled from London—"

"I don't care if she flew from the moon. She had no business coming here. I left a message two weeks ago with the service. That woman knows perfectly well I've fired them. I didn't ask her to come. And it's not my problem she wasted her time."

Speaking of which, Elizabeth thought, rubbing at the back of her neck to ease the pinch of pain, she *was* wasting time standing here. It was time to introduce herself, get the meeting underway.

Shoulders squared, Elizabeth took a deep breath and pushed the tall door open. As she entered the room, her low heels made a faint clicking sound on the hardwood floor.

"Good afternoon, Mr. Koumantaros," she said. Her narrowed gaze flashed across the shuttered windows, cluttered coffee table, newspapers stacked computer-high on a corner desk. Had to be a month's newspapers piled there, unread.

"You're trespassing, and eavesdropping." Kristian jerked upright in his wheelchair, his deep voice vibrating with fury.

She barely glanced his way, heading instead for the small table filled with prescription bottles. "You were shouting, Mr. Koumantaros. I didn't need to eavesdrop. And I'd be trespassing if your care weren't my responsibility, but it is, so you're going to have to deal with me."

At the table, Elizabeth picked up one of the medicine bottles to check the label, and then the others. It was an old habit, an automatic habit. The first thing a medical professional needed to know was what, if anything, the patient was taking.

Kristian's hunched figure in the wheelchair shuddered as he tried to follow the sound of her movements, his eyes shielded by a white gauze bandage wrapped around his head, the white gauze a brilliant contrast to his thick onyx hair. "Your services have already been terminated," he said tersely.

"You've been overruled," Elizabeth answered, returning the bottles to the table to study him. The bandages swathing his eyes exposed the hard, carved contours of his face. He had chiseled cheekbones, a firm chin and strong jaw shadowed with a rough black beard. From the look of it, he hadn't shaved since the last nurse had been sent packing.

"By whom?" he demanded, leaning crookedly in his chair.

"Your physicians."

"My physicians?"

"Yes, indeed. We're in daily contact with them, Mr. Koumantaros, and these past several months have made them question your mental soundness."

"You must be joking."

"Not at all. There is a discussion that perhaps you'd be better cared for in a facility—"

"Get out!" he demanded, pointing at the door. "Get out now."

Elizabeth didn't move. Instead she cocked her head, coolly examining him. He looked impossibly unkempt, nothing like the sophisticated powerful tycoon he'd reportedly been, with castles and estates scattered all over the world and a gorgeous mistress tucked enticingly in each.

"They fear for you, Mr. Koumantaros," she added quietly, "and so do I. You need help."

"That's absurd. If my doctors were so concerned, they'd be here. And you…you don't know me. You can't drop in here and make assessments based on two minutes of observation."

"I can, because I've managed your case from day one, when you were released from the hospital. No one knows more about you and your day-to-day care than I do. And if you'd always been this despondent we'd see it as a personality issue, but your despair is new—"

"There's no despair. I'm just tired."

"Then let's address that, shall we?" Elizabeth flipped open her leather portfolio and scribbled some notes. One couldn't be too careful these days. She had to protect the agency, not to mention her staff. She'd learned early to document everything. "It's tragic you're still in your present condition— tragic to isolate yourself here on Taýgetos when there are people waiting for you in Athens, people wanting you to come home."

"I live here permanently now."

She glanced up at him. "You've no intention of returning?"

"I spent years renovating this monastery, updating and converting it into a modern home to meet my needs."

"That was before you were injured. It's not practical for you to live here now. You can't fly—"

"Don't tell me what I can't do."

She swallowed, tried again. "It's not easy for your friends or family to see you. You're absolutely secluded here—"

"As I wish to be."

"But how can you fully recover when you're so alone in what is undoubtedly one of the most remote places in Greece?"

He averted his head, giving her a glimpse of a very strong, very proud profile. "This is my home," he repeated stubbornly, his tone colder, flintier.

"And what of your company? The businesses? Have you given those up along with your friends and family?"

"If this is your bedside manner—"

"Oh, it is," she assured him unapologetically. "Mr. Koumantaros, I'm not here to coddle you. Nor to say pretty things and try to make you laugh. I'm here to get you on your feet again."

"It's not going to happen."

"Because you like being helpless, or because you're afraid of pain?"

For a moment he said nothing, his face growing paler against the white gauze bandaging his head. Finally he found his voice. "How dare you?" he demanded. "How dare you waltz into my home—?"

"It wasn't exactly a waltz, Mr. Koumantaros. It took me

two days to get here and that included planes, taxis, buses and asses." She smiled thinly. This was the last place she'd wanted to come, and the last person she wanted to nurse. "It's been nearly a year since your accident," she continued. "There's no medical reason for you to be as helpless as you are."

"*Get out.*"

"I can't. Not only have I've nowhere to go—as you must know, it's too dark to take a donkey back down the mountain."

"No, I don't know. I'm blind. I've no idea what time of day it is."

Heat surged to her cheeks. Heat and shame and disgust. Not for her, but him. If he expected her to feel sorry for him, he had another thing coming, and if he hoped to intimidate her, he was wrong again. He could shout and break things, but she wasn't about to cower like a frightened puppy dog. Just because he was a famous Greek with a billion-dollar company didn't mean he deserved her respect. Respect was earned, not automatically given.

"It's almost four o'clock, Mr. Koumantaros. Half of the mountain is already steeped in shadows. I couldn't go home tonight even if I wanted to. Your doctors have authorized me to stay, so I must. It's either that or you go to a rehab facility in Athens. *Your* choice."

"Not much of a choice."

"No, it's not." Elizabeth picked up one of the prescription bottles and popped off the plastic cap to see the number of tablets inside. Three remained from a count of thirty. The prescription had only been refilled a week ago. "Still not sleeping, Mr. Koumantaros?"

"I *can't.*"

"Still in a lot of pain, then?" She pressed the notebook to her chest, stared at him over the portfolio's edge. Probably addicted to his painkillers now. Happened more often than not. One more battle ahead.

Kristian Koumantaros shifted in his wheelchair. The bandages that hid his eyes revealed the sharp twist of his lips. "As if you care."

She didn't even blink. His self-pity didn't trigger sympathy. Self-pity was a typical stage in the healing process—an early stage, one of the first. And the fact that Kristian Koumantaros hadn't moved beyond it meant he had a long, long way to go.

"I do care," she answered flatly. Elizabeth didn't bother to add that she also cared about the future of her company, First Class Rehab, and that providing for Kristian Koumantaros's medical needs had nearly ruined her four-year-old company. "I do care, but I won't be like the others—going soft on you, accepting your excuses, allowing you to get away with murder."

"And what do you know of murder, Miss Holier-Than-Thou?" He wrenched his wheelchair forward, the hard rubber tires crunching glass shards.

"Careful, Mr. Koumantaros! You'll pop a tire."

"*Good.* Pop the goddamn tires. I hate this chair. I hate not seeing. I despise living like this." He swore violently, but at least he'd stopped rolling forward and was sitting still while the butler hurriedly finished sweeping up the glass with a small broom and dustpan.

As Kristian sat, his enormous shoulders turned inward, his dark head hung low.

Despair.

The word whispered to her, summing up what she saw, what she felt. His black mood wasn't merely anger. It was bigger than that, darker than that. His black mood was fed by despair.

He was, she thought, feeling the smallest prick of sympathy, a ruin of a great man.

As swiftly as the sympathy came, she pushed it aside, replacing tenderness with resolve. He'd get well. There was no reason he couldn't.

Elizabeth signaled to Pano that she wanted a word alone with his employer and, nodding, he left them, exiting the library with his dustpan of broken glass.

"Now, then, Mr. Koumantaros," she said as the library doors closed, "we need to get you back on your rehab program. But we can't do that if you insist on intimidating your nurses."

"They were all completely useless, incompetent—"

"All six?" she interrupted, taking a seat on the nearest armchair arm.

He'd gone through the roster of home healthcare specialists in record fashion. In fact, they'd run out of possible candidates. There was no one else to send. And yet Mr. Koumantaros couldn't be left alone. He required more than a butler. He still needed around-the-clock medical care.

"One nurse wasn't so bad. Well, in some ways," he said grudgingly, tapping the metal rim of his wheelchair with his finger tips. "The young one. Calista. And believe me, if she was the best it should show you how bad the others were. But that's another story—"

"Miss Aravantinos isn't coming back." Elizabeth felt her temper rise. Of course he'd request the one nurse he'd broken into bits. The poor girl, barely out of nursing school, had been putty in Kristian Koumantaros's hands. Literally. For a man with life-threatening injuries he'd been incredibly adept at seduction.

His dark head tipped sideways. "Was that her last name?"

"You behaved in a most unscrupulous manner. You're thirty—what?" She quickly flipped through his chart, found his age. "Nearly thirty-six. And she was barely twenty-three. She quit, you know. Left our Athens office. She felt terribly demoralized."

"I never asked Calista to fall in love with me."

"Love?" she choked. "Love didn't have anything to do with it. You seduced her. Out of boredom. And spite."

"You've got me all wrong, Nurse Cratchett—" He paused, a corner of his mouth smirking. "You *are* English, are you not?"

"I speak English, yes," she answered curtly.

"Well, Cratchett, you have me wrong. You see, I'm a lover, not a fighter."

Blood surged to Elizabeth's cheeks. "That's quite enough."

"I've never forced myself on a woman." His voice dropped, the pitch growing deeper, rougher. "If anything, our dear delightful Calista forced herself on me."

"Mr. Koumantaros." Acutely uncomfortable, she gripped her pen tightly, growing warm, warmer. She hated his mocking smile and resented his tone. She could see why Calista had thrown the towel in. How was a young girl to cope with him?

"She romanticized me," he continued, in the same infuriatingly smug vein. "She wanted to know what an invalid was capable of, I suppose. And she discovered that although I can't walk, I can still—"

"Mr. Koumantaros!" Elizabeth jumped to her feet, suddenly oppressed by the warm, dark room. It was late afternoon, and the day had been cloudless, blissfully sunny. She couldn't fathom why the windows and shutters were all closed, keeping the fresh mountain air out. "I do not wish to hear the details."

"But you need them." Kristian pushed his wheelchair toward her, blue cotton sleeves rolled back on his forearms, corded tendons tight beneath his skin. He'd once had a very deep tan, but the tan had long ago faded. His olive skin was pale, testament to his long months indoors. "You're misinformed if you think I took advantage of Calista. Calista got what Calista wanted."

She averted her head and ground her teeth together. "She was a wonderful, promising young nurse."

"I don't know about wonderful, but I'll give you naïve. And since she quit, I think you've deliberately assigned me nurses from hell."

"We do not employ nurses from hell. All of our nurses are professional, efficient, compassionate—"

"And stink to high heaven."

"Excuse me?" Elizabeth drew back, affronted. "That's a crude accusation."

"Crude, but true. And I didn't want them in my home, and I refused to have them touching me."

So that was it. He didn't want a real nurse. He wanted something from late-night T.V.—big hair, big breasts, and a short, tight skirt.

Elizabeth took a deep breath, fighting to hang on to her professional composure. She was beginning to see how he wore his nurses down, brow-beating and tormenting until they begged for a reprieve. *Anyone but Mr. Koumantaros. Any job but that!*

Well, she wasn't about to let Mr. Koumantaros break her. He couldn't get a rise out of her because she wouldn't let him. "Did Calista smell bad?"

"No, Calista smelled like heaven."

For a moment she could have sworn Kristian was smiling, and the fact that he could smile over ruining a young nurse's career infuriated her.

He rolled another foot closer. "But then after Calista fled you sent only old, fat, frumpy nurses to torture me, punishing me for what was really Calista's fault. And don't tell me they weren't old and fat and frumpy, because I might be blind but I'm not stupid."

Elizabeth's blood pressure shot up again. "I assigned mature nurses, but they were well-trained and certainly prepared for the rigors of the job."

"One smelled like a tobacco shop. One of fish. I'm quite certain another could have been a battleship—"

"You're being insulting."

"I'm being honest. You replaced Calista with prison guards."

Elizabeth's anger spiked, and then her lips twitched. Kristian Koumantaros was actually right.

After poor Calista's disgrace, Elizabeth had intentionally assigned Mr. Koumantaros only the older, less responsive nurses, realizing that he required special care. Very special care.

She smiled faintly, amused despite herself. He might not be walking, and he might not have his vision, but his brain worked just fine.

Still smiling, she studied him dispassionately, aware of his injuries, his months of painful rehabilitation, his prognosis. He was lucky to have escaped such a serious accident with his life. The trauma to his head had been so extensive he'd been expected to suffer severe brain damage. Happily, his mental faculties were intact. His motor skills could be repaired, but his eyesight was questionable. Sometimes the brain healed itself. Sometimes it didn't. Only time and continued therapy would tell.

"Well, that's all in the past now," she said, forcing a note of cheer into her voice. "The battleaxe nurses are gone. I am here—"

"And you are probably worse than all of them."

"Indeed, I am. They whisper behind my back that I'm every patient's worst nightmare."

"So I can call you Nurse Cratchett, then?"

"If you'd like. Or you can call me by my name, which is Nurse Hatchet. But they're so similar, I'll answer either way."

He sat in silence, his jaw set, his expression increasingly wary. Elizabeth felt the edges of her mouth lift, curl. He couldn't browbeat or intimidate her. She knew what Greek tycoons were. She'd once been married to one.

"It's time to move on," she added briskly. "And the first place we start is with your meals. I know it's late, Mr. Koumantaros, but have you eaten lunch yet?"

"I'm not hungry."

Elizabeth closed her portfolio and slipped the pen into the leather case. "You need to eat. Your body needs the nutrition. I'll see about a light meal." She moved toward the door, unwilling to waste time arguing.

Kristian shoved his wheelchair forward, inadvertently slamming into the edge of the couch. His frustration was written in every line of his face. "I don't want food—"

"Of course not. Why eat when you're addicted to pain pills?" She flashed a tight, strained smile he couldn't see. "Now, if you'll excuse me, I'll see to your meal."

The vaulted stone kitchen was in the tower, or *pyrgos,* and there the butler, cook and senior housekeeper had gathered beneath one of the medieval arches. They were in such deep conversation that they didn't hear Elizabeth enter.

Once they realized she was there, all three fell silent and turned to face her with varying degrees of hostility.

Elizabeth wasn't surprised. For one, unlike the other nurses, she wasn't Greek. Two, despite being foreign, she spoke Greek fluently. And three, she wasn't showing proper deference to their employer, a very wealthy, powerful Greek man.

"Hello," Elizabeth said, attempting to ignore the icy

welcome. "I thought I'd see if I could help with Mr. Koumantaros's lunch."

Everyone continued to gape at her until Pano, the butler, cleared his throat. "Mr. Koumantaros doesn't eat lunch."

"Does he take a late breakfast, then?" Elizabeth asked.

"No, just coffee."

"Then when does he eat his first meal?"

"Not until evening."

"I see." Elizabeth's brow furrowed as she studied the three staffers, wondering how long they'd been employed by Kristian Koumantaros and how they coped with his black moods and display of temper. "Does he eat well then?"

"Sometimes," the short, stocky cook answered, wiping her hands across the starched white fabric of her apron. "And sometimes he just pecks. He used to have an excellent appetite—fish, *moussaka, dolmades,* cheese, meat, vegetables—but that was before the accident."

Elizabeth nodded, glad to see at least one of them had been with him a while. That was good. Loyalty was always a plus, but misplaced loyalty could also be a hindrance to Kristian recovering. "We'll have to improve his appetite," she said. "Starting with a light meal right now. Perhaps a *horiatiki salata,*" she said, suggesting what most Europeans and Americans thought of as a Greek salad—feta cheese and onion, tomato and cucumber, drizzled with olive oil and a few drops of homemade wine vinegar.

"There must be someplace outside—a sunny terrace—where he can enjoy his meal. Mr. Koumantaros needs the sun and fresh air—"

"Excuse me, ma'am," Pano interrupted, "but the sun bothers Mr. Koumantaros's eyes."

"It's because Mr. Koumantaros has spent too much time

sitting in the dark. The light will do him good. Sunlight stimulates the pituitary gland, helps alleviate depression and promotes healing. But, seeing as he's been inside so much, we can transition today by having lunch in the shade. I assume part of the terrace is covered?"

"Yes, ma'am," the cook answered. "But Mr. Koumantaros won't go."

"Oh, he will." Elizabeth swallowed, summoning all her determination. She knew Kristian would eventually go. But it'd be a struggle.

Sitting in the library, Kristian heard the English nurse's footsteps disappear as she went in search of the kitchen, and after a number of long minutes heard her footsteps return.

So she was coming back. Wonderful.

He tipped his head, looking up at nothing, since everything was and had been dark since the crash, fourteen months and eleven days ago.

The door opened, and he knew from the way the handle turned and the lightness of the step that it was her. "You're wrong about something else," he said abruptly as she entered the library. "The accident wasn't a year ago. It was almost a year and a half ago. It happened late February."

She'd stopped walking and he felt her there, beyond his sight, beyond his reach, standing, staring, *waiting*. It galled him, this lack of knowing, seeing. He'd achieved what he'd achieved by utilizing his eyes, his mind, his gut. He trusted his eyes and his gut, and now, without those, he didn't know what was true, or real.

Like Calista, for example.

"That's even worse," his new nightmare nurse shot back. "You should be back at work by now. You've a corporation to run, people dependent on you. You're doing no one any good hiding away here in your villa."

"I can't run my company if I can't walk or see—"

"But you *can* walk, and there might be a chance you could see—"

"A less than five percent chance." He laughed bitterly. "You know, before the last round of surgeries I had a thirty-five percent chance of seeing, but they botched those—"

"They weren't botched. They were just highly experimental."

"Yes, and that experimental treatment reduced my chances of seeing again to nil."

"Not nil."

"Five percent. There's not much difference. Especially when they say that even if the operation were a success I'd still never be able to drive, or fly, or sail. That there's too much trauma for me to do what I used to do."

"And your answer is to sit here shrouded in bandages and darkness and feel sorry for yourself?" she said tartly, her voice growing closer.

Kristian shifted in his chair, and felt an active and growing dislike for Cratchett. She was standing off to his right, and her smug, superior attitude rubbed him the wrong way. "Your company's services have been terminated."

"They haven't—"

"I may be blind, but you're apparently deaf. First Class Rehab has received its last—*final*—check. There is no more coming from me. There will be no more payments for services rendered."

He heard her exhale—a soft, quick breath that was so uniquely feminine that he drew back, momentarily startled.

And in that half-second he felt betrayed.

She was the one not listening. She was the one forcing herself on him. And yet—and yet she was a woman. And he was—or had been—a gentleman, and gentlemen were supposed to have manners. Gentlemen were supposed to be above reproach.

Growling, he leaned back in his chair, gripped the rims on the wheels and glared at where he imagined her to be standing.

He shouldn't feel bad for speaking bluntly. His brow furrowed even more deeply. It was her fault. She'd come here, barging in with a righteous high-handed, bossy attitude that turned his stomach.

The accident hadn't been yesterday. He'd lived like this long enough to know what he was dealing with. He didn't need her telling him this and that, as though he couldn't figure it out for himself.

No, she—Nurse Hatchet-Cratchett, his nurse number seven—had the same bloody mentality as the first six. In their eyes the wheelchair rendered him incompetent, unable to think for himself.

"I'm not paying you any longer," he repeated firmly, determined to get this over and done with. "You've had your last payment. You and your company are finished here."

And then she made that sound again—that little sound which had made him draw back. But this time he recognized the sound for what it was.

A laugh.

She was laughing at him.

Laughing and walking around the side of his chair so he had to crane his head to try to follow her.

He felt her hands settle on the back of his chair. She must have bent down, or perhaps she wasn't very tall, because her voice came surprisingly close to his ear.

"But *you* aren't paying me any longer. Our services have been retained and we are authorized to continue providing your care. Only now, instead of you paying for your care, the financial arrangements are being handled by a private source."

He went cold—cold and heavy. Even his legs, with their only limited sensation. *"What?"*

"It's true," she continued, beginning to push his chair and moving him forward. "I'm not the only one who thinks its high time you recovered." She continued pushing him despite his attempt to resist. "You're going to get well," she added, her voice whispering sweetly in his ear. "Whether you want to or not."

CHAPTER TWO

KRISTIAN clamped down on the wheel-rims, holding them tight to stop their progress. "Who is paying for my care?"

Elizabeth hated played games, and she didn't believe it was right to keep anyone in the dark, but she'd signed a confidentiality agreement and she had to honor it. "I'm sorry, Mr. Koumantaros. I'm not at liberty to say."

Her answer only antagonized him further. Kristian threw his head back and his powerful shoulders squared. His hands gripped the rims so tightly his knuckles shone white. "I won't have someone else assuming responsibility for my care, much less for what is surely questionable care."

Elizabeth cringed at the criticism. The criticism—slander?—was personal. It was her company. She personally interviewed, hired and trained each nurse that worked for First Class Rehab. Not that he knew. And not that she wanted him to know right now.

No, what mattered now was getting Mr. Koumantaros on a schedule, creating a predictable routine with regular periods of nourishment, exercise and rest. And to do that she really needed him to have his lunch.

"We can talk more over lunch," Elizabeth replied, beginning to roll him back out onto the terrace once more. But, just like before, Kristian clamped his hands down and gripped the wheel-rims hard, preventing him from going forward.

"I don't like being pushed."

Elizabeth stepped away and stared down at him, seeing for the first time the dark pink scar that snaked from beneath the sleeve of his sky-blue Egyptian cotton shirt, running from elbow to wrist. A multiple fracture, she thought, recalling just how many bones had broken. By all indications he should have died. But he hadn't. He'd survived. And after all that she wasn't about to let him give up now and wither away inside this shuttered villa.

"I didn't think you could get yourself around," she said, hanging on to her patience by a thread.

"I can push myself short distances."

"That's not quite the same thing as walking, is it?" she said exasperatedly. If he could do more…if he could walk…why didn't he? *Ornio,* she thought, using the Greek word for ornery. The previous nurses hadn't exaggerated a bit. Kristian was as obstinate as a mule.

He snorted. "Is that your idea of encouragement?"

Her lips compressed. Kristian also knew how to play both sides. One minute he was the aggressor, the next the victim. Worse, he was succeeding in baiting her, getting to her, and no one ever—*ever*—got under her skin. Not anymore. "It's a statement of fact, Mr. Koumantaros. You're still in the chair because your muscles have atrophied since the accident. But initially the doctors expected you to walk again." *They thought you'd want to.*

"It didn't work out."

"Because it hurt too much?"

"The therapy wasn't working."

"You gave up." She reached for the handles on the back of his chair and gave a hard push. "Now, how about that lunch?"

He wouldn't release the rims. "How about you tell me who is covering your services, and then we'll have lunch?"

Part of her admired his bargaining skill and tactics. He was clearly a leader, and accustomed to being in control. But she was a leader, too, and she was just as comfortable giving direction. "I can't tell you." Her jaw firmed. "Not until you're walking."

He craned to see her, even though he couldn't see anything. "So you *can* tell me."

"Once you're walking."

"Why not until then?"

She shrugged. "It's the terms of the contract."

"But you know this person?"

"We spoke on the phone."

He grew still, his expression changing as well, as though he were thinking, turning inward. "How long until I walk?"

"It depends entirely on you. Your hamstrings and hip muscles have unfortunately tightened, shortening up, but it's not irreparable, Mr. Koumantaros. It just requires diligent physical therapy."

"But even with *diligent* therapy I'll always need a walker."

She heard his bitterness but didn't comment on it. It wouldn't serve anything at this point. "A walker or a cane. But isn't that better than a wheelchair? Wouldn't you enjoy being independent again?"

"But it'll never be the same, never as it was—"

"People are confronted by change every day, Mr. Koumantaros."

"Do not patronize me." His voice deepened, roughened, revealing blistering fury.

"I'm not trying to. I'm trying to understand. And if this is because others died and you—"

"Not one more word," he growled. "Not one."

"Mr. Koumantaros, you are no less of a man because others died and you didn't."

"Then you do not know me. You do not know who I am, or who I was before. Because the best part of me—the good in me—died that day on the mountain. The good in me perished while I was saving someone I didn't even like."

He laughed harshly, the laugh tinged with self-loathing. "I'm not a hero. I'm a monster." And, reaching up, with a savage yank he ripped the bandages from his head. Rearing back in his wheelchair, Kristian threw his head into sunlight. "Do you see the monster now?"

Elizabeth sucked in her breath as the warm Mediterranean light touched the hard planes of his face.

A jagged scar ran the length of the right side of his face, ending precariously close to his right eye. The skin was still a tender pink, although one day it would pale, lightening until it nearly matched his skin tone—as long as he stayed out of the sun.

But the scar wasn't why she stared. And the scar wasn't what caused her chest to seize up, squeezing with a terrible, breathless tenderness.

Kristian Koumantaros was beautiful. Beyond beautiful. Even with the scar snaking like a fork of lightning over his cheekbone, running from the corner of his mouth to the edge of his eye.

"God gave me a face to match my heart. Finally the outside and inside look the same," he gritted, hands convulsing in his lap.

"You're wrong." Elizabeth could hardly breathe. His words gave her so much pain, so much sorrow, she felt tears sting her eyes. "If God gave you a face to match your heart, your heart is beautiful, too. Because a scar doesn't ruin a face, and a scar doesn't ruin a heart. It just shows that you've lived—" she took a rough breath "—and loved."

He said nothing and she pressed on. "Besides, I think the scar suits you. You were too good-looking before."

For a split second he said nothing, and then he laughed, a fierce guttural laugh that was more animal-like than human. "Finally. Someone to tell me the truth."

Elizabeth ignored the pain pricking her insides, the stab of more pain in her chest. Something about him, something about this—the scarred face, the shattered life, the fury, the fire, the intelligence and passion—touched her. Hurt her. It was not that anyone should suffer, but somehow on Kristian the suffering became bigger, larger than life, a thing in and of itself.

"You're an attractive man even with the scar," she said, still kneeling next to his chair.

"It's a hideous scar. It runs the length of my face. I can feel it."

"You're quite vain, then, Mr. Koumantaros?"

His head swung around and the expression on his face, matched by the cloudiness in his deep blue eyes, stole her breath. *He didn't suit the chair.*

Or the chair didn't suit him. He was too big, too strong, too much of everything. And it was wrong, his body, his life, his personality contained by it. Confined to it.

"No man wants to feel like Frankenstein," Kristian said with another rough laugh.

She knew then that it wasn't his face that made him feel so broken, but his heart and mind. Those memories of his that haunted him, the flashes of the past that made him relive the accident over and over. She knew because she'd once been the same. She, too, had relived an accident in endless detail, stopping the mental camera constantly, freezing the lens at the first burst of flame and the final ball of fire. But that was her story, not his, and she couldn't allow her own experiences and emotions to cloud her judgment now.

She had to regain some control, retreat as quickly as possible to professional detachment. She wasn't here for him; she was here for a job. She wasn't his love interest. He had one in Athens, waiting for him to recover. It was this lover of his who'd insisted he walk, he function, he see, and that was why she was here. To help him recover. To help him return to her.

"You're far from Frankenstein," she said crisply, covering her suddenly ambivalent emotions. She rose to her feet, smoothed her straight skirt and adjusted her blouse. "But, since you require flattery, let me give it to you. The scar suits you. Gives your face character. Makes you look less like a model or a movie star and more like a man."

"A man," he repeated with a bitter laugh.

"Yes, a man. And with some luck and hard work, soon we'll have you acting like a man, too."

Chaotic emotions rushed across his face. Surprise, then confusion, and as she watched the confusion shifted into anger. She'd caught him off guard and hurt him. She could see she'd hurt him.

Swallowing the twinge of guilt, she felt it on the tip of her tongue to apologize, as she hadn't meant to hurt his feelings so much as provoke him into taking action.

But even as she attempted to put a proper apology together, she sensed anything she said, particularly anything sympathetic, would only antagonize him more. He was living in his own hell.

More gently she added, "You've skied the most inaccessible mountain faces in the world, piloted helicopters in blizzards, rescued a half-dozen—"

"Enough."

"You can do anything," she persisted. His suffering was so obvious it was criminal. She'd become a nurse to help those wounded, not to inflict fresh wounds, but sometimes patients were so overwhelmed by physical pain and mental misery that they self-destructed.

Brilliant men—daring, risk-taking, gifted men—were particularly vulnerable, and she'd learned the hard way that these same men self-destructed if they had no outlet for their anger, no place for their pain.

Elizabeth vowed to find the outlet for Kristian, vowed she'd channel his fury somehow, turning pain into positives.

And so, before he could speak, before he could give voice to any of his anger, or contradict her again, she mentioned the pretty table setting before them, adding that the cook and butler had done a superb job preparing their late lunch.

"Your staff have outdone themselves, Mr. Koumantaros. They've set a beautiful table on your terrace. Can you feel that breeze? You can smell the scent of pine in the warm air."

"I don't smell it."

"Then come here, where I'm standing. It really is lovely. You can get a whiff of the herbs in your garden, too. Rosemary, and lemongrass."

But he didn't roll forward. He rolled backward, retreating back toward the shadows. "It's too bright. The light makes my head hurt."

"Even if I replace the bandages?"

"Even with the bandages." His voice grew harsh, pained. "And I don't want lunch. I already told you that but you don't listen. You won't listen. No one does."

"We could move lunch inside—"

"*I don't want lunch.*" And with a hard push he disappeared into the cooler library, where he promptly bumped into a side-table and sent it crashing, which led to him cursing and another bang of furniture.

Tensing, Elizabeth fought the natural inclination to hurry and help him. She wanted to rush to his side, but knew that doing so would only prolong his helpless state. She couldn't become an enabler, couldn't allow him to continue as he'd done—retreating from life, retreating from living, retreating into the dark shadows of his mind.

Instead, with nerves of steel, she left him as he was, muttering and cursing and banging into the table he'd overturned, and headed slowly across the terrace to the pretty lunch table, with its cheerful blue and white linens and cluster of meadow flowers in the middle.

And while she briefly appreciated the pretty linens and fresh flowers, she forgot both just as quickly, her thoughts focused on one thing and only one—Kristian Koumantaros.

It had cost her to speak to him so bluntly. She'd never been this confrontational—she'd never needed to be until now—but, frankly, she didn't know what else to do with him at this point. Her agency had tried everything—they'd sent every capable nurse, attempted every course of therapy—all to no avail.

As Elizabeth gratefully took a seat at the table, she knew her exhaustion wasn't just caused by Kristian's obstinance, but by Kristian himself.

Kristian had gotten beneath her skin.

And it's not his savage beauty, she told herself sternly. It couldn't be. She wasn't so superficial as to be moved by the violence in his face and frame—although he had an undeniably handsome face. So what was it? Why did she feel horrifyingly close to tears?

Ignoring the nervous flutter in her middle, she unfolded her linen serviette and spread it across her lap.

Pano appeared, a bottle of bubbling mineral water in his hand. "Water, ma'am?"

"Please, Pano. Thank you."

"And is Mr. Koumantaros joining you?"

She glanced toward the library doors, which had just been shut. She felt a weight on her heart, and the weight seemed to swell and grow. "No, Pano, not today. Not after all."

He filled her glass. "Shall I take him a plate?"

Elizabeth shot another glance toward the closed and shuttered library doors. She hesitated but a moment. "No. We'll try again tonight at dinner."

"So nothing if he asks?" The butler sounded positively pained.

"I know it seems hard, but I must somehow reach him. I must make him respond. He can't hide here forever. He's too young, and there are too many people that love him and miss him."

Pano seemed to understand this. His bald head inclined and, with a polite, "Your luncheon will be served immediately," he disappeared, after leaving the mineral water bottle on the table within her reach.

One of the villa's younger staff served the lunch— *souvlaki,* with sliced cucumbers and warm fresh pitta. It wasn't the meal she'd requested, and Elizabeth suspected it was intentional, the cook's own rebellion, but at least a meal had been prepared.

Elizabeth didn't eat immediately, choosing to give Kristian time in case he changed his mind. Brushing a buzzing fly away, she waited five minutes, and then another five more, reflecting that she hadn't gotten off to the best start here. It had been bumpy in more ways than one. But she could only press on, persevere. Everything would work out. Kristian Koumantaros would walk again, and eventually return to Athens, where he'd resume responsibility for the huge corporation he owned and had once single-handedly run. She'd go home to England and be rid of Greece and Greek tycoons.

After fifteen minutes Elizabeth gave up the vigil. Kristian wasn't coming. Finally she ate, concentrating on savoring the excellent meal and doing her best to avoid thinking about the next confrontation with her mulish patient.

Lunch finished, Elizabeth wiped her mouth on her serviette and pushed away from the table. Time to check on Kristian.

In the darkened library, Kristian lifted his head as she entered the room. "Have a nice lunch?" he asked in terse Greek.

She winced at the bitterness in his voice. "Yes, thank you. You have an excellent cook."

"Did you enjoy the view?"

"It is spectacular," she agreed, although she'd actually spent most of the time thinking about him instead of the view. She hadn't felt this involved with any case in years. But then, she hadn't nursed anyone directly in years, either.

After her stint in nursing school, and then three years working at a regional hospital, she'd gone back to school and earned her Masters in Business Administration, with an emphasis on Hospital and Medical Administration. After graduating she had immediately found work. So much work she had realized she'd be better off working for herself than anyone else—which was how her small, exclusive First Class Rehab had been born.

But Kristian Koumantaros's case was special. Kristian Koumantaros hadn't improved in her company's care. He'd worsened.

And to Elizabeth it was completely unacceptable.

Locating her notebook on the side-table, where she'd left it earlier, she took a seat on the couch. "Mr. Koumantaros, I know you don't want a nurse, but you still need one. In fact, you need several."

"Why not prescribe a fleet?" he asked sarcastically.

"I think I shall." She flipped open her brown leather portfolio and, scanning her previous notes, began to scribble again. "A live-in nursing assistant to help with bathing, personal hygiene. Male, preferably. Someone strong to lift you in and out of your chair since you're not disposed to walk."

"I can't walk, Mrs.—"

"*Ms.* Hatchet," she supplied, before crisply continuing, "And you could walk if you had worked with your last four physical therapists. They all tried, Mr. Koumantaros, but you were more interested in terrifying them than in making progress."

Elizabeth wrote another couple of notes, then clicked her pen closed. "You also require an occupational therapist, as you desperately need someone to adapt your lifestyle. If you've no intention of getting better, your house and habits will need to change. Ramps, a second lift, a properly outfitted bathroom, rails and grabs in the pool—"

"No," he thundered, face darkening. "No bars, no rails, and no goddamn grabs in this house."

She clicked her pen open again. "Perhaps its time we called in a psychiatrist—someone to evaluate your depression and recommend a course of therapy. Pills, perhaps, or sessions of counseling."

"I will never talk—"

"You are now," she said cheerfully, scribbling yet another note to herself, glancing at Kristian Koumantaros from beneath her lashes. His jaw was thick, and rage was stiffening his spine, improving his posture, curling his hands into fists.

Good, she thought, with a defiant tap of her pen. He hadn't given up on living, just given up on healing. There was something she—and her agency—could still do.

She watched him for a long dispassionate moment.

"Talking—counseling—will help alleviate your depression, and it's depression that's keeping you from recovering."

"I'm not depressed."

"Then someone to treat your rage. You *are* raging, Mr. Koumantaros. Are you aware of your tone?"

"*My* tone?" He threw himself back in his chair, hands flailing against the rims of the wheels, furious skin against steel. "*My* tone? You come into my house and lecture me about my tone? Who the hell do you think you are?"

The raw savagery in his voice cut her more than his words, and for a moment the library spun. Elizabeth held her breath, silent, stunned.

"You think you're so good." Kristian's voice sounded from behind her, mocking her. "So righteous, so sure of everything. But would you be so sure of yourself if the rug was pulled from beneath *your* feet? Would you be so callous then?"

Of course he didn't know the rug *had* been pulled from beneath her feet. No one got through life unscathed. But her personal tragedies had toughened her, and she thought of the old wounds as scar tissue…something that was just part of her.

Even so, Elizabeth felt a moment of gratitude that Kristian couldn't see her, or the conflicting emotions flickering over her face. Hers wasn't a recent loss, hers was seven years ago, and yet if she wasn't careful to keep up the defenses the loss still felt as though it had happened yesterday.

As the silence stretched Kristian laughed low, harshly. "I got you on that one." His laughter deepened, and then abruptly ended. "Hard to sit in judgment until you've walked a mile in someone else's shoes."

Through the open doors Elizabeth could hear the warble of a bird, and she wondered if it was the dark green bird, the one with the lemon-yellow breast, she'd seen while eating on the patio terrace.

"I'm not as callous as you think," she said, her voice cool enough to contradict her words. "But I'm here to help you, and I'll do whatever I must to see you move into the next step of recovery."

"And why should I want to recover?" His head angled, and his expression was ferocious. "And don't give me some sickly-sweet answer about finding my true love and having a family and all that nonsense."

Elizabeth's lips curved in a faint, hard smile. No, she'd never dangle love as a motivational tool, because even that could be taken away. "I wasn't. You should know by now that's not my style."

"So tell me? Give it to me straight? Why should I bother to get better?"

Why bother? Why bother, indeed? Elizabeth felt her heart race—part anger, part sympathy. "Because you're still alive, that's why."

"That's it?" Kristian laughed bitterly. "Sorry, that's not much incentive."

"Too bad," she answered, thinking she *was* sorry about his accident, but he wasn't dead.

Maybe he couldn't walk easily or see clearly, but he was still intact and he had his life, his heart, his body, his mind. Maybe he wasn't exactly as he had been before the injury, but that didn't make him less of a man…not unless he let it. And he was allowing it.

Pressing the tip of her finger against her mouth, she fought to hold back all the angry things she longed to say, knowing she wasn't here to judge. He was just a patient, and her job was to provide medical care, not morality lessons. But, even acknowledging that it wasn't her place to criticize, she felt her tension grow.

Despite her best efforts, she resented his poor-me attitude, was irritated that he was so busy looking at the small picture he was missing the big one. Life was so precious. Life was a gift, not a right, and he still possessed the gift.

He could love and be loved. Fall in love, make love, shower someone with affection—hugs, kisses, tender touches. There was no reason he couldn't make someone feel cherished, important, unforgettable. No reason other than that he didn't want to, that he'd rather feel sorry for himself than reach out to another.

"Because, for whatever reason, Mr. Koumantaros, you're still here with us, still alive. Don't look a gift horse in the mouth. Live. Live fully, wisely. And if you can't do it for yourself, then do it for those who didn't escape the avalanche that day with you." She took a deep breath. "Do it for Cosima. Do it for Andreas."

CHAPTER THREE

COSIMA and Andreas. Kristian was surprised his English Nurse Cratchett knew their names, as it was Cosima and Andreas who haunted him. And for very different reasons.

Kristian shifted restlessly in bed. His legs ached at the moment. Sometimes the pain was worse than others, and it was intense tonight. Nothing made him comfortable.

The accident. A winter holiday with friends and family in the French Alps.

He'd been in a coma for weeks after the accident, and when he'd come out of it he'd been immobilized for another couple weeks to give his spine a chance to heal. He'd been told he was lucky there was no lasting paralysis, told he was lucky to have survived such a horrific accident.

But for Kristian the horror continued. And it wasn't even his eyes he missed, or his strength. It was Andreas, Andreas—not just his big brother, but his best friend.

And while he and Andreas had always been about the extreme—extreme skiing, extreme diving, extreme parasailing—Andreas, the eldest, had been the straight arrow, as good as the sun, while Kristian had played the bad boy and rebel.

Put them together—fair-haired Andreas and devilish Kristian—and they'd been unstoppable. They'd had too much damn fun. Not that they hadn't worked—they'd worked hard—but they had played even harder.

It had helped that they were both tall, strong, physical. They'd practically grown up on skis, and Kristian couldn't even remember a time when he and Andreas hadn't partici-pated in some ridiculous, reckless thrill-seeking adventure. Their father, Stavros, had been an avid sportsman, and their stunning French mother hadn't been just beautiful, she'd once represented France in the Winter Olympics. Sport had been the family passion.

Of course there had been dangers, but their father had taught them to read mountains, study weather reports, discuss snow conditions with avalanche experts. They'd coupled their love of adventure with intelligent risk-taking. And, so armed, they had embraced life.

And why shouldn't they have? They'd been part of a famous, wealthy, powerful family. Money and opportunity had never been an issue.

But money and opportunity didn't protect one from trag-edy. It didn't insure against heartbreak or loss.

Andreas was the reason Kristian needed the pills. Andreas was the reason he couldn't sleep.

Why hadn't he saved his brother first? Why had he waited?

Kristian stirred yet again, his legs alive and on fire. The doctors said it was nerves and tissue healing, but the pain was maddening. Felt like licks of lightning everywhere.

Kristian searched the top of his bedside table for medicine but found nothing. His nurse must have taken the pain meds he always kept there.

If only he could sleep.

If he could just relax maybe the pain would go away. But he wasn't relaxing, and he needed something—anything—to take his mind off the accident and what had happened that day on Le Meije.

There had been ten of them who had set off together for a final run. They'd been heli-skiing all week, and it had been their next to last day. Conditions had looked good, the ski guides had given the okay, and the helicopter had taken off. Less than two hours later, only three of their group survived.

Cosima had lived, but not Andreas.

Kristian had saved Cosima instead of his brother, and that was the decision that tormented him.

Kristian had never even liked Cosima—not even at their first meeting. From the very beginning she'd struck him as a shallow party girl who lived for the social scene, and nothing she'd said or done during the next two years had convinced him otherwise. Of course Andreas had never seen that side in her. He'd only seen her beauty, her style, and her fun—and maybe she was beautiful, stylish, but Andreas could have done better.

Driven to find relief, Kristian searched the table-top again, before painfully rolling over onto his stomach to reach into the small drawers, in case the bottles had been put there. Nothing.

Then he remembered the bottle tucked between the mattresses, and was just reaching for it when his bedroom door opened and he heard the click of a light switch on the wall.

"You're still awake." It was dear old Cratchett, on her night rounds.

"Missing the hospital routine?" he drawled, slowly rolling onto his back and dragging himself into a sitting position.

Elizabeth approached the bed. "I haven't worked in a hospital in years. My company specializes in private home healthcare."

He listened to her footsteps, trying to imagine her age. He'd played this game with all the nurses. Since he couldn't see, he created his own visual images. And, listening to Elizabeth Hatchet's voice and footsteps, he began to create a mental picture of her.

Age? Thirty-something. Maybe close to forty.

Brunette, redhead, black-haired or blonde?

She leaned over the bed and he felt her warmth even as he caught a whiff of a light fresh scent—the same crisp, slightly sweet fragrance he'd smelled earlier. Not exactly citrus, and not hay—possibly grass? Fresh green grass. With sunshine. But also rain.

"Can't sleep?" she asked, and her voice sounded tantalizingly near.

"I never sleep."

"In pain?"

"My legs are on fire."

"You need to use them, exercise them. It'd improve circulation and eventually alleviate most of the pain symptoms you're experiencing."

For a woman with such a brusque bedside manner she had a lovely voice. The tone and pitch reminded him of the string section of the orchestra. Not a cello or bass, but a violin. Warm, sweet, evocative.

"You sound so sure of yourself," he said, hearing her move again, sensing her closeness.

"This is my job. It's what I do," she said. "And tell me, Mr. Koumantaros, what do *you* do—besides throw yourself down impossibly vertical slopes?"

"You don't approve of extreme skiing?"

Elizabeth felt her chest grow tight. Extreme skiing. Jumping off mountains. Dodging avalanches. It was ridiculous—ridiculous to tempt fate like that.

Impatiently she tugged the sheets and coverlet straight at the foot of the bed, before smoothing the covers with a jerk on the sheet at its edge.

"I don't approve of risking life for sport," she answered. "No."

"But sport is exercise—and isn't that what you're telling me I must do?"

She looked down at him, knowing he was attempting to bait her once again. He wasn't wearing a shirt, and his chest was big, his shoulders immense. She realized that this was all just a game to him, like his love of sport.

He wanted to push her—had pushed her nurses, pushed all of them. Trying to distract them from doing their job was a form of entertainment for him, a diversion to keep him from facing the consequences of his horrific accident.

"Mr. Koumantaros, there are plenty of exercises that don't risk life or limb—or cost an exorbitant amount of money."

"Is it the sport or the money you object to, Nurse?"

"Both," she answered firmly.

"How refreshing. An Englishwoman with an opinion on everything."

Once again she didn't rise to the bait. She knew he must be disappointed, too. Maybe he'd been able to torment his other nurses, but he wouldn't succeed in torturing her.

She had a job to do, and she'd do it, and then she'd go home and life would continue—far more smoothly once she had Kristian Koumantaros out of it.

"Your pillows," she said, her voice as starchy as the white blouse tucked into cream slacks. Her only bit of ornamentation was the slender gold belt at her waist.

She'd thought she'd given him ample warning that she was about to lean over and adjust his pillows, but as she reached across him he suddenly reached up toward her and his hand became entangled in her hair.

She quickly stepped back, flustered. She'd heard all about Kristian's playboy antics, knew his reputation was that of a lady's man, but she was dumbfounded that he'd still try to pull that on her. "Without being able to see, you didn't realize I was there," she said coolly, wanting to avoid all allegations of improper conduct. "In the future I will ask you to move before I adjust your pillows or covers."

"It was just your hair," he said mildly. "It brushed my face. I was merely moving it out of the way."

"I'll make sure to wear it pulled back tomorrow."

"Your hair is very long."

She didn't want to get into the personal arena. She already felt exceedingly uncomfortable being back in Greece, and so isolated here on Taygetos, at a former monastery. Kristian Koumantaros couldn't have found a more remote place to live if he'd tried.

"I would have thought your hair was all short and frizzy," he continued, "or up tight in a bun. You sound like a woman who'd wear her hair scraped back and tightly pinned up."

He was still trying to goad her, still trying to get a reaction. "I do like buns, yes. They're professional."

"And you're so *very* professional," he mocked.

She stiffened, her face paling. An icy lump hit her stomach.

Her former husband, another Greek playboy, had put her through two years of hell before they were finally legally separated, and it had taken her nearly five years to recover. One Greek playboy had already broken her heart. She refused to let another break her spirit.

Elizabeth squared her shoulders, lifted her head. "Since there's nothing else, Mr. Koumantaros, I'll say goodnight."

And before he could speak she'd exited the room and firmly shut the door behind her.

But Elizabeth's control snapped the moment she reached the hall. Swiftly, she put a hand out to brace herself against the wall.

She couldn't do this.

Couldn't stay here, live like this, be tormented like this.

She despised spoiled, pampered Greeks—particularly wealthy tycoons with far too much time on their hands.

After her divorce she'd vowed she'd never return to Greece, but here she was. Not just in Greece, but trapped on a mountain peak in a medieval monastery with Kristian Koumantaros, a man so rich, so powerful, he made Arab sheikhs look poor.

Elizabeth exhaled hard, breathing out in a desperate, painful rush.

She couldn't let tomorrow be a repeat of today, either. She was losing control of Koumantaros and the situation already.

This couldn't continue. Her patient didn't respect her, wasn't even listening to her, and he felt entirely too comfortable mocking her.

Elizabeth gave her head a slight dazed shake. How was this happening? She was supposed to be in charge.

Tomorrow, she told herself fiercely, returning to the bedroom the housekeeper had given her. Tomorrow she'd prove to him she was the one in charge, the one running the show.

She could do this. She had to.

The day had been warm, and although it was now night, her bedroom retained the heat. Like the other tower rooms, its plaster ceiling was high, at least ten or eleven feet, and decorated with elaborate painted friezes.

She crossed to open her windows and allow the evening breeze in. Her three arched windows overlooked the gardens, now bathed in moonlight, and then the mountain valley beyond.

It was beautiful here, uncommonly beautiful, with the ancient monastery tucked among rocks, cliffs and chestnut trees. But also incredibly dangerous. Kristian Koumantaros was a man used to dominating his world. She needed him to work with her, cooperate with her, or he could destroy her business and reputation completely.

At the antique marble bureau, Elizabeth twisted her long hair and then reached for one of her hair combs to fasten the knot on top of her head.

As she slid the comb in, she glanced up into the ornate silver filigree mirror over the bureau. Glimpsing her reflection—fair, light eyes, an oval face with a surprisingly strong chin—she grimaced. Back when she'd done more with herself, back when she'd had a luxurious lifestyle, she'd been a paler blonde, more like champagne, softer, prettier. But she'd given up the expensive highlights along with the New York and London stylists. She didn't own a single couture item anymore, nor any high-end real estate. The lifestyle she'd once known—taken for granted, assumed to be as much a part of her birthright as her name—was gone.

Over.

Forgotten.

But, turning back suddenly to the mirror, she saw the flicker in her eyes and knew she hadn't forgotten.

Medicine—nursing—offered her an escape, provided structure, a regimented routine and a satisfying amount of control. While medicine in and of itself wasn't safe, medicine coupled with business administration became something far more predictable. Far more manageable. Which was exactly what she prayed Kristian would be tomorrow.

* * *

The next morning Elizabeth woke early, ready to get to work, but even at seven the monastery-turned-villa was still dark except for a few lights in the kitchen.

Heartened that the villa was coming to life, Elizabeth dressed in a pale blue shirt and matching blue tailored skirt— her idea of a nursing uniform—before heading to find breakfast, which seemed to surprise the cook, throwing her into a state of anxiety and confusion.

Elizabeth managed to convince her that all she really needed was a cup of coffee and a bite to eat. The cook obliged with both, and over Greek coffee—undrinkable—and a *tiropita,* or cheese pie, Elizabeth visited with Pano.

She learned that Kristian usually slept in and then had coffee in his bed, before making his way to the library where he spent each day.

"What does he do all day?" she asked, breaking the pie into smaller bites. Pano hesitated, and then finally shrugged.

"He does nothing?" Elizabeth guessed.

Pano shifted his shoulders. "It is difficult for him."

"I understand in the beginning he did the physical therapy. But then something happened?"

"It was the eye surgery—the attempt to repair the retinas." Pano sighed heavily, and the same girl who'd served Elizabeth lunch yesterday came forward with fresh hot coffee. "He'd had some sight until then—not much, but enough that he could see light and shadows, shapes—but something went wrong in the repeated surgeries and he is now as you see him. Blind."

Elizabeth knew that losing the rest of his sight would have been a terrible blow. "I read in his chart that there is still a slight chance he could regain some sight with another treatment. It'd be minimal, I realize."

Elderly Pano shrugged.

"Why doesn't he do it?" she persisted.

"I think…" His wrinkled face wrinkled further. "He's afraid. It's his last hope."

Elizabeth said nothing, and Pano lifted his hands to try to make her understand.

"As long as he postpones the surgery, he can hope that one day he might see again. But once he has the surgery, and it doesn't work—" the old man snapped his fingers "—then there is nothing else for him to hope for."

And that Elizabeth actually understood.

But as the hours passed, and the morning turned to noon, Elizabeth grew increasingly less sympathetic.

What kind of life was this? To just sleep all day?

She peeked into his room just before twelve and he was still out, sprawled half-naked between white sheets, his dark hair tousled.

Elizabeth went in search of Pano once more, to enquire into Kristian's sleeping habits.

"Is it usual for Kirios Koumantaros to sleep this late?" she asked.

"It's not late. Not for him. He can sleep 'til one or two in the afternoon."

Unable to hide her incredulity, she demanded, "Did his other nurses allow this?"

Pano's bald head shone in the light as he bent over the big table and finished straightening the mail and papers piled there. "His other nurses couldn't control him. He is a man. He does as he wants to do."

"No. Not when his medical care costs thousands and thousands of pounds each week."

Mail sorted and newspapers straightened, Pano looked up at her. "You don't tell a grown man what to do."

She made a rough sound. "Yes, you do. If what he's doing is destructive."

Pano didn't answer, and after a glance at the tall library clock—it was now five minutes until one—she turned around and headed straight for Kristian's bedroom. What she found there, on his bedside table, explained his long, deep sleep.

He'd taken sleeping pills. She didn't know how many, and she didn't know when they'd been taken, but the bottle hadn't been there earlier in the evening when she'd checked on him.

She'd collected the bottles from the small table in the library and put them in her room, under lock and key, so for him to have had access to this bottle meant he had a secret stash of his own to medicate himself as he pleased.

But still, he couldn't get the prescriptions filled if Pano or another staff member weren't aiding him. Someone—and she suspected Pano again—was making it too easy for Kristian to be dependent.

Elizabeth spoke Kristian's name to wake him. No response. She said his name again. "Mr. Koumantaros, it's gone noon—time to wake up."

Nothing.

"Mr. Koumantaros." She stepped closer to the bed, stood over him and said, more loudly, "It's gone noon, Mr. Koumantaros. Time to get up. You can't sleep all day."

Kristian wasn't moving. He wasn't dead, either. She could see that much. He was breathing, and there was eye movement beneath his closed lids, but he certainly wasn't interested in waking up.

She cleared her throat and practically shouted, "Kristian Koumantaros—it's time to get up."

Kristian heard the woman. How could he not? She sounded as if she had a bullhorn. But he didn't want to wake.

He wanted to sleep.

He needed to keep sleeping, craved the deep dreamless sleep that would mercifully make all dark and quiet and peaceful.

But the voice didn't stop. It just grew louder. And louder.

Now there was a tug on the covers, and in the next moment they were stripped back, leaving him bare.

"Go away," he growled.

"It's gone noon, Mr. Koumantaros. Time to get up. Your first physical therapy session is in less than an hour."

And that was when he remembered. He wasn't dealing with just any old nurse, but nurse number seven. Elizabeth Hatchet. The latest nurse, an English nurse of all things, sent to make his life miserable.

He rolled over onto his stomach. "You're not allowed to wake me up."

"Yes, I am. It's gone noon and you can't sleep the day away."

"Why not? I was up most of the night."

"Your first physical therapy session begins soon."

"You're mad."

"Not mad, not even angry. Just ready to get you back into treatment, following a proper exercise program."

"No."

Elizabeth didn't bother to argue. There was no point. One way or another he would resume physical therapy. "Pano is on his way with breakfast. I told him you could eat in the dining room, like a civilized man, but he insisted he serve you in bed."

"Good man," Kristian said under his breath.

Elizabeth let this pass, too. "But this is your last morning being served in bed. You're neither an invalid nor a prince. You can eat at a table like the rest of us."

She rolled his wheelchair closer to the bed. "Your chair is here, in case you need it, and I'll be just a moment while I gather a few things." And with that she took the medicine bottle from the table and headed for the bathroom adjoining his bedroom. In the bathroom she quickly opened drawers and cupboard doors, before returning to his room with another two bottles in her hands.

"What are you doing?" Kristian asked, sitting up and listening to her open and close the drawers in his dresser.

"Looking for the rest of your secret stash."

"Secret stash of what?"

"You know perfectly well."

"If I knew, I wouldn't be asking."

She found another pill bottle at the back of his top drawer, right behind his belts. "Just how much stuff are you taking?"

"I take very little—"

"Then why do you have enough prescriptions and bottles to fill a pharmacy?"

It was his turn to fall silent, and she snorted as she finished checking his room. She found nothing else. Not in the armchair in the corner, or the drawer of the nightstand, nor between the mattresses of his bed. Good. Maybe she'd found the last of it. She certainly hoped so.

"Now what?" he asked, as Elizabeth scooped up the bottles and marched through the master bedroom's French doors outside to the pool.

"Just finishing the job," she said, leaving the French doors open and heading across the sunlit patio to the pool and fountain.

"Those are mine," he shouted furiously.

"Not anymore," she called back.

"I can't sleep without them—"

"You could if you got regular fresh air and exercise." Elizabeth was walking quickly, but not so fast that she couldn't hear Kristian make the awkward transfer from his bed into his wheelchair.

"Parakalo," he demanded. "Please. Wait a blasted moment."

She did. Only because it was the first time she'd heard him use the word *please*. As she paused, she heard Kristian hit the open door with a loud bang, before backing up and banging his way forward again, this time managing to get through. Just as clumsily he pushed across the pale stone deck, his chair tires humming on the deck.

"I waited," she said, walking again, "but I'm not giving them back. They're poison. They're absolutely toxic for you."

Kristian was gaining on her and, reaching the fountain, she popped the caps off the bottles and turned toward him.

His black hair was wild, and the scar on his cheek like face paint from an ancient tribe. He might very well have been one of the warring Greeks.

"Everything you put in your body," she said, trying to slow the racing of her heart, as well as the sickening feeling that she was once again losing control, "and everything you do to your body is my responsibility."

And with that she emptied the bottles into the fountain, the splash of pills loud enough to catch Kristian's attention.

"You did it," he said.

"I did," she agreed.

A line formed between his eyebrows and his cheekbones grew more pronounced. "I declare war, then," he said, and the edge of his mouth lifted, tilted in a dark smile. "War. War against your company, and war against you." His voice dropped, deepened. "I'm fairly certain that very soon, Ms. Hatchet, you will deeply regret ever coming here."

CHAPTER FOUR

ELIZABETH'S heart thumped hard. So hard she thought it would burst from her chest.

It was a threat. Not just a small threat, but one meant to send her to her knees.

For a moment she didn't know what to think, or do, and as her heart raced she felt overwhelmed by fear and dread. And then she found her backbone, and knew she couldn't let a man—much less a man like Kristian—intimidate her. She wasn't a timid little church mouse, nor a country bumpkin. She'd come from a family every bit as powerful as the Koumantaros family—not that she talked about her past, or wanted anyone to know about it.

"Am I supposed to be afraid, Mr. Koumantaros?" she asked, capping the bottles and dropping them in her skirt pocket. "You must realize you're not a very threatening adversary."

Drawing on her courage, she continued coolly, "You can hardly walk, and you can't see, and you depend on everyone else to take care of you. So, really, why should I be frightened? What's the worst you can do? Call me names?"

He leaned back in his wheelchair, his black hair a striking contrast to the pale stone wall behind him. "I don't know whether to admire your moxie or pity your naïveté."

The day hadn't started well, she thought with a deep sigh, and it was just getting worse. Everything with him was a battle. If he only focused half his considerable intelligence and energy on healing instead of baiting nurses he'd be walking by now, instead of sitting like a wounded caveman in his wheelchair.

"Pity?" she scoffed. "Don't pity me. You're the one that hasn't worked in a year. You're the one that needs your personal and business affairs managed by others."

"You take so many liberties."

"They're not liberties; they're truths. If you were half the man your friends say you are, you wouldn't still be hiding away and licking your wounds."

"Licking my wounds?" he repeated slowly.

"I know eight people died that day in France, and I know one of them was your brother. I know you tried to rescue him, and I know you were hurt going back for him. But you will not bring him back by killing yourself—" She broke off as he reached out and grasped her wrist with his hand.

Elizabeth tried to pull back, but he didn't let her go. "No personal contact, Mr. Koumantaros," she rebuked sternly, tugging at her hand. "There are strict guidelines for patient-nurse relationships."

He laughed as though she'd just told a joke. But he also swiftly released her. "I don't think your highly trained Calista got that memo."

She glanced down at her wrist, which suddenly burned, checking for marks. There were none. And yet her skin felt hot, tender, and she rubbed it nervously. "It's not a memo. It's an ethics standard. Every nurse knows there are lines that cannot be crossed. There are no gray areas on this one. It's very black and white."

"You might want to explain that one to Calista, because she *begged* me to make love to her. But then she also asked me for money—confusing for a patient, I can assure you."

The sun shone directly overhead, and the heat coming off the stone terrace was intense, and yet Elizabeth froze. "What do you mean, she asked you for money?"

"Surely the UK has its fair share of blackmail?"

"You're trying to shift responsibility and the blame," she said, glancing around quickly, suppressing panic. Panic because if Calista *had* attempted to blackmail Mr. Koumantaros, one of Greece's most illustrious sons…oh…bad. Very, very bad. It was so bad she couldn't even finish the thought.

Expression veiled, Kristian shrugged and rested his hands on the rims of his wheelchair tires. "But as you say, Cratchett, she was twenty-three—very young. Maybe she didn't realize it wasn't ethical to seduce a patient and then demand hush money." He paused. "Maybe she didn't realize that blackmailing me while being employed by First Class Rehab meant that First Class Rehab would be held liable."

Elizabeth's legs wobbled. She'd dealt with a lot of problems in the past year, had sorted out everything from poor budgeting to soaring travel costs, but she hadn't seen this one coming.

"And you *are* First Class Rehab, aren't you, Ms. Hatchet? It is your company?"

She couldn't speak. Her mouth dried. Her heart pounded. She was suddenly too afraid to make a sound.

"I did some research, Ms. Hatchet."

She very much wished there was a chair close by, something she could sit down on, but all the furniture had been exiled to one end of the terrace, to give Mr. Koumantaros more room to maneuver his wheelchair.

"Calista left here months ago," she whispered, plucking

back a bit of hair as the breeze kicked in. "Why didn't you come to me then? Why did you wait so long to tell me?"

His mouth slanted, his black lashes dropped, concealing his intensely blue eyes. "I decided I'd wait and see if the level of care improved. It did not—"

"You refused to cooperate!" she exclaimed, her voice rising.

"I'm thirty-six, a world traveler, head of an international corporation and not used to being dependent on anyone—much less young women. Furthermore, I'd just lost my brother, four of my best friends, a cousin, his girlfriend, and her best friend." His voice vibrated with fury. "It was a lot to deal with."

"Which is why we were trying to help you—"

"By sending me a twenty-three-year-old former exotic dancer?"

"She wasn't."

"She was. She had also posed topless in numerous magazines—not that I ever saw them; she just bragged about them, and about how men loved her breasts. They were natural, you see."

Elizabeth was shaking. This was bad—very bad—and getting worse. "Mr. Koumantaros—" she pleaded.

But he didn't stop. "You say you personally hire and train every nurse? You say you do background reports and conduct all the interviews?"

"In the beginning, yes, I did it all. And I still interview all of the UK applicants."

"But *you* don't personally screen every candidate? You don't do the background checks yourself anymore, either. Do you?"

The tension whipped through her, tightening every muscle and nerve. "No."

He paused, as though considering her. "Your agency literature says you do."

Sickened, Elizabeth bit her lip, feeling trapped, cornered. She'd never worked harder than she had in the past year. She'd never accomplished so much, or fought so many battles, either. "We've grown a great deal in the past year. Doubled in size. I've been stretched—"

"Now listen to who has all the excuses."

Blood surged to her cheeks, making her face unbearably warm. She supposed she deserved that. "I've offices in seven cities, including Athens, and I employ hundreds of women throughout Europe. I'd vouch for nearly every one of them."

"*Nearly?*" he mocked. "So much for First Class Rehab's guarantee of first-class care and service."

Elizabeth didn't know which way to turn. "I'd be happy to rewrite our company mission statement."

"I'm sure you will be." His mouth curved slowly. "Once you've finished providing me with the quality care I so desperately need." His smile stretched. "As well as deserve."

She crossed her arms over her chest, shaken and more than a little afraid. "Does that mean you'll be working with me this afternoon on your physical therapy?" she asked, finding it so hard to ask the question that her voice was but a whisper.

"No, it means *you* will be working with *me.*" He began rolling forward, slowly pushing himself back to the tower rooms. "I imagine it's one now, which means lunch will be served in an hour. I'll meet you for lunch, and we can discuss my thoughts on my therapy then."

Elizabeth spent the next hour in a state of nervous shock. She couldn't absorb anything from the conversation she'd had with Kristian on the patio. Couldn't believe everything she'd thought, everything she knew, was just possibly wrong.

She'd flown Calista into London for her final interview. It

had been an all-expenses paid trip, too, and Calista had impressed Elizabeth immediately as a warm, energetic, dedicated nurse. A true professional. There was no way she could be, or ever have been, an exotic dancer. Nor a topless model. Impossible.

Furthermore, Calista wouldn't *dream* of seducing a man like Kristian Koumantaros. She was a good Greek girl, a young woman raised in Piraeus, the port of Athens, with her grandmother and a spinster great-aunt. Calista had solid family values.

And not much money.

Elizabeth closed her eyes, shook her head once, not wanting to believe the worst.

Then don't, she told herself, opening her eyes and heading for her room, to splash cold water on her face. Don't believe the worst. Look for the best in people. Always.

And yet as she walked through the cool arched passages of the tower to her own room a little voice whispered, *Isn't that why you married a man like Nico? Because you only wanted to believe the best in him?*

Forty-five minutes later, Elizabeth returned downstairs, walking outside to the terrace where she'd had a late lunch yesterday. She discovered Kristian was already there, enjoying his coffee.

Elizabeth, remembering her own morning coffee, grimaced inwardly. She'd always thought that Greek coffee—or what was really Turkish coffee—tasted like sludge. Nico had loved the stuff, and had made fun of her preference for *café au lait* and cappuccino, but she'd grown up with a coffee house on every corner in New York, and a latte or a mocha was infinitely preferable to thick black mud.

At her footsteps Kristian lifted his head and looked up in her direction. Her breath caught in her throat.

Kristian had shaved. His thick black hair had been trimmed and combed, and as he turned his attention on her the blue of his eyes was shocking. Intense. Maybe even more intense without sight, as he was forced to focus, to really listen.

His blue eyes were such a sharp contrast to his black hair and hard, masculine features that she felt an odd shiver race through her—a shiver of awareness, appreciation—and it bewildered her, just as nearly everything about this man threw her off balance. For a moment she felt what Calista must have felt, confronted by a man like this.

"Hello." Elizabeth sat down, suddenly shy. "You look nice," she added, her voice coming out strangely husky.

"A good shave goes a long way."

It wasn't just the shave, she thought, lifting her napkin from the table and spreading it across her lap. It was the alert expression on Kristian's face, the sense that he was there, mentally, physically, clearly paying attention.

"I am very sorry about the communication problems," she said, desperately wanting to start over, get things off on a better foot. "I understand you are very frustrated, and I want you to know I am eager to make everything better—"

"I know," he interrupted quietly.

"You do?"

"You're afraid I'll destroy your company." One black eyebrow quirked. "And it would be easy to do, too. Within a month you'd be gone."

There wasn't a cloud in the sky, and yet the day suddenly grew darker, as though the sun itself had dimmed. "Mr. Koumantaros—"

"Seeing as we're going to be working so closely together, isn't it time we were on a first-name basis?" he suggested.

She eyed him warily. He was reminding her of a wild

animal at the moment—dangerous and unpredictable. "That might be difficult."

"And why is that?"

She wondered if she should be honest, wondered if now was the time to flatter him, win him over with insincere compliments, and then decided against it. She'd always been truthful, and she'd remain so now. "The name Kristian doesn't suit you at all. It implies Christ-like, and you're far from that."

She had expected him to respond with anger. Instead he smiled faintly, the top of his finger tapping against the rim of his cup. "My mother once said she'd given us the wrong names. My older brother Andreas should have had my name, and she felt I would have been better with his. Andreas—or Andrew—in Greek means—"

"Strong," she finished for him. "Manly. Courageous."

Kristian's head lifted as though he could see her. She knew he could not, and she felt a prick of pain for him. Vision was so important. She relied on her eyes for everything.

"I've noticed you're fluent in Greek," he said thoughtfully. "That's unusual, considering your background."

He didn't know her background. He didn't know anything about her. But now wasn't the time to be correcting him. In an effort to make peace, she was willing to be conciliatory. "So, you are the strong one and your brother was the saint?"

Kristian shrugged. "He's dead, and I'm alive."

And, even though she wanted peace, she couldn't help thinking that Kristian really was no saint. He'd been a thorn in her side from the beginning, and she was anxious to be rid of him. "You said earlier that you were willing to start your therapy, but you want to be in charge of your rehabilitation program?"

He nodded. "That's right. You are here to help me accomplish my goals."

"Great. I'm anxious to help you meet your goals." She crossed her legs and settled her hands in her lap. "So, what do you want me to do?"

"Whatever it is I need done."

Elizabeth's mouth opened, then closed. "That's rather vague," she said, when she finally found her voice.

"Oh, don't worry. It won't be vague. I'll be completely in control. I'll tell you what time we start our day, what time we finish, and what we do in between."

"What about the actual exercises? The stretching, the strengthening—"

"I'll take care of that."

He would devise his own course of treatment? He would manage his rehabilitation program?

Her head spun. She couldn't think her way clear. This was all too ridiculous. But then finally, fortunately, logic returned. "Mr. Koumantaros, you might be an excellent executive, and able to make millions of dollars, but that doesn't mean you know the basics of physical therapy—"

"Nurse Hatchet, I haven't walked because I haven't wanted to walk. It's as simple as that."

"Is it?"

"Yes."

My God, he was arrogant—and overly confident. "And you want to walk now?"

"Yes."

Weakly she leaned back in her chair and stared at him. Kristian was changing before her eyes. Metamorphosing.

Pano and the housekeeper appeared with their lunch, but Kristian paid them no heed. "You were the one who told me I need to move forward, Cratchett, and you're absolutely right. It's time I moved forward and got back on my feet."

She watched the myriad of small plates set before them. *Mezedhes*—lots of delicious dips, ranging from eggplant purée to cucumber, yoghurt and garlic, cheese. There were also plates of steaming *keftedhes, dolmadhes, tsiros*. And it all smelled amazing. Elizabeth might not love Greek coffee, but she loved Greek food. Only right now it would be impossible to eat a bite of anything.

"And when do you intend to start your...program?" she asked.

"Today. Immediately after lunch." He sat still while Pano moved the plates around for him, and quietly explained where the plates were and what each dish was.

When Pano and the housekeeper had left, Kristian continued. "I want to be walking soon. I need to be walking this time next week if I hope to travel to Athens in a month's time."

"Walking next *week?*" she choked, unable to take it all in. She couldn't believe the change in him. Couldn't believe the swift turn of events, either. From waking him, to the pills being dumped into the fountain, to the revelation about Calista—everything was different.

Everything, she repeated silently, but especially him. And just looking at him from across the table she saw he seemed so much bigger. Taller. More imposing.

"A week," he insisted.

"Kristian, it's good to have goals. But please be realistic. It's highly unlikely you'll be able to walk unaided in the next couple of weeks, but with hard work you might manage short distances with your walker—"

"If I go to Athens there can be no walker."

"But—"

"It's a matter of culture and respect, Ms. Hatchet. You're not Greek; you don't understand—"

"I *do* understand. That's why I'm here. But give yourself time to meet your goals. Two or three months is far more realistic."

With a rough push of his wheelchair, he rolled back a short distance from the table. "Enough!"

Slowly he placed one foot on the ground, and then the other, and then, leaning forward, put his hands on the table. For a moment it seemed as though nothing was happening, and then, little by little, he began to push up, utilizing his triceps, biceps and shoulders to give himself leverage.

His face paled and perspiration beaded his brow. Thick jet-black hair fell forward as, jaw set, he continued to press up until he was fully upright.

As soon as he was straight he threw his head back in an almost primal act of conquest. *"There."* The word rumbled from him.

He'd proved her wrong.

It had cost him to stand unassisted, too. She could see from his pallor and the lines etched at his mouth that he was hurting, but he didn't utter a word of complaint.

She couldn't help looking at him with fresh respect. What he had done had not been easy. It had taken him long, grueling minutes to concentrate, to work muscles that hadn't been utilized in far too long. But he had succeeded. He'd stood by himself.

And he'd done it as an act of protest and defiance.

He'd done it as something to prove.

"That's a start," she said crisply, hiding her awe. He wasn't just any man. He was a force to be reckoned with. "It's impressive. But you know it's just going to get harder from here."

Kristian shifted his weight, steadied himself, and removed one hand from the table so that he already stood taller.

Silent emotion flickered across his beautiful scarred face. "Good," he said. "I'm ready."

Reaching back for his wheelchair, he nearly stumbled, and Elizabeth jumped to her feet even as Pano rushed forward from the shadows.

Kristian angrily waved both off. *"Ohi!"* he snapped, strain evident in the deep lines shaping his mouth. "No."

"Kyrios," Pano pleaded, pained to see Kristian struggle so.

But Kristian rattled off a rebuke in furious Greek. "I can do it," he insisted, after taking a breath. "I *must* do it."

Pano reluctantly dropped back, and Elizabeth slowly sat down again, torn between admiration and exasperation. While she admired the fact that Kristian would not allow anyone to help him be reseated, she also knew that if he went at his entire therapy like this he'd soon be exhausted, frustrated, and possibly injured worse.

He needed to build his strength gradually, with a systematic and scientific approach.

But Kristian had a different plan—which he outlined after lunch.

Standing—walking—was merely an issue of mind over matter, he said, and her job wasn't to provide obstacles, tell him no, or even offer advice. Her job was to be there when he wanted something, and that was it.

"I'm a handmaid?" she asked, trying to hide her indignation. After four years earning a nursing degree, and then another two years earning a Masters in Business Administration? "You could hire anyone to come and play handmaid. I'm a little over-qualified and rather expensive—"

"I know," he said grimly. "Your agency charged an exorbitant amount for my care—little good did it do me."

"You chose not to improve."

"Your agency's methods were useless."

"I protest."

"You may protest all you like, but it doesn't change the facts. Under your agency's care, not only did I fail to recover, but I was harassed as well as blackmailed. The bottom line, Kyria Hatchet, is that not only did you milk the system—and me—for hundreds and thousands of euros, but you also dared to show up here, uninvited, unwanted, and force yourself on me."

Sick at heart, she rose. "I'll leave, then. Let's just forget this—pretend it never happened—"

"What about the doctors, Nurse? What about those specialists who insisted you come here or I go to their facility in Athens? Was that true, or another of your lies?"

"Lies?"

"I know why you're here—"

"To get you better!"

"You have exactly ten seconds to give me the full name and contact number of the person now responsible for paying my medical bills or I shall begin dismantling your company within the hour. All it will take is one phone call to my office in Athens and your life as you know it will be forever changed."

"Kristian—"

"Nine seconds."

"Kris—"

"Eight."

"I promised—"

"Seven."

"A deal is—"

"Six."

Livid tears scalded her eyes. "It's because she cares. It's because she loves you—"

"Four."

"She wants you back. Home. Close to her."

"Two."

Elizabeth balled her hands into fists. *"Please,"*

"One."

"Cosima." She pressed one fist to her chest, to slow the panicked beating of her heart. "Cosima hired me. She's desperate. She just wants you home."

CHAPTER FIVE

COSIMA?

Kristian's jaw hardened and his voice turned flinty. How could Cosima possibly pay for his care? She might be Andreas's former fiancée and Athens's most popular socialite, but she had more financial problems than anyone he knew.

"Cosima hired you?" he repeated, thinking maybe he'd heard wrong. "She was the one that contacted you in London?"

"Yes. But I promised her—*promised*—I wouldn't tell you."

"Why?"

"She said you'd be very upset if you knew, she said you were so proud—" Elizabeth broke off, the threat of tears evident in her voice. "She said she had to do something to show you how much she believed in you."

Cosima believed in him?

Kristian silently, mockingly, repeated Elizabeth's words. Or maybe it was that Cosima felt indebted to him. Maybe she felt as guilt-ridden as he did. Because, after all, she lived and Andreas had died, and it was Kristian who'd made the decision. It was Kristian who'd played God that day.

No wonder he had nightmares. No wonder he had nightmares during the day.

He couldn't accept the decision he'd made. Nor could he accept that it was a decision that couldn't be changed.

Kristian, wealthy and powerful beyond measure, couldn't buy or secure the one thing he wanted most: his brother's life.

But Elizabeth knew nothing of Kristian's loathing, and anger, and pressed on. "Now that you know," she continued, "the contract isn't valid. I can't remain—"

"Of course you can," he interrupted shortly. "She doesn't have to know that I know. There's no point in wrecking her little plan."

His words were greeted by silence, and for a moment he thought maybe Elizabeth had left, going God knew where, but then he heard the faintest shuffle, and an even softer sigh.

"She just wants what is best for you," Elizabeth said wearily. "Please don't be angry with her. She seems like such a kind person."

It was in that moment that Kristian learned something very important about Elizabeth Hatchet.

Elizabeth Hatchet might have honest intentions, but she was a lousy judge of character.

It was on the tip of his tongue to ask if Elizabeth was aware that Cosima and Calista had gone to school together. To ask her if she knew that both women had shared a flat for more than a year, and had gone into modeling together, too.

He could tell her that Calista and Cosima had been the best of friends until their lives had gone in very different directions.

Cosima had met Andreas Koumantaros and become girl-friend and then fiancée to one of Greece's most wealthy men.

Calista, unable to find a rich enough boyfriend, or enough modeling jobs to pay her rent, had turned to exotic dancing and questionable modeling gigs.

The two seemed to have had nothing more in common after

a couple years. Cosima had traveled the world as the pampered bride-to-be, and Calista had struggled to make ends meet.

And then tragedy had struck and evened the score.

Andreas had died in the avalanche, Cosima had survived but lost her lifestyle, and Calista, who had still been struggling along, had thought she'd found a sugar-daddy of her own.

Albeit a handicapped one.

The corner of his mouth curved crookedly, the tilt of his lips hiding the depth of his anger as well as his derision. Calista hadn't been the first to imagine he'd be an easy conquest. A dozen women from all over Europe had flocked to his side during his hospital stay. They'd brought flowers, gifts, seductive promises. *I love you. I'll be here for you. I'll never leave you.*

It would have been one thing if any of them had genuinely cared for him. Instead they'd all been opportunists, thinking a life with an invalid wouldn't be so bad if the invalid was a Greek tycoon.

Again Kristian felt the whip of anger. Did women think that just because he couldn't see he'd lost his mind?

That his inability to travel unaided across the room meant he'd enjoy the company of a shallow, self-absorbed, materialistic woman? He hadn't enjoyed shallow and self-absorbed women before. Why would he now?

"You've met Cosima, then," he said flatly.

"We've only spoken on the phone, but her concern—and she *is* concerned—touched me," Elizabeth added anxiously, trying to fill the silence. "She obviously has a good heart, and it wouldn't be fair to punish her for trying to help you."

Kristian ran his hand over his jaw. "No, you're right. And you said, she seems most anxious to see me on my feet."

"Yes. Yes—and she's just so worried about you. She

was in tears on the phone. I think she's afraid you're shutting her out—"

"*Really?*" This did intrigue him. Was Cosima possibly imagining some kind of future for the two of them? The idea was as grotesque as it was laughable.

"She said you've become too reclusive here."

"This is my home."

"But she's concerned you're overly depressed and far too despondent."

"Were those her actual words?" he asked, struggling to keep the sarcasm from his voice.

"Yes, as a matter of fact. I have it in my notes, if you want to see—"

"No. I believe you." His brows flattened, his curiosity colored by disbelief. Cosima wasn't sentimental. She wasn't particularly emotional or sensitive, either. So why would she be so anxious to have him return to Athens? "And so," he added, wanting to hear more about Cosima's concern, "you were sent here to rescue me."

"Not rescue, just motivate you. Get you on your feet."

"And look!" he said grandly, gesturing with his hands. "Today I stood. Tomorrow I climb Mount Everest."

"Not Everest," Elizabeth corrected, sounding genuinely bemused. "Just walk in time for your wedding."

Wedding?

Wedding?

Kristian had heard it all now. He didn't know whether to roar with amusement or anguish. His wedding. To Cosima, his late brother's lover, he presumed. My God, this was like an ancient Greek comedy—a bold work conceived of by Aristophanes. One full of bawdy mirth but founded on tragedy.

And as he sat there, trying to take it all in, Cosima and Calista's scheming reminded him of the two Greek sisters: Penia, goddess of poverty, and Amakhania, goddess of helplessness. Goddesses known for tormenting with their evil and greed.

But now that he knew, he wouldn't be tormented any longer.

No, he'd write a little Greek play of his own. And if all went well his good Nurse Cratchett could even help him by playing a leading role.

"Let's not tell her I know," Kristian said. "Let's work hard, and we'll surprise her with my progress."

"So where do we start?" Elizabeth asked. "What do we do first?"

He nearly smiled at her enthusiasm. She sounded so pleased with him already. "*I've* already hired a physical therapist from Sparta," he answered, making it clear that this was not a joint decision, but his and his alone. "The therapist arrives tomorrow."

"And until then?"

"I'll probably relax, nap. Swim."

"Swim?" she asked. "You're swimming?"

Her surprise made his lip curl. She really thought he was in dreadful shape, didn't she? "I have been for the past two weeks."

"Ever since your last nurse left?" she said quietly.

He didn't answer. He didn't need to.

"Maybe you could show me the pool?" she asked.

For a moment he almost felt sorry for her. She was trying so hard to do what she thought was the right thing, but her idea of right wasn't necessarily what he wanted or needed. "Of course. If you'll come with me."

Together they traveled across the stone courtyard with its trellis-covered patio, where they'd just enjoyed lunch, with

Kristian pushing his own wheelchair and Elizabeth walking next to him.

They headed toward the fountain and then passed it, moving from the stone patio to the garden, with its gravel path.

"The gardens are beautiful," Elizabeth said, walking slowly enough for Kristian to push his chair at a comfortable pace.

His tires sank into the gravel, and he wrestled a moment with his chair until he found traction again and pushed faster, to keep from sinking back into the crushed stones. "You'd do better with a stone path here, wouldn't you?" she asked, glancing down at his arms, impressed by his strength.

Warm color darkened his cheekbones. "It was suggested months ago that I change it, but I knew I wouldn't be in a wheelchair forever so I left it."

"So you planned on getting out of your wheelchair?"

His head lifted, and he shot her a look as though he could see, his brow furrowing, lines deepening between his eyes. He resented her question, and his resentment brought home yet again just who he was, and what he'd accomplished in his lifetime.

Watching him struggle through the gravel, it crossed her mind that maybe he hadn't remained in the wheelchair because he was lazy, but because without sight he felt exposed. Maybe for him the wheelchair wasn't transportation so much as a suit of armor, a form of protection.

"Are we almost to the hedge?" he asked, pausing a moment to try and get his bearings.

"Yes, it's just in front of us."

"The pool, then, is to the left."

Elizabeth turned toward her left and was momentarily dazzled by the sun's reflection off brilliant blue water. The long lap pool sparkled in its emerald-green setting, making it appear even more jewel-like than it already was.

"It's a new pool?" she guessed, from the young landscaping and the gorgeous artisan tilework.

"I wish I could say it was my only extravagance, but I've been renovating the monastery for nearly a decade now. It's been a labor of love."

They'd reached a low stone wall that bordered the pool, and Elizabeth moved forward to open the pretty gate. "But why Taygetos? Why a ruined monastery? You don't have family from here, do you?"

"No, but I love the mountains—this is where I feel at home," he said, lifting a hand to his face as if to block the sun. "My mother was French, raised in a small town at the base of the Alps. I've grown up hiking, skiing, rock-climbing. These are the things my father taught us to do, things my mother enjoyed, and it just feels right living here."

Elizabeth saw how he kept trying to shield his eyes with his hand. "Is the sun bothering you?"

"I usually wear bandages, or dark glasses."

"You've that much light sensitivity?"

"It's painful," he admitted.

She didn't want him in pain, but the tenderness and sensitivity gave her hope that maybe, one day, he might get at least a little of his vision back. "Shall I call Pano to get your glasses?"

"It's not necessary. We won't be here long."

"But it's lovely out," she said wistfully, gazing around the pool area and admiring the tiny purplish campanula flowers that were growing up and over the stone walls. The tiny violet-hued blossoms were such a pretty contrast to the rugged rock. "Let me get them. That way you can relax a little, be more comfortable."

"No, just find me a little shade—or perhaps position me away from the sun."

"There's some shade on the other side of the pool, near the rock wall." She hesitated. "Shall I push you?"

"I can do it myself."

But somehow in the struggle, as Elizabeth pushed forward and Kristian grappled for control, the front castors of his chair ran off the stone edge and over the side, and once the front casters went forward, the rest of the chair followed.

He hit the pool with a big splash.

It all happened in slow motion.

Just before he hit the water Elizabeth could see herself grabbing at his chair, hanging tight to the handles and trying to pull him back, but she was unable to get enough leverage to stop the momentum. In the end she let go, knowing she couldn't stop him and afraid she'd fall on him and hurt him worse.

Heart pounding, Elizabeth dropped to her knees, horrified that her patient and his wheelchair had just tumbled in.

How could she have let this happen? How could she have been so reckless?

Elizabeth was close to jumping in when Kristian surfaced. His chair, though, was another matter. While Kristian was swimming toward the side of the pool, his chair was slowly, steadily, sinking to the bottom.

"Kristian—I'm sorry, I'm sorry," she apologized repeatedly as she knelt on the pool deck. She'd never felt less professional in her entire life. An accident like this was pure carelessness. He knew it, and so did she.

"I cut the corner too close. I should have been paying closer attention. I'm so sorry."

He swam toward her.

Leaning forward, she extended her hand as far as it would

go. "You're almost at the wall. My hand's right in front of it. You've almost got it," she encouraged as he reached for her.

His fingers curled around hers. Relief surged through her. He was fine. "I've got you," she said.

"Are you sure?" he asked, hand tightening on hers. "Or do I have you?"

And, with a hard tug, he pulled her off her knees and into the pool.

Elizabeth landed hard on her stomach, splashing water wildly. He'd pulled her in. Deliberately. She couldn't believe it. So much for poor, helpless Kristian Koumantaros.

He was far from helpless. And he'd fooled her three times now.

Spluttering to the surface, she looked around for Kristian and spotted him leaning casually against the wall.

"That was mean," she said, swimming toward him, her wet clothes hampering her movements.

He laughed softly and ran a hand through his hair, pushing the inky black strands back from his face. "I thought you'd find it refreshing."

She squeezed water from her own hair. "I didn't want you to fall in. I'd never want that to happen."

"Your concern for my wellbeing is most touching. You know, Cratchett, I was worried you might be like my other nurses, but I have to tell you, you're worse."

She swallowed hard. She deserved that. "I'm sorry," she said, knowing a responsible nurse would never have permitted such a thing to happen. Indeed, if any of her nurses had allowed a patient in their care to fall into a pool she'd have fired the nurse on the spot. "It's been a while since I actually did any in-home care. As you know, I'm the head administrator for the company now."

"Skills a little rusty?" he said.

"Mmmm." Using the ladder, she climbed out and sat down on the deck, to pluck at her shirt and tug her soggy shoes off.

"So why are *you* here and not another nurse?"

Wringing water from her skirt, she sighed. Defeated. "The agency's close to bankruptcy. I couldn't afford to send another nurse. It was me or nothing."

"But my insurance has paid you, and I've paid you."

Elizabeth watched the water trickle from her skirt to the stone pavers. "There were expenses not covered, and those costs were difficult to manage, and eventually they ate into the profits until we were barely breaking even." She didn't bother to tell him that Calista had needed counseling and compensation after leaving Kristian's employment. And covering Calista's bills had cost her dearly, too.

"I think I better get your chair," she said, not wanting to think about things she found very difficult to control.

"I do need it," he agreed. "Are you a strong swimmer?"

"I can swim."

"You're not inspiring much confidence, Cratchett."

She smiled despite herself. "It'll be okay." And it would be. She wasn't going to panic about holding her breath or swimming deep under water. She'd just go down and grab the chair, and haul it back up.

He sighed, pushed back wet hair from his face. "You're scared."

"No."

"You're not a very good swimmer."

She made a little exasperated sound. "I can swim laps. Pretty well. It's just in deep water I get…nervous."

"Claustrophobic?"

"Oh, it's silly, but—" She broke off, not wanting to tell him.

She didn't need him making fun of her. It was a genuine fear, and there wasn't a lot she could do about it.

"But what?"

"I had an accident when I was little." He said nothing, and she knew he was still waiting for the details. "I was playing a diving game with a girl I'd met. We'd toss coins and then go pick them up. Well, in this hotel pool there was a huge drain at the bottom, and somehow—" She broke off, feeling a little sick from the retelling. "There was a lot of suction, and somehow the strings on my swimsuit got tangled, stuck. I couldn't get them out and couldn't get my suit off."

Kristian didn't speak, and Elizabeth tried to smile. "They got me out, of course. Obviously. Here I am. But…" She felt a painful flutter inside, a memory of panic and what it had been like. Her shoulders lifted, fell. "I was scared."

"How old were you?"

"Six."

"You must have been a good swimmer to be playing diving games in the deep end at six."

She laughed a little. "I think as a little girl I was a bit on the wild side. My nanny—" She broke off, rephrased. "Anyway, after that I didn't want to swim anymore. Especially not in big pools. And since then I've pretty much stuck to the shallow end. Kind of boring, but safe."

Elizabeth could feel Kristian's scrutiny even though he couldn't see her. He was trying to understand her, to reconcile what he'd thought he knew with this.

"I'll make you a deal," he said at last.

Her eyes narrowed. So far his deals had been terrible. "What kind of deal?"

"I'll go get my own chair if you don't look while I strip. I can't dive down in my clothes."

Elizabeth pulled her knees up to her chest and tried not to laugh. "You're afraid I'll see you naked?"

"I'm trying to protect you. You're a nurse without a lot of field experience lately. I'm afraid my…nudity…might overwhelm you."

She grinned against her wet kneecap. "Fine."

One black eyebrow arched. "Fine, what? Fine, you'll look at me? Or fine, you'll politely avert your gaze?"

"Fine. I'll politely avert my gaze."

"Endaxi," he said, still in the pool. "Okay." And then he began peeling his clothes off one by one.

And although Elizabeth had made a promise not to look, the sound of wet cotton inching its way off wet skin was too tempting.

She did watch, and as the clothes came off she discovered he had a rather amazing body, despite the accident and horrific injuries. His torso was still powerful, thick with honed muscle, while from her vantage point on the deck his legs looked long and well shaped.

Clothes gone, he disappeared beneath the surface, swimming toward the bottom with strong, powerful strokes. Even though he couldn't see, he was heading in the right direction. It took him a moment to find the chair's exact location, but once he found it he took hold of the back and immediately began to swim up with it.

Incredible.

As Kristian surfaced with the chair, Pano and one of the housemaids came running through the small wrought-iron gate with a huge stack of towels.

"Kyrios," Pano called, "are you all right?"

"I'm fine." Kristian answered, dragging the chair to the side of the pool.

Pano was there to take the chair. He tipped it sideways and water streamed from the spokes and castors. He tipped it the other way and more water spurted from open screwholes, and then he passed the chair to the maid, who began vigorously toweling the wheelchair dry.

In the meantime Kristian placed his hands on the stone deck and hauled himself up and out, using only his shoulders, biceps and triceps. He was far stronger than he let on, and far more capable of taking care of himself than she'd thought.

He didn't need anyone pushing him.

He probably didn't need anyone taking care of him.

If everyone just stepped back and left him alone, she suspected that soon he'd manage just fine.

And, speaking of fine, Elizabeth couldn't tear her eyes from Kristian's broad muscular back, lean waist, and tight hard buttocks as he shifted his weight around. His body was almost perfectly proportioned, every muscle shaped and honed. He didn't look ill, or like a patient. He looked like a man, an incredibly physical, virile man.

Once his thighs had cleared the water he did a quick turn and sat down. Pano swiftly draped a towel over Kristian's shoulders and threw another one over his lap, but not before Elizabeth had seen as much of Kristian's front as she had seen of his back.

And his front was even more impressive. His shoulders broad and thick, his chest shaped into two hard planes of muscle, his belly flat, lean, and his…

His…

She shouldn't be staring at his lap, it was completely unprofessional, but he was very, very big there, too.

She felt blood surge to her cheeks, and she battled shyness, shame and interest.

His body was so beautiful, and his size, that symbol of masculinity—wow. Ridiculously impressive. And Elizabeth wasn't easily impressed.

No wonder Kristian was so comfortable naked. Even after a year plus in a wheelchair he was still every inch a man.

"I thought we had a deal," Kristian murmured, dragging the towel over his head and then his chest.

"We did. We do." Flushing crimson, Elizabeth jumped to her feet and twisted her damp skirt yet again. "Maybe I should go get some dry clothes."

"A good idea," Kristian said, leaning back on his hands, face lifted. He was smiling a little, a smile that indicated he knew she'd been looking at him, knew she'd been fascinated by his anatomy. "I wouldn't want you to catch a chill."

"No."

His lips curled, and the sunlight played over the carved planes of his face, lingering on the jagged scar, and she felt her heart leap at the savage violence done to his Greek beauty. "I'll see you at dinner, then."

See her at dinner.

He couldn't see her, of course, but he'd meet her, and her heart did another peculiar flutter. "Dinner tonight?"

"I thought I was to eat all my meals with you," he answered lazily. "Something about you needing to socialize me. Make me civil again."

Her heart was drumming a mile a minute. "Right." She forced a tight, pained smile. "I'll look forward to that…then."

Elizabeth turned so quickly that she stubbed her toe. With a hop and a whimper she set off at a run for the sanctuary of her room, lecturing herself the entire way. *Do not get personally involved, do not get personally involved, no matter what you do, do not get personally involved.*

But as she reached her tower bedroom and began to strip her wet clothes off she almost cried with vexation.

She already was involved.

CHAPTER SIX

OUTSIDE in the garden, as Kristian struggled to make his way back to the villa, water dripped from the chair and his cushion sagged, waterlogged.

Thank God he was almost done with this wheelchair.

Falling into the pool today had been infuriating and insightful. He hated how helpless he'd felt as he went blindly tumbling in. He'd hated the shock and surprise as he'd thrashed in his clothes in the water. But at the same time his unexpected fall had had unexpected results.

For one, Elizabeth had dropped some of her brittle guard, and he'd discovered she was far less icy then he'd thought. She was in many ways quite gentle, and her fear about the deep end had struck home with him. As a boy he'd been thrown from a horse, and he hadn't ridden again for years.

Getting back into the wet wheelchair had been another lesson. As he'd been transferred in, he'd realized the chair had served its purpose. He didn't want it anymore—didn't want to be confined or contained. He craved freedom, and knew that for the first time since his accident he was truly ready for whatever therapy was required to allow him to walk and run again.

Water still dripping, he cautiously rolled his way from grass to patio, and from patio toward the wing where his room was.

But as he rolled down the loggia he couldn't seem to find his bedroom door. He began to second-guess himself, and soon thought he'd gone the wrong way.

Pano, who'd been following several paces behind, couldn't keep silent any longer. "*Kyrie,* your room is just here." And, without waiting for Kristian to find it himself, the butler steered the wheelchair around the corner and over the door's threshold.

Kristian felt a tinge of annoyance at the help. He'd wanted to do it alone, felt an increasing need to do more for himself, but Pano, a good loyal employee of the past fifteen years, couldn't bear for Kristian to struggle.

"How did you end up in the pool?" Pano asked, closing the outside door.

Kristian shrugged and tugged the wet towel from around his shoulders. "Ms. Hatchet was pushing me toward the shade and misjudged the distance to the pool's edge."

"*Despinis* pushed you into the pool?" Pano cried, horrified.

"It was an accident."

"How could she push you into the pool?"

"It was a tight corner."

"How can that happen? How is that proper?" The butler muttered to himself as he opened and closed drawers, retrieving dry clothes for his master. "I knew she wasn't a proper nurse—knew she couldn't do the job. I *knew* it."

Kristian checked his smile. Pano was a traditional Greek, from the old school of hearth and home. "And how is she not a proper nurse?"

"If you could see—"

"But I can't. So you must tell me."

"First, she doesn't act like one, and second, she doesn't *look* like one."

"Why not? Is she too old, too heavy, what?"

"Ohi," Pano groaned. "No. She's not too old, or too fat, or anything like that. It's the opposite. She's too small. She's delicate. Like a little bird in a tiny cage. And if you want a little blonde bird for a nurse, fine. But if you need a big, sturdy woman to lift and carry…" Pano sighed, shrugging expressively. "Then Despinis Elizabeth is not for you."

So she was blonde, Kristian thought after Pano had left him alone to dress.

And Elizabeth Hatchet was neither old nor unattractive. Rather she was fine-boned, slender, a lady.

Kristian tried to picture her, this ladylike nurse of his, who hadn't actually nursed in years, who proclaimed Cosima kind, and as a child had stayed at hotels with a nanny to look after her.

But it was impossible to visualize her. He'd dated plenty of fair English and American girls, Scandinavians and Dutch, but he would have wagered a thousand euros Elizabeth was brunette.

But wasn't that like her? So full of surprises. For example her voice—melodic, like that of a violin—and her fragrance—not floral, not exotic spice, but fresh, clean, grass or melon. And then last night, when she'd leaned close to his bed to adjust his pillows, he'd been surprised she wore her hair down. Something about her brisk manner had made him assume she was the classic all-business, no-nonsense executive.

Apparently he was wrong.

Apparently his Cratchett was blonde, slender, delicate, *pretty*. Not even close to a battleaxe.

In trying to form a new impression of her, he wondered at her age, and her height, as well as the shade of her hair. Was she a pale, silvery blonde? Or a golden blonde with streaks of warm amber and honey?

But it wasn't just her age or appearance that intrigued him. It was her story, too, of a six-year-old who'd once been a daring swimmer now afraid to leave the shallow end, as well as the haunting image of a child trapped, swimsuit ties tangled, in that pool's powerful drain.

In her bedroom, after several lovely long hours devoted to nothing but reading and taking a delicious and much needed nap, Elizabeth was dressing for dinner as well as having a crisis of conscience.

She didn't know what she was doing here. Kristian didn't need a nurse, and he certainly didn't need the round-the-clock supervision her agency and staff had been providing.

How could she stay here? How could she take Cosima's money? It was not as if Kristian was even letting her do anything. He wanted to be in control—which was fine with her if he could truly motivate himself. He really would be better off with a sports trainer and an occupational therapist to help him adapt to his loss of sight rather than someone trained to deal with concussions, wounds, injuries and infections.

And, to compound her worry, she didn't have the foggiest idea how to dress for dinner.

She, who'd grown up in five-star hotels all over the world, was suffering a mild panic attack because she couldn't figure out what to wear for a late evening meal, at an old monastery, in the middle of the Taygetos.

One by one Elizabeth pulled out things from her wardrobe and discarded them. A swingy pleated navy skirt. Too school-girl. A straight brown gabardine skirt that nearly reached her ankles. She'd once thought it smart, but now she found it boring. A gray plaid skirt with a narrow velvet trim. She sighed, thinking they were all so serious and practical.

But wasn't that what she was supposed to be? Serious? Practical?

This isn't a holiday, she reminded herself sternly, retrieving the gray plaid skirt and pairing it with a pewter silk blouse. Dressing, she wrinkled her nose at her reflection. Ugh. So *not* pretty.

But why did she even care what she was wearing?

And that was when she felt a little wobble in her middle— butterflies, worry, guilt.

She was acting as if she was dressing for a dinner date instead of dinner with a patient. And that was wrong. Her being here, feeling this way, was wrong.

She was here for business. Medicine.

And yet as she remembered Kristian's smile by the pool, and his cool, mocking, "I thought we had a deal," she felt the wobble inside her again. And this time the wobble was followed by an expectant shiver.

She was nervous.

And excited.

And both emotions were equally inappropriate. Kristian was in her care. She'd been hired by his girlfriend to get him back on his feet. It would be professionally, never mind morally, wrong to think of him in any light other than as her patient.

A patient, she reminded herself.

Yet the butterflies in her stomach didn't go away.

With a quick, impatient flick of her wrist she dragged her brush through her hair. Kristian couldn't be an option even if he *was* single, and *not* her patient. It was ridiculous to romanticize or idealize him. She'd been married to a Greek and it had been a disaster from the start. Their marriage had lasted two years but scarred her for nearly seven.

The memory swept her more than ten years back, to when, as a twenty-year-old New York socialite, she had been toasted as the next great American beauty.

She'd been so young and inexperienced then, just a debutante entering the social scene, and she'd foolishly believed everything people told her. It would be three years before she fully understood that she was adored for her name and fortune, not for herself.

"No more Greek tycoons," she whispered to herself. "No more men who want you for the wrong reasons." Besides, marriage to a Greek had taught her that Mediterranean men preferred beautiful women with breasts and hips and hourglass figures—attributes slender, slim-hipped Elizabeth would never have.

With her hair a smooth pale gold curtain, she headed toward the library, since she didn't know where they were to eat tonight as the dining room had been converted into a fitness room.

Be kind, cordial, supportive, educational and useful, she told herself. But that is as far as your involvement goes.

Kristian entered the library shortly after she did. He was wearing dark slacks and a loose white linen shirt, and with his black hair combed back from his face his blue eyes seemed even more startling.

He wasn't happy, though, she thought, watching him push into the room, his wheelchair tires humming on the floor.

"Is something wrong?" she asked, still standing just inside the door, since she hadn't known where to go and didn't feel comfortable just sitting down. This was Kristian's refuge, after all, the place he spent the majority of his time.

He grimaced. "Now that I want to walk, I don't want to use the wheelchair."

"But you can't give up the chair yet. Though I bet you tried," she guessed, her tone sympathetic.

"I suppose I thought that, having stood, I could also probably walk."

"And you will. It'll take some time, but, considering your determination, it won't be as long as you think."

Pano appeared in the doorway to invite them to dinner. They followed him a short distance down the hall to a spacious room with a soaring ceiling hand-painted with scenes from the New Testament, in bold reds, blues, gray-greens and golds, although in places the paint was chipped and faded, revealing dark beams beneath.

A striking red wool carpet covered the floor, and in the middle of the carpet was a table set with two place-settings and two wood chairs. Fat round white candles glowed on the table and in sconces on the wall, and the dishes on the table were a glazed cobalt blue.

"It looks wonderful in here," she said, suddenly feeling foolish in her gray plaid skirt with its velvet trim. She should be wearing something loose and exotic—a flowing peasant skirt, a long jeweled top, even casual linen trousers came to mind. "The colors and artwork are stunning. This is the original ceiling, isn't it?"

"I had it saved."

"Is the building very old?"

"The tower dates to the 1700s while this part, the main monastery building, was put into service in 1802." Kristian drew a breath, held it, and just listened. After a moment he added more quietly. "Even though I can't see what's around me—the old stone walls, the beamed and arched ceilings. I feel it."

"That's good," she answered, feeling a tug on her heart. She could see why he loved the renovated monastery. It was atmospheric here, but it was so remote that she worried that Kristian wasn't getting enough contact with the outside world. He needed stimulation, interaction. He needed…a life.

But he's still healing, she reminded herself as they sat

down at the table, her place directly across from Kristian's. Just over a year ago he'd lost his brother, his cousin and numerous friends in the avalanche. He'd been almost fatally injured when his helicopter had crashed trying to look for survivors. Kristian had been badly hurt, and in the blunt trauma to his head he'd detached both retinas.

Sometimes, when she thought about it, it took her breath away just how much he'd lost in one day.

The housekeeper served the meal, and Pano appeared at Kristian's elbow, ready to assist him. Kristian sent him away. "We can manage," he said, reaching for the wine.

Kristian held the bottle toward Elizabeth, tilting it so she could read the label. "Will a glass hurt, Nurse Hatchet?"

His tone was teasing, but it was his expression which made her pulse quicken. He looked so boyish it disarmed her.

"A glass," she agreed cautiously.

He laughed and carefully reached out, found her glass, maneuvering the bottle so it was just over the rim. He poured slowly and listened carefully as he poured. "How is that?" he asked, indicating the glass. "Too much? Too little?"

"Just right."

He slowly poured a glass for himself, before finding an empty spot on the table for the bottle.

The next course was almost immediately served, and he was attentive during the meal, asking her questions about work, her travels, her knowledge of Greek. "At one point I spent a lot of time in Greece," she answered, sidestepping any mention of her marriage.

"The university student on holiday?" Kristian guessed.

She made a face. "Everyone loves Greece."

"What do you like most about it?" he persisted.

A half-dozen different thoughts came to mind. The water.

The people. The climate. The food. The beaches. The warmth. But Greece had also created pain. So many people here had turned on her during her divorce. Friends—close friends—had dropped her overnight.

A lump filled her throat and she blinked to keep tears from forming. It was long ago, she told herself. Seven years. She couldn't let the divorce sour her on an entire country. Maybe her immediate social circle hadn't been kind when she and Nico separated, but not everyone was so judgmental or shallow.

"You've no answer?" he said.

"It's just that I like it all," she said, smiling to chase away any lingering sadness. "And you? What do you like best about your country?"

He thought about it for a moment, before lifting his wine glass. "The people. And their zest for life."

She clinked her glass against his, took another sip, and let the wine sit on her tongue a moment before swallowing. It was a red wine, and surprisingly good. She knew from the label it was Greek, but she wasn't as familiar with Greece's red wines as she was the white, as Nico preferred white. "Do you know anything about this wine?"

"I do. It's from one of my favorite wineries, a local winery, and the grape is *ayroyitiko,* which is indigenous to the Peloponnese."

"I didn't realize there were vineyards here."

"There are vineyards all over Greece—although the most famous Greek wines come from Samos and Crete."

"That's where you get the white wines, right?"

"Samian wine is, yes, and the most popular grape there is the *moshato.* Lots of wine snobs love Samian wine."

It was all she could do not to giggle. Nico, her former husband, was the ultimate wine snob. He'd go to a restaurant, order an outrageously priced bottle, and if he didn't think it up to snuff imperiously send it away. There had been times when Elizabeth had suspected there was absolutely nothing wrong with the wine. It was just Nico wanting to appear powerful.

"You're a white wine drinker?" Kristian asked.

"No, not really. I just had…friends…who preferred white Greek wine to red, so I'm rather ignorant when it comes to the different red grape varieties."

Kristian rested his forearms on the table. The corner of his mouth tugged. "A friend?" His expression shifted, suddenly perceptive. "A *male* friend?"

"He was male," she agreed carefully.

"And Greek?"

"And Greek."

He laughed softly, and yet there was tension in the sound, a hint that not all was well. "Greek men are sexual as well as possessive. I imagine your Greek friend wanted more from you than just friendship?"

Elizabeth blushed hotly. "It was a long time ago."

"It ended badly?"

Her head dipped. Her face burned. "I don't know." She swallowed, wondered why she was protecting Nico. "Yes," she corrected. "It did."

"Did this prejudice you against Greek men?"

"No." But she sounded uncertain.

"Against me?"

She blushed, and then laughed. "Maybe."

"So that is why I got the fleet of battleaxe nurses."

She laughed again. He amused her. And intrigued her. And if he wasn't her patient she'd even admit she found him very, very attractive. "Are you telling me you didn't deserve the battleaxe nurses?"

"I'm telling you I'm not like other Greek men."

Her breath suddenly caught in her throat, and her eyes grew wide. Somehow, with those words, he'd changed everything—the mood, the night, the meal itself. He'd charged the room with an almost unbearable electricity, a hot tension that made her fiercely aware of him. And herself. And the fact that they were alone together.

"You can't judge all wine based on one vintner or one bottle. And you can't judge Greek men based on one unhappy memory."

She felt as though she could barely breathe, and she struggled to find safer topics, ones that would allow her more personal distance. "What kind of wine do *you* like?"

"It's all about personal preference." He paused, letting his words sink in. "I like many wines. I have bottles in my cellar that are under ten euros which I think are infinitely more drinkable than some eighty-euro bottles."

"So it's not about the money?"

"Too many people get hung up on labels and names, and hope to impress each other with their spending power or their knowledge."

"We are talking about wine?" she murmured.

"Do you doubt it?" he asked, his head lifting as though to see her, study her, drink her in.

She bit into her lower lip, her cheeks so warm she felt desperate for a frozen drink or a sweet icy treat. Something to cool her off. Something to take her mind off Kristian's formidable physical appeal.

And, sitting there, she could see how someone like Calista, someone young and impressionable, might be attracted to Kristian. But to threaten him? Attempt to blackmail him? Impossible. Even blinded, with shattered bones and scarred features, he was too strong, too overpowering. Calista was a fool.

And, thinking of the girl's foolishness, Elizabeth began to giggle, and then her giggle turned into full blown laughter. "What was Calista thinking?" she wheezed, touching her hand to her mouth to try and stifle the sound. "How could someone like Calista think she could get away with blackmailing *you?*"

Kristian sat across the table from Elizabeth and listened to her laugh. It had been so long since he'd heard a laugh like that, so open and warm and real. Elizabeth in one day had made him realize how much he'd been missing in life. He hadn't even known he'd become so angry and shut down until she'd arrived and begun insisting on immediate changes.

He'd at first resented her bossy manner, but it had worked. He'd realized he didn't want or need someone else giving him orders, or attempting to dictate to him. There was absolutely no reason he couldn't motivate himself.

Although he was still incredibly suspicious of Cosima, and mistrusted her desire to have him walking and returning to Athens, he was also grateful for her interference. Cosima had brought Elizabeth here, and, as it turned out, Elizabeth was the right person at the right time.

He needed someone like her.

Maybe he even needed *her.*

Sitting across the table from her, he focused on where he pictured her to be sitting. He hoped she knew that even if he couldn't see, he was listening. Paying attention.

He'd never been known for his sensitivity. But it wasn't that he didn't have feelings. He just wasn't very good at expressing them.

He liked this room, and he was enjoying the meal. Even if he couldn't see, he appreciated the small touches made by

Pano and Atta, his housekeeper—like the low warm heat from the candles, which smelled faintly of vanilla.

He knew they were eating off his favorite plates. He could tell by the size and shape that they were the glazed ceramic dinnerware he'd bought several years ago at a shop on Santorini.

The weave and weight of the table linens made him suspect they were also artisan handicrafts—purchased impulsively on one of his trips somewhere.

Despite his tremendous wealth, Kristian preferred simplicity, and appreciated the talent of local artists, supporting them whenever he could.

"Now you've grown quiet," Elizabeth said, as Atta began clearing their dishes.

"I'm just relaxed," he said, and he was. It had been so long since he'd felt this way. Months and months since he'd experienced anything so peaceful or calm. He'd forgotten what it was like to share a meal with someone, had forgotten how food always tasted better with good conversation, good wine and some laughter.

"I'm glad."

The warm sincerity in her voice went all the way through him. He'd liked her voice even in the beginning, when she had insisted on calling him Mr. Koumantaros every other time she opened her mouth.

He also liked the scent she wore. He still didn't know what it was, although he could name all the other battleaxes' favorite fragrances: chlorine, antiseptic, spearmint, tobacco and, what was probably the worst of all, an annoyingly cloying rose-scented hand lotion.

Elizabeth also walked differently than the battleaxes. Her step was firm, precise, confident. He could almost imagine her sallying forth through a crowded store, decisive and determined as she marched through Fortnum and Mason's aisles.

He smiled a little, amused by this idea of her in London. That was where she lived. His smile faded as the silence stretched. He wished he could see her. He suddenly wondered if she was bored. Perhaps she wanted to escape, return to her room. She had passed on coffee.

As the seconds ticked by, Kristian's tension grew.

He heard Elizabeth's chair scrape back, heard her linen napkin being returned to the table. She was leaving.

Grinding his teeth, Kristian struggled to get to his feet. It was the second time in one day, and required a considerable effort, but Elizabeth was about to go and he wanted to say something—to ask her to stay and join him in the library. It was very possible she was tired, but for him the nights were long, sometimes endless. There was no difference between night and day anymore.

He was on his feet, gripping the table's edge with his fingers. "Are you tired?" he said, his voice suddenly too loud and hard. He hadn't meant to sound so brusque. It was uncertainty and the inability to read her mood that was making him harsh.

"A little," she confessed.

He inclined his head. "Goodnight, then."

She hesitated, and he wondered what she was thinking, wished he could see her face to know if there was pity or resentment or something else in her eyes. That was the thing about not being able to see. He couldn't read people the way he'd used to, and that had been his gift. He wasn't verbally expressive, but he'd always been intuitive. He didn't trust his intuition anymore, nor his instinct. He didn't know how to rely on either without his eyes.

"Goodnight," she said softly.

He dug his fingers into the linen-covered table. Nodded. Prayed she couldn't see his disappointment.

After another moment's hesitation he heard her footsteps go.

Slowly he sat back down in his wheelchair, and as he sat down something cracked in him. A second later he felt a lance of unbelievable pain.

How had he become so alone?

Gritting his teeth, he tried to bite back the loss and loneliness, but they played in his mind.

He missed Andreas. Andreas had been his brother, the last of his family. Their parents had died a number of years earlier—unrelated deaths, but they had come close together—and their deaths had brought he and Andreas, already close, even closer.

He should have saved Andreas first. He should have gone to his brother's aid first.

If only he could go back. If only he could undo that one decision.

In life there were so many decisions one took for granted—so many decisions one made under pressure—and nearly all were good decisions, nearly all were soon forgotten. It was the one bad decision that couldn't be erased. The one bad decision that stayed with you night and day.

Slowly he pushed away from the table, and even more slowly he rolled down the hall toward the library—the room he spent nearly all his waking hours in.

Maybe Pano could find something on the radio for him? Or perhaps there was an audio book he could listen to. Kristian just wanted something to occupy his mind.

But once in the library he stopped pushing and just sat near his table, with his papers and books. He didn't want the radio, and he didn't want to listen to a book on tape. He just wanted to be himself again. He missed who he was. He hated who he'd become.

"Kristian?" Elizabeth said timidly.

He straightened, sat taller. "Yes?"

"You're in here, then?"

"Yes. I'm right here."

"Oh." There was the faintest hitch in her voice. "It's dark. Do you mind if I turn the lights on?"

"No. Please. I'm sorry. I don't know—"

"Of course you don't know."

He heard her footsteps cross to the wall, heard her flip the switch and then approach. "I'm not really that sleepy, and I wondered if maybe you have something I could read to you. The newspaper, or mail? Maybe you even have a favorite book?"

Kristian felt some of the tension and darkness recede. "Yes," he said, exhaling gratefully. "I'm sure there is."

CHAPTER SEVEN

THAT night began a pattern they'd follow for the next two weeks. During the day Kristian would follow a prescribed workout regimen, and then in the evening he and Elizabeth would have a leisurely dinner, followed by an hour or two in the library, where she'd read to him from a book, newspaper or business periodical of his choice.

Kristian's progress astounded her. If she hadn't been there to witness the transformation, she wouldn't have believed it possible. But being here, observing the day-to-day change in Kristian, had proved once and for all that attitude was everything.

Every day, twice a day, for the past two weeks, Kristian had headed to the spacious dining room which had been converted into a rehabilitation room. Months ago the dining room's luxurious carpets had been rolled back, the furniture cleared out, and serious equipment had been hauled up the mountain face to dominate the space.

Bright blue mats covered the floor, and support bars had been built in a far corner to aid Kristian as he practiced walking. The nine windows overlooking the garden and valley below were always open, and Kristian spent hours at a time in that room.

The sports trainer Kristian had hired arrived two days after

Elizabeth did. Kristian had found Pirro in Sparta, and he had agreed to come and work with Kristian for the next four weeks, as long as he could return to Sparta on the weekends to be with his wife and children.

During the week, when Pirro was in residence, Kristian drove himself relentlessly. A trainer for the last Greek Olympic team, Pirro had helped rehabilitate and train some of the world's most elite athletes, and he treated Kristian as if he were the same.

The first few days Kristian did lots of stretching and developing core strength, with rubber balls and colored bands. By end of the first week he was increasing his distance in the pool and adding free weights to his routine. At the end of the second week Kristian was on cardio machines, alternating walking with short runs.

From the very beginning Elizabeth had known Kristian would get on his feet again. She hadn't expected it would only take him fifteen days.

Elizabeth stopped by the training room on Friday, early in the afternoon, to see if Pirro had any instructions for her for the two days while he returned to Sparta for the weekend.

She was shocked to see Kristian running slowly on a steep incline on the treadmill.

Pirro saw her enter and stepped over to speak with her. *"Ti Kanis?"* he asked. "How are you?"

"Kalo." Good. She smiled briefly before pointing to Kristian on the treadmill. "Isn't that a bit extreme?" she asked worriedly. "He could hardly stand two weeks ago. Won't the running injure him?"

"He's barely running," Pirro answered, glancing over his shoulder to watch Kristian's progress. "Notice the extreme incline? This is really a cross training exercise. Yes, we're working on increasing his cardio, but it's really to strengthen and develop the leg muscles."

Elizabeth couldn't help but notice the incline. Nor Kristian's intense concentration. He was running slowly, but without support, with his shoulders squared, his head lifted, his gaze fixed straight ahead. And even though sweat poured off him, and his cheeks glowed ruddy red, she didn't think he'd ever looked better—or stronger. Yes, he was breathing hard, but it was deep, regular, steady.

She walked closer to the machine, glanced at the screen monitoring his heart-rate. His heart-rate was low. She returned to Pirro's side. "So it's really not too much?" she persisted, torn between pride and anxiety. She wanted him better, but couldn't help fearing he'd burn out before he got to where he wanted to be.

"Too much?" Pirro grinned. "You don't know Kirie Kristian, do you? He's not a man. He's a monster."

Monster.

Pirro's word lingered in her mind as she turned to leave Kristian to finish his training. It was the same word Kristian had used when she'd first met him—the day he'd torn the bandages from his head to expose his face. Monster. Frankenstein.

Yet in the past two weeks he'd demonstrated that he was so far from either…

And so much more heroic than he even knew.

Soon he'd be returning to Athens. To the woman and the life that waited for him there. He'd eventually marry Cosima—apparently his family had known her forever—and with luck he'd have many children and a long, happy life.

But thinking of him returning to Athens put a heaviness in her heart. Thinking of him marrying Cosima made the heaviness even worse.

But that was why she was here, she reminded herself, swallowing hard around the painful lump in her throat, that lump that never went away. She'd come to prepare Kristian for the life he'd left behind.

And he was ready to go back. She could see it even if he couldn't.

The lump grew, thickening, almost drawing tears to her eyes.

Kristian, the Greek tycoon, had done this to her, too. She hadn't expected to feel this way about him, but he'd amazed her, impressed her, touched her heart with his courage, his sensitivity, as well as those rare glimpses of uncertainty. He made her feel so many emotions. But most of all he made her feel tender, good, hopeful, new. *New.*

"Shall I give him a message for you?" Pirro asked, his attention returning to Kristian.

And Elizabeth looked over at Kristian, this giant of a man who had surprised her at every level, her heart doing another one of those stunning free falls. He was so handsome it always touched a nerve, and that violent scar of his just made him more real, more beautiful. "No," she murmured. "There's no message. I'll just see him at dinner."

But as Elizabeth turned away, heading outside to take a walk through the gardens, she wondered when she'd find the courage to leave.

She had to leave. She'd already become too attached on him.

Putting a hand to her chest, she tried to stop the surge of pain that came with thinking of leaving.

Don't think of yourself, she reminded herself. Think of him. Think of his needs and how remarkable it is that he can do so much again. Think about his drive, his assertiveness, his ability to someday soon live independently.

And, thinking this way, she felt some of her own sadness

lifted. He and his confidence were truly amazing. You wouldn't know he couldn't see from the way he entered a room, or the way he handled himself. In the past couple of weeks he'd become more relaxed and comfortable in his own skin, and the more comfortable he felt, the more powerful his physical presence became.

She'd always known he was tall—easily over six feet two—but she'd never felt the impact of his height until he'd begun walking with a cane. Instead of stumbling, or hesitating, he walked with the assurance of a man who knew his world and fully intended to dominate that world once more.

Her lips curved in a rueful smile as she walked through the garden, with its low, fragrant hedges and rows of magnificent trees. No wonder a monastery had been built here hundreds of years ago. The setting was so green, the views breathtaking, the air pure and clean.

Pausing at one of the stone walls that overlooked the valley below, Elizabeth breathed in the scent of pine and lemon blossoms and gazed off into the distance, where the Messenian plain stretched.

Kristian had told her that the Messenian plain was extraordinarily fertile and produced nearly every crop imaginable, including the delicious Kalamata olive. Beyond the agricultural plain was the sea, with what had to be more beautiful beaches and picturesque bays. Although Elizabeth had never planned on returning to Greece, now that she was here she was anxious to spend a day at the water. There was nothing like a day spent enjoying the beautiful Greek sun and sea.

"Elizabeth?"

Hearing her name called, she turned to discover Kristian heading toward her, walking through the gardens with his long narrow cane. He hadn't liked the cane initially, had said it emphasized his blindness, but once he'd realized the cane gave freedom as he learned to walk again, he had adapted to it with remarkable speed.

His pace was clipped, almost aggressive, bringing to mind a conversation she'd had with him a few days ago. She'd told him she was amazed by his progress and his confident stride. He'd shrugged the compliment off, answering, "Greeks like to do things well or not at all."

She couldn't help smiling as she remembered his careless confidence, bordering on Greek arrogance. But it had been a truthful answer and it suited him, especially now, as she watched him walk through the garden.

"Kristian, I'm here," she called to him, "I'm at the wall overlooking the valley."

It didn't take him long to reach her. He was still wearing the white short-sleeve T-shirt and gray baggy sweat pants he'd worked out in. His dark hair fell forward on his brow and his skin looked burnished with a healthy glow. Her gaze searched his face, looking for signs of exhaustion or strain. There were none. He just looked fit, relaxed, even happy. "You had a grueling workout," she said.

"It was hard, but it felt good."

"Pirro can be brutal."

Kristian shrugged. "He knows I like to be challenged."

"But you feel okay?"

White teeth flashed and creases fanned from his eyes. "I feel great."

And there went her heart again, with that painful little flutter of attraction, admiration and sorrow. He wasn't hers. He'd never be hers. All she had to do was watch one of his exhausting physical therapy sessions to see that his desire to heal was for his Cosima. And although that knowledge stung, she knew before long she'd be back in her office and immersed in her administrative duties there.

The desk would be a good place for her. At her desk she'd be busy with the phone and computer and email. She wouldn't feel these disturbing emotions there.

"You were in the training room earlier," he said. "Everything all right?"

The soft breeze was sending tendrils of hair flying around her face, and she caught one and held it back by her ear. "I just wanted to check with Pirro—see if he had any instructions for me over the weekend."

"Did he?"

"No."

"I guess that means we've the weekend free."

"Are you making big plans, then?" she asked, teasing him, knowing perfectly well his routine didn't vary much. He was most confident doing things he knew, walking paths he'd become familiar with.

"I'm looking forward to dinner," he admitted.

"Wow. Sounds exciting."

The corner of his mouth lifted, his hard features softening at her gentle mockery. "Are you making fun of me?"

"Me? No. Never. You're Mr. Kristian Koumantaros—one of Greece's most powerful men—how could I even consider poking fun at you?"

"You would," he said, grooves paralleling his mouth. "You do."

"Mr. Koumantaros, you must be thinking of someone else."

"Mmm-hmm."

"I'm just a simple nurse, completely devoted to your wellbeing."

"Are you?"

"Of course. Have I not convinced you of that yet?" She'd meant to continue in her playful vein, but this time the words came out differently, her voice betraying her by dropping, cracking, revealing a tremor of raw emotion she didn't ever want him to hear.

Instead of answering, he reached out and touched her face. The unexpected touch shocked her, and she reared back, but his fingers followed, and slowly he slid his palm across her cheek.

The warmth in his hand made her face burn. She shivered at the explosion of heat within her even as her skin felt alive with bites of fire and ice.

"Kristian," she protested huskily, more heat washing through her—heat and need and something else. Something dangerously like desire.

She'd tried so hard to suppress these feelings, knowing if she acknowledged the tremendous attraction her control would shatter.

Her control *couldn't* shatter.

"No," she whispered, trying to turn her cheek away even as she longed to press her face to his hand, to feel more of the comfort and bittersweet pleasure.

She liked him.

She liked him very much. Too much. And, staring up into his face, she felt her fingers curl into her palm, fighting the urge to reach up and touch that beautiful scarred face of his.

Kristian, with his black hair and noble but scarred face, and his eyes that didn't see.

She began talking, to try to cover the sudden awkwardness between them. "These past two weeks you've made such great strides—literally, figuratively. You've no idea how proud I am of you, how much I admire you."

"That sounds suspiciously like a goodbye speech."

"It's not, but I *will* have to be leaving soon. You're virtually independent, and you'll soon be ready to return to your life in Athens."

"I don't like Athens."

"But your work—"

"I can do it here."

"But your family—"

"Gone."

She felt the tension between them grow. "Your friends," she said quietly, firmly. "And you do have those, Kristian. You have many people who miss you and want you back where you belong." Chief among them Cosima.

Averting his head, he stood tall and silent. His brows tugged and his jaw firmed, and slowly he turned his face toward her again. "When?"

"When what?"

"When do you intend to leave?"

She shrugged uncomfortably. "Soon." She took a quick breath. "Sooner than I expected."

"And when is that? Next week? The week after that?"

She twisted her fingers together. "Let's talk about this later."

"It's that soon?"

She nodded.

"Why?" he asked.

"It's work. I've a problem in Paris, and my case manager is fed up, threatening to walk off the job. I can't afford to lose her. I need to go and try to sort things out."

"So when is this? When do you plan to go?"

Elizabeth hesitated. "I was thinking about Monday." The lump was back in her throat, making it almost impossible to breathe. "After Pirro returns."

Kristian just stood there—big, imposing, and strangely silent.

"I've already contacted Cosima," she continued. "I told her that I've done all I can do and that it'd be wrong to continue to take her money." Elizabeth didn't add that she'd actually authorized her London office to refund Cosima's money, because it was Kristian who'd done the work, not she. It was Kristian's own miracle.

"Monday is just days away," Kristian said, his voice hard, increasingly distant.

"I know. It is sudden." She took a quick breath, feeling a stab of intense regret. She wished she could reach out and touch him, reassure him, but it wasn't her place. There were lines that couldn't be crossed, professional boundaries that she had to respect, despite her growing feelings for him. "You know you don't need me, Kristian. I'm just in your way—"

"*No.*"

"Yes. But you must know I'm in awe of you. You said you'd walk in two weeks, and I said you couldn't. I said you'd need a walker, and you said you wouldn't." She laughed, thinking back to those first two intense and overwhelming days. "You've made a believer out of me."

He said nothing for a long moment, and then shook his head. "I wish I *could* make a believer out of you," he said, speaking so quietly the words were nearly inaudible.

"Monday is still three days from now," she said, injecting a note of false cheer. "Do we have to think about Monday today? Can't we think of something else? A game of blindman's bluff?"

Kristian's jaw drew tight, and then eased. He laughed most reluctantly. "You're a horrible woman."

"Yes, I know," she answered, grateful for humor.

"Most challenging, Cratchett."

"I'll take that as a compliment."

"Then you take it wrong."

Elizabeth smiled. When he teased her, when he played her game with her, it amused her to no end. Moments ago she'd felt so low, and yet she was comforted and encouraged now.

She loved his company. It was as simple as that. He was clever and sophisticated, handsome and entertaining. And once he'd determined to return to the land of the living, he had done so with a vengeance.

For the past week she'd tried to temper her happiness with reminders that soon he'd be returning to Athens, and marriage to Cosima, but it hadn't stopped her heart from doing a quick double-beat every time she heard his voice or saw him enter a room.

"I'm not sure of the exact time," Kristian said, "but I imagine it's probably close to five."

Elizabeth glanced at her silver watch. "It's ten past five now."

"I've made plans for dinner. It will mean dressing now. Can you be ready by six?"

"Is this for dinner here?"

"No."

"We're going *out*?" She gazed incredulously at the valley far below and the steep descent down. Sure, Pirro traveled up and down once a week to work with Kristian. But she couldn't imagine Kristian bumping around on the back of a mule or in a donkey's cart.

His expression didn't change. "Is that a problem?"

"No." But it kind of *was* a problem, she thought, glancing at the dwindling light. Where would they possibly go to eat? It would take them hours to get down the mountain, and it would be dark soon. But maybe Kristian hadn't thought of that, as his world was always dark.

Kristian heard the hesitation in Elizabeth's voice and he

tensed, his posture going rigid. He resented not being able to see her, particularly at times like this. It hadn't been until he couldn't see that he'd learned how much he'd depended on his eyes, on visual cues, to make decisions.

Why was she less than enthusiastic about dinner?

Did she not want to go with him? Or was she upset about something?

If only he could see her face, read her expression, he'd know what her hesitation meant. But, as it was, he felt as though he were stumbling blindly about. His jaw hardened. He hated this feeling of confusion and helplessness. He wasn't a helpless person, but everything was so different now, so much harder than before.

Like sleep.

And the nightmares that woke him up endlessly. Or, worse, the nightmares he couldn't wake from—the dreams that haunted him for hours when, even when he told himself to wake, even when he said in the dream, *This is just a dream,* he couldn't let go, couldn't open his eyes and see. Day or night, it was all the same. Black. Endless pitch-black.

"If you'd rather not go…" he said, his voice growing cooler, more distant. He couldn't exactly blame her if she didn't want another evening alone with him. She might say he didn't look like Frankenstein, but the scar on his face felt thick, and it ran at an angle, as though his face had been pieced together, stitched with rough thread.

"No, Kristian. No, that's not it at all," she protested, her hand briefly touching his arm before just as swiftly pulling away. And yet that light, faint touch was enough. It warmed him. Connected him. Made him feel real. And, God knew, between the darkness and the nightmares and the grief of losing Andreas, he didn't feel real, or good, very often anymore.

"I'd like to go," she continued. "I want to go. I just wasn't sure what to wear. Is there a dress code? Casual or elegant? How are you going to dress?"

He pressed the tip of his cane into the ground, wanting to touch her instead, wanting to feel the softness of her cheek, the silky texture that made him think of crushed rose petals and velvet and the softest lace edged satin. His body ached, his chest grew tight, pinched around his heart.

"I won't be casual." His voice came out rough, almost raw, and he winced. He'd developed edges and shadows that threatened to consume him. "But you should dress so that you're comfortable. It could be a late night."

In her bedroom, Elizabeth practically spun in circles.

They were going out, and it could be a late night. So where were they going and exactly how late was late?

Her stomach flipped over, and she felt downright giddy as she bathed and toweled off. It was ridiculous, preposterous to feel this way—and yet she couldn't help the flurry of excitement. It had been a little over two weeks since she'd arrived, and she was looking forward to dinner out.

Knowing that Kristian wouldn't be dressed casually, she flipped through her clothes in the wardrobe until she decided she'd wear the only dress she'd brought—a black cocktail-length dress with a pale lace inset.

Standing before the mirror, she blew her wet hair dry and battled to keep her chaotic emotions in check.

You're just his nurse, she reminded herself. Nothing more than that. But her bright eyes in the mirror and the quick beat of her pulse belied that statement.

Her hair shimmered. Elizabeth was going to leave it down, but worried she wouldn't appear professional. At the last minute she plaited her hair into two slender braids, then twisted the braids into an elegant figure-eight at the back of her head, before pulling some blonde wisps from her crown so they fell softly around her face.

Gathering a light black silk shawl and her small handbag, she headed for the monastery's library. As she walked through the long arched hallways she heard a distant thumping sound, a dull roar that steadily grew louder, until the sound was directly above and vibrating through the entire estate. Then abruptly the thumping stopped and everything was quiet again.

Elizabeth discovered Kristian already in the library, waiting for her.

He'd also showered and changed, was dressed now in elegant black pants and a crisp white dress shirt, with a fine leather black belt and black leather shoes. With his dark hair combed and his face cleanshaven, Elizabeth didn't think she'd ever met a man so fit, strong, or so darkly handsome.

"Am I underdressed?" he asked, lifting his hands as if to ask for her approval.

"No." Her heart turned over. God, he was beautiful. Did he have any idea how stunning he really was?

Kristian moved toward her, his cane folded, tucked under his arm. He looked so confident, so very sure of himself. "What are you wearing…besides high heels?"

"You could tell by the way I walked?" she guessed.

"Mmmm. Very sexy."

Blushing, she looked up into his face, glad he couldn't see the way she looked at him. She loved looking at him, and she didn't even know what she loved most about his face. It was just the way it came together—that proud brow, the jet-black eyebrows, the strong cheekbones above firm, mobile lips.

"I'm wearing a dress," she said, feeling suddenly shy. She'd never been shy around men before—had never felt intimidated by any man, not even her Greek former husband. "It's black velvet with some lace at the bodice. Reminds me of the 1920s flapper-style dress."

"You must look incredible."

The compliment, as well as the deep sincerity in Kristian's voice, brought tears to her eyes.

Kristian was so much more than any man she'd ever met. It wasn't his wealth or sophistication that impressed her, either—although she did admit that he wore his clothes with ease and elegance, and she'd heard his brilliant trading and investments meant he'd tripled his family fortune—those weren't qualities she respected, much less admired.

She liked different things—simple things. Like the way his voice conveyed so much, and how closely he listened to her when she talked to him. His precise word choice indicated he paid attention to virtually everything.

"Not half as incredible as you do," she answered.

His mouth quirked. "Ready?"

"Yes."

He held out his arm and she took it. His body was so much bigger than hers, and warm, the muscles in his arm dense and hard. Together they headed through the hall to the front entrance, where Pano stood, ready to open the front door.

At the door Kristian paused briefly, head tipped as he gazed down at her. "Your chariot awaits," he said, and with another step they crossed the monastery's threshold and went outside—to a white and silver helicopter.

CHAPTER EIGHT

A HELICOPTER.

On the top of one of Taygetos's peaks.

She blinked, shook her head, and looked again, thinking that maybe she'd imagined it. But, no, the silver and white body glinted in the last rays of the setting sun.

"I wondered how you got up and down the mountain," she said. "You didn't seem the type to enjoy donkey rides."

Kristian's deep laugh hummed all the way through her. "I suppose I could have sent the helicopter for you."

"No, no. I would have hated to miss hours bumping and jolting around in a wood cart.

He laughed again, as though deeply amused. "Have you been in a helicopter before?"

"I have," she said. "Yes." Her parents had access to a helicopter in New York. But that was part of the affluent life she'd left behind. "It's been a while, though."

The pilot indicated they were safe to board, and Elizabeth walked Kristian to the door. Once on board, he easily found his seatbelt and fastened the clip. And it wasn't until they'd lifted off, heading straight up and then over, between the mountain peaks, that Elizabeth remembered that the worst of

Kristian's injuries had come from the helicopter crash instead of the actual avalanche.

Turning, she glanced into his face to see what he was feeling. He seemed perhaps a little paler than he had earlier, but other than that he gave no indication that anything was wrong.

"You were hurt in a helicopter accident," she said, wondering if he was really okay, or just putting up a brave front.

"I was."

She waited, wondering if he'd say more. He didn't, and she touched the tip of her tongue to her upper lip. "You're not worried about being in one now?"

His brows pulled. "No. I know Yanni the pilot well—very well—and, being a pilot myself..."

"You're a pilot?"

His dark head inclined and he said slowly, "I was flying at the time of the crash."

Ah. "And the others?" she whispered.

"They were all in different places and stages of recovery." His long black lashes lowered, hiding the brilliant blue of his eyes.

She waited, and eventually Kristian sighed, shifted, his broad shoulders squaring. "One had managed to ski down the mountain to a lower patrol. Cosima..." He paused, took a quick short breath. "Cosima and the guide had been rescued. Two were still buried in snow and the others...were located but already gone."

The details were still so vague, and his difficulty in recounting the events so obvious that she couldn't ask anything else. But there were things she still wanted to know. Like, had he been going back for his brother when he crashed? And how had he managed to locate Cosima so quickly but not Andreas?

Thinking of the accident, she stole a swift side-glance in Kristian's direction. Yes, he was walking, and, yes, he was physically stronger. But what if he never saw again?

What if he didn't get the surgery—or, worse, did have it and the treatment didn't work? What if his vision could never be improved? What then?

She actually thought Kristian would cope—it wouldn't be easy, but he was tough, far tougher than he'd ever let on—but she wasn't so sure about Cosima, because Cosima desperately wanted Kristian to be "normal" again. And those were Cosima's words: "He must be normal, the way he was, or no one will ever respect him."

How would Cosima feel if Kristian never did get his sight back?

Would she still love him? Stay with him? Honor him?

Troubled, Elizabeth drew her shawl closer to her shoulders and gazed out the helicopter window as they flew high over the Peloponnese peninsula. It was a stunning journey at sunset, the fading sun painting the ground below in warm strokes of reddish-gold light.

In her two years of living in Greece she'd never visited the Peloponnese. Although the Peloponnese was a favorite with tourists, for its diverse landscape and numerous significant archeological sites, she only knew what Kristian had been telling her these past couple weeks. But, remembering his tales, she was riveted by three "fingers" of land projecting into the sea, the land green and fertile against the brilliant blue Mediterranean.

"We're almost there," Kristian suddenly said, his hand briefly touching her knee.

She felt her stomach flip and, breath catching, she glanced down at her knee, which still felt the heat of his fingers even though his hand was no longer there.

She wanted him to touch her again. She wanted to feel his hand slide inside her knee, wanted to feel the heat of his hand, his palm on her knee, and then feel his touch slide up the inside of her thigh. And maybe it couldn't happen, but it didn't make the desire any less real.

Skin against skin, she thought. Touch that was warm and concrete instead of all these silent thoughts and intense emotions. And they were getting harder to handle, because she couldn't acknowledge them, couldn't act on them, could do nothing but keep it in, hold it in, pretend she wasn't falling head over heels in love. Because she was.

And it was torture. Madness.

Her heart felt like it was tumbling inside her chest—a small shell caught in the ocean tide. She couldn't stop it, couldn't control it, could only feel it.

With an equally heart-plunging drop, the helicopter descended straight down.

As the pilot opened the door and assisted her and then Kristian out, she saw the headlights of a car in front of them. The driver of the car stepped out, and as he approached she realized it was Kristian's driver.

Whisked from helicopter to car, Elizabeth slid through the passenger door and onto the leather seat, pulse racing. Her pulse quickened yet again as Kristian climbed in and sat close beside her.

"Where are we?" she asked, feeling the press of Kristian's thigh against hers as the driver set off.

"Kithira."

His leg was much longer than hers, his knee extending past hers, the muscle hard against hers.

"It's an island at the foot of the Peloponnese," he added. "Years ago, before the Corinth Canal was built in the late nineteenth century, the island was prosperous due to all the ships stopping. But after the canal's construction the island's population, along with its fortune, dwindled."

As the car traveled on quiet roads, beneath the odd passing yellow light, shadows flickered in and through the windows. Elizabeth couldn't tear her gaze from the sight of his black trouser-covered leg against hers.

"It's nice to be going out," he said, as the car began to wind up a relatively steep hill. "I love living in the Taygetos, but every now and then I just want to go somewhere for dinner, enjoy a good meal and not feel so isolated."

She turned swiftly to look at him. There were no street-lights on the mountain road and she couldn't see his face well. "So you *do* feel isolated living so far from everyone?"

He shrugged. "I'm Greek."

Those two words revealed far more than he knew. Greeks treasured family, had strong ties to family, even the extended family, and every generation was respected for what it contributed. In Greece the elderly rarely lived alone, and money was never hoarded, but shared with each other. A father would never let his daughter marry without giving her a house, or land, or whatever he could, and a Greek son would always contribute to his parents' care. It wasn't just an issue of respect, but love.

"That's why Cosima wants you back in Athens," Elizabeth said gently. "There you have your *parea*—your group of friends." And, for Greeks, the circle of friends was nearly as important as family. A good *parea* was as necessary as food and water.

But Kristian didn't speak. Elizabeth, not about to be put off, lightly touched his sleeve. "Your friends miss you."

"My *parea* is gone."

"No—"

"Elizabeth." He stopped her. "They're gone. They died with my brother in France. All those that perished, suffocating in the snow, were my friends. But they weren't just friends. They were also colleagues."

Pained, she closed her eyes. Why, oh why did she push? Why, oh, why did she think she knew everything? How could she be so conceited as to think she could counsel him? "I'm sorry."

"You didn't know."

"But I thought… Cosima said…"

"Cosima?" Kristian repeated bitterly. "Soon you will learn you can't believe everything she says."

"Even though she means well."

Silence filled the car, and once again Elizabeth sensed that she'd said the wrong thing. She pressed her fists to her knees, increasingly uncomfortable.

"Perhaps I should tell you about dinner," Kristian said finally, his deep chest lifting as he squared his shoulders. "We're heading to a tiny village that will seem virtually untouched by tourism or time. Just outside this village is one of my favorite restaurants—a place designed by a Greek architect and his artist wife. The food is simple, but fresh, and the view is even better."

"You could go anywhere to eat, but you choose a rustic and remote restaurant?"

"I like quiet places. I'm not interested in fanfare or fuss."

"Have you always been this way, or…?"

"It's not the result of the accident, no. Andreas was the extrovert—he loved parties and the social scene."

"You didn't go with him?"

"Of course I went with him. He was my brother and my best friend. But I was content to let him take center stage, entertain everyone. It was more fun to sit back, watch."

As Kristian talked, the moon appeared from behind a cloud. Elizabeth could suddenly see Kristian's features, and that rugged profile of his, softened only by the hint of fullness at his lower lip.

He had such a great mouth, too. Just wide enough, with perfect lips.

To kiss those lips…

Knots tightened inside her belly, knots that had less to do with fear and more to do with desire. She felt so attracted to him it was hard to contain her feelings, to keep the need from showing.

What she needed to do was scoot over on the seat, put some distance between them—because with him sitting so close, with their thighs touching and every now and then their elbows brushing, she felt so wound up, so keenly aware of him.

She looked now at his hand, where it rested on his thigh, and she remembered how electric it had felt when his hand had brushed her knee, how she'd wanted his hand to slide beneath the hem of her dress and touch her, tease her, set her on fire…

That hand. His body. Her skin.

She swallowed hard, her heart beating at a frantic tempo, and, crossing her legs, she fought the dizzying zing of adrenaline. This was ridiculous, she told herself, shifting again, crossing her legs the other way. She had to settle down. Had to find some calm.

"You seem restless," Kristian said, head cocking, listening attentively.

She pressed her knees together. "I guess I am. I probably just need to stretch my legs. Must be the sitting."

"We're almost there."

"I'm not complaining."

"I didn't think you were."

She forced a small tight smile even as her mind kept spinning, her imagination working overtime. She was far too aware of Kristian next to her, far too aware of his warmth, the faint spice of his cologne or aftershave, the formidable size of him…even the steady way he was breathing.

"You're not too tired, are you?" he asked as the car headlights illuminated the road and what seemed to be a nearly barren slope before them.

"No," she said, as the car suddenly turned, swinging onto a narrow road.

"Hungry?"

She made a soft sound and anxiously smoothed the velvet hem of her dress over her knees. "No. *Yes.* Could be." She laughed, yet the sound was apprehensive. "I honestly don't know what's wrong with me."

He reached out, his hand finding hers in the dark with surprising ease. She thought for a moment he meant to hold her hand but instead he turned it over and put his fingers on the inside of her wrist, checking her pulse. Several seconds passed before his mouth quirked. "Your heart's racing."

"I know," she whispered, staring at her wrist in his hand as the lights of a parking lot and restaurant illuminated the car. His hand was twice the size of her own, and his skin, so darkly tanned, made hers look like cream.

"You're not scared of me?"

"No."

"But maybe you're afraid to be alone with me?"

Her heart drummed even harder, faster. "And why would that be?"

His thumb caressed her sensitive wrist for a moment before releasing her. "Because tonight you're not my nurse, and I'm not your patient. We're just two people having dinner together."

"Just friends," she said breathlessly, tugging her hand free, suddenly terrified of everything she didn't know and didn't understand.

"Can a man and a woman be just friends?"

Elizabeth's throat seized, closed.

The driver put the car into "park" and came around to open their door. Elizabeth nearly jumped from the car, anxious to regain control.

At the restaurant entrance they were greeted as though they were family, the restaurant owner clasping Kristian by the arms and kissing him on each cheek. "Kyrios Kristian," he said, emotion thickening his Greek. "*Kyrie.* It is good to see you."

Kristian returned the embrace with equal warmth. "It is good to be back."

"*Parakalo*—come." And the older man, his dark hair only peppered with gray, led them to a table in a quiet alcove with windows all around. "The best seats for you. Only the best for you, my son. Anything for you."

After the owner left, Elizabeth turned to Kristian. "He called you *son?*"

"The island's small. Everyone here is like family."

"So you know him well?"

"I used to spend a lot of time here."

She glanced out the window and the view was astonishing. They were high on a hill, perched above a small village below. And farther down from the village was the ocean.

The lights of the village twinkled and the moon reflected off the white foam of the sea, where the waves broke on the rocks and shore.

The restaurant owner returned, presenting them with a gift—a bottle of his favorite wine—pouring both glasses before leaving the bottle behind.

"*Yiassis,*" she said, raising her glass and clinking it with his. *To your health.*

"*Yiassis,*" he answered.

And then silence fell, and the stillness felt wrong. Something was wrong. She just knew it.

Kristian shifted, and a small muscle suddenly pulled in his cheek. Elizabeth watched him, feeling a rise in tension.

The mood at the table was suddenly different.

Kristian suddenly seemed so alone, so cut off in his world. "What's wrong?" she asked nervously, fearing that she'd said something, done something to upset him.

He shook his head.

"Did I do something?" she persisted.

"No."

"Kristian." Her tone was pleading. "Tell me."

His jaw worked, the hard line of his cheekbone growing even more prominent, and he laughed, the sound rough and raw. "I wish to God I could see you."

For a moment she didn't know what to say or do, as heat rushed through her. And then the heat receded, leaving her chilled. "Why?" she whispered.

"I just want to see you."

Her face grew hot all over again, and this time the warmth stayed, flooding her limbs, making her feel far too sensitive. "Why? I'm just another battleaxe."

"*Ohi.*" No. "Hardly."

Her hand shook as she adjusted her silverware. "You don't know that—"

"I know how you sound, and smell. I know you barely reach my shoulder—even in heels—and I know how your skin feels—impossibly smooth, and soft, like the most delicate satin or flower."

"I think you've found your old pain meds."

His dark head tipped. His blue eyes fixed on her. "And I think you're afraid of being with me."

"You're wrong."

"Am I?"

"Yes." She reached for her water glass and took a quick sip of the bubbly mineral water, but drank so much that the bubbles ended up stinging her nose. "I'm not afraid," she said, returning the glass to a table covered in white crisp linen and flickering with soft ivory candlelight and shadows. "How could I be afraid of you?"

His lips barely curved. "I'm not nice, like other men."

Her heart nearly fell. She looked up at him from beneath her lashes. "I'm not going to even dignify that with a response."

"Why?"

"Because you're baiting me," she said.

He surprised her by laughing. "My clever girl."

Her heart jumped again, and an icy hot shiver raced through her. Liquid fire in her veins. *His clever girl.* He was torturing her now. Making her want to be more than she was, making her want to have more than she did. Not more things, but more love.

His love.

But he was promised, practically engaged. And she'd been through hell and back with one man who hadn't been able to keep his word, or honor his commitments. Including his marriage vows.

"Kristian, I can't do this." She would have gotten up and run if there had been anywhere to go. "I can't play these games with you."

His forehead furrowed, emphasizing the scar running down his cheek. "What games?"

"These…this…whatever you call this. Us." She shook her head, unable to get the words out. "I know what you said earlier, that tonight we're not patient and nurse, we're just a man and…woman. But that's not right. You're wrong. I *am* your nurse. That's all I am, all I can be."

He leaned back and rested one arm on the table, his hand relaxed. His expression turned speculative. "And will you still be my nurse when you return to London in two days?"

"Three days."

"Two days."

She held her breath, her fingers balling into fists and then slowly exhaled.

His mouth tugged and lines deepened near his lips, emphasizing the beautiful planes of his face. "Elizabeth, *latrea mou,* let us not play games, as you say. Why do you have to go back?"

"I have a business to run—and, Kristian, so do you. Your officers and board of directors are desperate for you to return to Athens and take leadership again."

"I can do it from Taygetos."

She shook her head, impatient. "No, you can't. Not properly. There are appointments, conferences, press meetings—"

"Others can do it," he said dismissively.

Staring at him, she felt her frustration grow. He'd never sounded so arrogant as he did now. "But *you* are Koumantaros. You are the one investors believe in and the one your business partners want to meet with. *You* are essential to Koumantaros Incorporated's success."

He nearly snapped his fingers, rejecting her arguments. "Did Cosima put you up to this?"

"No. Of course not. And that's not the issue here anyway. The issue is you resuming your responsibilities."

"Elizabeth, I still head the corporation."

"But absent leadership?" She made a soft scoffing sound. "It's not effective, and, frankly, it's not you."

"How can one little Englishwoman have so many opinions about things she knows so little about?"

Elizabeth's cheeks flamed. "I know you better than you think," she flashed.

"I'm referring to the corporate world—"

"I am a business owner."

It was his turn to scoff. "Which we've already established isn't well managed at all."

Hurt, she abruptly drew back and stared at him. "That was unkind. And unnecessary."

He shrugged off her rebuke. "But true. Your agency provided me with exceptionally poor care. Propositioned and then blackmailed by one nurse, and demeaned by the others."

She threw her napkin down and pushed her chair back. "Maybe you were an exceptionally poor patient."

"Is that possible?"

"Possible?" she repeated, her voice quavering with anger and indignation. "My God, you're even more conceited than I dreamed. *Possible?*" She drew a swift breath. "Do you want the truth? No more sugar-coated words?"

"Don't start mincing words now," he drawled, sounding as bored as he looked.

Her fingers flexed, and blood pumped through her veins. She wanted to smack him, she really did. "Truth, Kristian— *you* were impossible. You were the worst patient in the history of my agency, and we take care of hundreds of patients every year. I've had my business for years, and never encountered anyone as self-absorbed and manipulative as you."

She took another quick breath. "And another thing—do you think I *wanted* to leave my office, put aside my obligations, to rush to your side? Do you think this was a holiday for me to come to Greece? No. And no again. But I did it because no one else would, and you had a girlfriend desperate to see you whole and well."

Legs shaking, Elizabeth staggered to her feet. "Speaking of your girlfriend, it's time you gave her a call. I'm done here. It's Cosima's turn to be with you now!"

CHAPTER NINE

ELIZABETH rushed out of the restaurant, past the three other tables of patrons. But no sooner had she stepped outside into the decidedly cooler night air than she felt assailed by shame. She'd just walked out on Kristian Koumantaros, one of Greece's most powerful and beloved tycoons.

As gusts of wind whistled past the building, perched on the mountain edge, she hugged her arms close, chilled, overwhelmed. She'd left a man who couldn't see alone, to find his own way out. And worst of all, she thought, tugging windblown tendrils behind her ears, she'd left in the middle of the meal. Meals were almost as sacred as family in Greece.

She was falling apart, she thought, putting a hand to her thigh to keep her skirt from billowing out. Her feelings were so intense she was finding it difficult to be around Kristian. She was overly emotional and too sensitive. And this was why she had to leave—not because she couldn't still do good here, but because she wondered if she couldn't manage her own emotions, how could she possibly help him manage his?

In London things would be different.

In London she wouldn't see Kristian.

In London she'd be in control.

A bitter taste filled her mouth and she immediately shook

her head, unable to bear the thought that just days from now she'd be gone and he'd be out of her life.

How could she leave him?

And yet how could she remain?

In the meantime she was standing outside Kristian's favorite restaurant while he sat alone inside. God, what a mess.

She had to go back in there. Had to apologize. Try to make amends before the evening was completely destroyed.

With a deep breath, she turned and walked through the front door, out of the night which was rapidly growing stormy. Chilly. She rubbed at her arms and returned to their table, where Kristian waited.

He was sitting still, head averted, and yet from his profile she could see his pallor and the strain at his jaw and mouth.

He was as upset as she was.

Heart sinking, Elizabeth sat down. "I'm sorry," she whispered, fighting the salty sting of tears. "I'm sorry. I don't know what else to say."

"It's not your fault. Don't apologize."

"Everything just feels wrong—"

"It's not you. It's me." His dense black lashes dropped. He hesitated, as though trying to find the right words. "I knew you'd need to go back, but I didn't expect you'd say it was so soon—didn't expect the announcement today."

She searched his face. It was a face she loved. *Loved.* And while the word initially took her by surprise, she also recognized it was true. "Kristian, I'm not leaving *you*. I'm just returning to my office and the work that awaits me there."

He hesitated a long time before picking up his wine glass, but setting it back down without taking a drink. "You couldn't move your office here?"

"Temporarily?"

"Permanently."

She didn't understand. "I didn't make this miracle, Kristian. It was you. It was your focus, your drive, your hours of work—"

"But I didn't care about getting better, didn't care about much of anything, until *you* arrived. And now I do."

"That's because you're healing."

"So don't leave while I'm still healing. Don't go when everything finally feels good again."

She closed her eyes, hope and pain streaking through her like twin forks of lightning. "But if I move my office here, if I remain here to help you…"

"Yes?"

She shook her head. "What about me? What happens to me when you're healed? When you're well?" She was grateful he couldn't see the tears in her eyes, or how she was forced to madly dash them away before anyone at the restaurant could see. "Once you've gotten whatever you need from me, do I just pack my things and go back to London again?"

He said nothing, his expression hard, grim.

"Kristian, forgive me, but sometimes being here in Greece is torture." She knotted her hands in her lap, thinking that the words were coming out all wrong but he had to realize that, while she didn't want to hurt him, she also had to protect herself. She was too attached to him already. Leaving him, losing him, would hurt so much. But remaining to watch him reunite with another woman would break her heart. "I like you, Kristian," she whispered. "Really like you—"

"And I like you. Very much."

"It's not the same."

"I don't understand. I don't understand any of this. I only know what I think. And I believe you belong here. With me."

He was saying words she'd wanted to hear, but not in the context she needed them. He wanted her because she was convenient and helpful, supportive while still challenging. Yet the relationship he was describing wasn't one of love, but usefulness. He wanted her company because it would benefit him. But how would *she* benefit by staying?

"Elizabeth, *latrea mou*," he added, voice deepening. "I need you."

Latrea mou. Darling. Devoted one.

His voice and words were buried inside her heart. Again tears filled her eyes, and again she was forced to brush them swiftly away. "No wonder you had mistresses on every continent," she said huskily. "You know exactly what women want to hear."

"You're changing the subject."

She wiped away another tear. "I'm making an observation."

"It's not accurate."

"Cosima said—"

"This isn't working, is it? Let's just go." Kristian abruptly rose, and even before he'd straightened the restaurant owner had rushed over. "I'm sorry," Kristian apologized stiffly, his expression shuttered. "We're going to be leaving."

"*Kyrie*, everything is ready. We're just about to carry out the plates," the owner said, clasping his hands together and looking from one to the other. "You are sure?"

Kristian didn't hesitate. "I am sure." He reached into his pocket, retrieved his wallet and cash. "Will you let my driver know?"

"Yes, Kyrie Kristian." The other man nodded. "At least let me have your meal packed to go. Maybe later you will be hungry and want a little plate of something, yes?"

"Thank you."

Five minutes later they were in the car, sitting at opposite ends of the passenger seat as the wind gusted and howled outside. Fat raindrops fell heavily against the windshield. Kristian stonily faced forward while Elizabeth, hands balled against her stomach, stared out the car window at the passing scenery, although most of it was too dark to see.

She didn't understand what had happened in the restaurant tonight. Everything had been going so well until they'd sat down, and then...

And then...what? Was it Cosima? Her departure? What?

As the car wound its way back down the mountain, she squeezed her knuckled fists, her insides a knot of regret and disappointment. The evening was a disaster, and she'd been so excited earlier, too.

"What happened?" she finally asked, breaking the miserably tense silence. "Everything seemed fine in the helicopter."

He didn't answer and, turning, she looked at him, stared at him pointedly, waiting for him to speak. He had to talk. He had to communicate.

But he wouldn't say a word. He sat there, tall, dark, impossibly remote, as though he lived in a different world.

"Kristian," she whispered. "You're being horrible. Don't do this. Don't be like this—"

His jaw hardened and his lashes flickered, but that was his only response, and she thought she could hate him in that moment—hate him not just now, but forever.

To be shut out, to be ignored. It was the worst punishment she could think of. So unbelievably hard to bear.

"The weather is going to be a problem," he said at last. "We won't be able to fly. Unfortunately we are unable to return to Taygetos tonight. We'll be staying in the capital city, Chora."

The driver had long ago merged with traffic, driving into

and through a harbor town. If this was the capital city it wasn't very big. They were now paralleling the coast, passing houses, churches and shops, nearly all already closed for the night. And far off in the distance a vast hulking fortress dwarfed the whitewashed town.

As the windshield wipers rhythmically swished, Elizabeth gazed out the passenger window, trying to get a better look at the fortress. It sat high above the city, on a rock of its own. In daylight the fortress would have an amazing view of the coast, but like the rest of Chora it was dark now, and even more atmospheric, with the rain slashing down.

"You've booked us into a hotel?" she asked, glimpsing a church steeple inside the miniature walled town.

"We won't be at a hotel. We'll be staying in a private home."

She glanced at him, her feelings still hurt. "Friends?"

"No. It's mine." He shifted wearily. "My home. One of my homes."

They were so close to the fortress she could see the distinct stones that shaped the mammoth walls. "Are we far from your home?"

"I don't think so, no. But I confess I'm not entirely sure where we are at the moment."

Of course—he couldn't see. And he wouldn't automatically know which direction they were going, or the current road they were traveling on. "We're heading toward a castle."

"Then we're almost there."

"We're staying near the castle?"

"We're staying *at* the castle."

"Your home is a castle?"

"It's one of my properties."

Her brows pulled. "How many properties do you have?"

"A few."

"Like this?"

"They're all a bit different. The monastery in Taygetos, the castle here, and other estates in other places."

"Are they all so…grand?"

"They're all historic. Some are in ruins when I purchase them; some are already in operation. But that's what I do. It's one of the companies in the Koumantaros portfolio. I buy historic properties and find different ways to make them profitable."

Elizabeth turned her attention back to the fortress, with its thick walls and towers and turrets looming before them. "And this is a real castle?"

"Venetian," he agreed. "Begun in the thirteenth century and finished in the fifteenth century."

"So what do you do with it?"

He made a soft, mocking sound. "My accountants would tell you I don't do enough, that it's an enormous drain on my resources, but after purchasing it three years ago I couldn't bear to turn it into a five-star luxury resort as planned."

"So you stay here?"

"I've reserved a wing for my private use, but I haven't visited since before the accident."

"So it essentially sits empty?"

The wind suddenly howled, and rain buffeted the car. Elizabeth didn't know if it was the weather or her question, but Kristian smiled faintly. "You're sounding like my accountants now. But, no, to answer your question. It's not empty. I've been working with an Italian architect and designer to slowly—carefully—turn wings and suites into upscale apartments. Two suites are leased now. By next year I hope to lease two or three more, and then that's it."

The car slowed and then stopped, and an iron gate

opened. The driver got out and came round to open their door. "We're here."

A half-dozen uniformed employees appeared from no-where. Before Elizabeth quite understood what was happening, she was being whisked in one direction and Kristian in another.

Left alone in an exquisite suite of rooms, she felt a stab of confusion.

Where on earth was she now?

The feeling was strongly reminiscent of how she'd been as a child, the only daughter of Rupert Stile, the fourth richest man in America, as she and her parents had traveled from one sumptuous hotel to the next.

It wasn't that they hadn't had houses of their own—they'd had dozens—but her mother had loved accompanying her father on his trips, and so they had all traveled together, the young heiress and her nannies too.

Back then, though, she hadn't Elizabeth Hatchet but Grace Elizabeth Stiles, daughter of a billionaire a hundred times over. It had been a privileged childhood, made only more enviable when she had matured from pampered daughter status to being the next high-society beauty.

Comfortable in the spotlight, at ease with the media, she'd enjoyed her debutante year and the endless round of parties. Invitations had poured in from all over the world, as had exquisite designer clothes made for her specifically.

It had been so much power for a twenty-year-old. Too much. She'd had her own money, her own plane, and her own publicist. When men wined her and dined her—and they *had* wined and dined her—the dates had made tabloid news.

Enter handsome Greek tycoon Nico. Being young, she'd had no intention of settling down so soon, but he'd swept her off her feet. Dazzled her completely with attention, affection, tender gifts and more. Within six months they'd been engaged. At twenty-three she'd had the fairytale wedding of her dreams.

Seven and a half months after her wedding she had discovered him in bed with another woman.

She'd stayed with him because he'd begged for another chance, promised to get counseling, vowed he'd change. But by their first anniversary he'd cheated again. And again. And again.

The divorce had been excruciating. Nico had demanded half her wealth and launched a public campaign to vilify her. She was selfish, shallow, self-absorbed—a spoiled little rich girl intent on controlling him and embarrassing him. She'd emasculated him by trying to control the purse strings. She'd refused to have conjugal relations.

By the time the settlement had been reached, she hadn't been able to stand herself. She wasn't any of the things Nico said, and yet the public believed what they were told—or maybe she'd begun to believe the horribly negative press, too. Because by the end, Grace detested her name, her fortune, and the very public character assassination.

Moving to England, she'd changed her name, enrolled in nursing school and become someone else—someone stable and solid and practical.

But now that same someone was back in Greece, and the two lives felt very close to colliding.

She should have never returned to Greece—not even under the auspices of caring for a wounded tycoon. She definitely shouldn't have taken a helicopter ride to a small Greek island. And she definitely, *definitely* shouldn't have agreed to stay in a thirteenth-century castle in the middle of a thunderstorm.

Exhausted, Elizabeth pivoted slowly in her room like a

jewelry box ballerina. Where had Kristian gone? Would she see him again tonight? Or was she on her own until morning?

As if on cue, the bedroom lights flickered once, twice, and then went out completely, leaving her in darkness.

At first Elizabeth did nothing other than move toward the bed and sit there, certain at any moment the power would come back on or one of the castle staff would appear at her room, flashlight, lantern or candle in hand. Neither happened. No power and no light. Minutes dragged by. Minutes that became longer.

Unable even to read her own watch, Elizabeth didn't know how much time had gone by, but she thought it had to have been nearly an hour. She was beyond bored, too. She was hungry, and if no one was coming to her assistance, then she would go to them.

Stumbling her way toward the door, she bumped into a trunk at the foot of the bed, a chair, a table—ouch—the wall, tapestry on the wall, and finally a door.

The hall was even darker than her room. Not a flicker of light anywhere, nor a sound.

A rational woman would return to her room and call it a night, but Elizabeth was too hungry—and a little too panicked—to be rational, and, taking a left from her room, began a slow, fearful walk down the hall, knowing there were stairs somewhere up ahead but not certain how far away, nor how steep the staircase. She couldn't even remember if there was one landing or two.

Just when she thought she'd found the stairs she heard a noise. And it wasn't the creak of stairs or a door opening, but something live, something breathing. Whimpering.

She stopped dead in her tracks. Her heart raced and, reaching for the wall, her hand shook, her skin icy and clammy.

There was something—someone—in the stairwell, something—someone—waiting.

She heard a heavy thump, and then silence. Ears, senses straining, she listened. It was breathing harder, heavier, and there was another thump, a muffled cry, not quite human, followed by a scratch against the wall.

Elizabeth couldn't take anymore. With one hand out, fingertips trailing the wall, she ran back down the hall toward her room—and yet as she ran she couldn't remember exactly where her room was, or where the door was located. She couldn't remember if there were many doors between her room and the stairs, or even if she'd left her bedroom door open or not.

The terror of not knowing where she was, of whatever was in the stairwell and what might happen next, made her nearly frantic. Her heart was racing, pounding as if it would burst, and she turned in desperate circles. Where was her room? Why had she even left it? And was that thing in the stairs coming toward her?

There was a thump behind her, and then suddenly something brushed her arm. She screamed. She couldn't help it. She was absolutely petrified.

"Elizabeth."

"Kristian." Her voice broke with terror and relief. "Help me. Help me, please."

And he was there, hauling her against him, pulling her into the circle of his arms, his body protecting her. "What is it? What's wrong?"

"There's something out there. There's something…" She could hardly get the words out. Her teeth began chattering and she shivered against him, pressed her face against his cheek, which was hard and broad and smelled even better than it felt. "Scary."

"It's your imagination," he said, his arm firmly around her waist, holding her close.

But the terror still seemed so real, and it was the darkness and her inability to see, to know what it was in the stairwell. If it was human, monster or animal. "There was something. But it's so dark—"

"Is it dark?"

"Yes!" She grabbed at his shirt with both hands. "The lights have been out for ages, and no one came, and they haven't come back on."

"It's the storm. It'll pass."

Her teeth still chattered. "It's too dark. I don't like it."

"Your room is right here," he said, his voice close to her ear. "Come, let's get you bundled up. I'm sure there's a blanket on the foot of the bed."

He led her into her room and found the blanket, draping it around her shoulders. "Better?" he asked.

She nodded, no longer freezing quite as much. "Yes."

"I should go, then."

"No." She reached out, caught his sleeve, and then slid her fingers down to his forearm, which was bare. His skin was warm and taut, covering dense muscle.

For a long silent minute Kristian didn't move, and then he reached out, touched her shoulder, her neck, up to her chin. His fingers ran lightly across her face, tracing her eyebrow, then moving down her nose and across her lips.

"You better send me away," he said gruffly.

She closed her eyes at the slow exploration of his fingertips, her skin hot and growing hotter beneath his touch. "I'll be scared."

"In the morning you'll regret letting me stay."

"Not if I get a good night's sleep."

He rubbed his fingers lightly across her lips, as if learning the curve and shape of her mouth. "If I stay, you won't be sleeping."

She shivered even as nerves twitched to life in her lower back, making her ache and tingle all over. "You shouldn't be so confident."

"Is that a challenge, *latrea mou?*"

He strummed her lower lip, and her mouth quivered. The heat in his skin was making her insides melt and her body crave his. Instinctively her lips parted, to touch and taste his skin.

She heard his quick intake when her tongue brushed his knuckle, and another intake when she slowly drew that knuckle into her mouth. Having his finger in her mouth was doing maddening things to her body, waking a strong physical need that had been slumbering far too long.

She sucked harder on his finger. And the harder she sucked the tighter her nipples peaked and her womb ached. She wanted relief, wanted to be taken, seized, plundered, sated.

"Is this really what you want?" he gritted from between clenched teeth, his deep voice rough with passion.

She didn't speak. Instead she reached toward him, placed her hand on his belt and slowly slid it down to cover his hard shaft.

Kristian groaned deep in his throat and roughly pulled her against him, holding her hips tight against his own. She could feel the surge of heat through his trousers, feel the fabric strain.

Control snapped. He covered her mouth with his and kissed her hard, kissed her fiercely. His lips were firm, demanding, and the pressure of his mouth parted her lips.

She shuddered against him, belly knotting, breasts aching, so that she pressed against him for desperate relief, wanting closer contact with his body, from his thighs to his lean hips to his powerful chest and shoulders. Pressed so closely, she could feel his erection against the apex of her thighs, and as exciting as it felt, it wasn't enough.

She needed him—more of him—more of everything with him. Touch, taste, pressure, skin. "Please," she whispered, circling his waist and slowly running her hands up his back. "Please stay with me."

"For how long?" he murmured, his head dropping to sweep excruciatingly light kisses across the side of her neck and up to the hollow beneath her ear. "Till midnight? Morning? Noon?"

The kisses were making it impossible to think. She pressed her thighs tight, the core of her hot and aching. Years since she'd made love, and now she felt as though she were coming apart here and now.

His mouth found hers again, and the kiss was teasing, light, and yet it made her frantic. She reached up to clasp his head, burying her fingers in his thick glossy hair. "Until as long as you want," she whispered breathlessly.

She'd given him the right answer with her words, and the kiss immediately deepened, his mouth slanting across hers, parting her lips again and drawing her tongue into his mouth. As he sucked on the tip of her tongue she felt her legs nearly buckle. He was stripping her control, seizing her senses, and she was helpless to stop him.

She'd given him a verbal surrender, she thought dizzily, but it wasn't enough. Now he wanted her to surrender her body.

CHAPTER TEN

KRISTIAN felt Elizabeth shiver against him, felt the curve of her hips, the indentation of her waist, the full softness of her breasts.

He'd discovered earlier she was wearing her hair pulled back, with wisps of hair against her face. Kissing her, he now followed one of the wisps to her ear, and he traced that before his fingers slid down the length of her neck.

He could feel her collarbone, and the hollow at her throat, and the thudding of her heart. Her skin was even softer than he remembered, and he found himself fantasizing about taking her hair down, pulling apart the plaits and letting her hair tumble past her shoulders and into his hands.

He wanted her hair, her face, her body in his hands. Wanted her bare and against him.

"Kristian," she said breathlessly, clasping his face in her hands.

Instantly he hardened all over again, his trousers too constricting to accommodate his erection. He wanted out of his clothes. He wanted her out of hers. *Now.*

Elizabeth shuddered as Kristian's hand caressed her hip, down her thigh, to find the hem of her velvet dress. As he lifted the hem she felt air against her bare leg, followed immediately by the heat of his hand.

She let out a slow breath of air, her eyes closing at the path his hand took. His fingers trailed up the outside of her thigh, across her hipbone to the triangle of curls between her legs.

Tensing, shivering, she wanted his touch and yet feared it, too. It had been so long since she'd been held, so long since she'd felt anything as intensely pleasurable as this, that she leaned even closer to him, pressing her breasts to his chest, her tummy to his torso, even as his fingers parted her cleft, finding the most delicate skin between. She was hot, and wet, and she pressed her forehead to his jaw as his fingers explored her.

She couldn't help the moan that escaped her lips, nor the trembling of her legs. She wanted him, needed him, and the intensity of her desire stunned her.

Flushed, dazed, Elizabeth pulled back, swayed on her feet. "The bed," she whispered breathlessly, tugging on his shirt. They walked together, reaching the bed in several steps.

As they bumped into the mattress Kristian impatiently stripped her dress over her head. "I want your hair down, too."

Reaching up, she unpinned her hair and pulled the elastics off the plaits. It was hard to pull her hair apart when Kristian was using her own body against her. With her arms up, over her head, he'd taken her breasts in his hands, cupping their fullness and teasing the tightly ruched nipples.

Gasping at the pressure and pleasure, she very nearly couldn't undo her hair. She hadn't worn a bra tonight due to the sheer lace at her bodice, and the feel of his hands on her bare skin was almost too much.

Hair loose, she reached for Kristian's belt, and then the button and zipper of his trousers. Freeing his shaft, she stroked him, amazed by his size all over again.

But Kristian was impatient to have her on the bed beneath him, and, nudging her backward, he sent her toppling down, legs still dangling over the mattress edge. With her knees parted he kissed her inner thigh, and then higher up, against her warm, moist core. He had a deft touch and tongue, and his expertise was almost more than she could bear. Suddenly shy, she wanted him to stop, but he circled her thighs with his arms, held her open for him.

The tip of his tongue flicked across her heated flesh before playing lightly yet insistently against her core. Again and again he stroked her with his tongue and lips, driving her mad with the tension building inside her. She panted as the pressure built, reached for Kristian, but he dodged her hands, and then, arching, hips bucking, she climaxed.

The orgasm was intense, overwhelming. She felt absolutely leveled. And when Kristian finally moved up, over her, she couldn't even speak. Instead she reached for his chest, slid her fingers across the dense muscle protecting his heart, up over his shoulder to pull him down on top of her.

His body was heavy, hard and strong. She welcomed the weight of him, the delicious feel of his body covering hers. Her orgasm had been intense, but what she really wanted—needed— was something more satisfying than just physical satisfaction. She craved him. The feeling of being taken, loved, sated by him.

He entered her slowly, harnessing his strength to ensure he didn't hurt her. Elizabeth held him tightly, awed by the sensation of him filling her. He felt so good against her, felt so good *in* her. She kissed his chest, the base of his throat, before he dipped his head, covering her mouth with his.

As he kissed her, he slowly thrust into her, stretching his body out over hers to withdraw and then thrust again. His chest grazed her breasts, skin and hair rubbing across her sensitive nipples. She squirmed with pleasure and he buried himself deeper inside her.

Elizabeth wrapped her legs around his waist as his hips moved against her. She squeezed her muscles, holding him inside, and the tantalizing friction of their bodies, the warm heated skin coupled with the deep impenetrable darkness, made their lovemaking even more mysterious and erotic.

As Kristian's tempo increased, his thrusts becoming harder, faster, she met each one eagerly, wanting him, as much of him as he would give her.

No one had ever made her feel so physical, so sexual, or so good. It felt natural being with him, and she gave herself over to Kristian, to his skill and passion, as he drove them both to a point of no return where muscles and nerves tightened and the mind shut out everything but wave after wave of pleasure in the most powerful orgasm of her life.

For those seconds she was not herself, not Grace Elizabeth, but bits of sky and stars and the night. She felt thrown from her body into something so much larger, so much more hopeful than her life. It wasn't sex, she thought, her body still shuddering around him, with him. It was possibility.

Afterwards, feeling dazed and nearly boneless, she clung to Kristian and drew a great gulp of air.

Amazing. That had been so amazing. He made her feel beautiful in every way, too. "I love you," she whispered, against his chest. "I do."

Kristian's hand was buried in her hair, fingers twining through the silken strands. His grip tightened, and then eased, and, dropping his head, he kissed her nose, her brow, her eyelid. "My darling English nurse. Overcome by passion."

"I'm not English," she answered with a supremely satisfied yawn, her body relaxing. "I'm American."

He rolled them over so that he was on the mattress and her weight now rested on him. "What?"

"An American."

"You're *American?*" he repeated incredulously, holding her firmly by the hips.

"Yes."

"Well, that explains a lot of things," he said with mock seriousness. "Especially your sensitivity. Americans are so thin-skinned. They take everything personally."

Her hair spilled over both of them, and she made a face at him in the dark. "I think you were the one who was very sensitive in the beginning. And you were attached to your pain meds—"

"Enough about my pain meds. So, tell me, your eyes... blue? Green? Brown?"

She felt a pang, realizing he might never really know what she looked like. She'd accepted it before, but now it seemed worse somehow. "They're blue. And I'm not that tall—just five-four."

"That's it? When you first arrived a couple weeks ago I was certain you were six feet. That you made Nurse Burly—"

"Hurly," she corrected with a muffled laugh.

"Nurse Hurly-Burly seem dainty."

Elizabeth had to stifle another giggle. "You're terrible, Kristian. You know that, don't you?"

"So you and a half-dozen other nurses keep telling me."

Grinning, she snuggled closer. "So you really had no clue that I was raised in New York?"

"None at all." He kissed the base of her throat, and then up by her ear. "So is that where home is?"

"Was. I've lived in London for years now. I'm happy there."

"Are you?"

"Well, I don't actually live in London. I work in Richmond, and my home is in Windsor. It's under an hour's train ride each way, and I like it. I read, take care of paperwork, sort out my day."

He was stroking her hair very slowly, leisurely, just listening to her talk. As she fell silent, he kissed her again. "My eye specialists are in London."

She wished she could see his face. "Are you thinking of scheduling the eye surgery?"

"Toying with the idea."

"Seriously toying…?"

"Yes. Do you think I should try?"

She considered her words carefully before answering. "You're the one that has to live with the consequences," she said, remembering what Pano had said—that Kristian needed to have something to hope for, something to keep him going.

"But maybe it's better to just know." He exhaled heavily, sounding as if the weight of the world rested on his shoulders. "Maybe I should just do it and get it over with."

Elizabeth put her hand to his chest, felt his heart beating against her hand. "The odds…they're not very good, are they?"

"Less than five percent," he answered, his voice devoid of emotion.

Not good odds, she thought, swallowing hard. "You're doing so well right now. You're making such good progress. If the surgery doesn't turn out as you hoped, could you cope with the results?"

He didn't immediately answer. "I don't know," he said at last. "I don't know how I'd feel. But I know this. I miss seeing. I miss my sight."

"I'm sure you do."

"And I'd love to get rid of the cane. I don't like announcing to the world that I can't see. Besides, I'm sure I look foolish, tapping my way around—"

"That's a ridiculous thing to say!" She pulled away, sat up cross-legged. "First of all, the cane doesn't look foolish, and secondly, it's not about appearances, either. Life and love shouldn't be based on looks. It's about kindness, courage, humility, strength." She paused, drew an unsteady breath. "And you have all those qualities in abundance."

With that, power restored, the lights suddenly flickered and came on.

Elizabeth looked down at them, aware that Kristian couldn't see what she could see and that she should have been embarrassed. They were both naked, he stretched out on his back, she sitting cross-legged, with his hand resting on her bare thigh. But instead of being uncomfortable she felt a little thrill. She felt so right with him. She felt like his—body and soul.

"The power's back," she said, gazing at Kristian, soaking up his dark erotic beauty. His black hair, the strong classic features, impossibly long eyelashes and that sensual mouth of his. "We have lights again."

"Am I missing anything?" he drawled lazily, reaching for her and pulling her back on top of him.

As she straddled his hips he caressed the underside of her breast, so that her nipple hardened and peaked. The touch of his hand against her breast was sending sharp darts of feeling throughout her body, making her insides heat, and clench, and begin to crave relief from his body again.

"No," she murmured, eyes closing, lips helplessly parting as he tugged her lower, allowing him to take her nipple into his mouth. His mouth felt hot and wet against the nipple, and she gripped his shoulders as he sucked, unable to stifle her whimper.

Her whimper aroused him further. Elizabeth could feel him grow hard beneath her. And all she could think was that she wanted him—again. Wanted him to take her—hard, fast—take her until she screamed with pleasure.

He must have been thinking the same thing, too, because,

shifting, he lifted her up, positioned her over him and thrust in. She groaned and shivered as he used his hands to help her ride him. She'd tried this position years ago and hadn't liked it, as she hadn't felt anything much but foolish, and yet now the positions and their bodies clicked. Elizabeth's cheeks burned hot, and her skin glowed as they made love again.

She came faster than before, in a cry of fierce pleasure, before collapsing onto his chest, utterly spent.

Her heart hammering, her body damp, she could do nothing but rest and try to catch her breath. "It just keeps getting better," she whispered.

He stroked her hair, and then the length of her back, until his hand rested on her bottom. "I think I've met my match," he said.

She pushed up on her elbow to see his face. "What does that mean?"

He cupped her breast, stroked the puckered aureola with his thumb. "I think you enjoy sex as much as I do."

"With you. You're incredible."

"It takes two to make it incredible." Reaching up, he pulled her head down to his and kissed her deeply, his tongue teasing hers in another sensual seduction.

In the middle of the kiss, her stomach suddenly growled. Elizabeth giggled apologetically against his mouth. "Sorry. Hungry."

"Then let's find our dinner. I'm starving, too."

They dressed in what they'd left strewn about the floor earlier. Elizabeth bent to retrieve their clothes before handing Kristian first his pants and then his shirt. Slipping on her dress, she struggled to comb her hair smooth with her fingers.

"I feel like I'm in high school," she said with a laugh. And then, and only then, it hit her—Cosima.

"My God," she whispered under her breath, blood draining, her body going icy cold. What had she done? What had she just done?

"Elizabeth?"

She pressed her hand to her mouth, stared at him as he struggled to rebutton his shirt. He'd got it wrong.

"What's the matter?" he demanded.

She could only look at him aghast, shocked, sickened.

She'd behaved badly. *Badly*. He wasn't hers. He'd never been hers. All along he'd belonged to another woman….

"Elizabeth?" Kristian's voice crackled with anger. "Are you still here? Or have you left? Talk to me."

He was right. He couldn't see. Couldn't read her face to know what she was thinking or feeling. "What did we just do, Kristian?" *What did I do?*

His hands stilled, the final button forgotten. A look of confusion crossed his features. "You already have…regrets?"

Regrets? She nearly cried. Only because he wasn't hers.

"Do you have someone waiting for you in London?" he asked, his voice suddenly growing stern, his expression hardening, taking on the glacier stillness she realized he used to keep the world at bay.

"No."

"But there is a relationship?"

"No."

Even without sight he seemed to know exactly where he was, he crossed to her, swiftly closing the distance between them. He took her by the shoulders.

She stiffened, fearing his anger, but then he slid his arms around her, held her securely against him. He kissed her cheek, and then her ear, and then nipped playfully at a particularly sensitive nerve in her neck. "What's wrong, *latrea mou?* Why the second thoughts?"

She splayed her fingers against his chest. Her heart thudded ridiculously hard. "As much as I care about you, Kristian, I cannot do this. It was wrong. *Is* wrong. Just a terrible mistake."

His arms fell away. He stepped back. "Is it because of my eyes? Because I can't see and you pity me?"

"No."

"It's something, *latrea mou*. Because one moment you are in my arms and it feels good, it feels calm and real, like a taste of happiness, and now you say it was…terrible." He drew a breath. "A *mistake*." The bitterness in his voice carved her heart in two. "I think I don't know you at all."

Eyes filling with tears, she watched him take another step backward, and then another. "Kristian." She whispered his name. "No, it's not that. Not the way you make it sound. I loved being with you. I wanted to be near you—"

"Then *what?* Is this about Cosima again? Because, God forgive me, but I can't get away from her. Every time I turn around there she is…even in my goddamn bedroom!"

"Kristian."

"*No,* No. None of that *I'm so disappointed in you* garbage. I've had it. I'm sick of it. What is it with you and Cosima? Is it the contract? The fact that she paid you money? Because if it's money, tell me the amount and I'll cut her a check."

"It's not the money. It's…you. You and her."

He laughed, but the sound grated on her ears. "*Cosima?* Cosima—the Devil Incarnate?"

"You're not a couple?"

"A couple? You're out of your mind, *latrea mou*. She's the reason I couldn't get out of bed, couldn't make myself walk, couldn't face life. Why would I ever want to be with a woman who'd been with my brother?"

Her jaw dropped. Her mouth dried. "Your…*brother?*"

Kristian had gone ashen, and the scar on his cheek tightened. "She was Andreas's fiancée. He's dead because she's alive. He's dead because I went to her aid first. I rescued her for him."

Elizabeth shook her head. Her mouth opened, shut. Of course. *Of course.*

Still shaking her head, she replayed her conversations with Cosima over again. Cosima had never said directly that she was in love with Kristian. She said she'd cared deeply for him, and wanted to see him back in Athens, but she never had said that there was more than that. Just that she hoped…

Hoped.

That was all. That was it.

"So, do you still have to go to Paris on Monday? Or was that just an excuse?" Kristian asked tersely, his features so hard they looked chiseled from granite.

"I still have to go," she answered in a low voice.

"And you still have regrets?"

"Kristian—"

"You do, don't you?"

"Kristian, it's not that simple. Not black and white like that."

"So what *is* it like?" Each word sounded like sharp steel coming from his mouth.

"I…" She closed her eyes, tried to imagine how to tell him who she'd been married to, how she'd been vilified, how she'd transformed herself to escape. But no explanation came. The old pain went too deep. The identities were too confusing. Grace Elizabeth Stiles had been beautiful and wealthy, glamorous and privileged, but she'd also been naïve and dependent, too trusting and too easily hurt.

"You *what?*" he demanded, not about to let her off the hook so easily.

"I can't stay in Greece," she whispered. "I can't."

"Is this all because of that Greek *ornio* you met on your holiday?"

"It was more serious than that."

He stilled. "How serious?"

"I married him."

For a long moment he said nothing, and then his lips pulled and his teeth flashed savagely. "So this is how it is."

She took a step toward him. "What does that mean?"

"It means I'm not a man to you. Not one you can trust or respect—"

"That's not true."

"It *is* true." His shoulders tensed. "We spent two weeks together—morning, noon and night. Why didn't you tell me you were married before? Why did you let me believe it was a simple holiday romance, a little Greek fling gone bad?"

"Because I…I…just don't talk about it."

"Why?"

"Because it hurt me. Badly." Her voice raised, tears started to her eyes. "It made me afraid."

"Just like swimming in the deep end of the pool?"

She bit her bottom lip. He sounded so disgusted, she thought. So irritated and impatient.

"You don't trust me," he added, his tone increasingly cold. "And you don't know me if you think I'd make love to one woman while involved with another."

Her heart sank. He was angry—blisteringly angry.

"What kind of man do you think I am?" he thundered. "How immoral and despicable am I?"

"You're not—"

"You thought I was engaged to Cosima."

"I didn't want to think so."

"But you did," he shot back.

"Kristian, please don't. Please don't judge me—"

"Why not? You judged me."

Tears tumbled. "I love you," she whispered.

He shrugged brusquely. "You don't know the meaning of love if you'd go to bed with a man supposedly engaged to another woman."

Elizabeth felt her heart seize up. This couldn't be happening like this, could it? They couldn't be making such a wretched mess of things, could they? "Kristian, I can't explain it, can't find the words right now, but you must know how I feel—how I really feel. You must know why I'm here, and why I even stayed this long."

"The money, maybe?" he mocked savagely, opening the door wider.

"*No.* And there is no money, I'm not taking her money—"

"Conveniently said."

He didn't know. He didn't see. And maybe that was it. He couldn't see how much she loved him, and how much she believed in him, and how she would have done anything, just about anything, to help him. Love him. Make him happy. "Please," she begged, reaching for him.

But there was no reaching him. Not when he put up that wall of his, that huge, thick, impenetrable ice wall of his, that shut him off from everyone else. Instead he shrugged her off and walked down the hall toward the distant stairwell.

His rejection cut deeply. For a moment she could do nothing but watch him walk away, and then she couldn't just let him go—not like that, not over something that was so small.

A misunderstanding.

Pride.

Ego.

None of it was important enough to keep them apart. None

of it mattered if they truly cared for each other. She loved him, and from the way he'd held her, made love to her, she knew he had to have feelings for her—knew there was more to this than just hormones. For Pete's sake, neither of them were teenagers, and both of them had been through enough to know what mattered.

What mattered was loving, and being loved.

What mattered was having someone on your side. Someone who'd stick with you no matter what.

And so she left the safety of her door, the safety of pride and ego, and followed him to the stairs. She was still wiping away tears, but she knew this—she wasn't going to be dismissed, wasn't going to let him get rid of her like that.

She chased after him, trailing down the staircase. Turning the corner of one landing, she started down the next flight of stairs even as a door opened and footsteps crossed the hall below.

"Kristian!" A man said, his voice disturbingly familiar. "We were just told you'd arrived. What a surprise. Welcome home!"

Nico?

Elizabeth froze. Even her heart seemed to still.

"What are *you* doing here?" Kristian asked, his voice taut, low.

"We—my girlfriend and I—live here part-time," Nico answered. "Didn't you know we'd taken a suite? I was sure you'd been told. At least, I know Pano was aware of it. I talked to him on the phone the other day."

"I've been busy," Kristian murmured distractedly.

Legs shaking, Elizabeth shifted her weight and the floorboard squeaked. All heads down below turned to look up at her.

Elizabeth grabbed the banister. This couldn't be happening. Couldn't be.

Nico, catching sight of her, was equally shocked. Staring up at Elizabeth, he laughed incredulously. "Grace?"

Elizabeth could only stare back.

Nico glanced at Kristian, and then back to his ex-wife. "What's going on?" he asked.

"I don't know," Kristian answered tightly. "You tell me."

"I don't know either," Nico said, frowning at Elizabeth. "But for a moment I thought you and Grace were...together."

"Grace who?" Kristian demanded tersely.

"Stile. My American wife."

Kristian went rigid. "There's no Grace here."

"Yes, there she is," Nico answered. "She's standing on the landing. Blonde hair. Black lace dress."

Elizabeth felt Kristian's confusion as he swung around, staring blindly up at the stairwell. Her heart contracted. "Kristian," she said softly, hating his confusion, hating that she was the source of it, too.

"That's not Grace," Kristian retorted grimly. "That's Elizabeth. Elizabeth Hatchet. My nurse."

"Nurse?" Nico laughed. "Oh, dear, Koumantaros, it looks like she's duped you. Because your Elizabeth is my ex-wife, Grace Stile. And a nasty gold-digger, too."

CHAPTER ELEVEN

KRISTIAN felt as though he'd been punched hard in the gut. He couldn't breathe, couldn't move, could only stand there, struggling to take in air.

Elizabeth wasn't Elizabeth? Elizabeth was really Grace Stile?

He tried to shake his head, tried to clear the fuzz and storm clouding his mind.

The woman he'd fallen in love with wasn't even who he thought she was. Her name wasn't even Elizabeth. Maybe she wasn't even a nurse.

Maybe she was a gold-digger, just like Nico said.

Gold-digger. The word rang in Elizabeth's head.

Shocked, she went hot, and then cold, and hot again. "I'm no gold-digger," she choked, finally finding her voice. Legs wobbling, she took one step and then another until she'd reached the hall. "*You* are," she choked. "You, you… you're…" But she couldn't get the words out, couldn't defend herself, could scarcely breathe, much less think.

Nico had betrayed *her.*

Nico had married *her* for her money.

Nico had poisoned the Greek media and public against her.

Stomach roiling, she was swept back into that short brutal marriage and the months following their divorce.

He'd made her life a living hell and she'd been the one to pay—and pay, and pay. Not just for the divorce, and not just his settlement, but emotionally, physically, mentally. It had taken years to heal, years to stop being so hurt and so insecure and so angry. *Angry.*

And she had been angry because she'd felt cheated of love, cheated of the home and the family and the dreams she'd cherished. They were supposed to have been husband and wife. A couple, partners.

But she'd only been money, cash, the fortune to supplement Nico's dwindling inheritance.

Nico, though, wasn't paying her the least bit of attention. He was still talking to Kristian, a smirk on his face—a face she'd once thought so handsome. She didn't find him attractive anymore, not even if she was being objective, because, next to Kristian, Nico's good-looks faded to merely boyish, almost pretty, whereas Kristian was fiercely rugged, all man.

"She'll seduce you," Nico continued, rolling back on his heels, his arms crossed over his chest. "And make you think it was your idea. And when she has you in bed she'll tell you she loves you. She'll make you think it's love, but it's greed. She'll take you for everything you're worth—"

"That's enough. I've heard enough," Kristian ground out, silencing Nico's ruthless character assassination. He'd paled, so that the scar seemed to jump from his cheekbone, a livid reminder of the tragedy that had taken so much from him over a year ago.

"None of it is true," Elizabeth choked, her body shaking, legs like jelly. "Nothing he says—"

"I said, *enough.*" Kristian turned away and walked down the hall.

Elizabeth felt the air leave her, her chest so empty her heart seized.

Somehow she found her way back to her room and stumbled into bed, where she lay stiff as a board, unable to sleep or cry.

Everything seemed just so unbelievably bad—so awful that it couldn't even be assimilated.

Lying there, teeth chattering with shock and cold, Elizabeth prayed that when the sun finally rose in the morning all of this would be just a bad, bad dream.

It wasn't.

The next morning a maid knocked on Elizabeth's door, giving her the message that a car was ready to drive her to meet the helicopter.

Washing her face, Elizabeth avoided looking at herself in the mirror before smoothing the wrinkles in her velvet dress and heading downstairs, where the butler ushered her to the waiting car.

Elizabeth had been under the impression that she'd be traveling back alone, but Kristian was already in the car when she climbed in.

"Good morning," she whispered, sliding onto the seat but being careful to keep as much distance between them as she could.

His head barely inclined.

She ducked her head, stared at her fingers, which were laced and locked in her lap. Sick, she thought, so sick. She felt as though everything good and warm and hopeful inside her had vanished, left, gone. Died.

Eyes closing, she held her breath, her teeth sinking into her lower lip.

She only let her breath out once the car started moving, leaving the castle for the helicopter pad on the other side of town.

"You were Nico's wife," Kristian said shortly, his deep rough voice splitting the car's silence in two. There was a brutality in his voice she'd never heard before. A violence that spoke of revenge and embittered passion.

Opening her eyes, she looked at Kristian, but she couldn't read anything in his face—not when his fiercely handsome features were so frozen, fixed in hard, remote, unforgiving lines. It was as if his face wasn't a face but a mask.

The car seemed to spin.

She didn't answer, didn't want to answer, didn't know *how* to answer—because in his present frame of mind nothing she said would help, nothing she said would matter. After all, Kristian Koumantaros was a Greek man. It wouldn't matter to him that she was divorced—had been divorced for years. In his mind she'd always be Nico's wife.

Elizabeth glanced down at her hands again, the knuckles white. She was so dizzy she didn't think she could sit straight, but finally she forced her head up, forced the world's wild revolutions to slow until she could see Kristian on the seat next to her, his blue eyes brilliant, piercing, despite the fact that she knew he couldn't see.

"I'm waiting," he said flatly, finality and closure in his rough voice.

Tears filling her eyes, she drew another deep breath. "Yes," she said, her voice so faint it sounded like nothing.

"So your name isn't really Elizabeth, is it?"

Again she couldn't speak. The pain inside her chest was excruciating. She could only stare at Kristian, wishing everything had somehow turned out differently. If Nico hadn't been one of the castle's tenants. If Cosima hadn't stood between them. If Elizabeth had understood just who and what Cosima really was...

"I'm still waiting," Kristian said.

Hurt and pain flared, lighting bits of fire inside her. "Waiting for what?" she demanded, shoulders twisted so she could better see him. "For some big confession? Well, I'm not going to confess. I've done nothing wrong—"

"You've done *everything* wrong," he interrupted through gritted teeth. "Everything. If your name isn't really Elizabeth Hatchet."

Colder and colder, she swallowed, her eyes growing wide, her stomach plummeting.

"If Nico was your husband, that makes you someone I do not know."

Elizabeth exhaled so hard it hurt, her chest spasming, her throat squeezing closed.

When she didn't answer, he leaned toward her, touched the side of her head, then her ear and finally her cheekbones, her eyes, her nose, her mouth. "You are Grace Stile, aren't you?"

"Was," she barely whispered. "I was Grace Stile. But Grace Stile doesn't exist anymore."

"Grace Stile was a beautiful woman," he said mockingly, his fingertips lingering on the fullness of her soft mouth.

She trembled inwardly at the touch. "I am not her," she said against his fingers. Last night he'd made her feel so good, so warm, so safe. *Happy.* But today...today it was something altogether different.

He ground out a mocking laugh. "Grace Stile, daughter of an American icon—"

"No."

"New York's most beautiful and accomplished debutante."

"Not me."

"Even more wealthy than the Greek tycoon she married."
Elizabeth stopped talking.

"Your father, Rupert Stile—"

She pulled her head away, leaned back in her seat to
remove herself from his touch. "Grace Stile is gone," she said
crisply. "I am Elizabeth Hatchet, a nursing administrator, and
that is all that is important, all that needs to be known."

He barked a laugh, far from amused. "But your legal name
isn't even Elizabeth Hatchet."

She hesitated, bit savagely into her lower lip, knowing
she'd never given anyone this information—not since that
fateful day when everything had changed. "Hatchet was my
mother's maiden name. Legally I'm Grace Elizabeth."

He laughed again, the sound even more strained and incredulous. "Are you even a registered nurse?"

"Of course!"

"Of course," he repeated, shaking his head and running a hand
across his jaw, which was dark with a day's growth of beard.

For a moment neither spoke, and the only sound was
Kristian's palm, rubbing the rough bristles on his chin and jaw.

"You think you know someone," he said, after a tense
minute. "You think you know what's true, what's real, and
then you find out you know nothing at all."

"But you do know I am a nurse," she said steadfastly. "And
I hold a Masters Degree in Business Administration."

"But I don't know that. I can't see. You could be just
anybody…and it turns out you are!"

"Kristian—"

"Because if I weren't blind you couldn't have pulled this off,
could you? If I could see I would have recognized you. I would
have known you weren't some dreary, dumpy little nursing administrator, but the famously beautiful heiress Grace Stile."

"That never crossed my mind—"

"No? Are you sure?"

"Yes."

He made a rough, derogatory sound. His mouth slanted, cheekbones pronounced. The car had stopped. They were at the small airport, and not far from their car waited the helicopter and pilot. As the driver of the car turned off the ignition, Kristian laid a hand on Elizabeth's thigh.

"Your degrees," he said. "Those are in which name?"

She felt the heat of his hand sear her skin even as it melted her on the inside. She cared for him, loved him, but couldn't seem to connect anything that was happening today with what had taken place in her bed last night.

"My degrees," she said softly, referring to her nursing degree and then the degree in Business Administration, "were both earned in England, as Elizabeth Hatchet."

"Very clever of you," he taunted, as the passenger door opened and the driver stood there, ready to provide assistance.

Elizabeth suppressed a wave of panic. It was all coming to an end, so quickly and so badly, and she couldn't figure out how to turn the tide now that it was rushing at her, fierce and relentless.

"Kristian," she said urgently, touching his hand, her fingers attempting to slide around his. But he held his fingers stiff, and aloof, as though they'd never been close. "There was nothing clever about it. I moved to England and changed my name, out of desperation. I didn't want to be Grace Stile anymore. I wanted to start over. I *needed* to start over. And so I did."

He didn't speak again. Not even after they were in the helicopter heading for Athens, where he'd told her a plane awaited. He was sending her home immediately. Her bags were already at Athens airport. She'd be back in London by mid-afternoon.

It was a strangely silent flight, and it wasn't until they were on the ground in Athens, exiting the helicopter, that he broke the painful stillness.

"Why medicine?" he demanded.

Kristian's question stopped her just as she was about to climb the private jet's stairs.

Slowly she turned to face him, tucking a strand of hair behind her ear even as she marveled all over again at the changes two weeks had made. Kristian Koumantaros was every inch the formidable tycoon he'd been before he was injured. He wasn't just walking, he stood tall, legs spread, powerful shoulders braced.

"You didn't study medicine at Smith or Brown or wherever you went in the States," he continued, naming universities on the East Coast. "You were interested in antiquities then."

Antiquities, she thought, her teeth pressed to the inside of her lower lip. She and her love of ancient cultures. Wasn't that how she'd met Nico in the first place? Attending a party at a prestigious New York museum to celebrate the opening of a new, priceless Greek exhibit?

"Medicine's more practical," she answered, eyes gritty, stinging with tears she wouldn't let herself cry.

And, thinking back to her move across the Atlantic, to her new identity and her new choices, she knew she'd been compelled to become someone different, someone better…more altruistic.

"Medicine is also about helping others—doing something good."

"Versus exploiting their weaknesses?"

"I've never done that!" she protested hotly.

"No?"

"No." But she could see from his expression that he didn't

believe her. She opened her mouth to defend herself yet again, before stopping. It didn't matter, she thought wearily, pushing another strand of hair back from her face. He would think what he wanted to think.

And, fine, let him.

She cared about him—hugely, tremendously—but she was tired of being the bad person, was unwilling to be vilified any longer. She'd never been a bad woman, a bad person. Maybe at twenty-three, or twenty-four she hadn't known better than to accept the blame, but she did now. She was a woman, not a punching bag.

"Goodbye," she said *"Kali tihi."* Good luck.

"Good luck?" he repeated. "With what?" he snapped, taking a threatening step toward her.

His reaction puzzled her. But he'd always puzzled her. "With everything," she answered, just wanting to go now, needing to make the break. She knew this could go nowhere. Last night she should have realized that nothing good would come out of an inappropriate liaison, but last night she hadn't been thinking. Last night she'd been frightened and uncertain, and she'd turned to him for comfort, turned to him for reassurance. It was the worst thing she could have done.

And yet Kristian still marched toward her, his expression black. "And just what is *everything?*"

She thought of all he had still waiting for him. He could have such a good life, such a rich, interesting life—sight or no sight—if he wanted.

Her lips curved in a faint, bittersweet smile. "Your life," she said simply. "It's all still before you."

And quickly, before he could detain her, she climbed the stairs, disappearing into the jet's cool, elegant interior where she settled into one of the leather chairs in the main cabin.

Except for the flight crew, the plane was empty.

Elizabeth fastened her seatbelt and settled back in the club chair. She knew it would be a very quiet trip home.

Back in London, Elizabeth rather rejoiced in the staggering number of cases piled high on her desk. She welcomed the billing issues, the cranky patients, the nurses needing vacations and personal days off, as every extra hour of work meant another hour she couldn't think about Kristian, or Greece, or the chaotic two weeks spent there.

Because now that she was back in England, taking the train to work at her office in Richmond every day, she couldn't fathom what had happened.

Couldn't fathom how it had happened.

Couldn't fathom why.

She wasn't interested in men, or dating, or having another lover. She wasn't interested in having a family, either. All she wanted was to work, to pay her bills, to keep her company running as smoothly as possible. Her business was her professional life, social life and personal life all rolled into one, and it suited her just fine.

Far better to be Plain Jane than Glamorous Grace Stile, with the world at her feet, because the whole world-at-your-feet thing was just an illusion anyway. As she'd learned the hard way, the more people thought you had, the more they envied you, and then resented you, and eventually they lobbied to see you fall.

Far better to live simply and quietly and mind your own business, she thought, shuffling papers into her briefcase.

She was leaving work early again today, tormented by a stomach bug that wouldn't go away. She'd been back home in England just over two months now, but she hadn't felt like herself for ages. Since Greece, as a matter of fact.

Her secretary glanced up as Elizabeth opened the office door.

"Still under the weather, Ms. Hatchet?" Mrs. Shipley asked sympathetically, pushing her reading glasses up on her head.

Mrs. Shipley had practically run the office single-handedly while Elizabeth was gone, and she couldn't imagine a better administrative assistant.

"I am," Elizabeth answered with a grimace, as her insides did another sickly, queasy rise and fall that made her want to throw up into the nearest rubbish bin. But of course she never had the pleasure of actually throwing up. She wasn't lucky enough to get the thing—whatever it was—out of her system.

"If you picked up a parasite in Greece, you'll need a good antibiotic, my dear. I know I'm sounding like a broken record, but you really should see a doctor. Get something for that. The right antibiotic will nip it in the bud. And you need it nipped in the bud, as you look downright peaky."

Mrs. Shipley was right. Elizabeth felt absolutely wretched. She ached. Her head throbbed. Her stomach alternated between nausea and cramps. Even her sleep was disturbed, colored with weird, wild dreams of doom and gloom.

But what she feared most, and refused to confront, was the very real possibility that it wasn't a parasite she'd picked up but something more permanent. Something more changing.

Something far more serious.

Like Kristian Koumantaros's baby.

She'd been home just over two months now and she hadn't had her period—which wasn't altogether unusual, since she was the least regular woman she knew—but she couldn't bring herself to actually take a pregnancy test.

If she wasn't pregnant—fantastic.

If she was…

If she was?

The next morning her nausea was so severe she huddled next to the toilet, managing nothing more than wrenching dry heaves.

Her head was spinning and she was gagging, and all she could think was, What if I really am pregnant with Kristian Koumantaros's baby?

Kristian Koumantaros was one of the most wealthy, powerful, successful men in Europe. He lived in ancient monasteries and castles and villas all over the world. He traveled by helicopter, private jet, luxury yacht. He negotiated with no one.

And she knew he wouldn't negotiate with her. If he knew she was pregnant he'd step in, take over, take action.

And, yes, Kristian *ought* to know. But how would he benefit from knowing? Would the baby—if there really was a baby—benefit?

Would *she?*

No. Not when Kristian viewed her as a heartless mercenary, a gold-digger, someone who preyed upon other's weaknesses.

Elizabeth somehow managed to drag herself into work, drag listlessly through the day, and then caught the train home to Windsor.

Sitting on the train seat, thirty minutes away from her stop, it hit her for the first time. She was pregnant. She knew deep down she was going to have a baby.

But Kristian. What about Kristian?

A wave of ice flooded her. What would he say, much less do, if he knew about the baby? He didn't even like her. He despised her. How would he react if he knew she carried his child?

Panic flooded her—panic that made her feel even colder and more afraid.

She couldn't let him find out. She wouldn't let him find out.

Stop it, she silently chastised herself as her panic grew. It's not as though you'll bump into him.

You live on opposite ends of the continent. You're both on islands separated by seas. No way to accidentally meet.

As heartless as it sounded, she'd make sure they wouldn't meet, either.

He'd take the baby. She knew he'd take the baby from her. Just the way Nico had taken everything from her.

Greek men were proud, and fierce. Greek men, particularly Greek tycoons, thought they were above rules and laws. And Kristian Koumantaros, now that he was nearly recovered, would be no different.

Elizabeth's nausea increased, and she stirred restlessly in her seat, anxious to be home, where she could take a long bath, climb into bed and just relax.

She needed to relax. Her heart was pounding far too hard.

Trying to distract herself, she glanced around the train cabin, studying the different commuters, before glancing at the man next to her reading a newspaper. His face was hidden by the back of the paper and her gaze fell on the headlines. Nothing looked particularly interesting until she read, *Koumantaros in London for Treatment.*

Koumantaros.

Kristian Koumantaros?

Breath catching, she leaned forward to better see the article. She only got the first line or two before the man rudely shuffled the pages and turned his back to her preventing her from reading more.

But Elizabeth didn't need to read much more than those first two lines to get the gist of the article.

Kristian had undergone the risky eye surgery at Moorfield's Hospital in London today.

CHAPTER TWELVE

WALKING from the train station to her little house, Elizabeth felt her nerves started getting the best of her. For the past three years she'd made historic Windsor her home, having found it the perfect antidote to the stresses of her career, but today the walk filled her with apprehension.

Something felt wrong. And it wasn't just thinking about the baby. It was an uneasy sixth sense that things around her weren't right.

Picking up her pace, she tried to silence her fears, telling herself she was tired and overly imaginative.

No one was watching her.

No one was following her.

And nothing bad was going to happen.

But tugging the collar of her coat up, and crossing her arms over her chest to keep warm, she couldn't help thinking that something felt bad. And the bad feeling was growing stronger as she left the road and hurried up the crushed gravel path toward her house.

Windsor provided plenty of diversion on weekends, with brilliant shopping as well as the gorgeous castle and the riverside walks, but as she entered her house and closed the door behind her, her quiet little house on its quiet little lane seemed very isolated.

If someone had followed her home, no one would see.

If someone broke into her house, no one would hear her cries for help.

Elizabeth locked the front door, then went through the kitchen to the back door, checking the lock on that before finally taking her coat off and turning the heat up.

In the kitchen she put on the kettle for tea, and was just about to make some toast when a knock sounded on her door.

She froze, the loaf of bread still in her hands, and stood still so long that the knock sounded again.

Putting the bread on the counter, and the knife down, she headed for the door, checking through a window first before she actually opened it.

A new model Jaguar was parked out front, and a man stood on her doorstep, his back to her as he faced the car. But she knew the man—knew his height, the breadth of his shoulders, the length of his legs, the shape of his head.

Kristian.

Kristian here.

But today was his surgery…he was supposed to have had surgery…the paper had said…

Unless he'd backed out.

But he wouldn't back out, would he?

Heart hammering, she undid the lock and opened the door, and the sound of the lock turning caught his attention. Kristian shifted, turning toward her. But as he faced her his eyes never blinked, and his expression remained impassive.

"Kristian," she whispered, cold all over again.

"Cratchett," he answered soberly.

And looking up into his face, a face so sculpturally perfect, the striking features contrasted by black hair and blue eyes, she thought him a beautiful but fearsome angel. One sent to judge her, punish her.

Glancing past him to the car, the sleek black Jaguar with tinted windows, she wondered how many cars he had scattered all over the world.

"You're…here," she said foolishly, her mind so strangely blank that nothing came to her—nothing but shock and fear. He couldn't know. He didn't know. She'd only found out today herself.

"Yes, I am." His head tipped and he looked at her directly, but still without recognition. She felt her heart turn over with sympathy for him. He hadn't gone through with the surgery. He must have had second thoughts. And while she didn't blame him—it was a very new, very dangerous procedure— it just reaffirmed all over again her determination to keep the pregnancy a secret…at least for now.

"How did you know I lived here?"

"I had your address," he said blandly.

"Oh. I see." But she didn't see. Her home address was on nothing—although she supposed if a man like Kristian Koumantaros wanted to know where she lived it wouldn't take much effort on his part to find out. He had money, and connections. People would tell him things, particularly private detectives—not that he'd do that…

Or would he?

Frowning, bewildered, she stared up at him, still trying to figure out what he was doing here in Windsor—on her doorstep, no less.

From the kitchen, her kettle began to whistle.

His head lifted, his black brows pulling.

"The kettle," she said, by way of explanation. "I was just

making tea. I should turn it off." And without waiting for him to answer she went to the kitchen and unplugged the kettle, only to turn around and discover Kristian right there behind her, making her small, old-fashioned kitchen, with its porcelain farm sink and simple farmhouse table, look tired and primitive.

"Oh," she said, taking a nervous step back. "You're here."

The corner of his mouth twisted. "I appear to be every-where today."

"Yes." She pressed her skirt smooth, her hands uncomfort-ably damp. How had he made his way into the kitchen so quickly? It was almost as if he knew his way already—or as if he could actually see…

Could he?

Her pulse quickened, her nerves strung so tight she felt dis-turbingly close to falling apart. It had been such an over-whelming day as it was. First her certainty about the baby, and now Kristian in her house.

"Have you been in England long?" she asked softly, trying to figure out just what was going on.

"I've spent part of the last month here."

A month in England. Her heart jumped a little, and she had to exhale slowly to try to calm herself. "I didn't know."

One of his black eyebrows lifted, but he said nothing else. At least some things hadn't changed, she thought. He was still as uncommunicative as ever. But that didn't mean she had to play his game.

"The surgery—it was scheduled for today, wasn't it?" she asked awkwardly.

"Why?"

"I read it in the paper…actually, it was on the train home. You were supposed to have the treatment done today in London."

"Really?"

She felt increasingly puzzled. "It's what the paper said," she repeated defensively."

"I see." He smiled benignly. And the conversation staggered to a stop there.

Uncertainly, she turned to pour her tea.

Good manners required her to ask if he'd like a cup, but the last thing she wanted to do was prolong this miserable visit.

She wrestled with her conscience. Good manners won. "Would you like some tea?" she asked, voice stilted.

White teeth flashed in a mocking smile. "I thought you'd never ask."

Hands shaking, she retrieved another cup and saucer from the cupboard before filling his cup.

He couldn't see…could he?

He couldn't possibly see…

But something inside her, that same peculiar sixth sense from earlier, made her suspicious.

"Toast?" Her voice quavered. She hated that. She hated that suddenly everything felt so wildly out of control.

"No, thank you."

Glancing at him, she put the bread away, too nervous now to eat.

"You're not going to eat?" he asked mildly.

"No."

"You're not hungry?"

Her stomach did another uncomfortable freefall. How did he know she wasn't going to eat?

"The surgery," she said. "You didn't have it today."

"No." He paused for the briefest moment. "I had it a month ago."

Her legs nearly went from beneath her. Elizabeth put a

hand out to the kitchen table to support herself. "A month ago?" she whispered, her gaze riveted to his face.

"Mmmm."

He wasn't helping at all, was he? She swallowed around the huge lump filling her throat. "Can you, can you…see?"

"Imperfectly."

Imperfectly, she repeated silently, growing increasingly light-headed. "Tell me…tell me…how much do you see?"

"It's not all dark anymore. One eye is more or less just shadows and dark shapes, but with the other eye I get a bit more. While I'll probably never be able to drive or pilot my own plane again, I can see you."

"And what do you see…now?" Her voice was faint to her own ears.

"You."

Her heart was beating so hard she was afraid she'd faint.

"The colors aren't what they were," he added. "Everything's faded, so the world's rather gray and white, but I know you're standing near a table. You're touching the table with one hand. Your other hand is on your stomach."

He was right. He was exactly right. And her hand was on her stomach because she felt like throwing up. "Kristian."

He just looked at her, really looked at her, and she didn't know whether to smile for him or burst into tears. He could see. Imperfectly, as he'd said, but something was better than nothing. Something meant he'd live independently more easily. He'd also have more power in his life again, as well as control.

Control.

And suddenly she realized that if he could see her, he'd eventually see the changes in her body. He'd know she was pregnant…

Her insides churned.

"Is that why you're here tonight?" she asked. "To tell me your good news?"

"And to celebrate your good news."

She swayed on her feet. "My good news?"

"You do have good news, don't you?" he persisted.

Elizabeth stared at Kristian where he stood, just inside the kitchen doorway. Protectively she rubbed her stomach, over her not yet existent bump, trying to stay calm. "I…I don't think so."

"I suppose it depends on how you look at it," he answered. His mouth slanted, black lashes lowering to conceal the startling blue of his eyes. "We knew each other only two weeks and two days, and that was two months and two weeks ago. Those two weeks were mostly good. But there was a disappointment or two, wasn't there?"

She couldn't tear her eyes off him. He looked strong and dynamic, and his tone was commanding. "A couple," she echoed nervously.

"One of the greatest offenses is that we flew to Kithira for dinner and we never ate. We were in my favorite restaurant and we never enjoyed an actual meal."

Elizabeth crossed her arms over her chest. "That's your *greatest* disappointment?"

"If you'd ever eaten there, you'd understand. It's truly great food. Greek food as it's meant to be."

She blinked, her fingers balling into knuckled fists. "You're here to tell me I missed out on a great meal?"

"It was supposed to be a special evening."

He infuriated her. Absolutely infuriated her. Pressing her fists to her ribs, she shook inwardly with rage. Here she was, exhausted from work, stressed and sick from her pregnancy, worried about his sight, deeply concerned about the future, and all he could think of was a missed meal?

"Why don't you have your pilot take you back to Kithira and you can *have* your delicious dinner?" she snapped.

"But that wouldn't help you. You still wouldn't know what a delicious meal you'd missed." He gestured behind him, to the compact living room. "So I've brought that meal to you."

"What?"

"I won't have you flying in your state, and I'm worrying about the baby."

"What baby?" she choked, her veins filling with a flood of ice water.

"Our baby," he answered simply, turning away and heading for the living room, which had been transformed while they were in the kitchen.

The owner of the Kithirian restaurant, along with the waiter who had served them that night, had set up a table, chairs, covering the table in a crisp white cloth and table settings for two. The lights had been turned down and candles flickered on the table, and on the side table next to her small antique sofa, and somewhere, she didn't know where, music played.

They'd turned her living room into a Greek taverna and Elizabeth stood rooted to the spot, unable to take it all in. "What's going on?"

Kristian shrugged. "We're going to have that dinner tonight. Now." He moved to take one of the chairs, and pulled it out for her. "A Greek baby needs Greek food."

"Kristian—"

"It's true." His voice dropped, and his expression hardened. "You're having our baby."

"My baby."

"Our baby," he corrected firmly. "And it is *our* baby." His blue gaze held hers. "Isn't it?"

With candles flickering on the crisp white cloth, soft Greek music in the background, and darkly handsome Kristian here before her, Elizabeth felt tears start to her eyes. Two months without a word from him. Two months without apology, remorse, forgiveness. Two months of painful silence and now this—this power-play in her living room.

"I know you haven't been feeling well," he continued quietly. "I know because I've been in London, watching over you."

Weakly she sat down—not at the table, but on one of her living room chairs. "You think I'm a gold-digger."

"A gold-digger? Grace Stile? A woman as wealthy as Athina Onassis Roussel?"

Elizabeth clasped her hands in her lap. "I don't want to talk about Grace Stile."

"I do." He dropped into a chair opposite her. "And I want to talk about Nico and Cosima and all these other sordid characters appearing in our own little Greek play."

The waiter and the restaurant owner had disappeared into the kitchen. They must have begun warming or preparing food, as the smell coming from the back of the house made her stomach growl.

"I know Nico put you through hell in your marriage," Kristian continued. "I know the divorce was even worse. He drove you out of Greece and the media hounded you for years after. I don't blame you for changing your name, for moving to England and trying to become someone else."

She held her breath, knowing there was a *but* coming. She could hear it in his voice, see it in the set of his shoulders.

"But," he added, "I minded very much not being able to see you. Much more not being able to see—and assess—the situation that night at the Kithira castle for myself."

She linked her fingers to hide the fact they were trembling.

"That evening was a nightmare. I just want to forget it. Forget them. Forget Grace, too."

"I can't forget Grace." His head lifted and his gaze searched her face. "Because she's beautiful. And she's you."

The lump in her throat burned, swelled, making everything inside her hurt worse. "I'm not beautiful."

"You were beautiful as a New York debutante, and you're even more beautiful now. And it has nothing to do with your name, or the Stile fortune. Nothing to do with your marriage or your divorce or the work you do as an administrator. It's you. Grace Elizabeth."

"You don't know me," she whispered, trying to silence him.

"But I do. Because for two weeks I lived with you and worked with you and dined with you, and you changed me. You saved me—"

"No."

"Elizabeth, I didn't want to live after the accident. I didn't want to feel so much loss and pain. But you somehow gave me a window of light, and hope. You made me believe that things could be different. Better."

"I wasn't that good, or nice."

"No, you weren't nice. But you were strong. Tough. And you wouldn't baby me. You wouldn't allow me to give up. And I needed that. I needed you." He paused. "I still do."

Her eyes closed. Hot tears stung her eyelids.

He reached over, skimmed her cheeks with his fingers. "Don't cry," he murmured. "Please don't cry."

She shook her head, then turned her cheek into his palm, biting her lip to keep the tears from falling. "If you needed me, why did you let me go?"

"Because I didn't feel worthy of you. Didn't feel like a man who deserved you."

"Kristian—"

"I realized that night that if I'd been able to see, I would have been in control at the castle in Kithira. I could have read the situation, understood what was happening. Instead I stood there in the dark—literally, figuratively—and it enraged me. I felt trapped. Helpless. My blindness was creating ignorance. Fear."

"You've never been scared of anything," she protested softly.

"Since the accident I've been afraid of everything. I've been haunted by nightmares, my sleep disturbed until I thought I was going mad, but after meeting you that began to change. I began to change. I began to find my way home—my way back to me."

She simply stared at him, her heart tender, her eyes stinging from unshed tears.

"I am a man who takes care of his woman," he continued quietly. "I hated not being able to take care of you. And you are my woman. You've been mine from the moment you arrived in the Taygetos on that ridiculous donkey cart."

Her lips quivered in a tremulous smile. "That was the longest, most uncomfortable ride of my life."

"Elizabeth, *latrea mou,* I have loved you from the very first day I met you. You were horrible and wonderful and your courage won me over. Your courage and your compassion. Your kindness and your strength. All those virtues you talked about in Kithira. You told me appearances didn't matter. You said there were virtues far more important and I agree. Yes, you're beautiful, but I couldn't see your beauty until today. I didn't need your beauty, or the Stile name, or your inheritance to win me. I just needed you. With me."

"Kristian—"

"I still do."

Eyes filmed by tears, she looked up, around her small living room. Normally it was a rather austere room. She lived off her salary, having donated nearly all of her inheritance to charity, and it never crossed her mind to spoil herself with pretty things. But tonight the living room glowed, cozy and intimate with candlelight, the beautifully set table and strains of Greek music, even as the most delectable smells wafted from the kitchen.

The restaurant owner appeared in the doorway. "Dinner is ready," he said sternly. "And tonight you both must eat."

Elizabeth joined Kristian at the table, and for the first time in weeks she enjoyed food. How could she not enjoy the meal tonight? Everything was wonderful. The courses and flavors were beyond brilliant. They shared marinated lamb, fish with tomatoes and currants, grilled octopus—which Elizabeth did pass on—and as she ate she couldn't look away from Kristian.

She'd missed him more than she knew.

Just having him here, with her, made everything feel right. Made everything feel good. Intellectually she knew there were problems, issues, and yet emotionally she felt calm and happy and peaceful again.

It had always been like this with him. It wasn't what he said, or did. It was just him. He made her feel good. He made her feel wonderful.

Looking across the table at him, she felt a thought pop into her head. "You know, Cosima said—" she started to say, before breaking off. She'd done it again. Cosima. Always Cosima. "Why do I keep talking about her?"

"I don't know. But you might as well tell me what she said. I might as well hear all of it."

"It's nothing—not important. Let's forget it."

"No. You brought it up, so it's obviously on your mind. What did Cosima say?"

Elizabeth silently kicked herself. The dinner had been

going so well. And now she'd done the same thing as at the castle in Kithira. Her nose wrinkled. "I'm sorry, Kristian."

"So tell me. What does she say?"

"That before you were injured you were an outrageous playboy." She looked up at him from beneath her eyelashes. "That you could get any woman to eat out of your hand. I was just thinking that I can see what she meant."

Kristian coughed, a hint of color darkening his cheekbones. "I've never been a playboy."

"Apparently women can't resist you…ever."

He gave her a pointed look. "That's not true."

"So you didn't have two dates, on two different continents, in the same day?"

"Geographically as well as physically impossible."

"Unless you were flying from Sydney to Los Angeles."

Kristian grimaced. "That was a one-time situation. If it hadn't been for crossing the time zones it wouldn't have been the same day."

Elizabeth smiled faintly, rather liking Kristian in the hot seat. "Do you miss the lifestyle?"

"No—God, no." Now it was his turn to smile, his white teeth flashing against the bronze of his skin. Sun and exercise had given him the most extraordinary golden glow. "Being a playboy isn't a picnic," he intoned mockingly. "Some men envied the number of relationships I had, but it was really quite demanding, trying to keep all the women happy."

She was amused despite herself. "You're shameless."

"Not as shameless as you were last August, checking me out by the pool…*despite* us having a deal."

"I *wasn't* looking."

"You were. Admit it."

She blushed. "You couldn't even see."

"I could tell. Some things one doesn't need to see to know. Just as I didn't need to see you to know I love you. That I will always love you. And I want nothing more than to spend the rest of my life with you."

Elizabeth's breath caught in her throat. She couldn't speak. She couldn't even breathe.

Kristian stood up from the table and crossed around to kneel before her. He had a ring box in his hand. "Marry me, *latrea mou*," he said. "Marry me. Come live with me. I don't want to live without you."

His proposal shocked her, and frightened her. It wasn't that she didn't care for him—she did, oh, she did—but *marriage*. Marriage to another Greek tycoon.

She drew back in her chair. "Kristian, I can't... I'm sorry, I can't."

"You don't want to be with me?"

All she wanted was to be with him, but marriage terrified her. To her it represented an abuse of power and control, and she never wanted to feel trapped like that again.

"I do want to be with you—but marriage..." Her voice cracked. She felt the old pressure return, the sense of dread and futility. "Kristian, I just had such a terrible time of it. And it shattered me when it ended. I can't go that route again."

"You can," he said, rising.

"No, I can't. I really can't." She slid off her chair and left the table. She felt cornered now, and she didn't know where to go. He was in her house. The restaurant owner and the waiter were in her house. And it was a little two-bedroom house.

Elizabeth retreated to the only other room—her bedroom—but Kristian followed. He put his hand out to keep her from closing the door on him.

"You accused *me* of being a coward by refusing to recover," he said, holding the door ajar. "You said I needed to get on my feet and back to the land of living. Maybe it's time you took your own advice. Maybe it's time you stopped hiding from life and starting living again, too."

Firmly, insistently, he pushed the door the rest of the way open and entered her room. Elizabeth scrambled back, but Kristian marched toward her, fierce and determined. "Being with you is good. It feels right and whole and healthy. Being with you makes me happy, and I know—even if I couldn't see before—it made you happy, too. I will not let happiness go. I will not let you run away, either. We belong together."

She'd backed up until there was nowhere else to go. She was against her nightstand, cornered near her bed, her heart thundering like mad in her chest.

"You," he added, catching her hands in his and lifting them to his mouth, kissing each balled fist, "belong with me."

And as he kissed each of her fists she felt some of the terrible tension around her heart ease. Just his skin on hers calmed her, soothed her. Just his warmth made her feel safe. Protected. "I'm afraid," she whispered.

"I know you are. You've been afraid since you lost your parents, the year before your coming-out party. That's why you married Nico. You thought he'd protect you, take care of you. You thought you'd be safe with him."

Tears filmed her eyes. "But I wasn't."

He held her fists to his chest. "I'm not Nico, and I could never hurt you. Not when I want to love you and have a family with you. Not when I want to spend every day of the rest of my life with you."

She could feel his heart pounding against her hands. His body was so warm, and yet hard, and even with that dramatic scar across his cheek he was beautiful.

"Everything I've done," he added, tipping his head to brush his lips across her forehead, "from learning to walk again to risking the eye surgery, was to help me be a man again—a man who was worthy of you."

"But I'm not the right woman—"

"Not the right woman? *Latrea mou,* look at you! You might be terrified of marriage, but you're not terrified of me." His voice dropped, low and harsh, almost mocking. "I know I'm something of a monster, I've heard people say as much, but you've never minded my face—"

"I *love* your face."

His hands tightened around hers. "You don't bow and scrape before me. You talk to me, laugh with me, make love with me. And you make me feel whole." His voice deepened yet again. "With you I'm complete."

It was exactly how he made her feel. Whole. Complete. Her heart quickened and her chest felt hot with emotion.

"You make sense to me in a way no one has ever made sense," he added, even more huskily. "And if you love me, but really can't face marriage, then let's not get married. Let's not do anything that will make you worry or feel trapped. I don't need to have a ceremony or put an expensive ring on your finger to feel like you're mine, because you already are mine. You belong with me. I know it, I feel it, I believe it—it's as simple and yet as complicated as that."

Elizabeth stared up at him, unable to believe the transformation in him. He was like a different man—in every way— from the man she'd met nearly three months ago.

"What's wrong?" he asked, seeing her expression. "Have I got it wrong? Maybe you don't feel the same way."

The sudden agony in his extraordinary face nearly broke

her heart. Elizabeth's chest filled with emotion so sharp and painful that she pressed herself closer. "Kiss me," she begged.

He did. He lowered his head to cover her mouth with his. The kiss immediately deepened, his touch and taste familiar and yet impossibly new. This was her man. And he loved her. And she loved him more than she'd thought she could ever love anyone.

Kissing him, she moved even closer to him, his arms wrapping around her back to hold her firmly against him. His warmth gave her comfort and courage.

"I love you," she whispered against his mouth. "I love you and love you and love you."

She felt the corner of his mouth lift in a smile.

"And I don't care if we get married," she added, "or if we just live together, as long as we're together. I just want to be with you, near you, every day for the rest of my life."

He drew his head back and smiled down into her eyes. "They say be careful what you wish for."

"Every day, forever."

"Grace Elizabeth…"

"Every day, each day, until the end of time."

"Done." He dropped his head and kissed her again. "There's no escaping now."

She wrapped her arms around him, reassured by the wave of perfect peace. "I suppose if you're not going to let me escape, we might as well make it legal."

Kristian drew his head back a little to get a good look at her face. "You've changed your mind?"

A huge knot filled her throat and she nodded, tears shimmering in her eyes. "Ask me again. Please."

"Will you marry me, *latrea mou?*" he murmured, his voice husky with emotion.

"Yes."

He kissed her temple, and then her cheek, and finally her mouth. "Why did you change your mind?"

"Because love," she whispered, holding him tightly, "is stronger than fear. And, Kristian Koumantaros, I love you with all my heart. I don't want to be with anyone but you."

COMING SOON!

We really hope you enjoyed reading this book. If you're looking for more romance, be sure to head to the shops when new books are available on

Thursday
23rd August

To see which titles are coming soon, please visit
millsandboon.co.uk

MILLS & BOON

LET'S TALK
Romance

For exclusive extracts, competitions
and special offers, find us online:

f facebook.com/millsandboon

◎ @millsandboonuk

𝕏 @millsandboon

Or get in touch on 0844 844 1351*

For all the latest titles coming soon, visit
millsandboon.co.uk/nextmonth

*Calls cost 7p per minute plus your phone company's price per minute access charge

Want even more

ROMANCE?

Join our bookclub today!

'Mills & Boon books, the perfect way to escape for an hour or so.'

Miss W. Dyer

'Excellent service, promptly delivered and very good subscription choices.'

Miss A. Pearson

'You get fantastic special offers and the chance to get books before they hit the shops'

Mrs V. Hall

Visit millsandbook.co.uk/Bookclub and save on brand new books.

MILLS & BOON